KENNETH BROWN

ZITA'S REVENGE

The Mountain King Series - Book 2
First Edition

Adgitize Press

COPYRIGHT PAGE

Zita's Revenge

Published by Adgitize Press

Copyright 2021 by Kenneth Brown

All rights reserved, including the right to reproduce this book, or portions thereof, in any form.

An Adgitize Press Book

Streamwood, IL

First Edition: January 2021

ISBN - 978-1-7322871-7-4

Library of Congress Control Number: 2021901904

ADGITIZE PRESS

https://www.adgitizepress.com

Cover Photo

Tomertu

Cover Design

Kenneth Brown

Editor

Joan H Young

THANK YOU

Thank you for purchasing this Adgitize Press Book.

To find out more about the author, Kenneth Brown, and get advance notification about future books, check out the website, Adgitize Press, https://www.adgitizepress.com.

Join the Adgitize Press Readers Group to receive these great benefits.

- Get the latest information on New Releases

- Insider Looks at Outlines, Plots, Characters, Deleted Scenes and Exclusive behind the Scenes looks at Kenneth Brown's Writing

- Sneak Peeks at Chapters of Upcoming Books

- Ask the Author Questions

- Exclusive Offers

- And MORE

Go to https://www.adgitizepress.com for more information.

Adgitize Press

DEDICATION

Dedicated to my mother and father
Betty Brown - Robert Brown
Remarkable parents who passed down their love for
great novels and wonderful adventures.

CHAPTER 1

Princess Zita huddled in the corner of a small cabin fifteen miles from Velidred Castle in the forested hills of the Velidred Forest. She had eaten little since the eclipse when she sent the fireball that killed her father, King Haskell. Zita focused on a plan for revenge against Erik Anderson and his friends from Earth for their part in what occurred at the volcano.

A knock sounded at the door.

Zita stood, opened the door a crack, and saw the servant girl she had sent to the Velidred village.

That wretched servant better have an answer for me. "Come in," Zita said.

A girl in her late teens entered the hut and removed her traveling cape. "Good morning, Princess Zita."

"Did you find him?"

"Yes, Master Gadiel comes, but he is angry at you and King Haskell. You should run, my lady. He's an evil man."

"Don't worry about him. Bring firewood, it's cold in here."

"Yes, my lady. Please don't meet with the man, my lady."

"Go."

An hour later the fire warmed the room, but Zita walked back and forth hugging herself. She feared Gadiel based on stories Dad told about the man. Many kings bowed to Gadiel, but stories of his power and wealth had to be exaggerated.

"What's the news in the village?" Zita asked.

"The resistance has taken over the castle, my lady. Prince Krunal's forces stormed the castle for a week and defeated the castle guards."

"What happened to the wizards at the volcano? Weren't the king's loyal warrior wizards supposed to return and protect the castle?" *Glad I didn't return to the castle after the eclipse.*

"The warrior wizards scattered after King Haskell died. They returned to their homelands and kingdoms." The servant twisted long, brunette hair around an index finger.

A loud knock on the door startled Zita.

"Gadiel." The servant darted out the back door.

The man with the white beard arrived, and Zita's pulse quickened. *Should she answer the knock or pretend not to be home?*

She brushed her dirty, torn clothing damaged at the volcano. Zita considered scurrying out the back, but remembered Dad's command to find Gadiel if the king should ever die.

With her right hand, she lifted the latch and swung open the wooden door.

There he stood, his white beard bright in the sunshine through the trees. The man lifted a black brimmed hat in acknowledgement and pushed open the door with his cane. He was tall and lanky and wore a long, black, wool jacket that ended just above his knees. The ensemble included black pants and a grey vest woven in red and grey diamonds.

"How do you do, Master Gadiel?"

"Forget the niceties, child. You have a problem, don't you? Your dad is dead and the prophecies have come true." Gadiel removed his hat and laid a cane and the hat on the table. "I warned your father about his plan to bring the teens back early, but he didn't listen and now you're living in this squalid environment instead of the castle. What are you going to do about it?"

Zita bowed her head.

He slammed his hand on the table. "Answer me."

She jumped at the force of the blow and looked into his black eyes. A red mark in his left eye glowed in the cabin's dim light. Zita's hand shook as she said, "I don't know, sir. I need your help."

"Why?"

"I seek revenge against Erik Anderson and his friends. They've killed my father and I want their lives."

"Revenge is a nasty business and has ruined many a kingdom. I recommend against it. Go to another kingdom, marry a lord, and raise a family. Forget revenge."

If Gadiel wouldn't help, then what could she do? Who could help her punish the teens from Earth for ruining her life?

Gadiel grabbed her chin in his manicured hands and looked into her eyes. "How's your magic?"

"Fine. I practiced with Dad's wizards twice a week before the eclipse."

"Are you skilled enough to commit to the Fire and Ice experience?" Gadiel asked with a deep, steady voice. "That would help you more than revenge and could improve your magic and wisdom."

"Isn't that an ancient cult practice and dangerous to wizards who participate in the experience?"

"Ha, dangerous? Yes, to inexperienced pretty boys with no natural abilities who want to wander around with a staff in their hands and pretend to be wizards. The ceremony is dangerous, but for individuals striving to be the best wizard in the world, it can make you a legend."

"But sir, I've heard one in four wizards who take the challenge don't survive."

"Your father hesitated the first time I mentioned it to him after an unfortunate friend, Max, didn't survive the experience. After the ceremony he became a premier wizard and king."

"Yet, he lost his life to a bunch of teenagers."

Gadiel slapped the table once more. "Your father," he yelled, "didn't lose his life to a bunch of teenagers."

Zita looked up at Gadiel. "What do you mean?"

"Do you want revenge?"

"Yes, sir."

"Will you endure the Fire and Ice experience to get it?"

She wanted to say no, because she couldn't get revenge if the experience left her dead or a drooling lunatic, as she knew it could.

Gadiel said, "I don't like revenge, but I have a task for the teens from Earth. There is a treasure I seek in the Pit of Wretchedness, and the boys can acquire it for me. But I will not help you if you don't do the Fire and Ice ceremony."

"The danger, sir, is it worth it? The teenagers from Earth shredded my life, killed Dad, and stole my kingdom. Now you want me to risk becoming an unintelligent lunatic.

"Like your father, you have talent. When he was young, I searched for him in the streets of the city. A dirty boy living day to day. I watched him make contacts, steal food, plan escapes and survive in a tough city. The boy had that extra bit that set him apart. I snatched him, cleaned him up, educated him, taught him ancient magic and yes, made the boy take the Fire and Ice ceremony. He had few dreams before the ceremony, but after the experience, he became a king. You have that something extra, as well, Zita. You're beautiful like your mother, but your father's brain is what will make you a leader and the best queen the country has ever known."

Zita smiled as goosebumps ran up her arm. She brushed at her dress, "Do I have to do the fire and ice thing, sir?"

"No, you can stay here in a little cabin in the forest, while strangers loot your castle and teenagers from Earth live the life you should be living." Gadiel stood, snatched the cane from the table and pointed it at her. "You aren't ready. I can't work with you."

She tried to meet his gaze, but couldn't. She looked at her shoes as Gadiel's magical darkness cloaked the room.

Gadiel grabbed his hat off the table and headed to the door.

"But, Sir."

"What?"

Zita's heart raced. She knew she wasn't ready, but she needed Gadiel's help and whispered. "Sir, I'm ready."

He kept walking and opened the door.

She raised her voice, "Mr. Gadiel, I'm ready."

Gadiel placed his black hat on his head and the cane made a clacking sound as it struck the wood floor. He marched through the door.

"Sir, I'm ready." Zita yelled the words at Gadiel's back.

He turned and stared. It unsettled her, but Zita returned the gaze.

"Be in Fairhaven in five days, I must make preparations. Wash yourself, and find warm clothes worthy of a princess."

CHAPTER 2

Zita arrived in Fairhaven prepared for the Fire and Ice ceremony. The village sat high in the mountains near glaciers and snow-covered peaks that never lost their snowfields, even during sweltering summers. A hundred people lived in the village during the summer, excavating blocks of ice from frozen ponds and transporting them to the castles.

She found Gadiel in a large, open tent in a mountain meadow outside the village. Zita followed his clothing advice and wore linen under layer tunic, a silk tunic and over all of those a wool gown and a green scarf. She stamped snow off her boots as she entered the tent. She hated snow, cold and the mountains.

Gadiel said, "Welcome to Fairhaven. This means you're serious about becoming an elemental force of nature and are ready to commit to the Order of the Ancients."

Zita wasn't sure she wanted to commit to the Order of the Ancients, as it included a painful branding. Yet, wizards who survived the Fire and Ice experience gained acclaim and recognition in a secret society. *First task, live through the initial phase.*

"Isn't this ceremony outdated?" Zita asked, her muscles twitchy as she brushed her dress and pulled on her collar for the hundredth time.

"Young wizards afraid of the challenge fear the experience, but you're in expert hands. Sit by the fire and we'll talk about the ceremony. Tea?"

She warmed her hands over the fire. Gadiel handed her a ceramic mug of hot tea, an unfamiliar mixture of sweet and savory. But as she drank, she felt the tea calming the nervous energy coursing through her body.

Gadiel said, "Before we start, you should learn the ceremony's history. A thousand years ago during the glorious age of wizards, the wizardress, Arcmelion, first performed the Fire and Ice experience on a student who showed great potential but who lived in fear of his magic. Arcmelion designed three incenses, infused with special herbs and supplemented with magic, and gave one to the student before each test. She traveled thousands of miles and bargained with dark-arts wizards and people of the mountain mines to acquire the incense mixtures.

She told me the student almost died three times during the experience, but found his confidence bolstered, and his ability for critical thinking and magic was strengthened.

Tension built in Zita's shoulders.

"After inhaling the incense, you'll drink a tea, something like the drink in your hand right now. Arcmelion designed the combinations of incense and tea to guide you on a unique spiritual journey. I will shepherd you through each step."

A loopy sensation circulated through Zita's head, as if she had drunk too much champagne at a castle party.

Gadiel continued, "The first journey is fire, which leads into past mistakes. You experience the pain of sins you committed against others."

That will be easy, thought Zita, as I haven't any sins against others.

"The second journey is ice, which shows the near future. Ice is the most jarring with the greatest risk of pain, suffering and a life of brain damage."

Zita squeezed the teacup and shook her head. *That's what she feared, a life of brain damage.*

"Are you ready to begin?"

"Yes," Zita tried to stand, but collapsed to the ground instead. *What's in this tea she wondered, and how could she make proper decisions feeling like this?* Her mind raced through feasible ways to escape the test. *Run away now,* she thought, but impossible without the ability to stand.

Gadiel lifted her to a chair and placed incense beneath her nose. "Breathe in deeply."

She inhaled the sweet aroma of the incense, a spring scent of honey blooms.

"Breathe out, in a long breath."

She exhaled and giggled at the thought of escaping down the mountain with Gadiel racing after her with his jacket wafting in the breeze like a black bird in flight.

"Another deep breath."

Zita closed her mouth and leaned near the incense and inhaled. She closed her eyes and experienced peace and tranquility.

"Remove jewelry and magical focusing devices as they will discombobulate the process."

She fingered the chain and pendant Mom had given her and hoisted it over her head. Gadiel held out his hand for the jewelry, but she held back. "I've never let this out of my possession." Memories of her mother presenting her the magic pendant flooded Zita's mind. The birthday party with servants dressed as animals and Zita receiving gifts of clothing, but then Mommy handing her the necklace. The turtle charm held magic powers and her mother showed Zita how to lift an item off the table using the focusing power of the turtle.

"It's okay. I promise to return it when we're finished." Gadiel stretched out his hand and stopped inches from taking the pendant.

Zita fingered the rough edges of the turtle and stared at Gadiel's hand. With a deep breath, she surrendered the object.

"Stand and take my hand."

Gadiel led her to a path of glowing charcoals. "Walk across these coals and re-live a painful memory. Embrace the pain. Live the experience."

The hot-charcoal path melted nearby snow. Zita rubbed clammy hands together as beads of sweat formed on her forehead. *Was this what she wanted? Would she remember her life or even her name or metamorphose into a mindless, muttering lunatic?* She remembered intelligent wizards who now begged at the castle walls for food and clothing after attempting the challenge.

Gadiel put incense under nose, "Breathe and let go of fears."

Three times Zita inhaled, and three times she followed with deep calming exhales.

Gadiel led her onto the burning coals, hot to her feet, but the bottom of her feet didn't burn or blister. The crisp outside air changed into a dense, black fog, making it difficult to see the path.

In the next moment, Zita stood as a child in the Velidred castle. Zita's mother, Queen Noreen, held little Zita's hand. The child looked at her mother and Zita experienced her mom's touch and bathed in the scent, a lavender fragrance, strong enough to overtake the smell of honey blooms. A multitude of questions rambled through Zita's mind at seeing her mother, and she opened her mouth to speak.

"Keep quiet, child, don't awaken the king."

A tall man with red hair led the way through the dark castle hallways. Ah, Cugbert the priest. Was it a dream or a faraway memory? Cugbert held Queen Noreen's hand. "My Queen, you and Zita will ride in the carriage out of the village. The driver is a friend of mine and will tell anyone who stops you that you're visiting your sick sister. We'll meet in the mountains where we agreed."

"Mommy?"

"Zita, it's important to be quiet." Queen Noreen put her index finger to her lips.

"But Mommy, I have a secret to tell you."

"Now is not the time." She whispered.

"I told Daddy our secret."

"You did what?" The queen's eyes widened and mouth slackened as she stopped.

"I told Daddy about our plan to escape. Daddy read me a story, and he asked me what I was doing today." She smiled at the queen.

Queen Noreen said, "Cugbert stop."

"What?" Cugbert pivoted toward the queen.

"Zita told the king our plans."

Cugbert tightened his fists as a pained expression crossed his face. "It's too dangerous to continue, my Queen. If the king knows, then we should stop the escape."

The queen took his hands in hers. "No, your life's in danger. Haskell won't let you stay in the castle knowing our plans. I'm surprised he didn't kill you in your sleep. We must continue, for you will be dead by morning if we go back."

"My Queen, we can't, it's too dangerous for you and the child." Cugbert whispered.

"No, we stick to our plan." She took Zita's hand and led the way.

The halls narrowed in this section of the castle, but they hastened down steps. Little Zita had to run to keep up. They sneaked through the servant's section of the castle into the kitchen. It was the first time Zita had visited the kitchen without the cooks talking, whisking, or making a delicious feast. A creepy shiver wriggled down her spine.

The door creaked as Cugbert pushed it open and they stepped out into the brisk night air. Clouds covered the Velidred moon, which outlined the clouds with a red glow. The queen pressed Zita against the wall as they waited for Cugbert. She bent to her daughter, placed a finger to her lip and whispered, "We need to be quiet so the king doesn't hear us, otherwise he'll stop us."

Cugbert gave a hand signal, and Queen Noreen and Zita crept along the wall to prevent notice by soldiers guarding high on the parapets. They inched toward the gate.

Zita's heartbeat raced in the darkness. *Could they make it to the carriage and out of the Velidred village without Daddy stopping them?*

Cugbert stopped, "Where's Fernando?"

Fifty-yards from the edge of the wall stood a carriage where a man held two horses by their harnesses.

"Why did he park the carriage so far from the walls? We were to meet him right next to the castle. Something is wrong."

Queen Noreen said, "It doesn't matter, we must get Zita to safety. Be safe my friend and if something happens to me, take care of my baby and get her out of the king's influence."

The queen stooped low to Zita. "You and Mommy will race to the carriage. No matter what happens, you run and hop on the carriage. Do you understand?"

Little Zita nodded. She was a fast runner, and even the nannies couldn't keep up when she bolted and dashed through the castle halls.

Mommy took Zita's hand, and they sprinted to the carriage. Halfway across the open space, three men jumped from behind the carriage and loosed arrows at Mommy.

Queen Noreen released Zita's hand and fell to the ground, clutching at two feathered shafts extending from her breast. She pushed Zita back toward the wall, "Run, run back to Cugbert."

Zita's father, King Haskell, stepped from the carriage.

The child knelt next to her mother.

A fog enveloped Zita as tears pooled in her eyes. She staggered across burning coals holding a man's hand, and the sun blazed in the sky. She came to the end of the hot coals, stepped into the snow. She released a wail.

Gadiel poured oil over her long, black hair, "Accept peace and forgiveness for past sins."

CHAPTER 3

Zita woke with a start. Where was she? She felt exhausted. She blinked in bright daylight, trying to orient herself. She was in a tent, and it was too hot for early morning. Zita opened her eyes and stared at the tent ceiling. A bright glow shining low through the canvas suggested it was afternoon. *How did she get here?*

A woman spoke, "My lady, it is good you awakened. Master Gadiel has inquired about your health."

Zita jumped at the woman's voice and then remembered Gadiel. The fire experience. Good, she lived through it. Memories flooded her consciousness, and she felt thrilled she hadn't lost her mental capabilities, but the pain of remembering her mother's death weighed heavy on her mind. She didn't need to re-hash that memory. A headache pounded at the front of her brain. Zita hated Gadiel.

She lay quietly, remembering the pain of the hot coals and wondered if she would survive the ice experience. *Could she expect it to be better or worse? Was there a way to stop this ceremony?* Her desire to continue retreated.

"My lady, are you all right?"

She rose from the mat. "Yes, tell Gadiel I'm fine."

* * * *

The servant returned to the tent as the last rays of the sun peeked between the mountain tops. "Master Gadiel has asked for you to get into your small-clothes and put on this robe, my lady."

Zita's stomach growled, and she realized she hadn't eaten since morning. "No, I will eat first."

"Oh my lady, you can't do that, Master Gadiel prohibits any food in your tent until he has finished the last ceremony."

"We'll see about that. Bring me my jacket. It's freezing out and I want to talk to Gadiel."

"Please, Master Gadiel —"

"Master Gadiel can wait until I eat. Hand me my jacket."

Zita put on a fur-trimmed, full-length leather jacket and walked out to the fire where Gadiel sat on a bench warming his hands.

He looked at her and scowled, "You should be in your small-clothes with a robe on, not a jacket and dressed for dinner."

"I'm cold and must have missed at least one meal."

"You may not survive this last test, so there's no need to waste food on you."

A cold emptiness blasted her core, and her head jerked back. *Gadiel wouldn't feed her because she might not survive the last test?*

"You promised to follow my commands, and yet you choose your own path."

She placed her hand on her chest. "I'm hungry."

The tall man slithered to her, grabbed her jaw with a tight grip and yanked her head to face him.

"Ow, that hurts." She tried to look into his eyes, but as he stared at her with his intense, black eyes, she pulled back.

He gripped tighter. "You agreed to this experience. I don't have time or patience for uncertain wizard wanna-bes. You have a goal to get revenge on the teens from Earth. That is the starting point for our relationship, but if you aren't interested in following through with the entire ceremony, then I will pack up and leave you to wallow in self-pity."

Zita glanced at his eyes, looked at his jacket, and then back at his eyes. The eye with the red dot changed and the red dot turned into a scorpion which crawled across the iris and grew larger. She felt mesmerized and troubled.

"What will it be, self-pity or revenge?"

If she refused the ceremony, would he let her go? How difficult would it be to track down the boys from Earth and inflict revenge on them? Did she need Gadiel? Was the risk of not surviving the ceremony worth the chance? And yet, Gadiel's years of experience had to make the process easier, and he had promised to look after her. Surviving this last event would provide her certain wizard honors. She stuttered, "Con-continue the ceremony."

"Then prepare yourself as I instructed. Now hurry, the sun has almost set."

She rushed back to the tent and stripped to her small-clothes, and the servant girl placed a blue velvet robe over her shoulders. Then Zita darted barefoot across the snow to the fire.

"Come with me," Gadiel commanded.

She slipped, skidded and stumbled up the mountain path, following in the man's footsteps as fast as possible, hoping to keep her feet and toes warm. A breeze picked up and flowed under the robe, chilling her legs. *Where were they going, and why couldn't she wear something warm?*

The trail leveled, and they entered an open meadow where a bonfire burned next to a frozen pond. Snow lay on top of the ice and was blown into interesting patterns. Two men stood next to a hole in the pond, moving a large oar in the water as if stirring a pot.

"What are men doing here?" She asked.

"They keep the hole open so you won't be trapped under the ice forever. Now, sit and drink tea with me."

Stuck under the ice? Her mind swam with numerous scenarios of drowning. *Gadiel planned to shove her into the water and under the ice? How could she allow that? Hadn't the spiritualist told her she'd drown in icy water? Did Gadiel know about the spiritualist's prophecy? Was this ceremony designed to find all the things she hated and force her to overcome them?* The blood drained from her face as she recognized the truth of that possibility and her hands turned clammy.

"I can't do this, not in icy water." She whirled back toward the tents.

"Stop." Gadiel's voice carried over the pond and echoed off the mountain peaks.

She stopped.

"Come by the fire, and warm yourself with hot tea. You'll be safe in the water, I'll be with you."

"But the spiritualist said I would drown in icy water. I don't want to die."

"Let's sit by the fire; everything will be fine." Gadiel's voice softened as he touched her elbow and led her to a log near the warm blaze.

She sat shivering, but unsure if from cold or fear. *Could this be when she dies?* She recalled Forest River Blossom's foretelling her death by drowning in an icy lake. She'd avoided open water ever since, and refused to ice skate on the local ponds with friends. *Was tonight the end the spiritualist predicted?*

"Have hot tea to warm you." Gadiel handed her a hot mug filled with a steaming, light-green liquid.

She held the mug in shaking hands, embracing the warmth.

Gadiel lighted two candles and burned incense.

Zita sipped the hot beverage, keeping her nose in the steam for warmth. The liquid burned her tongue. The more she drank, the more relaxed and comfortable she felt. Warmth entered her pores and loosened tight facial muscles and her jaw. The scent of peony flowers wafted about her head.

Gadiel said, "Relax, everything will be fine."

Zita drank more tea, burped and giggled. She swayed, and a grin played across her face as she thought how improper it was for a princess to burp.

"This next ceremony shows a potential future sin against your fellow man. It's dangerous, and we lose the most wizards during this step. The people you sin against will rebel and may attempt to fight back and kill you. Sometimes you encounter people you love, and your sin rips you from reality. Be careful, and hold on to the rope. If you release your grip, we might not save you."

Zita's face felt numb. She sipped more tea and giggled louder.

"Are you ready?" Gadiel extended his hand and steadied her as she rose. "Remember to hold on to the rope. Repeat that for me."

She tried focusing on Gadiel, but her eyes had trouble focusing. "Repeat what?"

He said, "Remember to hold the rope."

"Okay." She burped. "Hold the rope." The giggle continued to escape her lips, unbidden.

"Remove your robe and walk with me."

She dropped her robe to the log and walked with Gadiel to the ice.

They stood over the hole in the ice while the men stood back, holding their oars. One man had a stout cord wrapped around his waist. Gadiel tied the other end of this rope around Zita's waist.

A chill skittered down her back as if someone touched icy fingers to her neck. Zita's fear of the icy lake clutched at her chest.

Why had she agreed to such a stupid ceremony? She shook her head to try to release the tingling in her neck.

Gadiel held up the ceramic container of burning incense and placed it under Zita's nose. "Take a deep breath and hold it a second before exhaling."

Zita breathed in, held and enjoyed a lovely scent of sweet pea flowers. She exhaled.

"Once more. Grasp the rope," Gadiel said.

One deep breath, a pleasant scent, and Gadiel pushed her into the icy water. The shock of hitting the water forced the air from her lungs, and she struggled for a second. She opened her eyes in the water, but the sun had set, and she could see nothing but darkness. Then a light wavered and formed in the distance. She swam toward the light.

Her world changed as she swam, and in a moment, Zita stood next to a dining table set with fine china, exquisite silverware and sharp-cut crystal. Three servants dressed in formal serving attire stood in the room waiting to respond to her command. She brushed her emerald formal dress with her hands. *Where did this gown come from? What am I doing here?* Then her next thought— *everything is perfect, and I'm ready for the guests to arrive.*

She turned to a servant. "Where's the king? Is he in the castle?"

"The king's not back, my Queen."

The servant called her queen. What did that mean? She said, "What do you mean he's not back? He promised our daughter he wouldn't miss the banquet. If he's late, it will devastate Princess Sienna. It's her engagement announcement; he must be here."

"I'm sure he'll arrive any minute."

"I don't want empty assurances. Where is the king?" Zita examined the room and wondered what her husband thought more important than their daughter and her banquet.

"I will send someone to find him, my Queen." The servant waved his hand and other servants scurried away to search for the king.

"He better find him." Zita stomped across the room to face her chief of staff. "Where did the king go?"

The man's face colored red. "To visit a friend, my Queen."

"What friend?"

The man paused a beat. "The widow, Lily."

Zita's heartbeat pounded. *Be calm, everything will be okay, act like a queen and not a silly school girl.* She commanded, "Find him and bring him back."

The man didn't move.

"Now!"

Time jumped, and Zita found herself alone at the banquet room door, greeting guests that had come to celebrate the betrothal of her daughter to Prince Brian. An older couple came to her, "Welcome Lord and Lady Gustavson."

They bowed and said, "Where is King Erik?"

Through clinched teeth she said, "Visiting a sick friend." She rubbed clammy hands together.

"The king has a kind heart."

"Yes." Queen Zita scanned the doorway for the hundredth time.

Another couple entered, and she repeated the same routine. Then King Erik arrived and holding his arm, Lady Lily, his high-school friend and sweetheart from Earth. Zita struggled to swallow and felt nauseous.

They sashayed toward Queen Zita.

Erik said, "I'm sorry, I'm late, my dear, but I knew you wanted Lady Lily here for the celebration."

Zita stared at Erik and tightened her fists by her side. *How dare that woman?* "It is a pleasure to see you, Lady Lily. Are you well?" she asked.

"Yes, thank you so much for inviting me and sending the king personally to escort me to the celebration. You are gracious." Lily flipped her blonde hair off her face, which exposed flawless, smooth skin.

She hasn't aged in twenty-five years. "It wouldn't have been a celebration without your presence."

Lily proceeded into the dining room, and her lithe, dancer's body moved sensuously into the banquet hall with many a man turning his head to watch her entrance.

Zita grabbed Erik's wrist and dug her fingernails into his skin, drawing blood. "Why?"

"It's a celebration, my dear." His big, blue eyes sparkled, and he kissed Queen Zita on the cheek.

"We'll talk about this later." Zita said.

"About what?"

He better not play innocent with me. "I'll not have tongues wagging at my daughter's party and throughout the kingdom." *Everyone knows Erik loved Lily best, but he married me for power, not love.* "You know what I mean, and we'll have this conversation later," she said under her breath.

King Erik nodded and patted her hand.

They finished the second course, and then the meat service arrived at the table. Zita looked at King Erik. He smiled at her and squeezed her hand under the table. *He's gorgeous with a fine posture, and his radiant smile makes him more attractive as he ages. I love this man.*

Lady Lily, across the table, spoke to the woman on her right, "My servant girl was off visiting her sick mother. King Erik came and insisted I attend the celebration. Well, of course, I could do no such thing. How could I get into my corset and dress without my servant?"

Zita watched Erik turn his attention to Lily and smile. *What is she saying? Her servant girl wasn't there?* "Oh my," Zita said, "You look so lovely, how did you get dressed?"

"Well, I didn't know what to do, but King Erik insisted he accompany me to the celebration. How could I refuse the king?"

"Yes, but the dress and . . . corset, how did you manage?" The headache grew stronger, pounding beat upon beat into Zita's eyes. She blinked.

"The king offered to come back to the castle and find a housemaid to assist me, but I convinced him there wasn't time. Do you know what the dear man did for me?"

"No, what?" Zita's face turned feverish, and she scowled at Erik.

"He helped me. He fetched water, heated it, and poured me a bath. Then helped with my corset and dress, isn't he a dear?"

Zita's hand went to her lips, and she shook her head. She blew deep breaths from her mouth. She felt she might faint.

Erik looked at her. "It wasn't how you're picturing this."

She said nothing. *How could this man embarrass her so at his daughter's party?*

The butler bent to the queen, "They have served the meat, my Queen."

"What?"

"You need to cut the meat, your Highness."

"Oh, yes. Where are my manners?"

She grasped the steak knife and rotated it in her hands. Zita looked at the steak sitting on her plate and shook her head. "No, I'm not ready."

"Would you like me to prepare it for you?" King Erik asked.

"No!" Zita's fight-or-flight impulse clutched her stomach and twisted in her gut. With one brief story, Lily and Erik had embarrassed her unbearably. She couldn't take it anymore. The knife handle rotated in her hands as she studied Erik's beautiful blue eyes. She mouthed. "Why?"

"What is it, Love?" He smiled that same wonderful smile that attracted her the first day they met.

Queen Zita stood.

Everyone at the banquet table stopped talking and stood with the queen.

Erik said, "Your Highness?"

With a strong, quick jerk, she jammed the knife deep into his stomach and then again three times in his chest. Zita bolted from the room as blood blossomed on the king's dinner jacket.

She floated, unaware of her surroundings. Then she struggled in icy water. *Hold the rope.* Where was she? Tears formed in her eyes. *I can't kill Erik. Why did I kill the man I love?* She let go of the rope and dropped into the deep, black water.

CHAPTER 4

Erik Anderson noted the distinctive crack as lumberjacks dropped trees to build a cabin. Village loggers harvested their tenth tree of the morning, as men's voices echoed through the forest, "Clear the area, tree coming down."

In the nearby village, starving villagers shuffled in a line to receive food from Erik and Cugbert, who was a Pankratios Third-Braid Priest and healer. Cugbert's goal was to feed and heal anyone who needed his services, and this village ranked as the poorest Erik had seen this month. Erik trained to become a healer like Cugbert, and they worked the mountain villages that lost their harvest from the previous summer because of crimes by King Haskell of Velidred Castle.

Erik pulled twelve loaves of bread from the outdoor oven to serve the villagers. A hot soup of beans, barley, vegetables and deer meat boiled in a pot hung over an open flame in the village square.

From the forest he heard, "Watch out. Move, man. Move!"

A tree cracked, crashed and rumbled to the forest floor as a logger's scream drowned the reverberation of the thud echoing off surrounding mountain peaks.

Villagers, standing in line, stopped talking and gasped. Cugbert, examining a village woman complaining of difficulties breathing, raised his head.

Erik stopped slicing the bread and surveyed the forest. Cabins blocked Erik's direct view, which forced him to peer around a house.

His inspection showed nothing unusual through early summer leaves.

The village went quiet, and birds stopped chirping.

Cries of distress rose from the forest.

"Get help!"

"Move the tree!"

"I need men over here, now!"

Women waiting in line for soup and bread huddled in small groups, talking in whispers. Did the tree strike one's husband or a mother's son? How serious was the injury?

Cugbert scrambled to Erik. "A logging accident, I'll stay and feed the villagers, hurry; go find them and help."

Adrenaline spiked in Erik's core as he asked, "Do you think I can heal him myself?"

Cugbert whispered, "Loggers don't live long when a tree falls on them. Provide compassion. Heal if you are able, otherwise comfort him."

Erik removed his apron and sprinted around the village cabins toward the forest. What carnage, pain and suffering might he encounter? Was the injured man pinned by the tree? Could he survive? *Why did Cugbert leave this to him? He wasn't ready. He'd healed minor injuries on children. They were easy to heal, because children's bodies brought youthful self-healing.*

Two gangly boys dashed toward Erik.

"Where's the accident?"

"Back there." The boys slowed and said, "We're going after Cugbert."

"Cugbert sent me. Take me there."

The boys dawdled for a moment, in self-doubt.

"Lead the way. Move it," Erik shouted.

The boys pivoted and raced back into the forest with Erik close behind them.

A hard sprint for two minutes and Erik reached the downed tree, a giant oak with massive limbs splayed over the forest floor. Twelve loggers huddled around the trunk where a fellow sawyer lay pinned with both legs trapped.

Erik's core tensed tight, and he chewed his bottom lip. The trapped logger's eyes were closed; he appeared to be breathing, but his face was an ashen white mask.

"What are you boys doing back here without Cugbert?"

They were speechless for a moment, then the tallest pointed at Erik and said, "Boy says he's the healer."

A logger with enormous arms asked, "Is that true?"

Erik stuttered, "Y—Yes."

"Get over there. Can you heal him?"

Erik didn't know. He sprinted to the injured logger, having to leap over branches and limbs scattered on the forest floor. He knelt beside the wounded man. "What's your name?"

The logger wheezed with shallow breaths, but didn't respond.

Jumbo Arms answered, "Slater. His name's Slater."

Erik examined Slater's legs, bent at odd angles beneath the tree, and Erik's stomach felt queasy. "Can you move the tree off his legs?"

"Come on men, move this tree."

Thirteen loggers, three boys and two girls strained to lift the tree and tried to shove it. They didn't budge it in either direction, but managed to raise the trunk slightly.

Jumbo Arms said through clenched teeth, "Pull him out from underneath the tree."

Erik grabbed the injured man's armpits and yanked.

Slater jerked in Erik's hands and screamed in agony.

"Hurry boy, we can't hold this long." Sweat beaded on the man's brow.

Erik repositioned his feet and hauled the man through the fallen leaves and forest dirt.

Slater moaned and fell unconscious.

Erik dragged Slater's body free of the tree's branches, and the villagers dropped the massive trunk to the forest floor.

With slow, even breaths, Erik placed his hands on Slater's forehead. Cugbert had trained Erik to delve into the mind and body and search for healing energy from the host. If the host lost his desire to live, then survival decreased. Slater had passed out, and his breath was raspy and shallow.

Erik moved to Slater's legs. The tree struck Slater on the thighs, and Erik sensed both femurs were broken. The left shattered, causing the left leg to point skyward at an awkward, unnatural direction.

"Can someone bring me water?" Erik didn't need water. Slater wasn't conscious, but many onlookers hovered over Erik, and he felt self-conscious having the villagers watching him work.

"Josie, fetch water for the healer."

Slater had minimal chance to survive this accident. Should I comfort him or attempt to heal? What dangers lurked in Slater's body from this accident? Blood clots travel through veins from legs to brain and lungs. Should Erik amputate Slater's legs to offer the best chance to survive? Can Erik heal the smashed legs?

"Are you going to heal him or just put your hands on his legs?"

Erik's heart raced in his chest. He didn't need added pressure from these guys. "I'm delving the injury. Be quiet and give me space to work."

The crowd backed up as the big guy said, "Jackson, fetch Cugbert, this boy doesn't have it."

A youngster shot toward the village.

Why did Cugbert send him alone to heal this injured logger? I should feed the villagers while Cugbert healed. Maybe I should wait for Cugbert.

Erik grabbed the man's right leg, as it looked less damaged than the other. Maybe he'd only need to amputate one leg and not both of them. He discharged flows of mental pulses to delve into the leg, which showed this femur broken, but not crushed. Erik manipulated the leg and directed healing power to the damaged spot. He watched the leg mend.

This wasn't the first broken bone he mended, but the other times, Cugbert stood by his shoulder watching, offering hints and giving Erik confidence. *Why did the priest send me out here alone?*

The leg straightened, and the man moaned.

When a patient moaned during healing it was a positive sign, as healing caused as much pain as the original accident.

Slater's leg healed, and the men gasped in amazement as the exposed bone re-positioned, the contusion healed, and the skin color returned to a pale pink.

Erik drew a deep breath and placed his hand on Slater's shattered left leg. Many pieces of bone penetrated the muscle, and Erik sensed one bone shard perforated an artery, leaving the man with internal bleeding. He must fix the damaged artery first, or Slater risked bleeding out and dying. The injury site was swollen and puffy with blood and fluids.

A village woman reached the scene and screamed when she saw Slater. She dropped to her knees and kissed his face. She held Slater's head in her hands and rocked back-and-forth sobbing. She cried, "Will he live?"

Erik didn't dare tell her his honest belief, that Slater had moments to live. "Yes, I'm doing everything I can to save him."

He concentrated on patching the artery, as he manipulated the bone loose and used healing magic to stitch the bleeding hole. *Why don't loggers take more care to prevent accidents like this?*

"Slater stopped breathing," The woman screamed.

"Help me, Cugbert," Erik implored under his breath. He moved to the man's chest and delved into the lungs and heart. The man's heart had stopped. Erik had never attempted to re-start a heart using the healing Cugbert taught. How to manage that? Did Cugbert even have healing powers for that task? Erik had nothing but memories of TV-show doctors and emergency personnel. *It was worth a try.* He raised his right hand above his head, and slammed his fist into the man's chest.

"Hey, what're you doing to Slater," A logger yelled.

"He's breathing again," The woman shrieked.

Erik rolled his eyes and returned to Slater's left leg. He analyzed the many loose bone chips scattered through the leg and wondered where to start? The reconstruction resembled a thousand-piece puzzle. Erik evaluated a bone fragment and compared it to other fragments and the unbroken sections of bone. To piece the shards into a recognizable femur might take hours. He visualized the bone, piece after piece, mentally picking each one up and lining it into position or leaving it where it was for later evaluation.

As Erik rearranged each shard into its proper position, Slater moaned, the woman sobbed and loggers gasped. Erik knew they thought he was killing the man.

Cugbert arrived, and the loggers made space for him.

Erik moved to let Cugbert examine Slater, but Cugbert pushed Erik back down beside the man. "Continue your healing."

"So many pieces, it'll take hours to position each shard."

"Hmm, see if this helps." Cugbert removed a small, gold frog hanging from a chain around his neck and handed it to Erik.

"What's this?"

"A religious device designed for focused healing."

Erik examined the shining frog, an inch high, heavier than he expected, and wondered if the object was pure gold. He held the focusing device in his left hand and returned to his task. The pieces began to move. First one bone shard repositioned itself, followed by a second and a third, moving intelligently as if inspired by divine power.

Time passed. Was it five minutes or two hours? Erik finished rebuilding the femur and straightened the broken leg. He inspected Slater's head for other injuries but found none. Finally he began a cleansing routine designed to open airways and generate calm. This last step included a freezing factor that made patients gasp. Slater convulsed, bent at his waist, and jolted to a sitting position as Erik completed the procedure.

The woman screamed, then began to cry as Slater smiled and kissed her lips.

CHAPTER 5

Erik was one of four teenagers, along with Lily, Alpherge and Sherry, who came through a portal on Earth and ended up on the planet Aloheno. The portal closed before they could return to Earth, and now they were trapped on this planet until the pathway opened again. Erik rescued his friend Lily from becoming a sacrifice on the Velidred Volcano at the hands of King Haskell.

He lived with his friends in a small cabin in the village of Crossroads, and traveled to the mountain villages each day to help Cugbert feed people in need.

The next morning, Cugbert and Erik moved to the next village in the mountains.

Erik collected firewood in the mountain for the day's meals.

Cugbert had asked for twice as much firewood as normal, but gave no reason for the request.

Erik stoked the fire of the stone oven and tossed two more logs into the fire. He checked on the bread baking in the oven. The sun warmed them as Cugbert ladled soup and Erik handed out bread.

A woman carried a child in a cloth, wrapped over her shoulder and hanging on her chest. She took a slice of bread and Cugbert dipped a spoon into the hot chicken soup and ladled it into a wooden bowl the woman held.

She said, "You are so wonderful, Cugbert, for helping us, it's been a hard winter."

Cugbert touched the woman's shoulder and smiled.

Later, as Erik stoked the fires he asked, "Will I practice more healing, today? I'm getting better and I want a chance to use your frog again."

"You've grown in your powers, but today we won't be healing. Today you'll stretch your consciousness for guidance to reach the level of Pankratios single braid."

Lightness bloomed in Erik's chest, and a wide grin spread across his face. "Do you think I'm ready?"

"You showed mature wisdom and skill yesterday," Cugbert said. "Today's phase is the first step, like a baby learning to walk, you still have much to learn. You show promise and determination, which encourages me. The journey to the first braid contains three steps."

Erik's pulse quickened, and he leaned forward to make sure he didn't miss anything.

"You will experience the Fire and Ice challenge, and if you survive, we'll ask a loved one's permission to register you as a Pankratios monk in training."

Survive? Erik thought, "What do you mean Fire and Ice challenge, and how dangerous is it if you're worried about me surviving?"

"The practice is an ancient custom among priests and wizards to help discern your vocation and calling." Cugbert took a lump of dough, flipped it in the air, and pounded it on the wood counter. "One in four students struggles with the experience. We aren't sure what causes the problems, but yes, dangers exist. Students burn, or sometimes freeze to death. Sometimes surviving students suffer emotional issues upon completion.

Erik swallowed hard, "Emotional issues and freezing to death? Will I have burn scars all over my face from the fire part?"

"I can't predict outcome, or prevent dangers. The theory is adverse results prove that we chose students before they had adequate understanding and wisdom, or they weren't suitable for the priest role." Cugbert pressed his knuckles into the dough, kneading it.

"Shouldn't I wait to make sure? What's an extra month or year?"

"You'll be okay. I've lost no recruits over ten years and your expertise at healing the logger proves you're ready." Cugbert rolled the dough into a ball.

Erik took a deep breath. *Is this what I want?* Two months ago, on Earth, he prepared for life as a military pilot like his father. Now on Aloheno, he enjoyed newfound talents of healing, and he enjoyed helping the locals with food, but did he want to spend his entire life on Aloheno as a Pankratios monk?

"What happens if I have emotional issues? Will I live a normal life?"

"Family members take the unfortunate failures into their homes and comfort them. These students with adverse reactions die within a year from emotional pain and trauma."

"Can't you heal them?" Erik asked.

"It's interesting that despite probing their minds and bodies, healers can't help."

"What if I'm . . . not ready?"

"I wouldn't recommend it unless I knew you have the talent and mental fortitude to survive the experience." Cugbert created a nice round ball of dough, covered it with a clean cloth and placed it near the outdoor oven to give it time to rise.

* * * *

Ten hours later, Cugbert and Erik rested on a log near the tiny village. The thought of the Fire and Ice experience still weighed heavily on Erik's mind. Engaging in an activity that included fire seemed outrageous to him. A twenty-foot narrow path of coals, created from the extra wood collected for that morning's fires, glowed on the mountain side. Erik felt the heat even ten-feet from the hot embers. He rubbed his tired muscles. His feet were sore from standing and working all day, and he wanted to rest.

Cugbert stirred a mixture of water and herbs in a small metal pot. "Are you ready to begin the fire experience?"

Erik ran his hand through his hair. *Am I ready to be physically and mentally scarred and have my life shortened by sixty years? No. Is it too late to quit?*

The priest poured the mixture from the pot into a small, ceramic cup. "I can't give you this tea until you answer the question." The large red-headed monk stood above Erik. "Do you aspire to the life of a Pankratios monk?"

This was happening too fast. First, finding themselves on Aloheno, Al learning magic, the struggles to find Lily, the volcano ceremony during an eclipse, and now, only a few weeks later, he was considering committing his life to being a Pankratios monk? *Do I want this? What would Mom say? What will I do when the portal opens to Earth? Will I go home or stay on Aloheno? Can I marry as a Pankratios priest?*

Cugbert stood silently with the cup in his hand.

The power to heal and the joy of helping impoverished families had become a rewarding perk for Erik on this planet. At home in Montana, he sat in his room playing video games, but here he was helping create a better world. He thought back to a local village girl he healed. "Yes, I'm ready."

Erik accepted the cup; its heat warmed his hands. The tea smelled as if a chef had combined broccoli and curdled milk, but he sipped the liquid. He burned his lips, and blew on the surface. "This is horrible? What is it?"

"A tea designed by the ancients to enhance your senses and increase awareness of the spiritual world. This mixture displays the past and augments your reality to past actions and sins."

"Can you put in a tablespoon of honey to sweeten it?"

"The first step to Pankratios priesthood is to acknowledge your mistakes. The taste reminds you of imperfect decisions with friends and family."

A slight buzz built in his brain; it felt filled with cotton. His body warmed despite the cool air. He blinked his eyes, trying to focus on Cugbert.

"The first step is the fire challenge. It rids you of sins you've committed against others."

Erik's tongue felt heavy and thick, and he stuck it out a few times trying to work moisture into his mouth. "This doesn't feel right."

"It's important you finish your tea. You'll be fine."

The coals glowed brighter as dusk gathered. Erik gazed at the reds and oranges in the fire. He finished his drink, and Cugbert took Erik's hand and helped him to his feet. He stumbled at first until he centered himself. Smoke from the fire, the scent of burnt hickory, wafted in Erik's direction.

Cugbert said, "You'll hasten across the coals and experience the past from other's point of view."

Erik smiled. "Yes, I will walk across fire. Cool."

The priest positioned Erik before the glowing pathway and said, "Stay here. When I signal, walk toward me. Stay on the coals, keep walking and you'll be safe."

Erik laughed and said, "Cool. Get it? Fire. Cool." He laughed again.

The priest strode around the red coals and stood at the far end of the fire path.

Erik thought the smoke made it difficult to see Cugbert, or had the tea mixture made the large man appear out of focus? Erik couldn't tell for sure. Dusk turned to night, and silence settled over the mountain. When Erik exhaled, a small cloud formed around his mouth in the frigid mountain air.

Cugbert signaled Erik with a hand wave and said, "Begin the journey."

"I hope I don't die," Erik mumbled. He stepped onto the hot coals, moving quickly. He didn't want to linger. The smell of the burning charcoal reminded him of camping with his friends on Earth, memories from another lifetime.

The smoke switched from a wispy gray, turning to deep black, so dark he lost sight of Cugbert. *Stay the course, Cugbert's on the other side.*

The scene in front of Erik transformed, and a loud explosion broke the silence, startling Erik. His heart pounded in his chest. On his left, a volcano bubbled, spraying lava twenty feet into the air. A low stone altar appeared before him with his friend Lily sprawled on top.

Erik yelled, "Get up, Lily."

She didn't move.

He grasped a knife from the altar. Blood from an earlier sacrifice stained the knife. *Why am I holding this knife?* The knife's handle felt comfortable in his hands, as if he used it in other sacrifice ceremonies. Then he said words, nonsensical words, or maybe using an unfamiliar language? A strange power overtook him, and he realized his task was to drive the knife into Lily.

She lay on the altar in perfect peace and appeared asleep with a smile on her lips. She didn't tremble, scream or try to move. Her hands folded together on her chest, her white dress remained pristine despite the falling volcanic ash.

"Get up, Lily, get out of here." He yelled.

She didn't move.

Erik spoke more words and raised the knife above his head. Lily looked so beautiful and pure, her blond hair arranged behind her head like a halo or crown. He felt sad that he needed to drive the knife into her for the sacrifice. They should stop sacrificing the beautiful women. *I will recommend a change for the next sacrifice.* He gazed at the volcano but said to Lily, "I deliver you pure and blemish free to Velidred."

An arrow punctured his heart, and he fell. *No! Not on Lily, move the knife.* But the weight of his forward motion drove the knife into her chest.

Life drained from Erik's body. His breath came in brief gasps as his lungs filled with blood. "No," he yelled. His legs weakened, and black spots skittered across his vision. His hand grasping the altar failed, and he rolled to the ground.

I killed Lily. We're both dead.

Charcoal still burned, but the harsh, sulfuric stench dissipated in the cool mountain air. *Am I done; did I survive the fire?* The smoke turned black again.

No, not back to the volcano. His vision cleared, and he stood in a tiny cabin devoid of creature comforts. A table with two wooden stools stood near a window, but the fireplace lay empty and cold. A woman huddled in a corner. She was sobbing. Her clothes looked familiar to Erik. He knew this woman, but didn't quite recognize her thin, frail, dirt-streaked frame. *Should I comfort and feed her?*

Someone pounded on the door. The woman didn't move. She didn't lift her head, and her sobs grew more pronounced.

A man dressed all in black, with a white beard, opened the door, and he filled the small doorway. He entered and approached the woman touching her chin with a tender hand.

Erik felt a sudden giddiness. *Good, he will help. She's fine.*

The man grabbed the woman's hair and pulled her head at an angle to force her to look at him.

Erik's mouth fell open, and he tried to step back, but bumped into the wall instead. Coldness punched him in the core, and he gasped. The woman was Zita, emaciated, thin and in pain.

"Get up," the man yelled. "A princess doesn't cower." The tall man pulled her to her feet by her hair.

She let out a whimper and clutched her stomach.

Erik's nails bit into his palms, and his muscles quivered. *How dare this man treat Zita like a common servant?* Erik balled his fingers into a fist and moved toward the man. *Zita wasn't perfect, but I don't want her treated like garbage.* He yelled, "Get away from her. She's my friend."

Neither Zita nor the man reacted to Erik. The man continued his rough treatment, slapping her.

Erik placed his hands around the man's throat, but Erik's hands slid through the other's flesh. His body was useless here. He clenched his jaw tight, while his chest and lungs burned from the smoke.

The scent of the coals tainted his nostrils. Then the smoke cleared, heat warmed his legs, and Cugbert stood three-feet ahead. He completed the walk across the glowing charcoal and fell to the ground.

Cugbert poured oil over Erik's head. "You've experienced past sins and I absolve your sins. I purify you."

CHAPTER 6

Erik woke cold and hungry in the dark next to a fire, but the fire didn't warm him. Stiff muscles made it difficult to move. He remembered the fire experience like a dream. *Was it a dream? Did it occur? Are my feet okay? Are they burned?* He tried to sit, but fell back onto wet grass. He didn't remember walking to this location beside the fire.

In the fire experience, he killed Lily and watched a man hurt Zita. *Where is Zita?*

Cugbert said, "Good, you're awake. Talk to me."

"Zita's in trouble. I must go to her."

"No, the images you see during the experience may have happened many months or years ago. It's good that you survived and are well."

"I'm not well. Zita is alive and in trouble. She needs help."

"Do you know where she is?"

"She's in a cabin in the mountains. A man hurt her." Erik tried to stand, but his legs buckled, and he fell to the grass. "Something's wrong with my legs."

"The experience you had might have occurred before you arrived on Aloheno. Disregard it."

How can I forget about the fire experience? He couldn't sit without falling. He lay on his back looking at the stars. *Cugbert said he lost none of his students to the Fire and Ice experience. Will I be the first; am I paralyzed below the waist?*

"My legs aren't working." Erik struggled to swallow, his mouth dry and sticky. "Cugbert help me." He wrapped his arms around his chest. "I'm cold and can't feel anything." His lips and chin trembled.

"Relax."

Erik clenched his jaw as neck muscles bunched in pain.

"I've never seen this."

"Tell me it's temporary."

"I can't tell you that."

"Can you heal me?"

"Let's give it a few moments. I've heard of healers trying to resolve a problem but making it worse."

Erik took shallow breaths and tried to wiggle his toes and thought that worked. "I can wiggle my toes. If you're paralyzed, can you wiggle your toes?" *Maybe I wasn't ready for the Fire and Ice experience. Cugbert forced me to take the test too soon.*

"Each experience is unique." Cugbert stood over Erik.

"That's not helping me. I don't want to be paralyzed on this strange planet." Erik reached out to Cugbert. "Help me."

"Tell me about Zita." Cugbert asked.

"Forget Zita. I have a serious problem. Can't you do anything?"

Cugbert didn't take Erik's outstretched hand. "Tell me about Zita."

"There's nothing to tell. She's in trouble, that's all I know. Now help me." Erik's heart pounded as sweat bubbled on his forehead. *What happens to paralyzed people on Aloheno?* Unacceptable outcomes floated through his mind.

"Can you describe Zita's attacker?"

"Why are you worried about Zita? I can't walk or even sit. Will I die?"

Cugbert reached down to Erik and pushed his chest hard till he was flat on the ground. "Who attacked Zita?"

"Ouch, why are you hurting me?" Erik tried to push Cugbert away, but his arms seemed useless.

"Tell me."

Erik quit struggling. *What does this man want?* "I don't know. Zita huddled in a corner of a sparse cabin. This tall man with a white beard and black jacket yelled at Zita, pulled her hair and slapped her. I tried to help, but I slipped through him like a ghost."

Cugbert stood and wrinkled his brow. "She went to Gadiel. Dangerous."

"What does it mean?" Erik asked.

"Zita's not through with you and your friends. You're in danger if you go after her and yet . . ." He placed his chin in his cupped hand.

"And yet?"

"What did she wear?"

"I don't know, old rags or dirty clothes."

Cugbert reached down, grabbed the front of Erik's tunic, and hauled the boy to his feet. "What clothes did she wear? Were they the same clothes she wore to the volcano?"

Cugbert held Erik high enough that his feet didn't touch the ground, their faces inches apart. Erik took shallow breaths, afraid to do more.

"Tell me what she wore."

"Why does it matter?" Erik thought if Cugbert released him, he would crumple into a ball on the ground.

"It matters. We have to determine if she sent for Gadiel or if he found her for his own purpose. If she's branded, then she's connected with the old man, which permits him to control her mind. Power gained from the Fire and Ice experience. Did you see a brand on Zita?"

"A brand? She's branded like cattle?"

"Yes. Is she branded?"

"I don't know. I didn't see anything like that. It's not like we compared tattoos. She does have a volcano tattoo on her arm."

Cugbert placed Erik's feet on the ground and continued to hold his tunic while Erik swayed.

Erik smiled. "Feeling is coming back into my legs."

Cugbert let go, but Erik grabbed the man's arms. "Wait, don't let me fall."

"I think you'll be all right. I'm concerned. Zita's in danger.

"Isn't that what I told you five minutes ago?"

"I promised her mother I'd watch over her, yet Gadiel's influence will transform and twist her perceptions. I wanted to wait a day before doing the ice challenge, but we don't have time. It's more dangerous in your current condition, but we must hurry."

"Why can't we wait until tomorrow, or even after we find Zita? We don't want to rush into danger, do we?" Erik let go of Cugbert's arms, and though wobbly, his legs supported him.

"Hmm," Cugbert mused, "More dangerous, but we don't have time."

"What is the ice experience? Do you pour ice water over my head? That won't take long and I should be able to handle that."

Cugbert laughed. "No. Walk with me."

Erik followed the red-headed priest to a small frozen lake. The layer of ice looked thin and dangerous.

They stopped on the lakeshore. The night sky was dark above the lake where a sliver of the Pantaleon moon, shining in the firmament, reflected off the frozen water.

Cugbert said, "Strip to your small-clothes."

"Are you crazy? Don't you feel the cold? There's no fire, and I'll freeze to death. Are you trying to kill me?"

"Do you want to become a Pankratios Priest?"

Erik thought, maybe not. *This guy is crazy. I don't want to die.* He thought back to his trouble standing after the fire experience. *Will this ice experience complete the paralysis?* "Okay, but we'll make this fast, right? I don't want to freeze to death. I grew up in Montana and I know icy lakes even in summer can take your breath away and kill you in seconds or at least minutes."

"Yes, it's dangerous. Do you seek the Pankratios first braid?"

Erik hesitated. *What if I don't say yes or no?*

Cugbert stared at Erik.

Erik bowed his head and said, "Yes."

"Good, strip to your small-clothes." Cugbert produced a small bowl and a leather pouch from his cloak and emptied the powdered contents into the bowl.

Erik stood in the crisp night air and flapped his arms around his bare chest as he tried to stay warm. "I'm freezing here. Let's do this."

Cugbert recited words over the bowl, and the powder burst into a blue flame. "The ice experience guides you on a journey to see a hypothetical future sin against your fellow man. Be cautious. This may portend a future event or express an idle thought."

"Okay, okay, let's do this."

"Stand near me and breathe the incense."

Erik moved closer and took a deep breath. The incense smelled sweet, like a vanilla candle with a touch of cinnamon. The aroma reminded him of his mother baking cookies at Christmas.

"Once more," Cugbert whispered.

Erik closed his eyes and inhaled. Cugbert grabbed Erik's arms and dragged Erik toward the lake. Erik thought he should resist, but didn't. They stumbled to the shore and then walked on the ice. It cracked and they both plunged into the frigid water.

Cugbert pushed Erik into the deep water, and Erik wanted to draw another breath, but knew he would drown if he took in water. The sharp, cold shocked him, and he struggled, but Cugbert held him under the water.

Darkness surrounded him and his arms flailed uselessly. He thrashed for the surface, but in the murky water he couldn't tell which direction led to life giving oxygen.

A woman screamed.

A moment later, he stood on the ice of an enormous lake, where he couldn't see land in any direction. This ice held his weight, and he breathed deeply.

Another scream shrieked in the darkness.

Where is she? Should I try to rescue her? He searched the horizon, but saw no one.

The person screamed again, and water splashed. Erik got a bead on the woman's location and ran in the direction of the splash. Clouds muted the light from two moons. A red glow appeared in the clouds, and he knew that was from Aloheno's moon, Velidred. He must still be on this planet.

The splashing continued, and as Erik bounded toward the person, the ice cracked beneath him. He slowed, and it cracked again. He heard a splash nearby, and Erik said, "I'm here. Stop struggling and I'll help you."

"Hurry," the woman said.

"Zita is that you?"

"Please help."

Erik hurried, but took cautious steps as the ice thinned. Within five feet he saw her. Zita continued to splash as ice formed on her wet hair.

"Help." She pleaded.

Erik lay on his belly to reduce his body weight on the thin surface. He extended his hand toward Zita, and she grasped it.

"Thank you for rescuing me."

Then Erik put his hand on Zita's head and pushed her head downward. She struggled, but he was stronger and held her head under water.

Erik didn't know how long it took, but the water stopped churning, and he pulled his ice covered hand out of the water. He smiled as he returned to safe ice and whistled a cheerful tune he remembered from long ago. Warmth spread through his body.

A hand grabbed his arm and pulled.

CHAPTER 7

The sun shone through the trees as Erik sat by the fire contemplating the Fire and Ice experience. He remembered little from last night. He knew Cugbert pulled him out of the icy water. The cold gripped Erik like a vise as he shivered next to a roaring fire. The scent of pine trees filled the clearing.

Then the pain raced back into his mind. He rolled up the long sleeve on his tunic and studied the newly burned flesh.

He remembered the painful branding. Cugbert sat on Erik beside the fire. Erik couldn't move, and though he struggled, Cugbert's weight and strength overpowered him. Cugbert pulled a red-hot metal object from the fire.

Erik wriggled desperately.

Cugbert pressed the hot iron against Erik's upper arm. He screamed in pain. Cugbert released him, and prepared a different tea for Erik.

Cugbert said, "We need to get moving. We're running out of time. Drink that, it'll help the healing."

The brand displayed a castle on a mountain where the outline of two moons, one a sliver, hovered above the castle.

Erik pointed to his brand, "What's the castle?"

"That is the ancient city of Pankratios, the training ground for third-braid priests."

"Is that where you got your third braid?"

"No, the city of Pankratios is missing. Nothing but a bank of fog exists where the city once stood. Today we visit the Village of the Stone Warriors. I want you to meet your father."

Erik looked at Cugbert, "My father is alive on Aloheno?"

"You'll see." Cugbert said.

"Where is he? Why have you withheld this information from me?" Adrenaline swirled through Erik's body. "No, whoever is claiming to be my father is a fake, because Dad died in a war on Earth. My father was a United States, Air Force pilot. That's what Mom told me."

Cugbert poured a bucket of water on the fire.

Erik didn't move and wondered if his mother deceived him all these years. The frigid mountain air rushed into his lungs as he took a deep breath. He crossed his arms and stared at Cugbert.

"Your father was a brave commander of men for the Kallurian nation. He fought many battles against the Mountain King and led his courageous battalion to many a victory. But there was one battle he didn't win."

"No, I'm not of this planet. Maybe Al and Sherry came from Aloheno, but I was born on Earth and lived a normal Earth life." A lump formed in his throat and he raised his voice, "I'm not like the others. Mom wouldn't lie to me."

"All your mothers lied to you. In case spies on Earth searched for you. Your father convinced your mother to travel with you and the others to Earth to protect you. Come and meet your dad, you'll see." Cugbert walked up the mountain path.

Erik didn't move. He thought back to comments Prince Krunal made about the man Erik resembled. Was it true his dad and mom were from Aloheno? That Erik was born on Aloheno? He couldn't believe the man abandoned Erik and his mother. Why didn't

Cugbert tell him sooner? Erik looked at Cugbert's back as the third-braid priest of the Pankratios religion continued walking away.

Erik called after Cugbert, "I don't want to meet my father. Aren't there children and poor people to feed? Didn't you say we needed to find Zita because she's in trouble?"

Cugbert stopped and turned. "After meeting your father, we decide if you continue your Pankratios training."

"Why, because you think my father has a say in my life's direction? A man I've never met."

"It's the Pankratios way. We ask the family to get involved."

"Ask my mother. A man, a stranger to me, doesn't speak for me and my future." Erik walked away from Cugbert.

"I've been teaching you peace, forgiveness and patience and yet you've learned nothing."

Yes, Erik thought, you've taught me those concepts. It wasn't enough. He stopped walking and blurted out, "You don't understand how I feel."

"This is a test and you're failing. Do you want entrance into the Pankratios—"

"No, I don't want to be a part of a religion where the people training me lie and withhold information." Emotions swirled like a hurricane. Erik walked the opposite direction as his mentor. *Yes, I want to meet y father. Yes, I want to continue my training.* But this additional information rocked his mind in waves. One moment he thought Dad was dead, and now he's alive? *The man lived close to the portal to Earth, why didn't he visit? Why does Dad live in the Village of the Stone Warriors?*

Erik stopped. He looked up the mountain; Cugbert stood quietly studying him. The priest hadn't moved.

Erik rejoined Cugbert and protested, "My friends and I traveled to the cave entrance many times. You could have told me."

"You weren't ready."

"But he's my father."

They walked in silence past the village and continued to where the six thousand stone warriors stood, the same as they had the day the Mountain King used great magic to turn them to stone. Goosebumps rose on Erik's arms as they approached the immobile army. They were alive and talked, but couldn't move. On their visits to the portal, Erik saw families who had traveled to see a loved one. Were these birthday celebrations, anniversaries or times to share news of someone's death?

Cugbert led Erik to the commander of all the soldiers. The same man he met on the day he reached Aloheno. The man had cautioned his friends to return to Earth. Should they have turned back?

Cugbert stood at attention and said, "Commander John Anderson, I want to introduce you to your son, Erik Anderson."

"Hello, Son." The officer said.

The man stood three inches shorter than Erik. The stone soldier, a gray statue, showed no facial expressions, and his voice was muted. A bushy stone mustache covered his upper lip.

Erik stood motionless and silent in the presence of the man he thought was dead. He didn't know what to do. He couldn't shake his Dad's hand, it didn't seem right to hug the statue, so he stood and whispered, "Hello Dad."

"How's your mother?"

"She's probably worried sick, since we left without telling her where we were going. But she was doing well when we left Earth and she works in an office and is happy."

"Why did you return to Aloheno?"

"I told you, Dad, to rescue our friend, Lily. And we did, we succeeded, we defeated the Mountain King and saved Lily."

"I've heard news of the victory, was that your doing?"

It felt like talking to an automated phone service. The mouth on the stone soldier didn't move; no smile lines or arm movements exhibited joy or displeasure.

"I drove a spear into the man."

"You've become a skilled soldier then. Are you training to be a warrior and commander?"

Erik looked at Cugbert. *What would Dad's expectations be now that I'm living on Aloheno? Did Dad expect me to be a soldier? A military career on Earth would be cool, and I wanted to follow him into the Air Force and be a pilot, but a foot soldier on Aloheno?*

Cugbert said, "Your responsibility is to tell your parents your path."

"Dad . . . I'm . . . Cugbert is . . . I've decided to . . . be a Pankratios priest."

"A priest? You single-handedly defeat the Mountain King and you want to be a priest? Legions of men will follow you into battle, the boy who vanquished the Mountain King."

"I didn't kill the king myself. My friends, Alpherge and Sherry, and a girl named, Zita, helped kill the man. We just wanted to save Lily."

"You're a hero, my boy; men follow heroes. You can't waste gravitas being a priest. Cugbert is this your meddling?"

"I talked to him and showed him the life of a Pankratios priest. There's been no coercion, no trickery. He has the talent."

"Talent, bah. I don't want my son to be a poor priest when he has the skill to lead soldiers into battle."

"Dad, I don't want to be a soldier on Aloheno. I enjoy helping people and healing. You should have seen the man I helped the other day, when a tree fell on him. He broke both legs and I healed him. I have a gift."

"No, I can't give you my blessing to be a priest. The Kallurian army needs leaders and individuals like you to stop the aggression of destructive and power hungry kings. Priests are pacifist cowards, and I'd be ashamed to see you become a priest. You're the son of a commander, your grandfather was a commander, and your destiny is to be a commander. The army will teach you to accept success and defeat. As Commander you will earn people's respect. I would spit on the ground at Cugbert's feet if I could, to show distaste for your choice."

"I have talent to heal. Doesn't the world need healers, too?"

"A pacifist healer? Your grandfather is turning over in his grave right now."

"The Mountain King is dead and Prince Krunal and the resistance took over the Velidred Castle, Aloheno doesn't need warriors. We already brought peace to the land."

"There is never peace. Individuals lust for money, power and glory, and they achieve their goals on the backs of families, villages and kingdoms. A warrior protects families, friends and countries from bullies like the Mountain King. Behold these soldiers who gave their all for their country. Don't you want to imitate these brave men? I would turn my back on you if I could."

Erik ran his hand through his hair, "Dad, you don't understand. There are people hurting everywhere I've been. They're hungry, sick, impoverished and injured, and I bring them comfort and healing. Isn't that important, too?" *What can I do to show this man that helping others is an important and worthy goal?*

"Becoming anything other than a soldier brings dishonor to the family."

"Cugbert convinced me of the power and care that priests give, and he's told me of the pain, suffering and struggles of being a soldier. Things like being away from family, or returning home so crippled they can't work to support their family. Is that the future you picture for me?"

"There is risk of being injured and crippled, we all accept that risk, but the joy of serving your country is more important."

Erik couldn't believe this conversation. His father didn't see the power in healing instead of killing? He clinched his teeth so tight his jaw hurt. "Dad, I'm not becoming a soldier, I've decided to become a Pankratios priest, a peaceful healer and not a paid killer."

The commander took a sharp breath, "I sent you to Earth to save you from people who wanted to kill you. This is how you repay me by turning your back on your family and following this pacifist coward?"

Erik's hands tightened into a fist and his nails bit into his palms. He felt his body quivering. He shouted, "I won't be a soldier."

"I can't accept the path you've chosen. Never visit me, again."

"Don't worry, I'm leaving and never coming back." Erik turned and stormed away from his father.

Cugbert caught up with Erik and touched him on the shoulder. "Slow down, we need to talk."

"Don't you think there's been enough talking for today? Didn't you hear the man? He's ashamed of me. Fine."

"You can't be a Pankratios monk until we get his consent."

Erik stopped and looked at Cugbert. "Did you hear the man? I swear his expression changed to a look of disgust."

"He's old school. I've seen this in fathers. You can overcome it, but not by running."

"What am I supposed to do? Join the army? Get killed?"

Cugbert frowned and shook his head. "Have you learned nothing in the last six weeks? All the lessons on peacefulness, listening, healing and patience and at the first hint of conflict in your life you forget everything."

"My father turned his back on me. What would you do?"

"These lessons aren't idle suggestions. It's easy to be patient with someone who is sick, hungry or tired. But family members and friends can be difficult. You want to strike and yell, but you need to be peaceful, patient and attentive."

Erik exhaled. If blood could boil, then his was roiling. Peace. Gone. Patience. None. Each breath burned in his chest as it had the day Lily told him she was going to homecoming with the foreign student at school.

Cugbert stepped in front of Erik.

Erik sidestepped left.

Cugbert caught up with Erik and again stepped in front of him.

Erik stopped and looked at Cugbert.

The priest stood calmly rubbing his beard.

This time Erik stepped to his right, passed Cugbert and hurried down the mountain.

Cugbert laughed.

Erik jogged toward Crossroads. He wanted to be with his friends. Wait until he told them about his father. They wouldn't believe it, but they would comfort him.

Cugbert caught up and trotted beside Erik.

Erik accelerated. He was a fast runner, not the fastest on the cross-country team, but not one of the slackers.

Cugbert ran with an easy gait beside him.

The trail became steeper. They ran faster, and Erik lost his balance. He pin-wheeled his arms to keep from falling. He needed to change direction because the path curved around a tree, but he had too much momentum.

Cugbert made the turn.

Erik slammed hard into the tree.

Zita's Revenge

CHAPTER 8

The harsh smell of alcohol filled the small cabin where Erik lived with his friends in the village of Crossroads. Erik's three friends from Earth, Alpherge, Lily and Sherry sat on benches at the wooden table and watched Cugbert bandage the scratches to Erik's hands, arms and face where he hit the tree. Cugbert said nothing, although Erik expected a lecture on the dangers of not practicing patience and peacefulness at all times.

Alpherge, a tall, gangly teenager that they referred to as Al, said, "Are you serious; the stone warrior dude is your dad?"

Sherry, a redhead and the smartest person in their high school class on Earth, said, "He told you to never see him again?"

Lily said, "Oh my." She was a thin girl with a dancer's body. She pushed her long, blonde hair out of her eyes.

"I'm not going back to the stone warriors. Ow!" Erik yelped. "Cugbert, why can't you use gentle healing, why all the gunk and bandages?"

"It's a lesson in pain." Cugbert wrapped another layer of cloth over the scratches.

Al said, "I bet if we rescued the stone warriors, then your dad would let you become a priest, because at that point he would be commander again."

Erik wondered if that would work. *Could freeing Dad be a benefit?* "I don't know, Al. The man seemed adamant about me becoming a soldier and commander."

"Rescuing the warriors isn't the answer." Cugbert said.

With an exasperated sigh, Erik said, "What are we supposed to do?"

"Hold your arm high."

Cugbert wrapped the cloth higher on Erik's arm and above his elbow.

Erik tried to bend his elbow. "These scratches will heal without medicines. You're wrapping the cloth too tight, I can't bend my elbow."

"The cloth isn't for healing."

Erik shook his head. The ointment administered to the scratches burned, but he plastered a smile on his face. If the priest wanted to hurt Erik to teach him a lesson, then let it hurt, he could take it.

Erik said, "We need to find Zita."

Sherry stood. "Why?"

"She's in danger."

"From what?" Sherry asked.

He said, "I saw an image of a tall, thin man in a black outfit with a white beard beating her."

CHAPTER 9

The next day, seventeen-year-old, Alpherge Greystone, walked through the streets of Crossroads with the Staff of Ishwa in his hands. His high-school girlfriend, Sherry, walked beside him.

A boy approached and asked, "Are you a great wizard?"

"Yes, I'm Alpherge the Mighty, Defender of Velidred." He stuck out his chest. He loved the attention he received when he strolled through the village. With magic and Sherry's help, they killed the evil king of Velidred during the eclipse of the triple moons four weeks earlier.

Sherry said, "Really, you're going with Defender of Velidred?"

"Yeah, I like the sound of it. What do you think?"

"I think you're an egotistical bonehead. Why not use your magic to return to Earth? There must be a way we can open that cave and go home. Let's return to the Village of the Stone Warriors and see if anything changed."

Alpherge said, "We were up there a week ago and nothing changed. Master Ishwa told us it won't open for four years." He shook his head.

A group of children followed the wizard and Sherry through the streets.

"Don't you kids have to go to school?" Sherry asked. The children were dirty.

A girl with un-brushed hair and a dirt-smudged face said, "There's no school, that's for rich folk."

Sherry bent near the girl, "What's your name?"

"Sondra."

"How old are you?"

Sondra spent a moment thinking and said, "Ten."

"Where's your mother?"

"She's at the village well washing clothes."

"Who's watching you?" Sherry brushed hair out of the girl's eyes.

An older boy in the group spoke, "No one watches us. We watch ourselves."

All the kids nodded.

"This is horrible, you should be learning, not stampeding around the streets unattended."

Sherry stood, "Al, we should start a school for these kids."

"They're my entourage; if they're in school, who'll walk with me and adore me?" Al asked.

"Your entourage should learn math, science, and a language. Look at these kids. They're unkempt and don't know the basics of hygiene."

"The children will learn a trade as apprentices at the forge and tailor shops." Al's train of thought shifted, *I need a wizard robe to look more professional. Master Iswha's staff drew attention, but wearing a wizard's robe might bring me paying jobs.* He ran his hand across the three faces carved into the long wooden staff. The faces were trapped in the staff by magic allowing the entities to speak with Al.

"Yeah, and the ones who don't qualify run around the village causing trouble. That's no life for children. The best they can look forward to is work in the fields in hard physical labor, or to be like the women with their buckets of water washing clothes. Where are the schools?"

"Do you think I should buy a robe to wear instead of this tunic?"

"Are you even listening to me? Why do you need a robe? And where are you getting money for a robe?"

"A mighty wizard needs proper equipment to get respect. I'm like a wizened college professor."

"You know we got lucky on that volcano, and it wasn't skill that you survived. Forget wizarding and let's discover how to get off this planet."

Al waved at the people who glanced in his direction as he walked. The kids followed and mimicked his wave.

A man dressed in a black wool jacket approached the parading group.

The man stopped Al and bowed. "Kind wizard." His white beard sparkled in the sunlight, and he was nearly as tall as Al.

The children scattered.

"Yes?" Al asked.

"I've heard you're a wizard of considerable magic." The man's leathery face bore deep grooves and valleys.

Al brought his shoulders back, raised his head and smiled. "How may I serve you?"

Sherry said, "Oh brother."

"I've heard rumors. Is it true you killed the Mountain King?" The man leaned on his cane and lifted his black hat, exposing dark eyes to the sunlight.

Al stepped back from the leathery faced man. "Yes, that's true."

"I see. Can you help me?"

"Maybe." A shadow seemed to form between them.

"My name is Gadiel and my eldest grandson, Frank, is one of the stone warriors, a victim of the Mountain King. Are you strong enough in magic to release him from the curse and enable him to return to his mother, my daughter?" The man stepped closer to Al.

Al stepped back. "I've never tried, and I don't know any spells to do that. I'm still learning the craft." The man's eyes unnerved Al. They appeared black, but a red spot floated over his iris.

"My daughter is heartbroken over the loss of her son, and if a wizard released him from the spell, then my daughter could reunite with her boy. Could you free my grandson for us?"

"I must research how to perform a task like that." He touched his lip with his forefinger. *If I restore the stone warriors, then I'll become a legend and surpass my grandfather's legacy of magic. I'll be remembered as the wizard that killed the Mountain King and ended the pain and misery of the stone warriors.* "I'll do it."

Sherry said, "How can you say that? You don't have a clue what you're saying."

"That is wonderful, kind sir." Gadiel raised a dry, leathery hand and grasped Al's hand.

A tingle flowed through Al's arm like an electric shock. Al tried to shake off the man's grip, but Gadiel pulled him closer, forcing Al to look into his eyes.

Al met Gadiel's gaze, but leaned back.

Sherry said, "He can't do that, sir. He's making promises he can't keep."

"What do you mean?" Al raised his staff into the air and broke eye contact with Gadiel to look at Sherry. "With this staff I have great wizarding skills."

"But you don't know how to use it." Sherry stepped closer to Al.

"If I may interrupt." Gadiel thrust his cane between Sherry and Al.

"There are objects of immense magical power that may be beneficial to the release of the warriors." Gadiel spoke in a soothing, deep voice.

Al thought back to days on Earth playing Dungeons and Dragons where the adventures were quests to find magical items and gold. "Yes, a quest for powerful magical items." He nodded and smiled.

Sherry guffawed, "'A quest to find powerful magical items?' Do you hear yourself and the things you say? Look at me." Sherry touched his cheek and turned his face to hers. She lowered her voice, "This isn't some D&D game like we played on Earth. We don't want to wander around this planet fighting wild beasts and mucking through swamps on an adventure."

Gadiel squeezed Al's hand tighter, forcing Al to look at him.

Al said, "Sir, please," and pulled his hand from the man's grip. Al ran his hand through his oily, unwashed hair. He looked at Sherry, his jaw tight.

She looked into his eyes.

Her lips trembled. *Why won't Sherry let me have fun? She's nagged me ever since the eclipse. All I want is a brief adventure with treasures and magical items.*

Gadiel said, "I've heard of an object at the Ice Castle up north. A legend is told of a golden crown imbued with great magic. I'm sure a mighty wizard with your skills can retrieve it."

Sherry stepped between Al and Gadiel and pushed the elderly gentleman. "Al is busy solving other problems. Maybe another time he'll help with your grandson."

Gadiel removed his hat and looked at Sherry. "I'm sorry to bother you, Miss. I thought your friend was a powerful wizard, I see I'm wrong." He wiped his brow with a handkerchief and replaced his hat.

I am a powerful wizard, Sherry isn't my mother. Heat rushed through Al's body. "I'm a mighty wizard and can be more powerful, when I learn more about my staff."

The old man leaned toward the staff and squinted at the carved figures. "What if I taught you about the staff and its abilities?" He reached out and ran his fingers across patterns in the wood.

Sherry spoke, "Are you a wizard?"

He laughed, a dry coughing sound, "I'm no wizard, but I studied magical staffs over the years and will share my knowledge for the young wizard's aid."

Wow, someone to train me in the staff's use, instead of pointing at things and seeing what happens. "Sherry you should like that, I'll learn more about magic instead of vaporizing things and disintegrating stuff like my grandfather did."

"It's an awful idea." Sherry crossed her arms and raised her eyebrows. "Why can't Gadiel study the staff here, and you won't have to go to the Ice Castle?"

Al had seen this look on Sherry's face, the look that said, I read the book, and my answer is the right answer and nothing you say will convince me otherwise.

Sherry said, "You know I'm right, but you're thinking of a stupid answer, anyway."

Gadiel said, "I won't be staying in this area myself, I'm a business person with goods to deliver to the Ice Castle. The caravan leaves next week from Velidred. If you want help with the staff, you must come with us."

Sherry said, "If the golden crown is at the Ice Castle and you will be there anyway, why don't you retrieve it yourself?"

"Oh, I've tried to seize it numerous times when I was younger, but it requires the touch of someone with great magical ability, maybe a wizard with the skill of young Alpherge. That's your name, right? I've heard you're Alpherge the Great's grandson. I would ask Alpherge the Great himself to help if he were still alive."

This is a task the man might ask of my grandfather. I must do it for my family's name. "How far is it to the Ice Castle?" Al asked.

Gadiel said, "The trip takes about three months depending on weather and obstacles, but the caravan must return to Velidred before winter."

"You can't possibly be considering this, Al? It sounds like a trip to Alaska; if you don't make it back, you'll freeze to death."

Gadiel said, "I've traveled the route many times myself, and it's quite safe. We've an experienced crew that leads the caravan. You're welcome to join us."

"I don't want any more adventures on this planet." Sherry answered.

"What is it you want?" Gadiel leaned on his cane.

"I want to go home." She grabbed Al's hand.

Gadiel said, "A belief exists, which I don't hold to, that the gateway will open if you release the stone warriors."

"You know of the gateway?" Sherry cocked her head to the side.

"Rumors." Gadiel waved his hand. "Like I said, I don't subscribe to those beliefs."

"We should go to the Ice Castle," Al said. "Look at the opportunity, a quest, a golden crown, adventure, and a chance to save the stone warriors and open the portal."

"We can talk back at the cabin." Sherry said.

"You should commit now, and then I can make arrangements for your lodging."

Al said, "I'm ready to go, I don't have to talk it over with anyone."

"That's excellent, and I look forward to learning and sharing your staff's secrets."

Sherry grabbed a fistful of Al's tunic, "You can't be serious. Please let's talk, and then we'll decide. We should ask the others. Don't Al and I have time to talk about this, sir?"

"Yes, of course. I leave for Velidred tomorrow, you can leave with me or come a few days later. Did I tell you there will be compensation for working the animals needed for the caravan?"

"Perfect, I need cash. Then I can get that wizard's robe."

"We'll let you know," Sherry said.

The man walked away as heat flushed through Al's body, "Why are you fighting me on this? We can rescue the stone warriors, and I can learn more about my staff. It'll be great."

"So you can run off on a grand adventure?" Sherry huffed.

"It's a noble quest to recover the golden crown and rescue the stone warriors."

"You know nothing about the Ice Castle. What if Gadiel is a friend of the Mountain King and is setting a trap for you?"

"A trap? Are you serious? The old man has a grandson that's a stone warrior, and he wants to return him to his daughter. Why wouldn't you want that?"

"He mentioned you'd work with the animals. What do you know about animals? I'm better prepared for that task than you." She crossed her arms and bit her lower lip.

"You'll be right beside me. Imagine a real-life quest, not make believe like we played on Earth, but an exciting adventure as we search for a golden crown."

Sherry rubbed the back of her neck, "Listen, I'm scared. I got a bad vibe about that man."

"Come on, he's just an old man that wants to reunite his daughter and grandson. We should help."

CHAPTER 10

Al and Sherry entered the little cabin they lived in with their friends from Earth, Erik and Lily. The one-room, dirt-floored building had four straw-filled mattresses stacked in a corner. A large pot hung above the fireplace where a fire warmed the meager soup in the pot. The room felt crowded when they all packed in because it was the size of a bedroom on Earth.

Erik and Lily sat on a bench at the wooden table. When people from Aloheno kidnapped Lily, Erik convinced his friends to come with him to rescue Lily and they all became trapped on this planet when the portal to Earth closed.

Lily asked, "Where have you two been all day?"

Al said, "Erik, do you want to go on an adventure to retrieve a golden crown that will release the stone warriors? The caravan leaves in a week to the Ice Castle. We use wizardry to grab the magic crown and then come back and set the stone dudes free. We'll be heroes. What do you think?"

Al thought if he could convince Erik of the importance of the golden crown, then Erik would convince Sherry to help find the crown.

Sherry said, "I told him he's not going on a quest. He's staying right here and we're solving the portal issue."

"Wait," Erik said. "What adventure?"

Kenneth Brown

Al took a deep breath. "We met this man in the village, tall dude wearing all black, and he wants to save his grandson, one of the stone warriors. He asked for our help to turn the statues back to people, and if we capture the golden crown, we can release the warriors and the gateway opens."

Sherry said, "Look we have this cabin and need jobs to pay the rent. You can't go searching for imaginary treasures."

Erik rose from the table, "Wait, you two. Tell me from the start."

Sherry said, "Al wants to go on a quest to get a magic, golden crown."

"A quest sounds awesome. We should do it." Erik high-fived Al.

Al knew Erik would support his desire.

Sherry balled her hands into fists. "No, we shouldn't. It's dangerous and we don't know the man. He dressed differently from the rest of the people in Crossroads. Like a Southern, fire and brimstone preacher from the late eighteen hundreds. I don't trust him."

Al said, "Why don't you trust him, Sherry? He wants his family back. If Lily was a stone warrior you'd help her, wouldn't you?"

Sherry sat on the bench. "I don't think he's that harmless. The man is using you to either get a valuable item which he'll keep or use to hurt you. He was too smooth, like how TV shows picture a used car salesperson."

Lily asked, "Too smooth?"

"As the man spoke about the golden crown, all the pieces fit together like a jigsaw puzzle. He talked about his grandson and then how he just happens to know about the golden crown. And, oh yeah, by the way, I'm going that way next week, why don't you join me?"

Al thought about Sherry's comments. She was right. The man had a slick manner. "You've told us for a week we need to get jobs. The guy said he would pay us for handling the caravan animals."

"We discussed the animals. That's my skillset, not yours."

Al rubbed the back of his neck. "The guy said he's a business man, so yeah, he just noticed I was a wizard and I could handle the animals and get the magic, golden thingy."

"Remember in Montana when we all went to the dude ranch for the weekend? You were too afraid to ride the horses, and you didn't even feed them carrots or apples."

"Yeah, because they would eat my fingers . . .," Al wiggled his fingers, "they're the same size as carrots." Al remembered his friends laughing at him because he couldn't overcome his fear. But hadn't he grown into a fierce wizard not afraid of anything?

Sherry challenged Al, "What animals do they use? Horses? Mules? Donkeys or little ponies? He talked about a caravan. If you can't feed or ride a horse, how will you feed a camel or whatever crazy animals are used on this planet?"

Erik jumped into the conversation, "Where's the caravan going?"

Al said, "The Ice Castle."

"That sound's interesting." Erik said.

Lily asked, "How long will it take?"

"Three months."

Erik said, "What if the portal opens while we're traveling?"

"That's my point," Sherry said. "Erik, this man isn't your normal dude. He's slick and strange. At one point I thought he tried hypnotizing Al, and I stepped in between them."

"Ha! Hypnotizing?" Al thought back on the experience. The man grasped Al's hand and pulled him closer, which forced Al to gaze into the man's eyes. Then the red dot floated in his eye and got larger.

"Yes, hypnotizing. And you know it."

"It was a handshake." Al stared at the floor.

Sherry put her hands on her hips. "Why do you do this? Why do you deny all the evidence? You want to go on this quest more than you care about us."

Al felt heat rise to his face. "Yeah, I do want to go. A caravan, golden treasure, and a journey to a place called the Ice Castle sounds fun and exciting."

Sherry released an exasperated sigh, "Think about a month-long journey to this Ice Castle. You'll probably cross treacherous frozen lakes or encounter strange and dangerous animals, maybe worse than those weird stegox running around the forest. Where will you sleep and what will you eat? After you arrive at the Ice Castle, where's the golden crown? You might have to fight goblins, wizards, or enter a dungeon."

Erik said, "That sounds awesome." He gave Al another high-five. "We gotta do this."

Al stood erect, holding his staff. "Yes, imagine the glory we'll achieve after capturing the golden crown. Then we rescue the stone warriors. We'll be heroes and bards will recite our adventures for centuries."

Sherry said, "Oh brother. What if it's a trap? Imagine not one wizard but many wizards. Doesn't the name, Ice Castle, make you wonder about the environment where it's located? If you thought Montana was cold, how about Alaska or Canada?"

"Gadiel said it was safe, and goes there every year. I imagine it's like going to Billings, Montana, a normal road trip, with highways and everything."

"What about your plan to return to wizarding school?"

"One trainer at the wizard school, Jayanti, is working out the details; it might take a month or two to acquire needed resources. So, I have time."

"You're living safely in the fenced in section of Crossroads. You're getting three meals a day. Why do you want to disrupt that?"

"For fun and adventure." Erik said, grinning from ear to ear.

Sherry shook her head. "'Fun and adventure?' We're trying to stay alive long enough to get back to Earth, and you guys are talking fun and adventure? Why do I talk with you two? And Erik, you've been spending time with Cugbert, do you plan to throw that away?"

"He's teaching me the art of healing. I like it when we go to villages each day and feed, heal and help the residents." Erik rubbed his hand through his hair.

Al said, "Think about it Erik, adventure, treasure and a golden crown."

"Are you planning on walking away from learning about healing for 'fun and adventure?'" Sherry rubbed her hand across her eye and eyebrow. "Would a medical student at a university, walk away from college to take some crazy spontaneous trip?"

Erik said, "I don't know. It's been quiet around here, and I could use a little fun. I miss video games.

Lily said, "I miss school and my mom."

"Yeah, I'd like to see my mom, again." Erik said.

Silence descended on the room. Al thought of their mothers back on Earth whom they hadn't seen since coming through the rift between worlds, six weeks earlier.

Sherry said, "I want us all to stay close to the portal so we can go home when it opens."

Al realized how much he wanted to go home. "According to Master Wizard Ishwa, the portal won't open on its own for four years. We need this golden crown to open the gateway early. Isn't that what you want?"

"It's a trap. The man in black is lying to you. Either he wants to hurt you or get you to do something for him he can't do himself. He isn't an honest person. You saw the kids scatter when Gadiel approached. Children know to stay away from him." Sherry rose from the bench, walked to Al, put her arms around his waist and placed her head on his chest. "Please, stay, we'll all be together. If we have to wait four or five years then at least we'll be safe."

Al pulled her arms from around his waist and stepped back. "I don't understand you, Sherry. When Erik wanted to go rescue Lily, you didn't think twice about facing danger. We followed him to this strange world. Why won't you do the same for me? You learned how to handle animals when you were with the 4H club back on Earth. Come with us."

The room turned quiet. Al looked at Sherry's blue eyes shining bright in her freckled face haloed by red hair. She looked tired since coming to Aloheno. The food they ate wasn't like the food on Earth, and Sherry lost a lot of weight. She looked frail and vulnerable. Her hair, shiny and clean on Earth, now looked dirty and damaged.

"It's a ruse, and you'll die searching for a fake crown," she said, turning her back on him.

"Talk to her Erik, you see my point, don't you?" Al faced his friend of twelve years.

Erik sighed. "She's right, you know. The four of us shouldn't split up, because we might never get back together. Maybe you won't be in danger, but Sherry and Lily might. We should stay and protect them."

Al shook his head. "I can't believe you guys. Don't you see? We don't have to split up, because we can all go together. What will you do if you stay? Will you farm and work the fields with this planet's antiquated tools? Erik, I don't see you working in a forge as a blacksmith."

Erik said, "Sherry is right. I've been spending time with Cugbert, because I'm training to become a Pankratios priest."

"Really? It's okay for you to become a healing priest and use your skills, but I can't use my wizarding skills?"

Sherry paced back and forth in the compact space. "You can use your wizarding skills to help the townspeople. We can use our knowledge of Earth and the progress humans have made there to make this village better. Imagine running water, working toilets and not those horrible outhouses. And showers. I would give anything to take a shower with hot water." She grabbed a fistful of hair, "And shampoo and conditioner so my hair doesn't look like this rat's nest. You can't go on a quest. Stay and change this village, improve this civilization."

Al pinched his lips and shook his head. This felt like home when he wanted to spend money on a new D&D game or video game and his mom wouldn't let him. Sherry was trying to control him instead of Mom. He yelled, "You're not my mother and can't tell me what to do." His heart pounded in his chest and heat flushed through his body as he stormed out the cabin door.

CHAPTER 11

Al wandered the streets of Crossroads, his shoulders slumped, muttering to himself. "Why does Sherry want to control me? We're just friends and she can't tell me what to do. Maybe I'm not a skilled wizard, but if I was, I'd convince her to do what I wanted and not be at her mercy."

A boy yelled, "Alpherge the Mighty."

Al lifted his shoulders, and gave a half-hearted wave and a weak smile.

The boy dashed to Al and walked beside him.

Al scowled, "Go back to your mother." He bumped the boy with his staff. "Git."

The boy gave Al distance, but ambled behind the wizard.

The tension in Al's neck and shoulders increased. Is this what it meant to be a famous wizard? He needed alone time to reflect on problems and for introspection. Sure, he enjoyed the kid's attention, but right now he wanted to think. Al stopped, gritted his teeth, raised his staff and turned toward the boy. "Go away."

The boy raised his eyebrows and bolted.

Al didn't have a specific direction in mind as he meandered through the village. He was on the main road and walking toward the village gate. *Yes, that's what I need. Go straight through the gate and leave this village noise.* He missed being in his room at home, listening to music and working on a project where nobody told him what he could or couldn't do and nobody bossed him. His jaw ached from grinding his teeth.

He continued beyond the gate into a forested area two-hundred yards away. Only wind blowing the trees and an occasional bird broke the silence. No sounds of blacksmith's hammers or the normal background noise of commerce and daily, village living. A slight breeze ruffled his hair. He wasn't far into the forest, but the snow-covered peaks in the distance beckoned. He yearned to run into the mountains.

He sat with his back to an oak tree and whistled a song he knew from Earth. A catchy tune he liked from a rising rock group, Magic Giocoso.

Al didn't understand why everybody interfered in his business and told him what to do. He killed the Mountain King and should be entitled to do what he wanted, whenever he wanted. He was Alpherge the Mighty, a wizard entitled to quests and adventures for powerful magic items and grandiose treasures.

Al noticed a dead tree forty feet away and used magic to send a fireball at the tree, and a branch crashed to the ground. "Yes, a mighty wizard with impressive power. I am invincible." He said out loud.

Giggling erupted behind him.

Al noticed an audience of children and with a sly smile, launched another fireball at the tree. Another limb crashed to the forest floor.

Children cheered, and fifteen kids crowded around him.

"Hey you shouldn't be here. You're supposed to be in the village. It's dangerous in the forest. Go back where you belong."

A distant animal roared.

"Go home. There's a wild animal out here."

"But you will protect us, won't you Master Wizard Alpherge?" A little girl with large, brown eyes asked.

"I shouldn't have to protect you because you're supposed to be in the village behind the walls." He raised his staff and waved his arms. "Go home."

"You can't make us," a boy shouted at Al.

"I'll throw a fireball at you."

"No, you won't. That's against the laws of wizards. Do no harm to children. Didn't you learn that in wizard school?"

Al learned little in wizard school. He spent less than a week in classes before the enemy captured and placed him in a dungeon. It seemed like years, since studying with the other wizards. He should return to wizard school and learn the rules and laws governing wizards, or learn a spell to keep children away when you wanted peace.

The children wandered around the forest while three stayed near Al and stared at him. Two younger ones picked up pine cones. Others watched a squirrel climb a tree. Who brought all the kids? Al didn't know how to entertain children. He had no plans to babysit and ensure they didn't get eaten by wild creatures. What animals hunted in the forest that might want to eat kids? Did this forest contain jaguars, mountain lions or bears? A gigantic bird flew overhead, and Al watched its shadow creep across the forest floor.

A boy stood by the dead tree, watching the smoke curl in strange shapes from where Al's blast hit the dead limbs. "Is that fire?" The boy asked.

The tree burst into flames. *With all these children, a forest fire is horrible trouble.* Al tried to think of a spell to extinguish the fire.

A child tugged on his sleeve. "Can you do a magic trick for me?" The blue-eyed girl wore a plain brown tunic. She smiled at Al, showing missing front teeth.

"Not right now." Al turned her toward the village gates. "Time to go home; please go back to the village where it's safe." He raised his voice. "Go home, now!"

Two of the fifteen kids looked at Al. The rest ignored him and maintained their activities. Five girls clasped hands and sang a song as they danced around a sapling. Four kids raced around collecting pine cones stowing their treasures in their tunics. The others played tag, racing around trees and bushes.

The tree flared, sending out a blazing arm, reminding Al to forget the kids and concentrate on the spell to quench fire.

A bird of prey screeched overhead.

The kids made a racket singing, laughing and yelling.

Al found it difficult to concentrate.

A girl grab Al's sleeve. "I have to go to the bathroom."

Flames erupted on the dead tree and smoke rose on a second spot. Smoke and flames burst from the dead limb on the ground and the grass smoked. A boy, standing between Al and the dead tree, turned slowly in circles as the dry grass flared around him.

Al yelled, "This fire is dangerous." The tone of his voice got their attention. He grabbed the oldest boy, "Round up these kids and lead them back to the village. We have a problem."

The oldest boy didn't move, but watched the growing blaze.

The boy staring at the burning tree turned toward Al as the grass fire encircled him.

Al said, "Oh no, oh no!" Al raised his hands and placed them on top of his head as he paced back and forth. *What's the spell for putting out a fire? I can't let the boy burn.*

Kids stopped playing and stared at the burning grass. The girls dancing around the tree stopped and gawked.

Al pushed the older boy. "Grab those kids and take them to the village. Now!"

Sweat from the heat of the flames and from fear formed on Al's forehead. *This can't happen, all these kids will burn to death.* He scrubbed a hand across his face as his stomach knotted.

The oldest boy snapped to attention and ran toward the village, yelling. "Fire." The other kids stood and watched the flames lick toward them.

The boy entrapped in a circle of flames cried.

A girl who had been dancing got scared and raced toward Al. At that moment an enormous bird screeched, swooped low and rose into the sky with the girl in its claws.

"No!" Al yelled and threw a fireball at the bird. Breathing became difficult.

The fireball missed the bird, and the bird gained altitude grasping its prey tightly.

This can't be happening. I can't lose these children. He launched another fireball at the bird.

The bird turned south, and the fireball hit it square in the body. It hitched a second and then plummeted to the ground. The screaming girl fell with it.

CHAPTER 12

Erik Anderson watched motionless, as his friend Alpherge left the cabin. He'd never seen him react like that on Earth. "Should I go after him?" he asked.

"No, let him stew awhile." Sherry said. "He's impossible to live with and acting like a rock star. Al walks around the village with that stupid staff in his hands, and all the kids follow him. He's setting up to do something stupid."

"What's with you and Al?" Erik asked.

"Nothing. He's crazy with the popularity. Why can't he just stay here with us? Why does he have to chase after the stupid crown?"

Lily spoke, "Erik, go after him."

Sherry stamped her foot, "No, let him stew."

"Why are you getting bossy?" Erik asked. Was Sherry having a total mental breakdown? What was happening to his friends?

"Al is driving me crazy. He's not listening. You should've seen him in the village this morning. He's changing and acting arrogant and pushy. Not like the sweet Al we knew on Earth."

Lily said, "Are you kidding? Al's a gentle butterfly."

Sherry pinched her lips as she rubbed the back of her neck. She said, "He struts through the village waving at the villagers like royalty. When the children parade with him, he's worse."

"Should I check on him?" Erik asked as he studied Sherry.

"No! He needs to learn he can't behave like a teenager on Aloheno. We're adults on this planet, and he needs to act like one." She crossed her arms.

"Come on, Sherry, we're teenagers."

Sherry turned her back on Erik.

Bells rang in the village and people shouted in the streets.

"What's with the bells?" Erik asked. He opened the door. People holding buckets, raced along the street in front of their cabin.

Someone yelled, "Grab a bucket, there's a fire."

A sick feeling ran through Erik. "I think Al's in trouble."

"What?" Sherry asked.

He grabbed the wooden bucket they used for their daily water and joined the running crowd. Everyone ran toward the village gate.

"Where's the fire?" Erik yelled to people running beside him. He didn't see any houses with flames streaming from the roofs.

"In the forest. We have to control it before it reaches the village."

A two-horse wagon rolled through the street. Two men sat on a bench seat, and one rang bells while the second drove the horses. It bounced over ruts as four barrels in the wagon bed splashed water. People jumped out of the way.

Erik ran through the gate, his bucket in hand. The sun shone on his shoulders, the only cloud a dark billowing mass two hundred yards away. A crowd of a hundred villagers stood near the forest, many with buckets, and Erik expected a bucket line to form from the village well to the forest.

People stood gawking in a semi-circle outside a spot where rain gushed from the sky. Erik shoved his way through the crowd.

Al stood in the rain, his clothing soaked, holding a girl's limp body.

A young woman bulldozed through the crowd and dashed toward Al, screaming. "What did you do to my baby?"

Al stood motionless and said nothing. He laid the girl's body in the woman's arms.

The woman cried and dropped to the ground, hugging her child. Rain soaked the woman and her daughter.

Erik ran to Al. "Are you okay?"

Al nodded as water splattered off his hair and beard. He stared expressionless toward the woman.

Erik crouched next to the woman. "May I see your daughter?"

The woman pulled the girl's body closer to her chest.

"Please?" Erik held out his hand.

She shook her head.

"Please let me. I can help." He moved closer and touched the girl's neck, checking for a pulse.

"Don't touch her," the woman said, a grave expression outlined her eyes.

Rain cascaded from the one small spot in the sky.

"Al, stop the rain." Erik said.

The rain continued.

Erik stood and touched Al's arm. "Stop the rain. The fire's out."

Al blinked and mumbled unfamiliar words.

The rain stopped.

Erik slipped back to the sobbing woman. He saw her daughter's chest expand. Touching the woman's shoulder, he said, "Your daughter's alive. Please let me help."

She raised her swollen, red eyes to Erik.

He held out his hands.

She hesitated and pulled away from Erik, using her rounded shoulders as a shield.

What does she think I will do to her child? "I have power to heal injuries."

"What can you do?" The girl's mother asked.

"Please, I'm training with Cugbert, as a healer."

"Cugbert?"

Erik nodded.

The woman laid the limp body in Erik's arms. "Al, what happened to the girl?"

Al said nothing.

"Buddy, come on, what happened?"

A short, thin man with receding hair jostled out of the crowd. "I'll tell you what happened. The wizard shot a fireball at her and killed her."

The girl's dress was singed, but also torn at her shoulders as if an animal grabbed her.

"She's not dead, sir." Erik said.

A man, holding his son on his shoulders, elbowed through the crowd. "The wizard tried to burn my little Geoffrey, had the boy encircled in fire."

Al shook his head.

Erik placed the girl on the wet grass. He spread his hands on her forehead and whispered words the healing priest, Cugbert, had taught him. Words designed to delve into a person to see what maladies affected them. He said, "She has a nasty bump on her head, which caused a concussion. There are deep scratch marks on her shoulder and a broken leg."

The girl's mother cried louder.

"She will be okay."

Between sobs the mother said, "Can you really heal her?"

Erik struggled to speak the right words. "I'll repair her broken leg, and heal the scratches, but Cugbert will need to heal the concussion."

The bald-headed guy said, "The wizard tossed her in the sky and threw a fireball at her."

Al shook his head.

A tall man holding the hands of a boy said, "He waved his arms and chanted incantations that started a forest fire to encircle my son."

Someone in the crowd yelled, "The wizard tried to burn down the village."

Erik studied the aftermath of the fire. Flames blackened a dead tree and scorched a twenty foot section of grass, but Al extinguished the fire. There were no fire marks anywhere near the village walls.

He touched the girl's head and noticed a large bump. Cugbert showed him a technique for healing, which he thought might help the swelling. Erik placed his hands on her head and chanted healing words. The swelling dissipated, leaving a purple bruise.

The girl stirred.

Grabbing her daughter out of Erik's hands, the mother hugged the child.

Erik said, "I set her broken leg, but don't let her walk on it for two weeks. It still needs to heal." He took off his tunic and ripped the cloth into strips. He wrapped it tight around the girl's leg.

Sherry rushed through the crowd of people and threw her arms around Al. "Are you okay?"

Al said, "Yes, I'm okay. This is all my fault."

The bald man said, "Did you hear? The wizard acknowledges it's his fault. He lured the kids, your children, out into the wilderness and planned to use them as sacrifices for strange magic ceremonies."

Sherry plunked her hands on her hips. "Al did no such thing."

The other man said, "He threw fireballs at the kids and burned my little boy."

Geoffrey slid to the ground and hugged his dad's leg.

Geoffrey's clothing showed no burn marks, but the smell of smoke lingered in the air. Erik asked, "Al, what happened?"

"I came to the forest to be alone, and the kids followed. I told them to return to the village, the forest wasn't safe."

The bald man raised his hands to the crowd. "Liar. You lured them with spells to follow you for dangerous religious rituals. We see how children follow you through the village. He's manipulating them with magic."

Geoffrey's dad said, "Then you threw fireballs at them."

A woman yelled, "Keep those outsiders away from my children, Mayor. Not just the wizard boy, all four of them. They're not from around here, and they act strange and dangerous."

Sherry said, "That's ridiculous."

"Drive them from the village." A voice shouted.

Erik thought the bald dude must be mayor. That explained why his words excited the crowd.

The shouting increased, "We can't have an untrained wizard in the community. Someone will get hurt. Just like the girl. You should stop them, Mayor."

Al shouted, "I told the children to return to the village; they didn't listen to me."

Sherry hollered, "Your little children shouldn't run around the village unsupervised. They should be in school."

"Mayor, put these four in jail, or banish them from the village." A man yelled from behind the crowd.

Erik said, "The boy wasn't burned and the girl's okay. It's an accident."

Someone else yelled, "Banish them!"

The crowd chanted, "Banish them. Banish them."

Al kicked a rock on the ground.

Sherry's nostrils flared, and as her face reddened, she exhaled a growl.

Erik recognized this look. Sherry didn't get angry often, but when her body tensed and face turned red, someone received a mouthful from her. He scrambled toward Sherry before she made it worse.

The chant continued, "Banish them."

The mayor waved his hands in the air to silence the crowd.

Erik stood beside Sherry and said, "Relax, take deep breaths."

The mayor said, "I've decided."

The chanting subsided as people poked their neighbors, telling them to be quiet.

"As mayor of this fine village, I banish—"

Sherry screamed. "You'll do no such thing. That's the most ridiculous thing I've ever heard. You can't banish us." Sherry moved toward the mayor.

Erik grabbed her waist and prevented her from attacking the mayor. "Relax Sherry, don't make things worse."

Sherry said, "I won't let these thugs bully us. Al did nothing wrong. There's no way he tried to hurt a child."

Kenneth Brown

"I banish these four from Crossroads for a month for endangering children, starting a fire to burn the village and for destruction of forest property."

CHAPTER 13

Back on the road and homeless, Sherry thought as they trudged from Crossroads into the surrounding forest. She scrunched her brow as a headache pounded in her temples.

Erik asked, "Where are we going?"

Sherry harrumphed.

Al said, "I'm sorry, guys. I didn't know the kids followed me. I didn't mean to hurt them. A giant bird snatched the girl. I saved her."

Even in late spring, snow still covered the mountains that surrounded them. The forests were full of wild animals hungry from their winter hibernation.

The pain in Sherry's head flared. "We're banished from our home. It wasn't a pretty home, but it was home, safe from animals and weather." She rubbed her forehead. *We developed a routine, a family of sorts in Crossroads. Now what?*

Blonde-haired Lily said, "We should go to the Village of the Stone Warriors to stay close to the portal."

Sherry said, "We should stay in Crossroads and prove to the mayor and villagers we aren't dangerous."

"The villagers will hang us." Erik said.

"Maybe not. We used to have three meals a day, water with a fence and guards to protect us." Sherry stopped and scowled back at the village. "Now we're walking and I hate walking, I want to go home, return to Earth."

Al said, "That's why we need to seize the golden crown."

Sherry's body tensed as she shook her fist at Al.

Erik said, "Forget the crown for now."

"The crown opens the portal. Why can't you understand that?"

Sherry shouted. "Enough about the stupid golden crown. Can't *you* see it's a trap?" She pinched her eyes tight as pain like a hammer beat a steady bam, bam, bam on her forehead.

They walked in silence.

The forest shadows stretched across the road as they arrived in the village of Tanuku, a village of a hundred bright-colored homes painted yellow, red, green and blue.

Erik stopped. "It's decision time. The sun sets in two-hours. It's a twelve-hour walk to Velidred castle. What's our plan?"

"We should spend the night in Tanuku and sleep. I'm tired of walking." Al leaned on his staff, sucking in deep breaths.

"How far a walk to the Stone Warriors?" Lily asked.

"An hour north, all uphill. We can stay in the inn at the Village of the Stone Warrior's tonight and search for a cabin tomorrow." Erik plopped to the ground and rubbed his calves.

Sherry said, "I don't want to live in that tiny village. Why not sleep in Tanuku overnight and head to Velidred tomorrow? There're more jobs available in Velidred."

"Is Velidred safe?" Al asked. "The resistance seized the castle."

Erik said, "Prince Krunal's men captured us, and the resistance shot an arrow through my shoulder." He rubbed his shoulder.

"Now they've captured the castle, we should be fine. There's no reason to hold us captive." Sherry said. "Velidred is bigger than Crossroads, so they won't even notice us."

"I can't work with Cugbert if I'm living in Velidred. It's too far to travel back and forth each day. I would rather stay in the mountains where people need our help. You can't imagine the pain and suffering we encounter each day. The children aren't getting food to eat, and their parents are too weak to lift a bucket of water, much less plant crops."

Al said, "What if Sherry and I travel to Velidred while you and Lily hike to the Stone Warriors?"

"We can't split up," Sherry said. "It's important we stay together."

"Do we stay in Tanuku?" Erik asked.

"It doesn't have village walls to keep out animals, and there are no guards to protect the village," Sherry said.

"The people are carefree," Erik said.

Sherry lowered her voice. "Yeah, part of Forest River Blossom's cult. Do you want to reunite with her and those crazy barefoot dancers again?"

Al yawned. "Velidred works for me. We research the caravan and sign up for an adventure to the Ice Castle. Might be the best choice for us."

Sherry wanted to box his ears or slap him. She bent her head at odd angles, attempting to loosen a stiff neck.

"Who's Forest River Blossom?" Lily asked.

Sherry said, "She's a spiritualist who makes nasty predictions about you catching green spots all over your body and dying a horrible death. She's an awful person."

Erik said. "If we believed her predictions, Lily, you'd be dead along with Al. She didn't want us to rescue you."

"Oh my."

Al said, "Let's ask Forest River Blossom about the caravan."

"I'm not asking that terrible woman anything," Heat rose in Sherry's face. "She's a spiritualist, not a scientist. I want to deal in facts, not tea-leaf reading mumbo-jumbo."

Erik shook his head. "Don't worry about Forest River Blossom and her predictions. If we cross her path, we nod our heads, smile and continue on our merry way. I think we should trek to the Village of the Stone Warriors and sleep there."

Sherry said, "I'm not living in the wilderness high in the mountains. It's a great day-trip to examine the cave entrance, but no way I'll live there long term."

Erik said, "If we live in Velidred, it's a two-day trip to check the portal."

Sherry looked exasperated, "We should've stayed in Crossroads. Except for Mister, Grand Wizard—"

"Enough," Al shouted. "I didn't . . . the kids . . . a mistake . . . just leave it."

Sherry saw their lives unraveling. *We were a couple on Earth, but this planet, the harsh living conditions and the stress challenged their relationship. Should I end this relationship?* "We can't make it to Velidred before dark. We stay here tonight." Sherry crossed her arms and glared at Al.

Al scowled at the ground.

Lily draped an arm around Sherry's shoulders and said, "I'm staying with Sherry wherever she stays."

The beat of drums boomed in the distance, combined with the high pitched music of flutes and bells. A crowd of men and women swayed and danced approaching the teens in the dirt road. A petite woman led the group as other's in white dresses danced around the marching crowd.

Sherry said, "Oh brother."

"Say nothing," Erik said.

"Who is it?" Lily asked.

"Forest River Blossom." Sherry answered.

"I'm asking her what to do," Al said.

"You know she'll say, 'don't travel to the Ice Castle or you'll die a horrible death.' Just keep your mouth shut for once, please." Sherry's head pounded a beat to match the drums. She rubbed the back of her neck.

The women danced as the parade marched toward the teens. Forest River Blossom held impressive power over her people. This village managed itself and escaped the conflict and suffering the Mountain King inflicted on other mountain villages.

Erik said, "Speak her name, and boom, she appears." He smiled at Sherry, but she glared back.

Late afternoon sun lengthened the shadows of trees to grasping fingers. Beyond the parade, the Anticletus moon descended toward the horizon. Sherry never got used to how fast Anticletus changed its phases as it raced around the planet every six days.

The parade reached the teens and Lily swayed with the music. Forest River Blossom raised an arm and the music and dancing stopped.

She studied the teens. She extended her hand to Lily. "Child, you look well."

Lily smiled and grasped the woman's hand.

"What brings you to Tanuku? I heard you lived in Crossroads. Was the village not to your standards?"

Sherry turned bright red and her mouth moved, but she couldn't find the right words.

Erik spoke, "We had an incident in Crossroads and the mayor banned us from the village."

Al blurted in rapid speech, "We met this man, named Gadiel, and he wants us to travel to the Ice Castle with him and grab a golden crown, guaranteed to release the stone warriors. Should we go?"

Sherry took short, deep breaths and said through clenched teeth, "Why can't you keep your mouth shut?"

Forest River Blossom didn't answer Al, instead she said to Sherry, "The moon's pull is strong. Do you suffer from headaches?"

Sherry gasped.

The spiritualist released Lily's hand and touched Sherry's arm.

Sherry pulled away.

"All right, child. I predicted this to your mom, and she didn't believe me."

Sherry didn't move when the spiritualist touched her the second time. The spiritualist traced her fingers down Sherry's arm and grasped first one hand, and then the other. Forest River Blossom closed her eyes.

Sherry wanted to pull back. Her muscles tightened as her head leaned away from Forest River Blossom. Her body tensed, and Forest River Blossom released her grip. "Please stay as my guest in the village of Tanuku for a few days. I can help you alleviate the pain the moon's influence is causing. Herbs will help, but you need to control the moon's power, or it will consume you and lead to a premature death."

Sherry's face twitched. She smiled and then frowned. She prepared to unleash a scathing diatribe on how she felt about Forest River Blossom and her predictions. This woman scared them the first time they met and then tried to convince them to return to Earth instead of saving their friend, Lily, from being a sacrificial offering. Sherry's body tensed. Then she relaxed and said, "Thank you." Sherry searched the sky for the Anticletus moon.

The drums thrummed a rapid cadence, scaring squirrels up the trees. Birds preparing to roost for the evening flew off branches and scattered in the sky.

What happened? Sherry prepared to deliver a tongue lashing, but the intense head pain stopped. Did the spiritualist solve the problem, or did the Anticletus moon set? What witchcraft did the spiritualist perform?

Forest River Blossom raised her hand, bracelets jangled and silence descended on the villagers.

"I'll teach you techniques to reduce your pain. Cugbert can't help because it isn't organic pain, such as when a body part isn't working but your connection to Anticletus. It troubles you and induces meta-physical pain."

Sherry brought a shaky hand to her forehead and her voice quaked, "How did you know?"

"I examined you as a baby. Your mother asked about her child's changing moods when the moon was visible. This is another reason we escorted you and your friends off the planet. The lunar connection will ensure a premature death, and you must limit your exposure to Anticletus."

"How can you help?"

"Let me examine you and study ancient moon maps. I don't have answers right now."

Sherry wavered for a moment and Lily supported her.

Forest River Blossom touched Lily's arm, "Will you stay and dance with our troupe?"

"Yes, I love to dance."

Al said, "I want to travel to Velidred and check on the caravan."

Forest River Blossom's head pivoted sharply like a bird hearing a dangerous sound, "Gadiel's a scheming man, hiding evil by pretending to be an entrepreneur. Oh, he's a business owner, but his activities are illicit, dangerous and involve human trafficking. Avoid him."

Sherry smiled and stuck out her tongue at Al. *Maybe that'll stop him talking about the caravan. Keeping him involved in something else for a week will squash his focus on this quest.*

Al said, "If I capture the golden crown, then I'll release the stone warriors."

Forest River Blossom said, "It's a legend. The golden crown doesn't exist, and adventurers who seek it never return."

CHAPTER 14

S/ herry said, "We should stay together, no matter what."

Sherry and her friends talked long into the night, after Forest River Blossom found them a one-room cabin in the village. The pleasant weather turned to a hard rain, and a drip from the leaky roof puddled on the dirt floor near the fireplace. Erik added another log to the fire as chilly air seeped through holes in the log walls.

Sherry sat near the fire, holding Al's hand. "I can't let you two go on this caravan. I don't trust Gadiel, especially after what Forest River Blossom said about him."

Erik stirred the fire with a poker, and sparks exploded over the burning logs. He said, "Don't you feel that way about everybody on this planet? No one seems trustworthy. Everyone we meet wants us to do something for them or wants us dead."

"The crown can change everything," Al said.

Sherry winced at the mention of the golden crown, her posture stiffened and jaw tightened as she diverted her gaze from Al. *What injuries might the boys endure on the journey? How strong was the possibility of death?*

"You're not invincible," Sherry said.

"I can create a shield and I have the staff." Al's voice trailed off as he gazed at the long pole standing in the room's corner.

The staff said nothing.

"Your magic isn't perfect, you need more training and you may not always have your staff. What if you lose it or it doesn't respond to your commands?" Sherry asked.

"Hah, I'll always have my staff." Al grimaced, rubbed the back of his neck and said uncertainly, "No one can take it from me."

Sherry shook her head.

A knock sounded at the door.

"Who would come out in this rain?" Lily asked.

Erik opened the door, and Cugbert and Forest River Blossom stood beneath the dripping lintel.

Cugbert pushed Forest River Blossom into the room, "We need to talk." Water dripped off their clothing, making small circles in the dirt.

They entered, and the teens made room for them around the fire.

"What's this about?" Erik asked.

Forest River Blossom said, "Cugbert and I have discussed your problem and we have a plan."

Sherry huffed, "You have a plan for our problem? Isn't that something we should discuss and then we decide?

"You're children, and these decisions need to be made by adults."

Sherry felt heat rise to her freckled face. *Stay calm and hear them out.* "What plans have you made for us?"

Forest River Blossom glanced at Cugbert, and he nodded. She cleared her throat and said, "Gadiel's an evil man. He's ruined many good wizards with his lying and deception about his abilities. His motives to help wizards aren't pure. Anytime he says he can help you, I guarantee you'll be worse off at the end than when you started. He's manipulative and promises rewards that never pan out for people."

Sherry relaxed. She realized she'd been holding her breath. "Good. You don't want the boys to go on the caravan with Gadiel. I agree with that decision."

The spiritualist's eyes narrowed and she pinched her lips, as if displeased with Sherry's interruption.

Forest River Blossom forced a smile and said, "I checked the augur tokens."

"Augur tokens?" Sherry asked. "You're making decisions that affect our lives using divination objects?" *We're living on a planet where people decide life choices not on facts, but on objects tossed to the ground?*

"Hear her out," Cugbert said.

"We want the boys to search for the golden crown. If they find it, then it might have the power to rescue the stone warriors."

"After telling us how dangerous it is, then throwing dice or something on the table, you intend to send these boys to their deaths?"

Cugbert turned his large frame to face Sherry. "It's not just the tokens or the golden crown. We believe Zita is with Gadiel, and we need to rescue her from Gadiel's influence."

"Do you plan to go with the boys?" Sherry asked.

The healing priest gave a slight head shake. "No, summer is the only time of year I can heal in these mountain villages. During the winter, the villages are inaccessible, and if I don't check on them this summer, they won't last through the winter."

"What of Erik's training? Isn't that important?"

"I need Erik's help, because he's talented in healing and provides support to my ministry."

"Then Erik goes with you and you send Al by himself to this faraway Ice Castle?" *I have no intention of letting these two manipulate the boys like pawns on a chess board. I'll protect them, even if no one else will.*

Forest River Blossom said, "Al and Erik will go together. Let Cugbert finish the discussion, before interrupting."

"I keep interrupting because you're as bad as Gadiel at manipulating people for your personal agendas." She pointed at Cugbert and Forest River Blossom. "I'm doing something you two aren't. I'm thinking about my friends and not some grand scheme to give me personal power." Sherry felt so hot she wondered if she was sitting too near the fire.

Cugbert turned his head toward Forest River Blossom and said, "I told you it wouldn't be easy." Then he returned his gaze to Sherry, "I promised Zita's mother, on the night she died, to protect her daughter. We have information from reliable sources that Zita is with Gadiel. We need to break the bond between the two of them."

"You're using my friends to do a task you're not willing to do yourself? That's shameful."

"I know Erik wants to rescue his father from his existence as a stone warrior. We have ancient scrolls, information from wizards and documents that lead us to believe these two can succeed where others have failed."

Erik nodded.

"Where do the other wizards that gave you these documents land on their friendship with Gadiel? Are the boys being used to retrieve an object that'll never be used for the purpose they want?" Sherry crossed her arms across her chest. How could she stop these two people from exploiting her friends?

Forest River Blossom said, "I know an old wizard who retreated to the mountains years ago. He had a comrade that went into the Pit of Wretchedness—"

"The Pit of Wretchedness! You want to send my friends into the Pit of Wretchedness? Can this scenario get any worse?"

"Let her finish," Cugbert commanded.

Forest River Blossom let silence fill the room as she stared at Sherry.

Sherry took a deep breath. "Okay, go ahead, I'm sorry."

"My wizard friend gave us the scroll he found on the day his best friend died while attempting to retrieve the golden crown. The scroll's written in an old language, but we have interpreted the document to tease out the critical knowledge that will allow you to succeed."

"And you're willing to sacrifice my friends for your little treasure?"

"It's a powerful instrument for good, but if evil hands capture it, then we're all in more trouble than when King Haskell lived."

Al said, "A noble quest."

"A noble, but dangerous quest." Sherry corrected Al.

"I won't lie. Many young and old wizards have searched for the crown . . ." Forest River Blossom studied the dirt floor, "and never returned. But you two boys have a third key, one that wasn't available to the others."

"Oh, brother." Sherry rolled her eyes. "Can you show us this third key?" Each comment in this conversation made her legs twitchy and her skin itch.

"Zita's help in the search for the crown."

"Let me summarize what I'm hearing." Sherry numbered the important points on her fingers. "Gadiel is an evil man. He transformed Zita to an evil person." She touched her third finger. "You want my friends to find Zita, and destroy her evil bond with Gadiel. Then when no one's looking, the three of them will descend into the Pit of Wretchedness to find the magical golden crown." She snorted. "Oh, by the way, no one has ever returned from the Pit of

Wretchedness, with or without the golden crown. Did I summarize it right?" Sherry glowered at Forest River Blossom.

Cugbert muttered, "I told you all of them might not be on board with the plan."

Forest River Blossom said, "I intended to discourage any attempt to search for the golden crown, but after the tokens landed—"

"Stop with the stupid tokens. We're not deciding important life choices based on your interpretations of objects rolled across a table." *This planet is unreal,*

Al said, "It's a noble quest, and I say we take a chance."

Sherry lifted a single eyebrow. "You still believe you're at your mom's house playing a child's game. You don't even know if you'll survive the trip to the Ice Castle and you say, 'it's a noble quest.'" She stared at Forest River Blossom, who matched her stare.

The fire crackled and popped as a burnt log re-positioned. Sparks splattered in the fireplace. Rain continued to pound on the rooftop.

Erik asked, "If we find Zita, how do we break her bond with Gadiel?"

Sherry turned her back on everyone and faced the wall.

"We don't know." Forest River Blossom answered.

Sherry snorted.

Erik said, "Zita helped us at the volcano. If she's in trouble, then we should try to help her. That's the right thing to do isn't it?"

"That's the correct answer for a priest and healer." Cugbert said.

Sherry pivoted back toward the others with tears welling in her eyes. "Please don't go, we need you here. I don't want to tell your mom why you died."

Forest River Blossom handed Al a scroll. He unrolled the paper and said, "These words aren't in English, I can't read it."

"They're in the language of the ancients. Memorize the words and destroy the piece of paper. You'll need these words to find the golden crown."

"Words I can't read?"

Erik peeked over Al's shoulder, "Sure — that's our alphabet. You can just sound it out, like phonetics."

"Yeah, I guess I can do that, like those spells we find in the books." Al read from the scroll, "Oona ganna takkay goota, Nekkay akkay pakkee soota, Airay voomay meesay ketch. Nekkay ekkay moosmay wretch."

Erik said, "It has a nice rhyme to it. Reminds me of something."

Sherry exploded, "It's a nursery rhyme. Eenie, meenie, miney moe. Have you boys ever heard that one?" She faced Forest River Blossom. "You're sending my friends to their deaths with a nursery rhyme. Unbelievable."

CHAPTER 15

The next morning, the rain stopped by the time Al awoke. He tossed and turned throughout the night, and when he did open his eyes, Sherry and Lily weren't in the cabin. Al realized how mad Sherry must be if she chose not to see them off to Velidred. Dullness ached in his chest, and an overall feeling of heaviness enveloped him. He wished he knew what to do or say to keep Sherry happy. Would flowers help?

Al and Erik waited for the girls to return and even hoped Cugbert would reconsider, but after an hour during which their friends didn't show, they left Tanuku to meet the caravan in Velidred.

"Are you positive this is right?" Erik asked.

Al said, "Yes, I'm sure. I'm a wizard, and I need the challenge of finding the golden crown to enhance my magic. This gives me a chance to learn more about my grandfather's staff. Gadiel told me he can help develop my skills with the staff. The heads of the staff haven't talked since I met the man. I need to find out why."

"You've said nothing about the staff heads not talking."

Al lowered his voice, "I didn't want Sherry to know the staff stopped working."

"Will we be in danger?"

"No, I'm an excellent wizard without the staff, and I'll get better once I can speak to its wizards again."

"Have you tried talking to them? Did you offend them?"

"Well, there's the carved lady, Isabel, who seemed upset when I tried to drown her and then allowed the staff to catch on fire. What do I know about magic staffs? Who knows, maybe the three wizards are mad at each other. It was a big help when we rescued Sherry and Lily at the volcano, but since the morning we met Gadiel, nothing. Maybe I expended all its magic."

Erik asked, "Is there a switch, like a vacuum cleaner? You chant the right words and the heads turn on again."

"They don't work like that." Al studied the carved faces as he walked, tracing his fingers over the beard of the character carved into the top. The detailed craftsmanship amazed Al. How did his grandfather get so much expression into the wood? Did Al's grandfather manually carve the faces or did he use magic?

Erik said, "Imagine it's like a dog, and you say, 'speak staff.' Have you tried to say something simple?"

Al stopped in the street and held the staff in an outstretched hand. "Speak staff."

The boys waited.

Nothing happened.

Al tried. "I request your presence, oh Mighty Staff."

The staff didn't respond.

"Do you insert magic into the staff and then utter the words?" Erik asked.

"I've tried that and get nothing."

"Let me try." Erik held out his hand.

"Ha, what are you going to do? You don't have magical powers."

"Maybe it only works with non-magical people. Come on, hand it over so I can try it."

Al didn't want to give the staff to Erik. *What if Erik made it work?*

"Come on, man, let me try."

"Okay, but don't hurt it." Al handed the staff to Erik.

"What would I do, crack it over my leg?" Erik hefted it into the air a few times, "It's heavier than I expected."

"Yeah, when we traveled to the volcano, my arm was sore the entire day. I thought it would help me walk up hills, and it did, but my shoulder ached at the end."

Erik pointed the staff at a boulder and said, "Move, rock."

The rock didn't move.

"Talk to me, staff. What are your names?" He rotated the staff, studying the carved images. "The detail is amazing."

"I know, right? You can see crags and age lines in the carvings, like they created them from actual people's faces using a laser."

Al held out his hand. "Give it back."

"If I strut around with the staff, people will think I'm a wizard. That'd be fun." Erik raised the staff in the air, then handed it to Al.

Several miles later Erik asked, "Do you trust Gadiel? Will you let him handle the staff or let him study it when you aren't there?"

"I refuse to let the staff out of my sight. I'll let Gadiel handle it while I sit with him, but he can't study it without me."

"Does Gadiel have magical powers? What if you let him hold it and then he uses the staff to start you on fire or something?"

"Stop it. Gadiel will teach me about the staff and nothing more." But Al wondered if Gadiel might attempt to steal the staff. He didn't think Gadiel had magical powers, but could it be possible he had skills stronger than Al's? Can I *trust the old man to examine my most precious possession? Forest River Blossom didn't trust Gadiel. Maybe that was a message.*

As they rounded a grouping of pine trees, the landscape opened up. Sounds of hundreds of people working, talking and going about their everyday lives buzzed in the meadow. Black castle stone walls, the walls of Velidred Castle, rose ominously in the distance. But what amazed Al was several enormous animals outside the walls. Men directed the beasts with ropes, whips and spears.

Al stared at the hairy elephant-like animals milling about the grounds. The beasts had long curved tusks and towered over the men handling them. "Those amazing creatures are mastodons."

"How do you know they aren't wooly mammoths?" Erik asked.

"A mammoth's tusks curve more than a mastodon's, and mammoths are bigger." Al experienced a sobering realization. *These are the animals Gadiel wants us to manage for the caravan.*

He stopped walking and watched a boy wrestling a rope attached to a mastodon's leg. The boy tried to tie the rope to a stake pounded in the ground, but the hairy beast bellowed and moved his leg. The boy screeched as the beast moved toward a wagon loaded with evergreen branches and dragged his handler off his feet.

Shouting filled the air as two men scourged the beast, and another man snagged the boy by his tunic. The animal stopped and bellowed. The men with the sticks forced the animal back toward the stake in the ground and secured the rope.

An argument ensued between the boy and the man. After a few moments, the man pointed toward the castle. The boy shook his head, but the man yelled and pointed again. The boy's shoulders drooped as he plodded toward the castle walls.

Erik repeated Al's question. "Are these the animals Gadiel wants us to handle for the caravan?"

Al stood still, his jaw slack. He feared small horses. How could he handle an animal of this size that was obviously dangerous?

Four of the animals lifted their trunks and trumpeted. A smaller group of the animals shied away from the dominant, noisy ones.

"Will we ride them?" Al asked.

"Don't know." Erik said, "Who do we contact, now we're here?"

Al held the staff tightly to control his shaking limbs. Two mastodons, each led by one man, exited the forest, pulling carts filled with evergreens. "Let's find Gadiel."

CHAPTER 16

Al picked his way among shouting men, cursing women, wagons, boys and mastodon dung, his senses bombarded by noise, smells of animals and sweat of men, and the swirling motion of the animals, wagons and people. He felt overwhelmed by all the activity. Erik yelled at him, but Al couldn't understand what his friend said.

Erik yelled again, "Is that Gadiel's wagon there?" He pointed at a vehicle with wooden wheels six feet tall and an enclosed cabin on top.

The cart, trailer or wagon, Al wasn't sure what to call the dull gray structure, had a steep-sloped roof painted a fire engine red on one side and sunshine yellow on the other. Al shrugged and walked to the steps leading to the cabin, and as he prepared to climb the steps, the door opened.

A short man with a weathered face, a long unkempt beard, bulbous nose, and broad shoulders barreled out of the cart and hustled down the steps. "Out of my way, Boy. Obadiah," the man bellowed, "are the water carts filled?"

A wiry teen trotted to the wagon. "Two teams at the river right now will slosh the water wagons by nightfall."

"They better, because we're leaving in the morning. Spread the word. If we don't leave tomorrow we'll miss our window to the Ice Castle." The bulbous nose dude advanced toward a row of wagons and barked orders to the men standing around who were arguing about chickens.

Al followed the man, "Sir, can you help us?"

"Leave me alone, boy." The broad-shouldered man turned and pointed at a fat man sleeping under a covered cart. "Wagner, we're leaving in the morning. Is the food cart ready?"

The man under the cart didn't move.

Wagner moaned when the broad-shouldered man kicked him in the ribs. "Get up you lazy cook. Is the food packed for the journey?"

"Wha … aat? Hey. Oh. Yes sir, Hadrian, all supplies needed for the journey and the supplies requested by the Ice Castle. We're all set."

Al tried again. "Mr. Hadrian, sir, can you tell us where to find Gadiel."

"I'm busy. Stop bothering me." Despite the man's bulk, he moved with ease and headed toward a group of men tending the beasts.

Wagner under-the-cart yelled at Al. "Hey wizard, come here."

Al followed Hadrian, ignoring Wagner.

"Hey, Boy," Wagner tried again.

Erik grabbed Al's shoulder. "Al, wait. This guy might help us."

Al stopped. "What?"

"The man beneath the cart wants to talk." Erik spun Al toward Wagner.

Wagner crawled out and stood. "Are you a wizard, Boy?"

"What?"

"The staff. Is it real?"

Wagner stood close enough for the stink of strong alcohol to reach Al's nose. "Yeah, it's real. I'm a wizard."

Wagner laughed, "Ha, sure you are. Me too."

"Are you?" Al asked.

Two women sauntered from a nearby cart. They giggled. "Wagner's no wizard, but he does amazing tricks."

"I'll buy that staff. Give you genuine gold and jewels for it." Wagner said.

"It's not for sale. We're searching for Gadiel. Where is he?"

Wagner approached the staff and ran his hand up and down the carved images. "This is nice. I can sell it for you and make a lot of money, split the money with you. What do you say, Boy? Wanna sell it?"

"No, I don't want to sell the staff. It's my grandfather's." Al wrestled it out of Wagner's hands. "Where's Gadiel?"

"Gadiel." Wagner rubbed his hand across his stubbled chin. "Might help you. What's it worth to you."

"You want money to point us to Gadiel? Don't you think we can find him ourselves?"

"Ah, come on, Boy. A man needs food and drink," Wagner hitched his eyebrows at the women who watched the transaction.

The women giggled again.

"Forget it, we'll find him ourselves. Come on, Erik."

"Why do you want to see Gadiel?" Wagner grabbed the staff, almost ripping it from Al's grasp.

"Hey! Stop it, it's not for sale. We're meeting Gadiel and going to find an object for him." Al jerked the staff from Wagner's hand.

Erik whispered to Al, "Don't tell him why you want to see Gadiel."

"Oh, a secret object, eh?" A smile spread across Wagner's face. "I bet you're looking for the golden crown, aren't you?"

The women continued giggling.

"Maybe. What do you know about it?"

"What I know is if you value your life, you'll go back to your flea-bitten mountains and forget the golden crown."

"Why?"

"Every other trip to the Ice Castle, Gadiel convinces a wizard who thinks they're better than other wizards to retrieve the golden crown." Wagner moved closer to Al and lowered his voice. "The wizards never return. Young ones, old ones, wizards with staffs, wizards with wands, and female wizards go into the pit and . . ." His voice trailed off as he ran a finger across his neck.

Al and Erik said nothing.

"That staff won't help. Might as well give it to me and let me sell it. Maybe I can send the money to your momma for her old age when you don't return." The stench of alcohol saturated the air.

Erik pushed Al on the back, "Let's find Gadiel. This guy isn't helping."

"You can find Gadiel over in the southwest quadrant." Wagner pointed in the proper direction. "Give that green-eyed girl he's with a kiss for me." He waggled his eyebrows.

"Zita's here." Erik, his eyes bright, turned to Al. "Let's go."

The path to the southwest quadrant turned into a maze of horses, giant, hairy mastodons, men and women rushing to finish tasks, and carts of all kinds. Carts bearing little homes, carts full of pine and evergreen branches, carts holding water, carts smelling of animal waste and carts with canvas roofs.

Children ran through the maze of carts, animals, and handlers, and one or two stopped to admire Al's staff and ask him questions. Al stood straight and answered their questions until Erik pushed him further. "Come on, Zita's with Gadiel, we have to find her."

There were hundreds of conveyances in the meadow, and Al wondered if they would all be part of the expedition. How could you have so many carts in one caravan? When it traveled, it would stretch for three or four miles.

They asked more people for directions as they meandered through the commotion, and answers changed from a pointed finger to "three rows over" to "check the green and yellow wagon just over there."

Erik and Al stood ten feet from the biliously colored mobile home. Gadiel sat on a bench in front of a fire. The wagon, half the size of a railroad car with a rounded tin top, had a little chimney sticking from the left side of the roof. Three wooden steps led to a door with a curtained window. A blue canvas canopy, unfurled from the side of the cart with two poles for support.

Al whispered, "I don't see Zita. Should we ask Gadiel about her?"

"No, I don't think we should let him know we're looking for Zita." Erik whispered back.

Gadiel stood and addressed them. "Boys, I'm happy you made the right decision." He slithered over and shook their hands.

Al felt the old man's firm grip and weathered hands, like sandpaper to the touch. "We decided to join your caravan and," he lowered his voice, "find the golden crown."

"Excellent. I knew I could count on you. Did you bring your lady friends with you?"

Al shook his head.

"Hmm, I hoped they would join us. No worries, we can achieve our goals without them."

Erik asked, "Will we be riding with you?"

"No." Gadiel smiled, showing a mouthful of teeth, a crocodile waiting for a meal. "Go see Hadrian, the caravan leader; he'll set you up with an animal and wagons. Young Alpherge, I see you brought your staff. We'll make time to talk and examine it. The caravan departs tomorrow at sunrise. Find Hadrian and we'll discuss magic and treasures as we journey."

They changed directions to return to the wagon where they first met Hadrian.

Al asked, "Do you think we can find the guy again?"

"We'll ask. Should find him eventually. Can you work with the mastodons?" Erik asked.

Al had a sour taste in his mouth, like fermented sauerkraut and a tingling in his chest. "Don't know."

They waited at Hadrian's wagon a few minutes, and then a commotion erupted from a section of the camp near them. Mastodons bellowed and trumpeted, and men yelled, women screamed and sticks on leather whipped the air. The boys moved toward the disturbance.

Hadrian shouted over the cacophony, "Get that animal under control or I will butcher the beast."

"Don't worry Sir, we've got it."

The mastodon rose on its hind legs and pivoted toward a handler and crashed down hitting the man with its feet. The sound of breaking bones mingled with the man's screams. The beast rose again and lifted the second man holding the reins into the air. The man landed, dropped the reins, and ran away. Three men grabbed the injured handler and hauled him out of the beast's way.

Nearby animals moved, whickered, and shook at the bellowing beast.

Hadrian walked toward the boys, muttering under his breath. Al stopped him.

"Mr. Hadrian, Sir, Gadiel told us to report to you about getting assigned to a cart."

Hadrian perused the boys. "Can you handle animals?"

Erik said, "Yes sir, we grew up in farm country and can handle most any animal."

Al felt the blood drain from his face. He didn't like horses or even lambs, and had no wish to wrangle one of these monsters.

Hadrian studied them both and seemed to take their measure. "We lost two workers today to Roden." He pointed at the animal six men had finally wrestled into submission which was now tethered to two huge stakes in the ground. "Go see those men and tell them you're assigned to Roden. If the animal gets out of hand once more, he's dinner and you two walk home."

Hadrian grabbed a nearby boy, the same wiry dude working with the water carts. "Obadiah, set these boys up with Roden, assign them a wagon and collect more evergreens."

Obadiah looked like a twelve-year-old. He said, "You boys ever handle mastodons?"

"Nope." Erik said.

"Oy. Well, it's cactus. Roden will kill you in three days."

Two men carried Roden's victim in a litter and faltered toward the castle walls. Blood splattered the man's tunic and one leg bent at an improper angle at the knee.

Obadiah said, "Follow me, we'll find a wagon, tie Roden to the carts and get evergreens for the journey. We'll see if you mates can do a Bradbury."

Obadiah found an empty wagon. "Throw your stuff in the bassinet."

Erik and Al exchanged glances.

"Oy, boys, your stuff, in the sacks hanging from the wagon. This will be your home for the next nine to twelve weeks. You'll lead Roden, brush him, feed him, handle his waste, keep him calm and make him behave. We need the animals more than we need you, so stay alert. Don't bingle with the other wagons. There are no doctors on the trip. We leave you wherever you get hurt and you become something's next meal. Got a handle on that?"

Al and Erik put their meager possessions in one of the sacks.

"Let's hook up Roden to an empty wagon and fill it with food for the journey." Obadiah led them over to the red-haired beast, Roden.

"Is it sleeping now?" Al asked. His heart thumped in his chest. He couldn't do this. The animal stood twice as tall as he did.

"Roden is the largest mastodon we've ever had. This is his third year with the caravan. He's killed seven handlers. Hadrian talks about shredding the creature, but he never does. Roden tows twice as much as any other animal. So he's valuable, and you boys are brass razoos."

They stopped next to Roden, and Obadiah rubbed the beast's belly. "I like Roden and he's never been a problem for me. Rub him here and he'll be your mate for life."

Al stayed back from the beast while he watched Erik pat the animal.

Erik said, "I expected the hair to be soft, but it's rough."

"It's a pain to brush at night, and Roden hates it. If their hair gets knotted, it's painful and they get wild and crazy."

"I guess we'll keep it brushed then." Erik said.

Al wondered if he was hyper-ventilating. His breaths were shallow and inconsistent.

"Is your friend going to rub Roden? Is he sick? If he's as crook as Nookwood, then we have to leave you both here, can't have sick people on the journey. Eight years ago, a worker arrived with the plague and we lost fifteen handlers. Is your friend okay?"

Erik said, "Yeah, he's fine, come on over here Al, give Roden a little stomach rub."

Sweat beaded on Al's forehead.

Obadiah said, "Come on, Boy, give it a burl."

Erik said, "What does Roden eat?" He reached out to Al and pulled him close to Roden.

Obadiah rubbed Roden and patted the beast's shoulders. "These animals eat twigs, branches, leaves, pine needles and evergreen branches. We need more evergreens. Three months of traveling and they eat a fifth of a cart-full each day. Up North, we let them graze at night, which allows us to cut back on the amount from our supplies."

Erik whispered, "Come on Al, touch the animal." Erik pulled Al's arm and forced the wizard to touch Roden.

CHAPTER 17

Al's arm shook as Erik pulled him closer to Roden the mastodon. His knees locked as he leaned toward the animal, and he fastened his other hand on Erik's shoulder to keep from falling. Al wanted to scream, to cry out, to faint, but his body didn't cooperate.

The animal smelled like the boys' locker room at the high school. Would the animal eat him or just crush him like a worm in the dirt? At any moment the beast could grab Al with its trunk and sling him forty yards. The animal's coarse hair moved in and out with its every breath.

Roden turned its head in Al's direction, and Al feared to look at the beast's giant eyes. If the land giant took one more move toward Al he'd return to Crossroads and spend the next four years with Sherry and forget adventure.

Obadiah asked, "Is your friend okay?"

Al mouthed, "Help." He tried to speak but couldn't.

Erik smiled at Obadiah. "Yeah, Al's fine. He's tired."

"Knackered before we start? This journey takes months, he can't be tired already."

Erik whispered, "Get it together, and remember our goal, the golden crown."

Al's stomach roiled. One beat from emptying his last meal.

Erik released Al's arm and patted Roden's side. "Show us how to hook this beast to the carts. Gotta get food for the journey."

"You sure your friend's okay? I don't want him to cause the caravan to come down with a bug." Obadiah touched Al's arm, "The boy's sweating, does he have a fever?"

"No, we've been walking all day. He sweats a lot. Everything's fine, let's hook Roden to the carts."

"The harness is in your wagon. There are three pieces plus the chains." Obadiah headed in that direction.

Erik whispered, "Are you okay, buddy? Can you do this?" He grabbed Al's arm and pulled him toward the wagon.

They reached the wagon, and Obadiah threw an object at Erik. "The leather harness goes in front, which connects to the wooden harness on the mastodon's back. Stick this deer skin on its back under the harness."

Obadiah handed the deerskin and wooden frame to Al.

"It's gonna be easy for you to attach the harness as tall as you are. Center the deerskin on the animal's back."

Al didn't move from the wagon.

"Come on, Al. Bring those harness straps here."

Al responded. "Yeah, I'm coming right now." But he didn't move, just rocked back and forth. The shaking started in his legs and his jaw hurt as he ground his teeth. He tried self-talk, *I can do it. It's just an animal, like a fluffy dog.* It wasn't a fluffy dog, but a dangerous beast twice his height and three tons heavier. He knew if he got close to the animal, the beast would rise and stomp him into the ground.

"Al, move it, get over here." Erik said.

Do Erik and I need the golden crown? Maybe I can search for other adventures with no giant beasts.

Obadiah said, "I've seen this behavior. The kid's a bludger. Roden will sense fear and pound him into the ground. Tell your friend to go home, we'll find a battler."

Erik grabbed Obadiah's shoulder. "No, Al can do it. He's just not as comfortable with gigantic animals as I am. Give him a chance."

"This is one of our most productive beasts, we can't let a scaredy-cat, and bludger lead him. The animal leaders need to be brave, and steadfast. It's dangerous work, and not for everybody. I thought your friend's height would help, but he doesn't have it. He can join the cooks or help the women folk wash clothes."

Al stood motionless. Yes, he could join the cooks, though he knew even less about cooking than he did about working with animals. Roden now appeared to be sleeping and didn't look dangerous.

Erik scooted next to Al. "Come on man, you're a world-class wizard, Alpherge the Mighty, the wizard from Earth who killed the Mountain King. Nothing stops the wizard."

Something awoke in Al, the way magic surged through him at the volcano, the way he felt anytime he used magic.

A man in the crowd stepped forward. "That boy needs to learn how to lead a sheep first."

The onlookers laughed.

"Get the doctor to give the boy medicine to relieve his fears."

Another round of raucous laughter billowed.

"Bet Wagner's booze can stifle the fear."

Al hesitated. He feared animals, not just Roden, the horses in Montana, dogs in the neighborhood, and cats, though allergies topped the problem with cats. *Maybe I'd feel more comfortable if I had my inhaler.*

Erik chanted. "Alpherge the Mighty, Alpherge the Mighty." He raised his voice. "Alpherge the Mighty, Alpherge the Mighty."

The crowd picked up the chant. "Alpherge the Mighty, Alpherge the Mighty."

Al thought; visualize Roden as a fluffy puppy. Wizard Al could turn Roden into an animal the size of a fluffy puppy. *If Roden gets out of control, just shrink the beast before he hurts either of us.*

"Let's go, let's put this harness on Roden. How hard can it be?" Al approached the beast.

Obadiah said, "First we get Obadiah to kneel. Say the command, jilbajoog."

The beast didn't move.

"Yeah, if that doesn't work, touch Roden's trunk here and repeat the command, jilbajoog."

Roden dropped to his knees.

Al plopped the harness on the ground and tossed the deerskin over Roden's hairy back. Al looked at Erik and grinned. The wooden structure went on top of the deerskin and Obadiah showed Al how to place it on top.

"Once you have the harness on, then place the leather strap over the wood and under the mastodon's wide belly. Say istaag and Roden stands."

Roden stood.

They cinched it, pulling it tight.

Erik held the wide leather strap across the beast's breastbone, and attached it to the strap around the body.

Roden didn't seem to mind.

"Here's the hard part; we fasten these ropes to the harness, and each of you will hold one side and guide Roden with the ropes. We'll undo his leg stakes and you will walk him to the cart and we'll hitch him up." Obadiah went to the wagon and pulled out two large ropes, an inch thick and the length of a wagon.

Butterflies swirled in Al's stomach as the crowd closed in.

Obadiah showed the boys how to secure the ropes and handed one to each boy.

Roden lifted his head and eyeballed Al.

The moment of truth, Al's chance to handle Roden, arrived.

"When you want Roden to move forward say the word, 'fo', for back say, 'back', right say, 'yee', and left, 'yo.'" Obadiah tugged the rope Al held and said, "Roden, fo."

Roden turned his head from Obadiah, but didn't move.

"Sometimes he gets stubborn. Give it a burl. Move him forward so we can release his foot shackles."

Al said, "Roden, fo."

Roden looked at Al and moved forward three steps.

Erik smiled. "You did it."

"What's the word for stop?"

Obadiah responded, "'Stop.' He seems relaxed and ready to cooperate; you boys are lucky. But it's too early to celebrate, because Roden will test you when you secure his legs to the stakes."

Obadiah loosened the ropes around the stakes, pulled one loose and poked it under one side of the harness. This meant Al controlled the animal on that side.

"I'm releasing the last tether, and you two will have full control," Obadiah said.

A hush fell over the crowd, which moved back from the animal and its handlers.

Al held the slack rope tight in his hands, afraid to release it for fear Roden might stomp him or Erik.

Obadiah took the second tether and tucked it in the harness.

Roden flapped his enormous elephant like ears, but didn't move. Al thought the animal looked sad.

Obadiah said, "Use voice commands to move Roden to these empty carts over there." He pointed to the left.

Erik said, "Yo."

At the same time Al said, "Yee."

Obadiah yelled, "No, no, no. Only one of you gives the voice commands."

Erik said, "I'll do it."

Al responded by pulling the rope. "No, I should give the commands."

Roden bellowed.

The crowd moved back.

Al said, "Erik, you give the commands."

Erik said, "Yo."

Roden moved toward the carts.

Erik made mistakes, but continued the commands until Roden faced one of the open bed carts with three board sides and a gate in back.

Obadiah said, "Ace. Now turn him around and we'll attach the thills to the harness."

"What's the command to make him rotate one-hundred-eighty degrees?"

"No chuck a yewy. Move him right and then back him up and he'll be apples."

Al turned nervous when Roden backed him to the cart, leaving a foot between Al and the animal, but Erik's commands situated

Roden in the right spot and Obadiah showed them how to hook up the thills.

"Roden is a two person operation. The other mastodons only have one handler. Al, stand in front of Roden. Then we'll hook the second cart to the first and bounce into the forest. Notice the first cart has thills which we connect to the animal's harness. The other wagons have a single tongue to allow easier turning."

Al stood face to face with the noble beast, and he didn't believe fear had ever gripped him this tight. Knots tangled his stomach.

Erik managed the rope and told Al to move to the side. Erik yelled, "Fo."

Roden shrugged and leaned forward until the line stiffened.

Erik yelled, "Roden fo."

Roden bellowed. The carts inched forward until the first cart reached a dip in the meadow. Roden paused and then lunged forward like an NFL running back, driving through the defensive line. Giant legs the size of telephone poles lifted one by one, and the carts moved. Each step over the uneven ground became faster, and the mastodon gained speed. The cart hurtled forward on its giant wooden wheels.

It didn't take long before they entered the forest. Obadiah showed how to secure the mastodon to a tree with its leg ropes. "If Roden wants to pull this tree down and take off, there's nothing we can do to stop him. We've chained Roden to a strong stake since he was a young calf, and he doesn't know he has the power to pull this tree right out of the ground. Plus, with the added weight of the carts and soon the feed we gather, he'll stay calm."

Roden pulled needles from nearby trees and munched on them as the boys gathered larger branches for the feed cart.

Two hours later Al, Obadiah and Erik had filled both carts with a variety of plant materials Obadiah said the animals liked. The late afternoon sun threw long shadows across the forest floor.

Obadiah said, "Time to shoot to the caravan. Roden isn't always cooperative in the dark. If I didn't know better, I'd say he's afraid."

They untied Roden and Erik led the animal back to the caravan. Smoke rose from camp fires, making eerie shadows and turning the sinking sun into a golden haze. Roden plodded into the caravan enclosure and stopped near his two stakes.

"He knows it's near feeding time, so he'll cooperate. But be alert. Sometimes he knows we're tired and tries to escape."

Fear crept back into Al's tired body. He tried to will Roden to relax. *Just get him chained up and then I can sleep.*

Erik's commands guided Roden to a place to drop the carts, and Obadiah unhooked Roden. "Ace boys. Take him to the stakes and secure his legs."

They released the weight of the carts from the harness, and a tremendous shudder rippled through the animal's body.

Al gripped hard on the rope in case the beast wanted to make a run for it, although he knew they couldn't handle the mastodon if it raced for the mountains.

Erik continued his voice commands and Roden moved steadily to the stakes. "Al, hold him and I'll tie the rope on my side onto the stake."

"Okay."

Erik secured the second rope to the stake and Al relaxed. "Done. Dinner time."

"Oh, no, you don't." Obadiah said.

"First, brush Roden. We would usually feed him too, but he ate plenty in the forest. After he's brushed, scoop up the patties and toss them in the dung cart. We'll need that for campfires when we travel across the lake."

Erik gave Al a quizzical expression and mouthed the words. "Campfires on the lake?"

Al hunched his shoulders.

The sun set an hour before the boys finished their tasks with Roden. They requested food, but dinner hour was over and they wouldn't be given any food until tomorrow. Disappointment increased when they learned where they would sleep. The wagons had a strip of canvas tied across the fronts and on the sides. They were hammocks and the boys would sleep in them. They also were expected to travel in them when the caravan moved. They found scratchy mastodon-wool blankets inside the hammocks.

Before they drifted off to sleep Erik said, "Hey Al, is that a comet in the sky?"

Every muscle in Al's body ached and his empty stomach made a noise. He searched the night sky and found the object. "Wow that's the biggest, brightest comet I've ever seen."

CHAPTER 18

l woke the next morning to shouts echoing throughout the caravan camp, and someone poked him in the ribs.

"Get up, we're moving out. Master Hadrian is ready to speak to the handlers."

Al winced and rubbed his ribs as he tried to open his eyes in the bright sunlight streaming into his face. People from the camp walked by and urged him to get moving so he wouldn't miss Hadrian's speech.

Erik pushed Al and said, "Get up, Al. There's a ceremony of some kind we're supposed to attend."

Al groaned. "Five minutes."

"No, the dude is waiting for us. It might be important."

"Sleeping another five minutes is important." Al said.

Erik pushed Al again and ripped the blanket off him. "Rise and shine."

Al covered his eyes with his forearm and tried to roll over, but tangled in the hammock and couldn't move. "Okay, I'm awake."

"Hurry, I don't want to miss it."

"Okay, Okay." Al struggled to get out of the hammock without falling to the ground. He eased over the edge of the hammock, and when he stood, every muscle group in his body screamed from yesterday's hard work. He waddled, more than walked to where Master Hadrian waited for his crew to convene.

Hadrian, the caravan leader, stood on the back of his wagon. The caravan workers, a mix of sizes, shapes and colors, faced him in a semi-circle. Al noticed two guys about his own size, and he found it interesting they were thin like he was. A handful looked Kallurian, like the wizards he trained with at the wizard school in the mountains. A couple of them had red hair like Sherry and Cugbert. Wagner, the cook, stood near the platform as Master Hadrian eyed the people who had gathered.

Hadrian nodded to a man near the front who cried. "Quiet."

The message passed through the crowd and the talking stopped.

Hadrian waited.

A mastodon bellowed in the background.

Hadrian said, "Listen. This is an arduous, dangerous journey. Each year we lose people because they don't listen to our rules. Some get stomped, others are eaten by winter wolves or grass cats, some get lost in blizzards, fall through the ice or just do something fatally stupid."

Hadrian searched the crowd as if trying to locate the people he considered stupid, and his gaze landed on Al and Erik.

"The comet you saw last night is our clock and beacon. We must reach the Ice Castle before that comet disappears from view. Anyone who can't keep up because of sickness, incompetence or stupidity we leave behind, wherever we are. The animals are more important than humans. Unless you can move two to four carts by yourself, we need the animals more than you."

Al's mind wandered as the light breeze changed direction and the odor of fresh baked bread wafted in his direction. His stomach reminded him he went to bed without supper. He turned his head and scanned the camp for the source of the bread.

"You will listen to me as we travel, for if you get off course, your life will be in danger. I've made this trip eighteen times. I know the path to reduce the animals' workload, to get to our destination the fastest and to keep from getting eaten by wild animals or falling into the lake. If you lose your cargo for any reason, I take it out of your pay.

Erik poked Al on the arm, "Hey we get paid."

"Nice," Al said, "hey, let's move toward those carts over there where I smell fresh bread."

"We will encounter animals that look cute and cuddly. They'll pretend to be your friends. Do not feed them, for any reason. If you feed one winter wolf, I guarantee there will be a thousand winter wolves at your cart. Twenty wolves can take out half the caravan in one night."

Hadrian droned on about the trip and his expectations, but Al's stomach drove him toward the source of the baking bread, ". . . don't make it before the asteroids fall, you will die . . ."

Al and Erik had to slip between a group of men and women to reach the cook's cart. A large pot hung on a metal tripod over a fire, and delicious aromas of meat and spices wafted from the boiling liquid. A table next to the cart held row upon row of baked bread lined up like soldiers lying in a bunkhouse.

Al said, "Do you think we can grab a loaf of bread? Do you see any bowls for the soup? Or is that stew in the pot?"

". . . ride long hours each day. At night you take care of your animal first and then worry about your own needs. Everyone understand?"

Murmurs of acceptance rose among the crowd.

"Okay, feed your animals and harness the carts, we travel in one hour."

Al moved closer to the bread table. "Are we supposed to pay for a loaf? Is it part of our pay for the caravan to feed us? Were we supposed to bring our own food? How come Gadiel never told us this?"

Wagner, the camp cook, shuffled up to the boys. "Ah, my friend the wizard. Are you here to sell your staff, Boy?"

"My name is Al. No, like I told you yesterday, I'm not interested in selling the staff. It was my grandfather's."

"Sure it was kid. So what do you want?"

"How do we get food, I'm starving?" Al said. "Can we have a loaf of bread?"

"You want a loaf of bread, do ya?"

"Yeah."

"This bread isn't for you. I'm the cook for the caravan leaders. Go find the animal roustabout cooks. You better hurry, they eat at sunrise and we're hours past that. Scoot."

Erik whispered to Al, "I bet we could grab one of those loaves and get out of here before anyone could catch us."

Al thought about Erik's suggestion. It sounded tempting. Then he saw Master Hadrian and Gadiel walking toward the bread table.

Hadrian spotted the boys, "I told you to prepare your animals. Skedaddle, we leave in an hour and you better be ready."

Al touched Erik's shoulder and turned to leave.

"No, wait." Hadrian shouted.

"I saw you boys weren't listening. Let me tell you something. I'm only allowing you in the caravan because of Gadiel." Hadrian nodded at the old man. "He assured me you boys can carry your weight. Well, so far, I'm not convinced, but hear this." Hadrian covered the distance between them and poked Al in his sore ribs. "I have no qualms leaving you on Lake Destiny between the winter wolves and the asteroids. I will not go back for you, stop the caravan, look for you or wait for you. Do you understand?"

Al's empty stomach growled, and his face warmed as he lifted his gaze from his feet to Hadrian's steel-gray eyes. Al nodded.

"Get Roden equipped. You've lost ten minutes with your foolishness. Move!"

The boys scurried to Roden who was still anchored to the steel poles. Obadiah waited for them. "Let's go, where have you been?"

"We haven't eaten breakfast," Al said.

"Breakfast is at sunrise and you woke late, so you get ham and eggs and duck under the table. Get Roden's harness on, it takes thirty minutes to hook up the wagons. You better hope he wants to work today or it'll take longer. My job depends on you boys doing this right, and not just this morning, every morning. If you don't shape up, I'll replace you at the next castle. Now hustle."

Al glanced at the giant mastodon. Butterflies in his stomach replaced his hunger pains. Hook up the massive creature in the mornings? Dread crept down his spine, and he wondered if he had the mental fortitude to touch the beast. Last night's confidence blew away like dandelion's fluff.

Erik shook his head and pursed his lips. "What did he mean by, 'you get ham and eggs and duck under the table?'"

Al shrugged.

Erik went to the wagon and handed the animal deerskin harness pad and harness to Al. "Plop this across Roden's back."

Al hesitated. Could he wrangle Roden every day? Tension and stress built around his chest as he handled the equipment.

Roden eyed Al and bellowed.

Obadiah, working with another beast next to the boys, shouted. "Keep him calm. Don't let him stampede the whole encampment this morning. Steady Roden."

Roden lifted his massive trunk into the air and roared. He danced left and right as other animals bellowed.

Obadiah yelled, "Quiet him now."

Erik jumped from the wagon and ran to Roden, "Easy boy, easy." He rubbed Roden's hairy belly. "Easy."

Roden bellowed and stomped his feet.

Erik yelled at Al, "Get over here and help me calm him."

"Calm him? Who's calming me?"

"Rub his belly. Come on, we don't want to lose this job. We need to find the artifact, remember."

Every sinew of Al's body screamed to stay still. It was only the first day, and Roden would crush him like an ant, but the quest for the golden crown and the grand adventure still called to Al.

Roden bellowed and knocked Erik to the ground with its huge, rounded tusk.

Al stepped back.

Obadiah shouted, "Get control, boys. Hurry, that's how we lost two handlers yesterday."

Erik jumped to his feet and grabbed Roden's fur, "Al, I need help."

Al walked in front of the angry animal, staying clear of the tusks and trunk. Did Erik think Al could touch Roden and calm him? Was the quest for the crown worth risking your life with a wild beast?

Roden lunged toward Al.

Al fell to the ground, covering his head.

"Get up, Al."

The wooden anchors and giant ropes held the angry beast.

From the ground, Al looked into Roden's eyes and realized the animal outweighed the boy from Earth by two or three tons. If the beast took a single step forward, Al would die. He scrambled to his feet.

Roden stamped his feet and bellowed, and the animal's spit landed on Al's face.

"Ew, that's disgusting," Al moved to Roden's side and rubbed the smelly goo away with his sleeve. "That stinks."

"Good Al, now rub his belly."

"Really, we're still doing this?"

"Yes, I gotta save my dad, and that means we go on this journey. Now comfort Roden."

Al couldn't see Erik with the beast between them, but he suspected Erik's face was bright red. That's what happened when he got mad. Roden turned his body toward Al.

"Whoa, Roden, good buddy." Al placed his hand on the beast's shoulder, the rough red fur tangling between his fingers. Al knew one quick move by Roden and the beast would trample him to the ground, sending him to the hospital. Wait, they don't have hospitals on this world. Bloodletting would only make matters worse. "Easy Roden." Al patted the animal.

Roden settled, and began swinging his trunk back and forth.

Erik said, "Are you okay, Al?"

A sense of pride rolled through Al's body. "Yeah, I'm touching him."

Roden bellowed and rose on his back legs and stamped hard on the ground.

"Easy Roden," Al said.

Obadiah yelled, "Quit wasting time, grab Roden's harness and connect the wagons."

Roden pivoted back and forth between the two boys and relaxed.

"I think he's calming," Erik said.

Roden turned hard left and knocked Al to the ground, as the beast rose five feet onto his back legs and bellowed.

Al saw his life ending, but couldn't move. His chest locked, and he couldn't draw a breath. The giant beast moved in slow motion as it rotated its body toward Al and twisted to crash its feet into Al's body.

One foot, the size of a large cast iron pan, would crush Al's head, and the other would splinter his femur into a thousand pieces. Al wanted to scream, but all that came out was a whimper. His heart raced to the point of exploding. He knew he had to move, but he felt dizzy and his legs felt too weak to escape the deranged creature.

The creature's foreleg continued its downward movement toward Al's head.

He wanted to shut his eyes, but instead, studied the animal's footpad, cracked, dusty pink with toenails the size of Al's foot. He thought he should move, but wondered what sound his skull would make as it popped.

The creature's foreleg was only inches from Al's head.

Would he die immediately from the impact or lie wasting away for days like a drooling old man? Which would hurt more, his leg or his head? How long could he live on this planet in a vegetative state? Would Sherry come to his funeral?

Milliseconds separated Al from certain death.

Will Mom bury me on Aloheno or Earth?

Al felt the rush of air as the animal's massive foot descended.

Adrenaline clicked in and Al rolled.

Roden's feet hit the ground, and dust exploded from the impact.

Obadiah grabbed Al by the shoulders and pulled him to safety.

Erik yelled, "Easy boy."

Roden eyed Al as if in warning, "don't touch me." The animal calmed, blowing dust into the air with huge breaths.

Al gulped and gasped as he eyed Roden.

Obadiah pulled Al to his feet, "You're a bonehead bludger. You can't do this boy."

Al agreed with Obadiah, but what would Al do if he didn't handle the beast? Al imagined himself crushed under Roden's weight. *What happens if next time I can't move or don't move fast enough? I'll die.*

CHAPTER 19

Al disliked Obadiah calling him 'boy,' The trainer had to be at least three years younger. Although he didn't believe it, out of sheer annoyance, he said, "You're wrong, I can do this and I will do it. Roden is my new best friend. Come on, Erik, let's get the harness on this hairy beast. The caravan has to get moving. Obadiah, don't you have a beast to harness?"

Al trotted over to Erik and felt Obadiah watching him. Al mumbled under his breath. "Walk away Obadiah, go back to harness your animal, we got this."

Obadiah went back to his mastodon, and Al sighed and said, "You have to put on the harness, I can't get close to Roden right now. If animals can smell fear, then I'm in trouble. I will hand you the equipment, but you have to put them on."

Erik patted Al on the back. "No problem, buddy."

Roden settled down as Erik adjusted the harness. It took a little longer with only one person, but Erik yanked on the leather harness and all appeared tight and secure. "Okay, let's release Roden from the stakes and hook up the wagons."

Al held the guide rope while Erik loosed the tethers. Al looked Roden in the eye. He felt sure the crazy beast planned to escape for the hills.

Noise filled the air as caravan captains called out their status. "Section one complete and on the move."

"Section four moving into position."

The wagons creaked as the mastodons tugged their loaded wagons. Men and women shouted commands to ease their wagons into the caravan.

A woman shouted, "Section two moving."

Obadiah yelled, "Move it, boys. We're section three and should be done like a dinner."

Erik barked commands to shift Roden to the wagons and adjusted the animal to attach the carts. They had four wagons hooked up, two with feed, one with castle supplies and the fourth, at the tail end of their wagons, was the manure cart.

Al stood in front of Roden as Erik connected the ropes to the harness.

Erik said, "Let's move Roden. Fo!"

Roden gave Al the stink eye, but leaned forward. The first wagon started forward, but Roden stopped.

Erik said, "Roden, Fo."

Roden shook his head, his trunk moving like a pendulum.

"Come on, big boy. Fo."

Al looked at Roden and willed the animal to move. "Come on, you can do it."

Roden leaned forward and the first two carts gained momentum. The third cart caught and lurched forward. The fourth wagon stopped Roden's progress.

Obadiah shouted over the noise in the staging area. "Nudge the last wagon to get it started."

Erik grabbed the rope from Al. "Go back and shove the last wagon."

"Why me? You know what's in the fourth wagon, don't you?"

"Yeah, but I have to direct Roden. Come on, the wagon train is moving."

Al scanned the surrounding countryside as the wagon train advanced out of the meadow toward the mountain paths. He lumbered to the back of the fourth wagon and yelled, "Okay, Erik."

"Fo, Roden." Three carts moved.

"Push, Al."

Al planted his feet and leaned into the rough boards. Push? The manure stench made it difficult to breathe. He buried his nose in his shoulder and drove his legs. Al wanted to yell at Erik, but deep breaths proved impossible.

The wagon moved. The weight of the forward wagons had carved ruts in the soft field, and Al's extra push helped the final cart over the furrowed ground. A sense of accomplishment rushed through Al. With his help, Roden was moving four wagons. He continued shouldering the back of the cart while taking a last look at Velidred castle.

Awful memories of the Velidred dungeons flitted through his mind. The huge beetles that attacked his wizard friend, the room that wanted to kill them, and the brown mold that came within moments of finishing him off.

Busy looking over his shoulder at the castle, he stepped in an enormous pile of mastodon dung.

"Noooo!"

"Are you okay back there?"

Al hopped on one foot trying to shake off the muck clinging to his shoe. "No, no, no."

"Should I stop?"

"Keep going, I'm okay."

He released his hold on the wagon and wiped his shoe on the trampled grass.

"Hey, out of the way." A handler pushed Al to the ground as a mastodon pulling two carts passed Al.

I should shoot a fireball at that guy, Al thought, but instead wiped his shoe in the grass and trotted forward to catch Erik.

Erik walked next to Roden, patting the animal on the shoulder. "What happened?"

"I stepped in Roden's dung," Al said.

Erik laughed.

"How come Roden has to pull four wagons? The guy behind us, his mastodon has two, and Obadiah's animal has one to pull. Why are they so hard on Roden?"

"I don't know. Roden is larger than those other animals. Maybe he's experienced like a pro football player compared to a high school player, or maybe the others are young and this trip is their first caravan experience."

The convoy rolled out of Velidred, heading north. It stayed on the road which undulated through the mountains. Roden struggled on the uphill slopes, but the wagons rolled down the gentle hills without effort on Roden's part.

* * * *

The sun shone brightly at mid-day, and the caravan slowed. Obadiah strolled back to the boys.

"Is it lunch time?" Al asked.

Obadiah said, "No, there's a creek up ahead. When Roden reaches it, let him take a drink. Be careful, as sometimes these animals want to roll in the water and we can't let him do that with the harness tied to the carts. Control him. Let him drink and then force him forward for the next wagon master, and don't bunch up the group, the animals get angry being in each other's space."

"When do we eat?"

"We stop at sundown and then you eat."

"But, I'm hungry now."

"Tomorrow, get beef jerky to hold you till dinner." Obadiah stepped down the line, talking to handlers and checking the animals.

The wagon line slowed as each animal stopped for a drink. Al said, "I better get food tonight, I'm hungry enough to eat one of these mastodons."

Roden reached the creek which covered his toe nails when he stepped in the water. He put his trunk in the water, removed it and sprayed water into his mouth. Three times he repeated the process.

"How many times do we let him drink?" Erik asked.

"I suppose as much as he needs. He's been working hard."

Roden put his trunk into the water, and then moved his head right to left. Erik placed his hand on Roden's shoulder.

Roden sprayed Al with the water.

"Hey stop that!" Al spluttered.

Erik laughed. "Come on, big boy, time to move."

Roden's bellow sounded like a laugh, Al thought.

Later, Obadiah strolled back through the line of animals and wagons and saw Al dripping wet. He laughed, but sounded mean. "Oh yeah, I should warn you, Roden's got a trickster's instinct and a nasty streak. Now listen up, we're coming to a ridge and it's downhill for two miles. Halfway down it gets steep and takes a dangerous curve. You know how to use the brake system?"

"What brakes?" Al asked.

"The wagons have brakes. Going uphill keep them released, but on the downhill, set the brakes so the carts don't coast too fast. Don't ride the brakes otherwise Roden has to work too hard. When the hill gets steeper, set the brakes tighter and release them as the hill flattens. Got it?"

"Yeah, we know all about brakes, don't we, Al?" Erik asked.

"Sure, I guess. Same as car brakes, right?" Al asked.

Obadiah gave Al a quizzical expression and shrugged.

The caravan rolled on and sped up after all the animals cleared the creek. The mountain forest landscape changed to a meadow with wildflowers of purple, pink, white and yellow dotting the landscape. Sweet smells of lavender, honeysuckle and jasmine wafted on the breeze. Anuoura, large frogs the size of dogs and colored pink and purple, jumped between the flowers. Al wondered what the mastodons did if they faced off against a stygox, the bear-like animal the teens encountered when they first reached the planet. He figured it was best if they didn't find out.

The terrain and road slanted down, and the mountains opened to a glorious view of the valley. Several villages circled a lake, and a river flowed across the valley. A splashing waterfall resounded off the rocks. The serpentine road snaked back and forth along the mountain walls, winding down to the villages.

Al thought how wonderful it would be to sit here and enjoy nature and the beauty of the landscape.

Obadiah yelled, "Prepare to set your brakes."

The section-four leader hollered the same command.

Erik said, "Al, you got the brakes?"

"Where are the brakes?"

"You said you knew what you were doing."

The road inclined and Roden's speed increased.

"You tell me where the brakes are."

"Obadiah said they're on the wagons. Search for a wooden handle sticking up from the wheels. I remember that from the old, cowboy, TV shows."

Al hurried to the wagons, which accelerated. Roden walked faster, but the wagons pushed against the giant beast. Al searched for a wooden lever connected to the wheels, anything that might be a brake handle.

"I see nothing."

"Our speed is increasing, look harder."

Al scooted along the left side of the train of four wagons, but nothing resembled a brake. Boards underneath the wagon could work as brakes, but no levers were visible to engage them.

He scrambled around the back of the last wagon, holding his nose as he ran, but it became difficult to keep up with the quickening trailers.

"Slow down." Erik yelled.

"I can't."

"Find the brakes, and hurry, because we're heading toward a bend in the road with a steep drop.

Running faster became difficult. Flower pollen in the air caused congestion in Al's lungs as his allergies flared. He couldn't take a deep breath.

The mountain road narrowed as it reached the turn. The path tapered to a one lane wagon trail between a rocky wall and a one-thousand-foot plummet into the valley.

Al spotted the brake, a handle on the right side of the wagon, connected to a latch which winched a wooden board up against the wagon wheels. The problem was, the handle was inside the wheel, and to reach it, he needed to grab close behind the front wheel, and hope not to lose an arm. The lever had five positions, maybe slow braking to hard braking, Al didn't know.

"We'll miss the turn at this speed, Al, find the brakes."

"I found them. Do you want hard braking or a little braking?"

"I don't care, stop the carts."

"Hard braking then." Al reached his long arm toward the lever as he tried to keep pace with the wagon, while running close to the rocky mountain wall. He knew if he tripped, the wagon wheel in back would roll over him. It was now or never. He reached out and pulled the lever. The brake engaged, and the wheels locked and squealed, but the four wagons glided forward.

"It's not working." Al yelled.

"Did you set all four wagons? Hurry, we're sliding off the cliff."

Roden bellowed.

Al wheezed and squeezed past the locked, skidding wagon and raced up to the next one, as the space narrowed between the mountain wall and wagon wheels. He scraped his arm along a rock, and winced, but continued scurrying to the next wagon.

Erik said, "Hurry, I'm too young to die. Stop Roden, stop."

Al grabbed the next wagon brake handle and pulled it to the tightest position. Again the squeal, but despite locked wheels the wagon skidded down the sloped road.

"That's helping but hurry."

Al dashed to the next wagon. Running fast enough became easier as the wagon train slowed, but there was less room along the shoulder as bushes scratched and clawed him. Reaching the next wagon was a challenge. He worried that the giant, rolling wheels would crush and maim him if he slipped. Chilly water dripped off the walls and splashed his neck and dribbled under his tunic.

Erik yelled at Roden, "Stop, you big hairy beast."

When Al reached the next brake handle, he pulled, and the brakes set hard. Momentum still propelled the screeching wagon train down the road.

"Stop Roden and see if he can block the wagons."

"He won't stop."

The space between wall and wagon thinned to a mere sliver. Al had to stop the first wagon, but could he reach the lever in time? He noticed a concave spot in the rock, and if he hurried, he might sneak around the rear wheel and reach the brake lever.

Roden bellowed.

"Al, do something."

Al darted into the tiny opening as his heart throbbed in his chest. Would he get to the brake on the final wagon or die of a heart attack in the thin mountain air? He splashed through a puddle of water and almost fell as he passed the rear wheel.

Roden bellowed, kicking up dust, dirt and debris.

The wagons continued to slide forward. Even if Al reached the brake, would it be soon enough or would they all cascade over the cliff to their deaths? Al reached his long arm toward the brake, but he ran out of room between wagon and wall.

Roden neared the side of the mountain and raised his front legs as the wagon train slid toward the frightened animal.

Al's hand touched the brake lever, but then his other shoulder slammed into a rock outcrop. He fell to the ground. The unengaged brake remained useless as Roden was still being pushed by the heavy loads. Al rolled close to the mountain wall to prevent the wagon from smashing him. Erik and Roden would die as the wagons hurtled over the edge. They were doomed, and it was Al's fault.

He pictured Erik falling first, then Roden landing on top of Erik and the wagons crashing down on them both. How would he explain this to Lily and Sherry? They would never forgive him for allowing this to happen. He could have stopped it with magic.

Wait, yes, he could stop it with magic. He gestured with a hand and watched as the brake handle moved, locking the wheels.

It was too late, the wagons kept sliding. Between their forward momentum and the loose gravel the brakes couldn't stop the motion, and Roden continued to move forward, unable to come to a complete halt.

CHAPTER 20

Erik held Roden's rope as the animal came down hard on his front feet, less than a foot from the cliff's edge. The wagon train slid into Roden's back legs. Roden bellowed, the sound wave echoed off the mountain walls, and he stiffened to stop the wagons with his body.

The first wagon came to a stop because of Roden's strength.

The second wagon slid into the first and Roden held steady, stopping that one as well.

To Erik it was like watching a multiple car pile-up on the interstate expressway under icy conditions. You see it happening, but can't do anything about it.

The third wagon slowed and found a solid road. It, too, stopped skidding and halted.

The loose gravel and grass road surface couldn't impede the momentum, and the dung cart rammed into the third wagon. Erik thought it was like watching a movie of shock waves in science class. Three moved into two, causing it to bump into one.

Wagon one bumped into Roden's back legs. Roden bellowed in pain and stepped forward. One front foot landed inches from the edge, the other balanced half on the ledge. There was only air beneath the rest of the enormous foot. If Roden rose on his back legs, the wagons would nudge him forward and he'd never be able to bring his front feet down on the road.

Roden did not rear up. The wagon train stopped. Erik stood next to Roden as both breathed hard and trembled.

Obadiah ran back to the wagons. "What in the name of Anticletus are you guys doing? Are you trying to run the entire wagon train off the mountain? Will you kill my best animal?" He put his hands on Roden. "Are you okay, big guy?"

Roden didn't move.

Erik peeked over the edge, a thousand feet or more to the valley floor. Roden appeared glassy eyed and in shock.

The wagons were stopped but stranded in a precarious position. Roden had little room to turn, and couldn't maneuver with the attached wagons run up against the traces. If Roden became upset here, the entire wagon train could still plummet to the valley floor.

Obadiah checked for damage to the animal. "Fair crack of the whip. If you guys hurt Roden, I'll skin you alive. We have to move him and the wagons to see how bad he's injured. Un-hook Roden from the wagons."

Erik said, "Yes sir," and whispered, "I'm sorry."

"Oh, you'll be sorry all right. If Roden's injured and can't continue, you two yahoos are pulling these wagons yourself. I can't believe you damaged him on the first day. I've never seen that from even the most worthless bludgers."

Erik ran his hand through his hair and moved back to give Obadiah a chance to check Roden's legs. "We didn't know where the brakes were located."

"You didn't know where the brakes were located? Why didn't you say something? I asked you guys, and you acted like you knew how to apply the brakes. Are you just stupid, or were you lying to me?"

Erik's cheeks burned red; his knees felt weak as he moved away from the edge of the cliff. He scooted past Obadiah and loosened the straps holding Roden to the wagons.

Al came forward and asked, "Is Roden okay?"

"Is Roden okay?" Obadiah asked, "Look at these cuts on his legs. He's not okay. You better hope he can walk."

Erik released the last connection. "He's free of the wagons."

Obadiah said, "I'm taking Roden down the hill to check his gait. You two straighten out this mess, learn how to operate the brakes and bring the wagons to the valley with you. Can you handle that?"

"Yes, Sir," Erik said. He watched Roden walk away. The animal limped on its left back leg and blood dripped from the other side.

Erik glared at Al. "Why didn't you set the brakes?"

"The brake levers were on the mountain side and I couldn't reach them because of the mountain wall. You could have slowed the animal."

"Forget it," Erik said.

"I'm not forgetting it. It's not my fault. If I hadn't used magic, both you and Roden would be at the bottom of the mountain right now with six tons of wagons and manure on top of you."

Erik raised his voice, "I'm not taking the blame for this incident, we were going the proper speed. All you had to do was control the brakes." His jaw muscles clamped tight, and he wanted to punch Al in the face.

Al's nostrils flared. The tall skinny wizard's legs and arms were shaking with rage and shame.

Obadiah yelled, "Get those wagons moving, we're losing sunlight, and we have to be off the mountain before sunset.

Erik opened and closed his fists as heat rushed through his tired body.

Al walked back to the carts.

"You're just gonna walk away?"

"You heard Obadiah, we have to get these carts to the valley before night fall. Do you want to be out here with wolves and stegox in the dark?"

Two handlers approached the boys, actually willing to help. "It works best if you move them one at a time. There's room after this bend in the road to park the wagons along the mountain side. Take one cart to the valley and return for the others one at a time. We'll help you get them to the side so we can get past. We have to keep the caravan moving. No lost time right?"

Erik shook his head and stared dumbfounded at the animal handlers and Al. How could this be happening?

They hauled the wagons to the side crevice where three carts could sit while the end of the caravan rattled past. Al hoisted the wagon tongue and Erik lifted behind Al and they walked it down the mountain. Back and forth they zig-zagged down the winding mountain path, watching for loose gravel which might yet cause them to slip over the cliff. When they reached the valley floor, there was a wide meadow next to the lake where the caravan set up camp for the evening. Pulling the carts across the level ground was backbreaking.

Handlers pitched tents, or fed and brushed animals while food cooked. Al and Erik trudged up the mountain to retrieve the next wagon. Darkness arrived by the time they recovered the third wagon and parked it in the meadow next to the others.

As they walked up the mountain path to retrieve the last wagon, Al asked, "How did we think we could do this job? We're not farmers or cattle ranchers. We're high school students from Earth."

"Obadiah is younger than us and seems to handle the animals and the wagons like an expert, why couldn't we?"

"He only has to worry about the one wagon and not four wagons like Roden. Plus, he's probably done this his entire life."

Erik proposed, "They want us to fail and get satisfaction watching city folk like us crash and burn."

Al said, "What are we doing tomorrow? I have blisters on my hands from pulling these wagons. My muscles ache, I can't lift my arms and we still have to haul the heaviest wagon to the camp site. I can't go on much longer without food."

"Do you think we've crippled Roden? It sounds like they will put him down if he gets injured. I don't suppose they have an animal hospital he can stay at while we finish the journey."

"I'm sure our employment is finished." They reached the manure wagon. Al said, "My arms are so tired, it'll take us all night to walk it to the valley floor and then another half mile to the lake."

"Don't you have magic spells to solve this problem?" Erik's legs quivered like jelly, his chest muscles throbbed, and his back ached.

"Hmm, magic."

"What're you thinking? We don't want to lose this load of manure. I'm not spending the rest of the night shoveling manure."

"I'm not picking it up, but I will lighten the load."

Al pointed his hands at the wagon and mumbled. "There done."

"I don't see any difference."

"Try to pull it, you won't need me."

Erik lifted the wagon tongue and pulled. It felt light as a child's red toy wagon. The cart rolled down the mountain, and Erik controlled it with precision and ease. "Brilliant. Can you do this when Roden pulls the wagons?"

"Maybe when we go uphill, that'll make it easier on Roden. He won't be so tired."

Campfires had burned down to red embers when they arrived, and the camp slept except for people talking around a fire near Master Hadrian's wagon.

Erik whispered, "We missed another meal."

"I don't care; I'm too tired to eat." Al grabbed his blanket and struggled into the hammock.

"I want to check on Roden first."

"Don't do it; the animal is probably sleeping. Let him be, and check on him in the morning."

"No, I won't feel right unless I examine him now." As they walked down the mountain the final time, Erik thought he might try to use healing techniques on Roden the same way he did on humans. If Roden healed by morning, maybe Obadiah and Hadrian wouldn't expel them from the caravan. Their only hope to find the way to the golden crown was to stay with the group. They couldn't lose this opportunity.

A few wagons beyond, Roden's stake had been pounded in the ground, close to Obadiah's and Gadiel's animals. Near Gadiel's wagon three figures sat whispering around the fire. Erik hid behind a wagon, trying to catch snatches of the conversation. Obadiah said something unintelligible from Erik's location. Gadiel whispered, "We need those boys to stay with the caravan."

A female voice whispered, and Erik couldn't hear her response. He needed to get closer.

The fire had burned down, and Erik was sure he could sneak closer to the conversation.

The woman said something else. Then Erik saw her rise and slip into Gadiel's wagon. *Who is that with Gadiel?*

Obadiah said, "Okay, we'll give them another chance. We'll take one wagon off Roden until he heals. But we can't afford to lose the animal."

Erik pumped his fist. He snuck around looking for Roden. The gigantic beast slept on the ground snoring.

He checked the animal's back legs in the dark. Without light, Erik couldn't see how bad the injuries were. It didn't matter; with humans he put his hands on them and could feel their injuries and pain. Would it work with an animal the size of Roden? Even if Erik sensed the injury, did his healing powers extend to livestock and service animals?

Erik placed his hands on Roden's haunches. The snoring stopped and Roden moved. Erik pulled his hands off the animal. "Nope, stay here, buddy." He attempted a second time, and Roden didn't move when Erik stroked the animal's rump.

Cugbert taught Erik to delve deep with his mind and to explore an injured person's pain. But Roden didn't seem to have any pain. Erik's process required putting hands on the person, perceiving wounds, and delivering healing power to the affected areas. But the animal didn't respond. Was it because Roden slept? Would the healing process improve if the animal was awake? Erik didn't want to wake the creature for fear Obadiah would find him and expel them.

He moved his hands closer to the injuries. Roden's leg muscles quivered, but he didn't awaken. *Ah, found it.* The animal didn't feel pain the way humans did. But Erik realized the injury was confined to the back leg. The bone wasn't broken, but an enormous bruise had developed at the site where the wagon crashed into his legs. That was something Erik could fix.

Twenty minutes later, after healing both legs, Erik felt the injury mitigated enough that Roden would walk without pain.

Two of the planet's moons shone in the sky as Erik walked back to his hammock. The red Velidred moon waned and the fast moving Anticletus moon rose over the horizon, full and bright. Erik thought of Sherry when he saw Anticletus. Was she still having headaches?

Erik grabbed his blanket and clambered into the hammock. As he drifted off to sleep, his attention wandered to the woman traveling with Gadiel. Was that the man's wife or daughter? Who was she and how could Erik find out more? Could it be Zita?

CHAPTER 21

Zita stormed into her wagon. *Erik was snooping around the wagons. Did he recognize me?* She hoped not. Images raced through her mind from the eclipse of the triple moons as her dad prepared to finish the last sacrifice and Erik raced to rescue his friend from being a sacrificial victim. That night on the volcano, she tried to kill Erik with a fireball because he wanted to kill her dad, but everything went wrong and her dad died instead.

Zita wanted to send a fireball at Erik, but Gadiel squeezed her leg moments before she released one. Gadiel wasn't a skilled wizard, so how had he sensed her wish?

Gadiel entered the compact space inside the wagon, and his tall frame crowded the tiny room. "What were you thinking? I told you not to kill the boys until they seize the golden crown."

She looked at her feet and smirked. "The boys will kill themselves with these animals."

Gadiel said, "The boys will learn to drive the wagons and handle the animals."

"You promised to teach me new skills."

"Obadiah was in the way tonight."

"I'll go crazy if I have to stay in the wagon every day." She imagined the walls of the wagon closing in on her, squeezing her lungs, heart and head. Gadiel grew in the confining space, displacing more air.

Gadiel sighed, "I will teach you a technique which will allow you freedom during the day. Have patience."

"Patience! The boy walks while Dad is dead."

"We had a deal; you won't harm the boys until the crown is mine. Then you can kill them. I need to check the caravan for the evening. Go to bed." Gadiel left the wagon.

Zita thought, the boys are close, they don't know I'm in the caravan. How easy would it be to kill them in their sleep? Sneak out of the wagon. Find them. Finish them.

She waited until Gadiel left the area. Gadiel, a stickler for details, took twenty minutes each night to walk the camp. This would give Zita plenty of time to exterminate the boys.

She raised her hood to keep from being recognized. This high in the mountains, the temperature dropped at night, and nobody would think twice about a figure strolling among the sleeping caravan crew with head and face covered. She hated the plain grey dress Gadiel made her wear; this was not like the nice clothes at the castle. What happened to her fine dresses? Were her dresses handed to the vermin that defeated the Mountain King's army and now worn by common folk?

Zita lifted the latch and opened the wagon door. Cool air, smelling of campfires, entered the warm wagon. She checked for Gadiel around the smoldering fire. He was elsewhere, and she hurried down the stairs.

Where are the boys?

Zita passed beast handlers snoring under their wagons or immobilized in hammocks. The mastodons, tied down for the night, stunk of urine and manure. A mosquito buzzed her face, but a quick slap finished the insect. Ruts filled the grassy meadow where the wagons had rolled. A million stars filled the sky as two moons danced across the firmament.

Zita didn't know where the boys parked their wagons, but knew she had little time to dawdle. Gadiel's examination of the caravan lasted twenty minutes max, so she rushed from wagon to wagon checking on sleeping handlers. The task proved difficult in the dark.

Anger built within Zita as each place she checked yielded no results. She must finish this and eliminate Erik and the tall wizard boy, too. *Erik professed he loved me, but he killed my dad.* She held no love for the boy from planet Earth. Zita bent to check under the next wagon where two men, one with graying hair, lay. She kicked the wagon wheel, but the men only snored louder. Where are the boys?

She shoved her hands in her pockets. Her flesh was cold despite droplets of sweat that ran between her breasts. How much time did she have left? What would Gadiel do if he found out she vanquished the boys? Zita reached the outside edges of the caravan where four wagons stood alone. She had heard the boys had animal and wagon problems on the mountain path and had to struggle down the mountain with the wagons one by one, and it made sense they parked them on the outskirts of the caravan. She clenched her fists and took a deep breath.

Three wagons had no bodies underneath, but shapes clung like cocoons from the first wagon. Erik and Al hung limp in their hammocks. How best to do the deed? Make it look like an accident, or maybe like an animal ate them or fire ignited under the wagon.

The shorter shape rolled, and she stared at Erik and clenched her teeth. The man who killed her dad slept before her, ready for death. She wanted to kick him first, but a wagon fire would work best.

Using magic, she built a wall of air around the wagon, barricading the boys in the structure. When she lit the fire, they wouldn't be able to escape. They slept on a feed wagon filled with flammable, dry brush. After walking all day and dragging the wagons down the mountain, they would be so exhausted they would sleep until nobody could save them. This far from the rest of the caravan, no one would notice the fire until the boys were dead.

Her heart pounded and pressure built in her ears.

"What's a young lady doing this far from her wagon at this time of night?"

Zita jumped.

Wagner the cook said, "Wild animals search for food this time of night, dangerous for you on the outskirts of the caravan."

"What are you doing here?" Zita whispered. She wanted to shout at Wagner, to punch him in the stomach, but she didn't want to wake the boys.

"Come back to the cook wagons, I have a drink that'll warm you." He leaned over and put his hand on her shoulder.

"Leave me alone." She smacked his arm.

One hammock bounced against the wagon wall as the inhabitant rolled and moaned.

"Are you sweet on one of those boys?" He asked.

Zita smelled alcohol on his breath and imagined Wagner lifting his eyebrows like he did when flirting with the cooking women. "Ugh, get away." She pushed him. *This man will ruin my plan.*

"Gadiel asked me to locate you. He sounded surprised you weren't in the wagon sleeping."

"I needed air. Now go away."

"Well you came to the right area to get air, but you're a little close to the manure cart don't you think?"

The man talked so loud she knew others were awake and listening even this far from the other wagons. Her opportunity to blast the boys and make it seem like an accident had expired. She glared and sent a swarm of mosquitoes into the boy's enclosed hammocks. *Tonight you will be in discomfort, but live.*

CHAPTER 22

Gadiel never yelled at Zita for leaving the wagon and almost attacking the boys, but for three days and nights, he didn't allow her out of the wagon. Zita grew restless. If Gadiel didn't release her, she would sneak out and never return. He had promised to teach her magic techniques and ways to disguise herself. He didn't know magic, so she wasn't sure what he could teach.

The caravan rolled on as the uneven road tossed her around the interior of the cabin. She was only able to peek outside through the curtained windows. She caught glimpses of Erik and Al whose wagons were several behind hers as turns in the road revealed the rear of the caravan. On two rainy days, she watched the boys slog through the mud with their beast. Zita stayed dry, but as the days wore on, being sequestered in the cabin made her legs ache, hair itch and body smell. Time to escape.

Zita missed the spacious rooms of the Velidred castle where she walked the halls, or played within the interior courtyards. She'd been free to venture to other villages. Now she felt imprisoned like the margo bird, caged at the castle as a pet. *Am I Gadiel's pet? I must escape.*

The fourth day, the road evened out, and the path smoothed. An hour after the caravan began rolling, Gadiel entered the cabin. Zita told herself to act domesticated, subdued, and to control her desires to scurry out the door.

Gadiel said, "Are you ready to behave?"

"Yes, sir." Zita bent her head, not making eye contact with Gadiel. A volcano rumbled in the pit of her stomach, forcing a sour taste into her mouth. She wanted to push past him into the sun, but he blocked the exit.

"It is time for your training. I teach an old skill, limited these days to elderly wizards hundreds of years old."

Zita thought, yeah, old geezers like you. No one knew Gadiel's age or how he lived so long. "Does it concern magic?"

"Yes and no."

"Well, what is it, yes or no?"

"I don't like your attitude. Maybe I will teach it another day."

"No, let's do this. I'm going crazy in here."

"Sit."

Zita plopped down on the bench, used as a couch during the day, but converted into a bed for sleeping at night. Gadiel stood above her, and her neck hurt, staring up at him.

The tall man settled on the floor, his eyes level with hers. "In the old days, before wizarding was a recognized profession, other skill sets were popular to give one an advantage. One skill required magic, while another did not. I have a little magic power, nothing compared to the strength of you and your father. No wizarding school wanted me. My trick was to make things disappear into my pockets. If I was caught, I found a technique to hide the objects, to make it look like I didn't have them."

"Sleight of hand, like a carnival showman?" She crossed her arms. "How lame."

"If you want to downgrade this ability, I can find someone else to teach. Maybe Alpherge the Great's grandson." Gadiel didn't move.

Zita sighed. "Okay, go ahead, what can you do that you want to show me?"

The pots and pans hanging on the walls shook. First, they banged against the wall and then swung harder and clanged against each other. The clatter increased, and she placed her hands over her ears.

Zita didn't think the ground surface had changed. The wagon didn't feel like it was heaving on an uneven road, so what caused the pots to shake?

The blue pot they used to cook soup the day before jumped from its hook on the wall. It fell to the floor, but didn't make a noise like you would expect a pot to make. The pot grew legs and landed on its feet, silent and dangerous as the handle grew into the head of a wolf. A wolf's body formed around the pot and grew hair. The wolf growled.

She gasped. There was no place to run in this tiny space. Even as she gawked, the animal grew to outweigh Zita.

Two more pots, one blackened by fire, and the other a shiny gray metal, fell to the floor and transformed into wolves. The available air diminished as Zita felt cramped and imprisoned. The animals snarled and barked.

Gadiel sat on the floor, his eyes closed.

Zita searched for an escape route from the cabin, but the animals blocked the exit. The wolves approached her and ignored Gadiel.

These animals were bigger and nastier than dogs. She became lightheaded but didn't lose control. "Mr. Gadiel. Can you do something about the wolves?"

They circled closer to Zita with drool dripping from their fangs. The hungry wolves snarled and snapped at each other as if sparring to see who earned first bite.

Gadiel opened his eyes and petted the closest animal, calming it. The other two continued to snarl and threaten Zita. "Do you fear carnival magic?"

Zita held her hands close to her body to protect herself. "Please get rid of them."

"Sit my friends."

The wolves sat on the floor, snarling at Zita.

"This is an elementary example of the potential power of this technique. Imagine you're at a dinner that requires security, but you're alone with no protection. You can conjure friends to augment your safety. There's a wisp of magic involved, but the power comes from your imagination." Gadiel stroked the blue-haired wolf. "You know wizards sense when another wizard uses magic? This technique uses such an insignificant amount of magic that others can't discern its use."

"I didn't hear you say any words. You didn't wave your hands at the pots. How did you do it?" She leaned toward Gadiel.

Gadiel asked, "Are you ready to learn?"

He spent an hour teaching and explaining the old magic.

It was nothing like what she learned growing up in the castle with Dad's wizards. Gadiel explained clearing your mind, thinking of the original object and then transforming it in your mind to transfigure into the semblance of different matter.

"Okay, you try." Gadiel floated a ceramic cup from the cabinet and placed it on the bench beside Zita. "Don't turn it into a wolf. Make the cup shake first. That is where we start. Close your eyes and empty the mind."

Zita closed her eyes. It was difficult to empty her mind as many thoughts and emotions washed through her brain.

Gadiel said, "Many of the old masters taught me to imagine a small fire with a wisp of smoke snaking above the wood. Concentrate on the smoke. Tune out distractions. Breathe in the smoke. Smell the wood."

She smelled a sweet but sharp fragrance, as if the wood of an apple tree burned in the forest.

Kenneth Brown

"Push all troubles and thoughts away from you. In your mind, see those problems shrinking and moving out past the horizon, out of your sight. Smaller."

Erik popped into her mind, but she pushed him away. She imagined him shrinking to the size of a tiny mouse as he moved toward the horizon. Zita stood alone in the woods where a fire burned in the darkness, and she enjoyed the sweet smell of the burning apple branches. Darkness consumed the space, forcing the light from the fire back. Peace surrounded the fire.

"Take a deep breath."

Zita inhaled.

"Hold. Imagine total silence."

Zita thought of the darkness and relaxed.

Erik wandered near her and said, "What cha doing, Zita?" Then he leaned in and kissed her.

Gadiel said, "Exhale."

A rush of air flew from her lips. She lost the peace. She opened her eyes, ready to slap Erik.

Gadiel sat on the floor observing while running his hands through the blue wolf's fur. "What happened?"

"I couldn't hold my breath that long."

"No, you lost focus. What distracted you?"

Her cheeks warmed, and she felt her ears turn red. She couldn't tell Gadiel that she imagined Erik walking into the peaceful circle by the fire and kissing her. "My leg cramped and I couldn't hold my breath. I'm tired of being confined in here. I need air." She stood.

"Sit. You can roam tonight. Today, you have lessons to learn."

Zita fidgeted, trying to get Erik out of her mind. He was right there; she had felt his touch and enjoyed his warm kiss. She ached for the embrace of his powerful arms and muscular body.

"I said, sit. Try again."

Zita said, "Don't you have incense and some of that drink from the other ceremony? That gave me a delicious kick."

"No, for this skill you must be open to possibilities, not drugged. Sit and relax." Gadiel pointed to the bench.

She felt a tingle run up her back, to her neck and then across her face. She shook her head. *What was that? What is he doing to me? Can I get past Gadiel?* The wolves now guarded the door.

The black wolf snarled and bared its teeth.

Gadiel can read my mind. How does he do that? This can't be happening. If he could read her thoughts, that meant he knew about Erik's kiss. *I can't let that happen again.* She sat and settled on the bench.

"Clear your mind."

Zita returned to the imaginary forest setting, and the three wolves sat around the fire.

Gadiel said, "Push all distractions away from you."

Zita imagined the wolves growing smaller and their growls became little yaps. She shooed them away, and they ran into the forest. A smile crossed her face.

"Take a deep breath; breathe in for ten seconds. Fill your lungs with air."

She tried to inhale while Gadiel counted.

"Smell the smoke and imagine it drifting into the sky."

She concentrated on the smoke.

"Imagine total darkness, you're floating like a feather, in total safety, nothing will harm you."

There was no up, no down, no noise, only perfect total darkness as Zita floated in seclusion.

Gadiel moved the cup beside Zita, "Breathe out and when you breathe in again, picture the ceramic cup."

She leaned forward as the cup appeared in her mind.

"Imagine the cup jumping on its own free will."

The cup didn't jump up and down in her mind, but floated next to her, ignoring her commands. Her expression changed to a scowl. She wanted to pace back and forth. The cup floated in the dark, but a light formed beyond the darkness as in the minutes before the sunrise.

"Focus on the darkness." Gadiel whispered.

She focused on the darkness, the cup, the smoke, and then Erik entered the darkness carrying a lantern. The cup disappeared. Zita lost focus and opened her eyes.

The cup sat next to her on the bench. She grabbed it and hurled it at the door, shattering the cup and the moment.

"What happened?"

"I don't know."

"Tell me about it."

"Is this all you plan to teach me? Are we done now?"

"It's the boy, isn't it? You have feelings for him."

"You're right, we should try again. Let me grab another cup from the cabinet."

The wolves growled.

"Tell me."

She tilted her head to look at the canvas ceiling and sighed. Tension built in her shoulders. She wanted to eliminate these feelings, not talk to Gadiel about them. She could talk to another girl, but not prickled, craggy Gadiel.

"I can wait all day."

She knew he wouldn't. Later tonight, the caravan would stop and Gadiel would do the rounds, checking on the animals, the cargo and the handlers. He didn't have all day. In fact, she had never seen him stay in one place this long. Could he persist? Could she have a staring contest with him to find out which of them would surrender first?

Zita stared into Gadiel's black eyes, and the red, scorpion figure floated across his left eye. The scorpion spooked her; she broke eye contact and scrutinized the door.

"Tell me about the boy. Which one is it, the wizard or the other one?"

"Not the wizard," she gave a nervous laugh. Everything in her body and mind wanted to lash out at Gadiel and stop this game he played. "You already knew it was Erik. How do you read my mind?"

"You're not ready."

"How dare you say I'm not ready? You have no right to read my thoughts."

He smiled a crooked, brief smile. Scary.

CHAPTER 23

Zita's brain hurt from trying to shape-shift the ceramic mug. Would Gadiel's trick work for her? The caravan stopped for the night. Zita decided to skip the evening meal in hopes of eluding Gadiel. By the time darkness arrived, most of the beast handlers were sleeping.

But Gadiel entered the wagon for the third time that day.

He insisted they repeat the same process. Relax. Breathe deep. Empty the mind. Turn everything to darkness and then concentrate on the object to transform.

Mid-way through this third session, Zita's face tightened, and she crossed her arms. *Gadiel has only a little magic ability. How can he accomplish shape-shifting, but it's so difficult for me?* She rubbed the back of her neck.

"Relax, remove all tension." Gadiel instructed again.

"I can't." She threw her hands in the air. "I give up, I can't do it."

Gadiel took a deep breath.

Zita's fingernails bit into her palms, as her fists tightened. "There must be an easier way; you aren't teaching it right."

Gadiel examined the ceiling, his lips pressed tight together.

Minutes passed, and anger flowed in Zita's veins. Through clenched teeth, she said, "Get out."

Gadiel narrowed his eyes, his brow furrowed in stony defiance.

Zita's head ached, and tension stiffened her jaw. "I'm done with this. I can't."

Gadiel snorted like an angry bull.

"Why won't you say something?" Zita's eyes pooled, but she didn't want Gadiel to see her cry. She wiped her sleeve across her eyes before the tears spilled down her cheeks. She desperately wanted to run from the wagon, but, once again, Gadiel blocked the door. At least there were no wolves this time.

Gadiel said, "King Haskell was an impatient man. I tried to teach him this technique at your age, but he pursued other treasures. A girl he desired disrupted the training."

A tear rolled down Zita's cheek, and she brushed it away with a finger.

"Shape-shifting is a valuable and powerful skill. I wished I knew it at your age." Gadiel touched Zita's wrist. "Empty the mind. Relax."

She wanted to learn, but it wasn't coming easily. Each time she neared the concentration needed, a distraction disrupted her thoughts. Erik wandered into the darkness. He would smile and touch Zita's hand, speak to her or kiss her. How could she concentrate when he confused her? Zita wondered what would happen if she threw a fireball at him in the darkness of her imagination?

"Ready to try again?" Gadiel removed his hand.

Zita sniffled. "Sure."

"Take a deep breath."

Darkness returned to the forest. Smoke drifted into the night air. She pushed away all distractions. A light shone among the trees. Zita resisted the light until it hovered, a dim splotch far in the distance. Alone in the darkness, she drifted.

Kenneth Brown

Zita pictured the cup floating next to her in the darkness. Her mind melded with the cup, and she knew the ability to transform the cup was within her grasp.

A bearded man with a lantern approached Zita in the forest.

Focus on the darkness and the cup.

The man raised the lantern, searching in the darkness. Erik.

Her mind drifted, and she lost mental contact with the cup.

Erik said, "Zita is that you?"

In her imagination, she ran to him and pushed him to the ground.

"Why?" He picked up the fallen lantern. "I'm here to help. Good, the flame still burns." He smiled.

Erik's smile caught her off guard with his full lips and straight, white teeth. She must resist the temptation to touch him.

He reached for her. "I looked for you at the volcano. I miss you."

"No. Leave. It's dangerous."

Erik stroked her cheek.

His hand felt warm and coarse. The boy's hands had been soft like a prince's hands when she first met him, but now they were rough, weathered and masculine. Her body trembled. Zita felt her skin flush; she moistened her lips, and with half-closed eyes waited for Erik's delicious kiss. Warmth inundated her body, and her heartbeat galloped as she leaned toward him.

He leaned toward Zita for the kiss.

She opened her eyes. *I can't kiss him, not now.* "No," she yelled.

Zita threw a fireball, hitting Erik in the chest. A red blaze erupted on his shirt, and blood oozed from the blast site.

Erik's mouth fell open, and he gaped at Zita with wide eyes, dazed and incredulous. His head jerked, and he shuffled back a step.

He mouthed, "Why?" dropped the lantern and closed his eyes as his fingers spread out over the open wound.

A smile crossed her face as she smoothed out the front of her dress and straightened her shoulders. Erik faded into the darkness. Her mind emptied, she floated in the smoke, and concentrated on the cup. It shook.

CHAPTER 24

Erik walked beside the mastodon, Roden, guiding him with his hand. He said to Al, "You're gonna think I'm crazy, but I dreamed about Zita last night."

Al said, "Why are you so transfixed by her? We killed her dad; she ran off; just forget her."

They traveled through the grasslands, and a strong, warm wind blew from the south. Though it felt hot, at least the winds kept the mosquitoes from biting. It hadn't rained in a week, and they walked on a path of packed, dry dirt with six-foot tall grasses waving on either side.

Why did he fantasize about Zita, and what caused these dreams?

"I wonder what Lily would say if she knew you were thinking about Zita instead of her?"

"The dream was so real. I touched Zita, and we kissed." Roden turned his head, and Erik scratched Roden's rough fur. Roden needed little attention here, for he was content to follow the caravan wagon in front. The tall grasses stood like living walls which defined a clear path.

Al raised his stick. "When will Gadiel teach me about this staff?"

"Really, you're gonna change the conversation to talk about Gadiel and the staff? I'm trying to tell you about the dream I had last night."

"It's a dream, it means nothing. Stop worrying about Zita. She found a prince, told him she's a princess, and they married. End of story. She's fine."

"You're wrong, Al. Zita isn't fine, and she didn't marry a prince. She's in the convoy with us right now."

"In this convoy? You've got to be kidding. Do you think the princess is feeding the mastodons? Brushing them each night and eating the poor excuse for food they give us? She's a princess. She's in a castle far, far away, just like in the fairytales."

"I think she's in the wagon with Gadiel." The dream felt so real. He still remembered touching Zita and the pain of the fireball. The way his chest felt today, he knew it wasn't just a dream.

Al said, "Why hasn't she come out? She doesn't eat or walk. Never leaves the wagon. Who would do that? Is she injured so she can't get around? Who's taking care of her? Zita isn't part of this journey. Forget her."

Roden stopped walking and shook his head. The smell of a dead animal drifted on the wind. "Keep marching, Roden. Yeah, it smells nasty." Erik patted the mastodon's side.

Animals scurried in the grasses, a cat-like creature, and small deer. Obadiah told them the cats kill the deer, and anything the cats didn't finish eating decayed where it lay. Vultures never settled into the grasses after the carrion because of the poor sight lines to potential predators.

Erik forced Roden to keep moving because if they stopped, the flies feeding on the carcasses would annoy the mastodons. The boys needed to walk beside the harnessed animals when the path snaked through the tall prairie, because of the cats.

After they passed the decaying meat, Erik said, "She threw a fireball at me."

"Who?"

"Zita. In the dream. I met her in a forested area at night."

"Were you chasing her?"

"No, I was not chasing her."

"Then why did she throw a fireball at you? Do fireballs hurt you in a dream?"

"That's what I'm trying to tell you." Erik rubbed his chest, still tender to the touch.

A roar sounded in the grasses to his right, followed by answering roars on his left. Roden stopped again. Erik slapped Roden hard on the haunches to get the beast moving. "Can't stop, Roden, gotta keep moving." Obadiah said he had never seen the cats attack the caravan, but he mentioned the cats appeared more energetic than normal today. *What does that mean, more energetic, like they might attack us? Is it mating season?*

"Knock on the door and see who answers."

Erik stopped and gaped at Al, "What are you talking about?"

"Find out who's in the wagon with Gadiel. Knock, and see if Zita answers."

Erik caught up with Roden. What would be the downside? He couldn't see one if he arranged it while Gadiel was walking around or he found a way to distract the old man. "Yeah, knock, peek in a window or sneak in, and check the interior."

"No way! Be careful. Remember the penalties about entering wagons that aren't yours and I quote, 'Anybody found breaking into cabins, wagons or food storage will be stripped, beaten and tied spread-eagled onto the top of their wagon for a day.'"

"Okay." Erik thought of the cats sneaking around in the grasses. *I can do it myself. I'll sneak around the campground at night after we stop and manage a quick glimpse into the cabin window.*

"And don't forget," Al pointed his staff at Erik, "the person has to go without food for a day. Whatever you do, make sure I'm not included in your little scheme. I don't get enough food now."

Erik thought about Al's magic skills. "Can you make me invisible? You know with your magic and wizardry skills."

"I will not help you with this, and no, I can't make you invisible. Maybe if I learn more about the staff, I could make you look like someone else. I remembered the other students at the wizardry school camouflaged themselves. But I never got to those lessons."

"My chest is red and blistered where Zita's fireball hit me in the dream." Zita's fireball surprised Erik. "We were in the forest and I held her—"

"Zita's fireball from the dream left a mark? Can I see it?"

Erik peeled back his clothing and exposed his chest. His skin showed a ragged circle in red with a black outline like a burn mark. The blisters itched. "See?"

"From the dream? You sure you didn't sleep in a patch of itchwort plant?"

"I slept next to you on the ground, and there was no itchwort."

"Maybe you slept on a fire ant nest."

Erik shook his head. "Ants would attack you, too. This only hit my chest. Zita threw a fireball, and I need to know for sure if she's in the caravan."

"So tell me about this dream."

Erik grinned to the point of laughing, hunched his shoulders and raised his hands, "That's what I'm trying to do. You keep interrupting me."

"I'm listening now."

"I met Zita in the forest. She smiled at me; she has a beautiful smile, and then we held hands. But when I leaned in to kiss her, she pushed me away. I left her for a while, but then I came back and held her hand, and when I went to kiss her the second time, she told me to beat it and threw a fireball at me." He rubbed his chest.

"What did you do?"

"I woke up on the hard ground we call a bed, underneath the wagon. My chest hurt so much I thought I would die."

Al asked, "Should we go back to sleeping in the hammocks."

"No, they're hot and confining, I'm sleeping on the ground like the other guys."

"Why do you think she's in the caravan?"

"In the dream, I saw Gadiel's wagon in the background."

"I thought you said you met her in the forest. They didn't park the wagon in the forest, did they?"

Erik thought about that for a moment. He didn't remember seeing the rest of the caravan around Zita. Darkness had surrounded the dream forest, and off to one side, a tiny campfire burned. Someone sat on a log by the fire. A man. Erik carried a lantern with a candle in it, the only light he remembered. Where was the wagon? Did Zita come from the wagon? The details of the dream faded. "No, the dream wagon wasn't part of the caravan, just alone in a small clearing in the forest."

"See, that proves Zita isn't in the caravan. Case closed. What you should try to discover is a way to put your hands on the bacon Wagner cooks for Gadiel each morning. Now that's a quest worthy of great adventurers."

"Ha! Funny," Erik said. But Al was right. The wagon in the dream wasn't Gadiel's, just painted similar colors. He didn't recognize the guy by the fire. A thin man, but was it Gadiel? Erik couldn't be sure. But a quick gander inside the wagon would resolve it. How could he convince Al to help him with this quest? Maybe if they just took a quick peek with limited risk and then hurried back to their campsite. If they waited till dark, when most of the laborers and animal handlers were asleep, they could sneak to the wagon. Gadiel and Wagner usually sat around a fire and talked at night when everybody else was preparing to bed down.

Al said, "You're thinking about actually doing this, aren't you? Are you planning on running ahead of us in the tall grass? A guy running alone—the cats will drag you down like a deer."

As if on cue, the cats' roars resumed, though they remained hidden in the swaying grasses.

Erik's developed a plan, "No, I agree we can't do it during the day. We do it at night. You're helping me."

"I'm not helping. I don't plan to get whipped, sun-burned and deprived of food for a day."

"What if I could arrange it so Gadiel helps you with your staff?"

Al asked, "You can do that?"

"Maybe. You won't have to help me break in or peek in the window, just warn me if somebody snoops around that might catch me in the act."

"Like you want me to yell, hey watch out, someone's behind you?"

"Don't be stupid. Of course not. Can you whistle?"

Al proved it by whistling a song he knew from Earth. The song was on his phone playlist from the rock group, Magic Giocoso. He didn't care much for the lyrics, but loved the fast-paced guitar fingering from the lead guitarist.

"Yeah, like that," Erik said, "only we need a specific signal."

"There was this boy in junior high school that could do this." Al put two fingers in his mouth and blew out a shrill three note song. High whistle, low whistle, and higher than the first note whistle.

The cats stopped their growling and the tall, dry grasses rippled as if something moved through them. Dried seed pods at the tips of the stalks rubbed together, creating a rustling sound.

"That's perfect. Can you do that every time?"

"Yeah. Once I heard the boy do it twice, I must have practiced it a thousand times at home. Mom used to yell at me to stop making so much noise in the house, so I practiced outdoors. The whistle is automatic now, never misses and always clear and perfect."

A plan formed in Erik's mind. "You sit down and visit with Gadiel and Wagner, keep them distracted after everybody else is asleep, and then I do a quick walk by the cabin and glance in the window. Show them your staff. Let Wagner touch it and look it over. Ask Gadiel about it. Keep them busy. Won't take me but a second to sneak and peek. No one will notice me. And they won't suspect you because you'll be with them the whole time showing off something they want to see. It's perfect."

"All I have to do is whistle if somebody walks toward the wagon?"

A cry sprang up from the wagons in front of Erik. Roden let out an enormous roar and rocked back onto his hind legs. Then there were cats everywhere. They looked like a genetic mutation between a house-cat and a tiger but the size of a border collie. They held their long ears erect above their heads, thin ears, four inches or more in length, coming to a point at the top.

Erik raced to the wagon and pulled out a barbed stick used as a defensive weapon. Three of the animals jumped atop Roden, who tried to buck them off, but the harness restricted his movement.

Al waved his staff at a pair of cats, keeping them at arm's length.

"Throw a fireball at them," Erik yelled. He used the weapon and pounded a cat clinging to Roden's back, and the predator fell unconscious to the ground.

A mastodon behind them roared, then tore through the grass pulling two wagons. A handler held onto the animal's harness with five cats attacking the mastodon's back. As the beleaguered mastodon and wagon passed by, Erik batted another cat off Roden.

The last cat on Roden's back screeched as a fireball exploded near its tail. Flaming, it leaped to the ground. Another cat jumped toward Al, but in mid-air, struck an invisible shield and tumbled to the ground.

Erik shouted, "Put the shield around Roden." Another two cats jumped toward Roden's neck and Erik swung his weapon at one, but his club hit the shield Al had just set. The cats clawed and bit Roden's neck, and the mastodon jumped and bucked, which tore a thill from the wagon. "Al let me in the shield."

Two fireballs flew from Al's hands and the cats caught fire and dashed back into the grass. "Get next to Roden and you'll be okay."

Erik huddled next to Roden and tried to calm the massive beast. "Easy big fellow." He liked to think Roden had gotten more comfortable with him around.

Roden flinched where Erik touched him and swung his giant ivory tusks back and forth as a protective measure.

Three cats leaped toward Roden's head, and Roden swung his tusks into position to fling them off, but they hit the shield and slumped to the ground.

Turmoil boiled throughout the caravan. Human cries, cat screams and mastodon roars filled the air.

"Easy Roden, you're okay." Erik rubbed Roden behind the ears, talking in soothing tones.

Another mastodon and wagon train thundered off to their right, half in the grass and half in the path, with one wagon dragging on its side. Two handlers chased after it as two cats bounded toward them.

Al's fireballs knocked the cats to the ground.

And as fast as it began, the cats retreated. Was there a signal? A roar or cry from a lead cat? Erik didn't know. One second the cats were scrambling everywhere and then they disappeared.

Roden swung his head in large lazy figure eights as Erik rubbed him behind the ears. Were the cats regrouping for another attack?

Kenneth Brown

Did the cats kill any mastodons? How many of the mastodons that bolted had dragged their handlers to death?

CHAPTER 25

Obadiah sprinted past Erik. "Get the wagons moving!"

Erik said, "What's the hurry?" He didn't want to move Roden until he delved into Roden's injuries and healed any scratches and bites. A quick visual examination suggested Roden suffered only minor injuries.

The wagoner behind the boys yelled, "Move."

Erik said, "What's the big hurry?"

Al pointed into the prairie and gaped.

Smoke billowed from the dry grasses as flames licked the sky.

The adrenalin from the cat attack hadn't worn off and Erik's heart pounded. He wondered how much farther the caravan needed to travel through the grasslands. Did they have time to beat the fire to safety?

The wagon ahead of them on the path moved forward.

Erik took a deep breath, and smoke filled his nostrils. "Let's go, Roden." He poked the animal in the side, which nudged him forward, and the wagons behind creaked and groaned into motion.

The wooden thill attached to the harness on Roden's right side flopped in the air, broken, no longer secured to the wagon. The wagon moved, but skewed to the left at an awkward angle. Erik realized the other thill would break if they continued. Erik stopped Roden.

The handlers behind Roden hollered, "Move."

Erik waved for them to pass. "The thill is broken."

Other teams moved past Erik and Al, guiding their mastodons and wagons, trampling the grasses on the right. Handlers prodded their mastodons to speed up. First, one wagon went past and a second followed.

Erik examined the broken bar, a long, wooden pole that attached the wagon to the harness. The milled thill was three inches in diameter, but it had cracked for two feet of its length, and the pieces had separated. "How do we fix this?"

Al hunched his shoulders. "Not a clue. We can't go to the lumberyard and get more lumber, and we wouldn't have time or tools to mill it."

"Do you have magic glue?"

"Negative. No duct tape either."

The smoke thickened in dark, threatening tendrils behind the boys and blew toward them. Another two wagons passed them.

The strong thill ran from Roden's shoulder harness to the wagon and attached there with a tongue-and-groove arrangement. A quick examination showed no way to remove the broken shaft without tearing the wagon apart. The wagon carried a ton of mastodon feed.

Erik ran his hands through his hair as he gazed, glassy eyed, at the broken shaft. He dropped his shoulders and looked at the billowing black smoke rising from the grass. How were they going to get out of this jam? If they couldn't pull the wagons away from the fire, the caravan might not have enough food to feed the animals for the long trip to the ice castle.

Roden bellowed and tossed his head.

"Don't worry, we'll get it fixed." Erik didn't feel so confident but he didn't want to display fear to the mastodon.

Al said, "I know how we can shore up the brace."

"What do you mean?"

"We need a stick to run alongside the broken part."

Erik eyeballed Al's staff. "Like your staff."

"No way are we using my grandfather's staff." Al pulled the precious rod to his chest. "How about that tool you used to whack the cats?"

"Yeah, that might work." Erik picked the tool up off the ground and walked back to the broken thill. He put the two split pieces together and held the wooden tool against the broken pole. "Too short. There's no way it would hold." He threw the pole to the ground where the spiked point planted itself in the ground.

"How will you attach the pole to the brace? We don't have nails, duct tape or glue."

"I don't know. Give me that staff." Erik grabbed the staff and pulled.

Al yanked back. "We aren't using the staff."

"The staff is the perfect size, plus, your fireballs placed us in this predicament." *Doesn't Al see the problems we are facing?* "If Roden dies, then our trip to the castle is finished."

The stench and smoke of the grass fire swelled behind them.

Roden bellowed as his body shuddered, and he leaned forward.

"We're running out of time." Erik's gaze darted over his shoulder.

The last two wagons passed, and the handler advised, "Unharness the mastodon. Gadiel will be furious if you lose Roden. Drop the broken wagon and save the other three."

"Don't worry, we're dealing with it." Erik waved him past as he considered alternatives to losing the wagon.

"Is the wind blowing in the opposite direction?" Al asked.

Black smoke billowed and swirled toward Erik, clouding his eyes. "It's heading right for us. The staff is the best choice."

"No."

Erik swept his arm in a wide arc. "Do you see trees in the grass, with wood the perfect size to support this pole?"

Al shook his head.

Erik inhaled, and the rush of smoke caused a coughing spasm. Despite convulsing lungs, he smiled. He held up his hand while he bent over, coughing. An idea bloomed in his mind, causing a jolt of giddiness.

"Are you okay?" Al patted Erik on the back.

"Yeah," he wheezed. "I . . . have," he coughed, "an . . . idea." It took another ten seconds to clear his lungs. Then he held his tunic over his nose and mouth and took a deep breath. The acrid smoke burned his throat. He pointed to the grass, "We'll use that."

"Grass? Grass isn't strong enough."

"Yeah, it will, like fiber. Hemp rope. The break is horizontal, and we can wrap the grass tight around the break and secure it."

"Will it hold?"

Roden bellowed and stood on his hind legs, then crashed with a hard stomp and jerked the wagon forward as the broken thill bobbed in the air.

"Easy, Roden. Hold. Stop." Erik raced in front of the animal to calm him. "Grab a handful of long grasses, hurry."

Roden moved his head from side to side, and the long curved tusk whacked Erik and threw him to the ground. Roden rose to his haunches.

Two giant feet rose above Erik as he tried to unscramble his brain. A twinge in his side made him wonder if he broke a rib. Erik rolled into the grasses, away from Roden's descending feet, and the ground rumbled as Roden pounded the soil.

Roden rose on his haunches again, and Erik felt dizzy. He wanted to breathe, but the smoke choked his lungs. If they lost control of Roden now, the animal might die. He could run into the grass where the cats were or worse, into the fire. Erik hurried to his feet, but his legs felt like jelly. "Easy, big boy." Erik coughed out the words.

The smoke grew thicker and blacker as the fire sizzled and burned closer. How much time did they have? He danced around the gigantic beast. He had to get Roden under control. Their quest couldn't end like this.

Roden lunged, and the wagons jerked in weird directions.

The manner Erik normally used to control Roden was to rub the animal's belly, but the way Roden's head gyrated, getting near Roden right now might prove fatal.

Al hollered, "I have grass."

"Wrap it around the broken pole."

"Make Roden stop twitching. The pole is twisting, making it worse."

"I'm trying," Erik yelled.

Roden lunged and halted. He threw his head back and forth.

Erik couldn't approach Roden to soothe the animal. He ran in front of Roden and raised his hands.

Giant tusks rolled in fast figure eights just out of Erik's reach.

"Look at me, big boy. We're gonna be okay. Relax." If Roden whacked him again with those tusks, Erik might not survive.

Roden brayed and reared again.

Erik retreated, his heartbeat racing and his throat sore. "No. Easy." He tried to talk in a calming voice, but knew the coughing and jerky arm movements weren't soothing. What could he do?

The animal landed hard and lunged toward Erik.

Erik wormed past the moving tusks and huddled next to the animal's side. He rubbed the beast's belly, "Easy, I'm with you, everything will be okay."

Roden calmed, he stopped jerking his head. Instead of rising to his haunches, he stamped his front feet, but only lifted one at a time.

"Wrap it quick, I don't know how long he'll stay calm."

Time passed. The heat and crackle of dry, burning grass painfully warmed Erik's neck. He covered his nose against the stench from the grass fire.

"It's not great, try it." Al shouted.

"Okay, big fella, let's march." Erik said.

Roden didn't move.

"Fo, Roden."

Roden leaned forward, and the harness strained, but the fix held. The wagons advanced, creaking with the familiar comfort of wheels on uneven ground.

"Is it holding?" Erik peered through the thick smoke where Al waddled, hunched over, with his left hand grasping grasses wrapped around the pole.

"Okay, for now." He gave a thumb up sign.

Roden picked up the pace, and they moved ten yards, fifteen yards and then fifty yards. They cleared the billowing smoke.

Erik took a deep breath and wondered if he had been holding his breath. The clean air felt wonderful. Everything worked. The fire crossed the road behind them, the wind now pushing it away. They could safely join the rest of the caravan.

In another ten yards, Roden quickened the pace. Erik reasoned that meant Al used magic to make the wagons lighter. Smart move, Al. The animal and carts lumbered on another twenty yards.

Al shouted, "Stop."

Erik glared at Al, who stood waving his arms.

"The winds keep shifting. We gotta escape the fire again." Erik's voice rose in pitch.

"The grass rope isn't holding."

The thill whipped and splintered.

"Hold, Roden." He touched the mastodon. "Stop."

Roden slowed and stopped.

A new area of grass kindled in the near distance. The main fire was farther away than before, but they needed to cover more ground to fully escape the danger. Flames licked the sky. Time was short.

Together they hauled large clumps of grass out of the ground, six-foot lengths of stalks. The edges were rough, and the leaves scratched Erik's fingers with long thin slices like paper cuts.

Roden bellowed nervously.

"How much grass did you use before?" Erik asked.

"About ten or twelve strands, but we should double it."

They pulled more stalks and ran to the broken pole with grass and dirt flying.

Al said, "I can't get it tight, it's a two-person job."

Twelve cats ran past them on the open trail, ears back, intent on escaping the fire. They did not bother the boys or Roden.

Al said, "Can we entwine it like a rope?"

"We don't have time. Besides, braiding is something the girls know how to do. Do you?"

"Yes, I think so. The cord will be stronger and hold better."

Erik pointed to the dark billows which were increasing as new areas caught fire. "Roden doesn't like the smoke, and he'll bolt if he gets spooked. I need to be near his head if he panics."

"Okay, then hold the two pieces of the pole together." Al began braiding the strands. Then he stopped as if he was thinking how to do it.

"Hurry up, Al. You said you knew how to do this."

"Give me a second; I'm trying to remember how Sherry and Lily do it."

"That's about all the time you have."

Al concentrated and began to put the outside strand over the middle, and then the inside one over that one, which was now the middle one. In a few seconds he had braided six inches of cord. He began wrapping it around the thill, starting a foot before the break. He tightened the braid as he neared the break, but kept wrapping the homemade rope until he ran out of grass. He tucked the end under and pulled it tight.

Roden bellowed and stomped.

Erik yelled at Roden to hold. "Give us two minutes." The animal didn't know minutes, but they needed time to finish the patch.

Al started from the other direction with a new braid. He tied off the beginning, ran it loose for a foot and then wrapped tighter around the broken section. Sweat soaked through Al's clothing from the heat and the stress of his effort to stabilize the break.

More cats escaped from the burning grasses, fleeing along the path. Would the cats become a problem once they got ahead of the fire again? Erik hoped not. Smoke blew into his face and he coughed. How was Al handling this smoke with his asthma?

Al tore up another plant by the roots, tore off the seed heads, smashed the bundle to the ground to remove the dirt and pulled out a single strand.

"Hurry, it doesn't have to be pretty," Erik snarled.

"I think it will hold now, but we need more stability. This will rub and break. Grab a strand and do what I'm doing." He wound strands of grass around the braid to bind it to the thill.

Erik grabbed a grass strand and wrapped the braid behind Al. Twenty times they encircled the makeshift bandage to the thill. Around and around they wound the patch, tighter and tighter.

Roden lunged, and the wagons jerked forward.

Al plopped one hand on his knee and waved his other hand. "Let him pull and test it. We need a stronger weave than this, but let's see how well this patch holds."

CHAPTER 26

l lay on the ground ruminating on the day's events. Darkness settled over the camp and he simply felt ecstatic to be alive and back with the rest of the caravan.

Obadiah walked by the boys and said, "You guys are not worth a goat's chin hair. Gadiel wants you to have dinner with him tonight."

Al shook his head and looked at Erik, whose complexion had gone pale and sickly.

Erik said, "Don't look at me, I didn't throw the fireballs at the cats."

Al crossed his arms over his chest and sputtered, "I tried to save Roden. How can Gadiel be angry with us? We saved all the feed, the wagons and Roden. They should thank us and throw us a parade."

Obadiah snorted, "A parade?

"Well, something for saving this caravan from starvation and rescuing Roden from certain death." Al swallowed hard and used a shaky hand to wipe his forehead.

* * * *

He remembered their journey as they made it out of the grassland. Alive. Three times they had repaired the broken thill. After they had reached safety from the fire, the cats became bold enough to attack once more. But they still fought off the cats. They hurried to catch up with the rest of the caravan.

Obadiah had warned them that the cats were less likely to attack when the wagons traveled as a group, but cats attack a single mastodon and wagon traveling alone every time.

As Erik and Al twined the grass into rope, eight large cats attacked them. They used every tool at their disposal to fight them off. Roden whacked a few with his mighty tusks. Erik used his wooden tool with the spike at the end to remove cats from Roden's back.

Al had learned his lesson about throwing fireballs. They couldn't afford another grass fire incident. So he shot hard, fast bursts of air at the cats. Their fur blew back as if in hurricane-force winds, and the animals slid from Roden's back, buffeted to the ground. Al set the shields once the cats were beaten back, and that prevented them from coming close again.

"What do you think Gadiel will do to us?" Erik asked.

"I hope we don't get kicked out of the caravan. We can't walk to the Ice Castle by ourselves, and people aren't around to give us directions."

That was strange, too. The caravan's path avoided villages, towns and castles. They didn't stop in towns to re-supply. Even though Al saw villages off in the distance, they camped in open fields beside lakes, rivers and creeks, resupplying the animal feed wagons.

Wagner would take a wagon to the nearest village each night to re-fill their human needs. Obadiah had said the convoy wasn't allowed in the villages.

Their most recent attempt at making rope worked best. It handled the stresses of being pulled by Roden against the weight of the wagons. While they walked beside Roden, they twined two grass strands together, grabbed another grass strand and twined that with the first two. They continued to twist the grasses together, staggering the locations of the ends, until they created a strong rope. When the earlier repair broke, they replaced the braid with the new rope which lasted the last twelve miles of the day's journey.

Once they had left the prairie, they followed the ruts created by the rest of the caravan. They stopped once near a creek to let Roden rest, and Erik used his healing power to ease the injuries sustained from the cat attacks.

Al was struggling. The walking and the aftereffects of the adrenalin release from the cats, the fire, and handling Roden's reactions had worn him down. He was stumbling often. He knew their survival hinged on locating the rest of the caravan. He didn't like being alone in this environment. The dangers of this strange world lurked around each tree, hill and shrub. The familiarity and safety of the caravan brought him comfort.

While they rested at the creek, they looked back at the still-burning grasses where black smoke still rose into the sky. Had Al destroyed the prairie? Where did the cats go? How many died from the fire or would now suffer from loss of habitat? What else lived in the grasses? Al worried about villages bordering the prairie and their abilities to manage the grass fires.

After resting, they continued following the caravan. Dusk came, and Al feared being alone after dark.

Then the familiar shape of the caravan camp appeared in the distance. Wagons were circled with the mastodons in the center. The boys traveled another hour to reach the encampment.

* * * *

Obadiah spoke, bringing Al back to the present, "Hadrian carries a whip. And remember that animal handler that got drunk the second night of the trip? The next morning they tied him between two trees and Hadrian whipped him fifty strokes." Obadiah made hand motions as if using a whip and made sounds of the whip striking flesh, "Ker-thwack. Ker-thwack."

Al shuddered each time Obadiah made the noise.

"After they released the man, they told him to never let it happen again. I heard he ran away later that day."

"Do you think that's what's in store for us?" Al curled his shoulders forward and caved in his chest. He dreaded the thought of being whipped. A twig snapped nearby and Al flinched. What could he do to prevent this? Apologize to Gadiel. Apologize to Hadrian. Promise to never do it again? "We saved Roden and all the feed, they won't forget about that, will they?"

Obadiah said, "And remember that handler they caught stealing food? Made him sleep in the forest outside the safety of the caravan. It's lucky for him he survived the night. Sometimes you hear screams in the dark, and the next morning you'll find traces of body parts."

Al craved the safety of the caravan. Al needed that safety. He had a sour taste in the back of his throat. Would Gadiel allow Erik and Al to eat first and then whip them, or force them to watch Gadiel and Hadrian eat while they received no food? He tried to take a deep breath, but his chest hitched and he coughed.

"We lost three mastodons and seven wagons," Obadiah said, "Gadiel said whoever whistled caused the cats to attack. Remember, Hadrian warned us this morning not to whistle in the grasses, and yet some fool did and almost killed us all."

Al's face grew hot. He remembered the morning meeting before entering the prairie. Hadrian stood before the caravan. Each morning Hadrian instructed the caravan handlers on what to expect from the terrain, wildlife dangers, and how to manage the mastodons.

Al thought Hadrian's comment strange, "We've seen in the past that whistling causes the cats' distress. Perhaps they were formerly domesticated cats and their owners used whistling as an attack signal, so don't whistle."

Al mused that when you're walking and looking at the landscape and get caught up in conversation you forget little things. Things like not whistling.

"Gadiel wants you to bring your staff," Obadiah stood. "Come boys, punishment time."

A chill shivered down Al's back as he took a deep breath, exchanged a glance with Erik, and struggled to his feet. *Should I disappear and find my way back to Sherry? Could I even do that? Maybe I could just lie low until this subsides.*

Erik pushed him in the back.

"Wait, the staff."

CHAPTER 27

Al smelled bacon as he approached Gadiel's campsite. A small fire had been kindled twenty feet from Gadiel's wagon, and three small benches had been placed around the fire. Gadiel and Hadrian sat on one bench, deep in conversation, as Wagner bent over a pot on a metal rack. He stirred the concoction. It smelled wonderful, and Al's mouth watered.

He held his staff more for support than as a prop for a mighty wizard. Al's shoulders curled forward as he entered the small camp, dragging his feet and kicking up dust. He studied Gadiel's and Hadrian's expressions, looking for signals concerning his fate. The men gazed only at the fire and spoke in low tones.

Al noticed Erik's hands trembled when he scratched his beard.

Gadiel and Hadrian stopped their conversation when they heard the boys. Gadiel stared at Al with his impenetrable black eyes, and the old man's eyelids flicked only once. "Come boys, sit." His voice revealed neither anger nor joy.

With clenched stomach, and taking a deep breath, Al parked on the bench furthest from the two men.

"I'm happy you boys survived the cat attacks and fires." Gadiel said, still in an even tone.

Al looked at Hadrian. The caravan leader's face showed tightness in his eyes and his lips flattened.

Gadiel said, "Wagner, serve the boys crackers and meat." The light from the fire threw shadows across Gadiel's crinkled face. "Roden is my favorite mastodon. I was worried."

Wagner brought a small tin bowl containing crackers and strips of bacon and handed it to the boys. He studied Al's staff and lingered a moment until moving back to the fire.

Al leaned forward and took a slice of bacon. The crisp meat crunched in his mouth as he bit off a piece. His mouth watered, and he used his sleeve to wipe away a drip of saliva escaping from the corner of his lips. Joyful, wonderful bacon. He took a deep breath, inhaling the scents of the food and campfire. *Is punishment off the table?*

A woman stepped from a wagon off to the right. She offered Al and Erik tin cups containing a brownish liquid. Gadiel nodded at the boys, giving permission. Al took the offered cup. After the rough day of fighting the cats, the fire, the broken harness and handling Roden, he wasn't about to question anything that looked like food. The salty bacon and crackers enhanced Al's thirst. He drank from the cup, a deep gulp. It was a sweet liquid with a hint of peaches followed by the long slow burn of alcohol.

Al coughed and waved his hand over his open mouth to reduce the drink's immediate effects. He shook his head. "Wow, that's powerful stuff."

Wagner said, "Yes, that's known as Ouuzool. A fermented fruit found in these regions. Goes down easy and then bites you."

Al ate another slice of bacon and then drained the cup. *If we're being fed bacon and this drink, then there's no danger of being reprimanded.*

Gadiel said, "Obadiah tells me you boys did a masterful job managing Roden, and the broken harness. You made a wise decision to braid the grasses into rope to wrap the pole. Most handlers in the caravan prefer to drop everything and run. In fact, two handlers did, and they were killed by the cats."

The woman returned with a pitcher, and looked at Gadiel, who nodded, and then she refilled the boy's cups.

Al smiled at the woman. His mind felt foggy. He straightened his back and shoulders, stuck his chest out and extended the cup out toward Erik as if to propose a toast. Erik wore a ridiculous grin on his face as he stared at the fire but did not lift his cup to tap Al's. Al turned and lifted his cup in the air toward Gadiel in a salute and took another long drink.

Gadiel nodded.

An excellent idea to use the grasses, Al thought. Gadiel recognized their brilliance and maybe they weren't getting a parade, but at least recognition for a job well done. He finished his bowl of crackers and bacon and stared at the empty bowl in wonder that it was all gone.

Wagner said, "Here, catch, Boy," and threw a roll at Al.

Al raised his hand a moment too late, and the roll went careening across the ground.

Erik laughed.

Abruptly, Gadiel said, "I want to study your staff."

Al hesitated as he considered letting Gadiel handle the precious possession. Since acquiring it in the Velidred Castle dungeon, he had let no one touch the staff. Sure, his friends handled it, but could he allow it of a stranger? And this was not any stranger, but Gadiel, whose motives were mysterious at best. He looked into Gadiel's dark eyes. Was it the drink that caused his brain to be fuzzy?

Erik slurred his words, "What are you waiting for? Give him the staff. You said you wanted Gadiel to help you."

Al shook his head. What would Gadiel do with it? The staff had the family connection coming from his grandfather, plus, when he walked with the staff he felt more confident.

Gadiel raised his hand, "I can teach you its secrets, and I knew Alpherge the Great."

"You knew my grandfather?"

"Years ago we met, when we were both younger men. Your grandfather was a powerful wizard. Smarter than most, he created and manipulated powerful spells."

"How do you know the staff's secrets?" Al shook the fuzziness from his brain and attempted to decide whether to hand the staff to Gadiel. He knew he shouldn't drink more Ouuzool, but took another swig.

"Legends speak of Alpherge the Great's staff. I've studied many staffs over the years and have desired a chance to examine the one you carry. I might tease out its secrets." The old man reached for a stick and poked at the logs in the fire, whipping-up sparks, and the flame flared. A sweet and savory aroma wafted from the burning hickory.

If Al handed the staff to Gadiel, would the old man use it against him or throw it in the fire? Maybe he'd give it to Wagner to sell. That would be even worse. Al could rescue it from the fire. "Are you a wizard?"

"I've dabbled with magic through the years, but my magic is weak compared to yours. My skill-sets run better toward people and businesses than wizardry."

The drink distorted Al's thinking and hampered a rational decision. Give the staff to Gadiel? He looked to Erik, who stared at the fire with unfocused eyes. It was just a walking stick. What harm could Gadiel do? Maybe he'll give Al a new spell or get the heads on the staff to talk to him again. Why had they stopped talking?

Gadiel said, "I understand your reluctance, and if you're not ready for me to handle the staff, then we can do it another day."

Gadiel is going to retract his offer to teach me, Al thought. "No, that's okay, you can examine it. What's the harm?"

"You're as wise as your grandfather."

Al picked up the staff and tried to stand, but toppled over. "Whoa, I'm a little unsteady."

Erik guffawed.

Al planted the staff in the ground, used it to rise, and staggered toward Gadiel. "There's powerful magic in that drink."

"There is that," Wagner raised his cup to Al.

Al stood next to Gadiel holding the staff.

Gadiel placed his hand on the rod and gave a slight tug.

Magic coursed through the staff. Al felt it. Weeks had passed since he felt power in the staff. He didn't let go. "What did you do?"

"Put my hand on the staff. No more. Do you plan to release it?"

Gadiel's black eyes gleamed in the darkness, and light from the fire reflected off the man's pupils. Was Gadiel good or evil? Could Al trust the man to handle the staff? Al yanked on the staff, but Gadiel also held tight.

"I can't examine the staff unless you let me handle it, touch it, inspect it, pulse magic into it and tease secrets from it." The man smiled, an innocent smile, a smile a grandfather might give while playing with a toy with his grandson.

Buzzing filled Al's brain, but it wasn't a sound from outside, it came from within. Was it the drink or Gadiel's touch on the staff? Al tugged at the staff.

Erik shouted from the bench, "Let him examine it Al, what are you waiting for?"

Al took a deep breath and exhaled slowly, trying to think this through. What was he doing? Gadiel had not requested the staff before today. If he wanted it for himself, there had been plenty of opportunities to snatch it during the journey.

Gadiel released his grip on the staff.

Kenneth Brown

The buzzing faded in Al's brain. Why did the buzzing stop when Gadiel released the staff? He wanted the wizards on the staff to talk to him, to share wisdom with him, not Gadiel.

Gadiel said, "I recognize the faces carved into the staff. Isabel the Invidious. She wasn't a nasty person by nature, but love of drink and men led to her downfall. And I can't forget Callahan the Curious, always putting his nose in places where it didn't belong. Did you know that your grandfather didn't put him in the staff, but it was his own curiosity that captured him?

Al considered Gadiel's words. Al, a fledgling wizard on Aloheno for mere weeks, understood little compared to this aging man. It was obvious Gadiel knew these witches and wizards, and he claimed to know staffs.

"And I would be remiss if I didn't tell you about the wizard's image at the top of the staff, which is your own grandfather."

Al felt a fluttery feeling in his belly and in a shaky voice said, "Seriously, the top figure is my grandfather?" *Why didn't Master Wizard Ishwa tell me this when he showed it to me the first time?*

"I can recognize that face anywhere."

"Tell me about my grandfather."

"Are you here to bargain with me? Let me examine the staff and I will share stories of your grandfather and his power."

Confusion befuddled Al's mind, making him reluctant to hand over the staff to Gadiel. Cugbert said not to trust Gadiel. Sherry begged him not to trust the old man. Al needed time to cleanse his head and get a firm grip on Gadiel's motives, but what if Gadiel's knowledge could help liberate the staff's secrets and his grandfather's magic? Would Gadiel leave if Al rebuffed him too many times?

Gadiel relaxed and took a pipe from his jacket pocket, stuffed it with tobacco, lit a small stick from the fire and puffed a flame into the pipe bowl. "I can light my pipe with magic, I need not do it with a stick and fire, but some secrets, like the staff contains, need a human touch, not magic to make them work."

"Can you help me find out why the staff's wizards stopped talking to me?"

"They stopped talking to you? Interesting." A puff of smoke blew from the pipe toward Al.

Al inhaled an aroma of apples, tobacco and cinnamon. He closed his eyes and reminisced of home and his mother. The scent reminded him of his mom baking cookies on a fall day in Montana. "People told me you used to sell staffs."

"There are times I arrange a sale, but it has to be an important transaction. Rare these days. But I won't sell your staff without your approval, though I'm sure this valuable piece could return a great price."

Fog was rising from the plain where they camped, mixing with the smoke from the fire and the sweet vapor from Gadiel's pipe.

Al didn't know why, but he said, "Guarantee I'll get it back and I'll let you examine it."

The man's thin lips lifted in a smile, showing no teeth. "You'll let me examine it, will you?" Gadiel's eyes glowed red in the light fog. "You are a great wizard, and if the stories are true, you defeated the Mountain King, and yet you want a guarantee I'll hand the staff back to you?"

"I know it's a powerful staff and I want to make sure I get it back is all. Wagner's always asking me if I want to sell it."

"I guarantee I won't let Wagner sell your staff." The man didn't blink.

Could he trust Gadiel's word? Should he be more worried about Gadiel and less worried about Wagner? Al held tight to the staff, willing the wizards to guide him, but they remained silent. Suddenly, he decided. "I'm sorry, here you go."

The old man's smile broadened as he nodded and touched the staff again. "If you're sure."

Al released the staff. He stood above the seated man, unsure whether to return to the bench or wait for Gadiel to finish his examination.

Gadiel rotated the staff slowly in his hands, and the firelight danced strange shadows from the carved images of past wizards.

Gadiel hummed as he examined the staff. Al thought the tune sounded familiar.

"Sit and have some more crackers and bacon. It's been a long day for you boys and you'll need strength for tomorrow's journey."

Al stood motionless. The offer seemed disingenuous. There was no food left.

"Wagner, help the boy back to the bench. We don't want him to fall into the fire." Gadiel resumed humming the familiar tune.

Wagner grabbed Al's arm and led him back to the bench.

Al sat next to Erik, and Wagner did bring him more crackers and bacon. The woman returned with the pitcher and refilled the boy's cups.

The old man spent the next fifteen minutes examining the staff and humming the tune. Al wracked his brain trying to identify the tune. He knew the tune, it was an Earth song. But what?

Erik leaned in and whispered. "Al, remember our signal?"

"What signal?"

"I'm going to check on the wagon. Gadiel is busy and I can get a quick peek inside the window."

"Are you crazy? Leave it be."

"Do you remember the signal?"

"Yes, but you're not serious are you?"

"Just watch these three. If one of them moves, then whistle." Erik stood and swayed side to side, unsteady on his feet.

This can't be happening. It must be the drink. Why does Erik think he can sneak a look right now with the wagon a mere twenty feet away?

Erik wobbled a moment, steadied his legs and ambled around the fire, but away from Gadiel's wagon.

A quick glance showed Gadiel deep in thought over the staff, still humming the tune. Hadrian and Wagner chatted up two of the women helping with the meal. Al surveyed the nearby campsite, searching for Erik.

A few moments passed and Gadiel said, "That wasn't smart throwing fireballs at the cats in dry grass, was it?" His voice turned toward displeasure.

The comment startled Al, "What?"

"The fireballs to fight the cats, did you not see the danger of the fire and the dry grasses?"

Al said nothing. His mouth hung open.

Gadiel went back to humming the tune.

Hadrian stopped his conversation with Wagner. "Do you know how many mastodons we lost today?"

Al looked around for Erik, for someone to help. "Three?"

"Three mastodons lost to the cats, and seven wagons and their supplies." Hadrian stood and moved toward Al. "Someone didn't listen to the instructions before we entered the grasses. Did you?"

"I heard the instructions," Al stammered. "I always listen." The door to Gadiel's wagon opened, and an animal scampered out. A dog, he thought, because he heard barking.

"The instructions we give aren't suggestions."

The dog continued to bark, as if it cornered a nearby animal.

Gadiel said, "Go check on the dog, Wagner."

Hadrian said, "Did you not hear the command for no one to whistle while we traveled through the grasses?"

It clicked in Al's brain. The song Gadiel hummed. The barking dog. Erik sneaking a peek in Gadiel's wagon and Wagner heading in his direction. The song Gadiel hummed was the Earth song Al had whistled in the prairie, which caused the cats to attack. Gadiel stood and held the staff, and a red glow emanated around him. Al must warn Erik. He put his fingers in his mouth to whistle, but the salty crackers and bacon dried his mouth to silence.

CHAPTER 28

ita laughed and clapped her hands when she heard the dog barking near the wagon window. The shape-shifting spell worked. She had transformed the pot that hung on the wall into a dog. It wasn't a big dog, but wow, she did it.

She had sensed a presence by the window. A man lurked near the window, trying to peer into the cabin. She felt Erik's nearness rather than saw him, and knew he was trying to look inside.

Her hand flew to her mouth, suppressing a yelp. How dare he try to peer into her cabin? *Does he know I'm here? That ruins everything.* Zita used magic and extinguished the cabin candles.

In the darkness, Zita had cleared her mind and focused on the pot.

The blackened metal pot made a racket when it fell from the wall, and she worried the sound might spook Erik, but he continued to peer through the window. She lost focus for a moment as she thought of Erik. Her stomach fluttered, then she reached out with magic and felt the pot transform. The pot handle turned into a dog's snout and face, and then the bowl became the dog's body and fur covered it all. She struggled with the dog's legs, but then they sprouted.

She took a deep breath, expanding her chest. Her heart pounded. The dog lived, panted, trotted to her and licked her face. "Oh, aren't you cute?" Zita had rubbed her hands across its short hair. She couldn't make out the dog's color in the darkness, but the pot had been a blackened one.

Zita suppressed a desire to whoop and dance. She had transformed a pot into a dog, an inanimate object into a living animal.

A shadow moved by the window, which brought her attention back to Erik. Yes, she made the dog to irritate Erik. Could it live outside of the cabin? She feared Gadiel's reaction if she released the dog.

Adrenaline rushed through her and she didn't care what Gadiel thought. Erik was snooping around the wagon and needed dissuading. Would the pot hold its dog shape? Zita opened the cabin door a crack. Gadiel sat near the fire with Al's staff in his hands, running his fingers over the carvings. Hadrian and Wagner chatted with the women. Tall, gawky Al sat on the bench, his eyes focused on Gadiel and the staff. How did Gadiel get Al to give up his staff?

She whispered, "Get that mean boy by the window. Go, girl." Zita opened the door just enough to stay hidden and yet release the dog.

The mutt leapt to the ground and sped around the wagon, barking.

Zita giggled, put her hands over her mouth to keep from being heard and swallowed a shout of glee.

The dog barked as if it had cornered an animal. "Good girl."

Wagner spotted Erik. He stood and said, "Get away from the wagon."

The dog barked.

Zita heard muffled shouts and peeked through the window. Wagner had pinned Erik to the ground, with a boot planted firmly on the boy's back. Hadrian walked Alpherge back toward the boys' wagon. Would Gadiel whip them and leave them in the woods for the animals? A smile formed on Zita's lips as she imagined the boys screaming in pain as wild animals shredded their flesh.

A few minutes later Gadiel entered the wagon carrying the pot in one hand and the staff in the other. Gadiel threw the pot to the wagon floor. It banged as it hit the wood, wobbled and rotated until it came to rest.

Gadiel said, "You lost focus." He pointed to the ordinary metal pot lying on the floor. "That's what happens when you don't concentrate. You maintain focus until you want the spell to end. I told you to practice inside and you disobeyed me."

Doom replaced Zita's glee at shape-shifting the pot. Her breath hitched, and she stuttered, "But I . . ."

"You'll ruin your ability to fool people. The magic's power comes from others ignorance that you have the skill."

Zita folded her arms across her chest, elbows pressed hard against her sides. Had she ruined everything? The hard training and cramped quarters in the cabin day after day with no companionship spun her emotions. She needed release.

Gadiel said, "Hopefully no one saw it transform. Tell me what happened to your focus. Was it the boy?"

She looked at the floor and curled her hair around her fingers. *Yes, it was the boy, Erik. He ruins everything.*

"Well, why did you lose focus?"

Zita needed someone to talk with other than Gadiel, and then she could keep focus. The confined space of the wagon closed in on her. She clenched her jaw so hard it was painful. "Yes, I peeked out the window and saw the boy and I lost focus." Would he keep training her if someone else noticed the skill? Why did it matter if they knew?

Gadiel towered above her with an accusing stare.

Zita's cheeks burned as she stood solidly in front of Gadiel and squeezed her fists.

He said, "You have the power. You're almost ready to transform animals into other animals. You may be able to transform yourself into an animal or make yourself look like someone else." He grabbed her chin and forced her to look at him. "Listen to my instructions or you throw away all this training."

"You expect me to transform myself into something else?" She never imagined that as an end goal. "Who? And why would I want to change myself into someone else?"

"There are many possibilities when you transform. It's better than being invisible because then you can involve yourself in events rather than just watch what happens." Gadiel leaned Al's staff in the corner.

Zita shivered at the thought of transforming herself. "Is it possible I might get stuck in the animal's body after shape-shifting and never change back to my body?"

"That's why you need to listen and practice, instead of playing pranks and losing focus. I'm going out to inspect the caravan. You practice with the pot and keep your focus." He walked to the door and lifted the handle.

"Sir, what happens to the boys?"

"They'll be punished for whistling and setting the grass fires." Gadiel's face tightened as he brushed lint off his black jacket.

Zita smiled.

CHAPTER 29

Three mornings later, Al stretched his aching muscles yet again as he listened to Hadrian bark out commands for the day's journey.

Gadiel and Hadrian had punished Al and Erik by stretching them naked, on their backs, on the top of their wagons, tied by hands and feet to the corners for two days and two nights. The boys lay on the feed stored in the wagon, an uneven pile of brush, limbs and insects. Obadiah said the mastodons enjoyed the insects, which provided a superb source of protein, as much as the limbs. However, the insects' bites left nasty welts on humans.

Hadrian said, "We wasted two days repairing the broken equipment and allowing the mastodons to rest and heal." He focused his gaze on Al. "We will travel at night to make up for lost time. Tomorrow is the longest day of the year and all three moons will shine in the night sky, so we expect enough light for safe travel. Even so, you still must be diligent and aware of your surroundings."

Al thought lying in the brush had been painful, but not being able to turn was worse, causing his legs and arms to ache. The sun burned hot each day, but the insects were worst of all.

Hadrian droned on. "We have to reach the ice in five days. If the comet reaches the eastern star, Myverius, before we reach the frozen lake, then the caravan will not make it to the Ice Castle, and we die. I won't allow that to happen and I will push you harder to insure we don't die."

Kenneth Brown

The insects had been small, with tiny legs, and Al hadn't even noticed them until late the first day. Obadiah said human's smells attracted the insects and handlers encountered them when they pulled the feed for the mastodons.

Hadrian's voice broke into Al's reverie. "We're ten days from the Ice Castle. It turns colder as we travel north, and even if we run into blizzards, winter wolves or other animals, we continue moving. Nothing stops the caravan, we'll jettison handlers instead of stopping."

Al stared at the ground when Hadrian fixed him with a steely gaze. Whatever winter wolves were, they couldn't be worse than these spruce ticks that had fed on him the last two days and nights. Al considered leaving the caravan. No one deserved the kind of punishment he and Erik had received, but they needed to get to the Ice Castle to find the golden crown.

The insect bites and sunburn had combined to fester into electrifying pain. After they were freed, Obadiah had given him cream to smear on the insect bites, which hadn't helped much. And he couldn't scratch because his entire front was sunburned. Spruce ticks had bitten him on his back, unreachable by scratching.

Erik remained silent this morning. His only comment was to blame Al for not whistling in time for him to escape being caught looking for Zita. His face was oddly swollen from a reaction to the insect bites. Would the bites scar their faces for life? Erik had always thought himself a ladies' man, but maybe the scars would change that.

Would Hadrian's instructions never end? "The terrain becomes rocky with small rolling hills, so be alert to dangers your animals might face. Since we lost mastodons, we're forced to take extra care with the ones that remain."

Two days without food, no food this morning and the mastodons worry Hadrian? Al hadn't been able to eat this morning because the tick bites had painfully swollen his lips. He pulled three of the blood filled parasites from the inside of his lips after three handlers had untied him, lifted him off the wagon and dumped him to the ground.

"That's enough instructions, we ride in an hour."

Al glared at Erik and prepared the wagons for the day's travel. They had built a rhythm in their morning routine, and so, despite their weakened condition, they harnessed and hitched Roden. They were ready for the day's travels in fifteen minutes.

Roden appeared rested and frisky compared to earlier days of travel. The mastodon snorted and began pulling the wagons toward the road.

Al lost his magical ability after the night of drinking the Ouuzool and had no means to help make the load seem lighter. How might the full weight affect the day's travels? Al hadn't seen Gadiel this morning and worried what the man had been doing with his staff. How long did Ouuzool affect magic?

Erik mumbled something Al couldn't understand, but Roden moved and fell into step, taking his place in the wagon train.

What was in that drink? Could he get his staff back without magic now that Gadiel held it? Al worried Gadiel might attune to the staff and become the new master. Or he might give it to Wagner to sell despite saying that he wouldn't. How much magic did Gadiel control? He said he wasn't strong in magic, and Al sensed little magic in the man. Maybe he was a low level wizard.

The caravan cleared the end of a large lake, and the animals strained as they began pulling their loads into the rolling hills Hadrian mentioned in his morning speech. The trees transitioned from deciduous to spruce and pine.

Al started to scratch an itch on the side of his face and stopped when his fingers touched one of the bites that was scabbing over. Instead, he rubbed his cheek with the cloth of his cloak. How long till the effects of the drink dissipated so he could do magic again? Ten days to the Ice Castle, Hadrian had said. Al resolved to restore his magic and staff by that time.

The path entered a small canyon which forced them to snake around large boulders. In some places the jumbled rocks narrowed the path so much the wagons cleared them by mere inches. Al walked behind the wagons to insure they didn't scrape against the walls of rock, while Erik guided Roden in front. Al studied the cliffs for animals and other dangers, though he didn't remember Hadrian mentioning concerns about dangerous animals on today's travels. Trees lined the top of the canyon fifty feet above. The rock walls and trees threw dark shadows across the trail.

Al imagined confronting Gadiel, "Gadiel, I demand my staff back." and Gadiel might say, "No, and I sentence you to three more nights tied to the top of the wagon."

Al should ask Erik to rub more cream on his back; it itched, a lot. He stopped a moment and leaned against the canyon wall to scratch his back. He felt like a cow, but it helped. He watched the four wagons hitched to Roden traverse a creek running through the canyon. A trickle of a waterfall fed it, and it fell away into a hole on the lower side of the trail. Wet sand sloshed, and the wagon slowed, but Roden kept the load moving.

He would go to Gadiel tonight at supper time and ask for the staff back. Gadiel would understand. Al hadn't told Gadiel he could keep the staff. In fact, he expected the man to give him hints, magic spells, and techniques to use the staff. Gadiel had promised as much.

That afternoon, the sides of the canyon narrowed and rose higher with moss growing thickly on the tan sandstone rocks. The light faded in the steep canyon. Shadows lurked everywhere, but Al's eyes adjusted to the darkness. If he had his magic, Al could call the staff. He assumed that would still work, but he hadn't used that command in a while. Now he realized the staff's power had diminished since he first met Gadiel in the village. In fact, that's when the voices on the staff quit talking to him. Coincidence?

He heard a grinding of wood against rock.

Erik yelled something unintelligible, and the wagon train stopped.

There wasn't room for Al to maneuver between the wagons and rocks to determine the problem.

More shouting from Erik, though garbled. Did he want Al to climb over the wagons? Al yelled, "What?"

The wagons moved backwards a foot and then started forwards again, only to grind against the canyon wall. Al realized that Erik was trying to back up and reposition the wheels.

Al shouted, "You have to move back farther to get a straighter path." He wondered if his voice sounded as garbled as Erik's.

Two handlers, approaching from behind with their beasts and carts said, "The handler has to go straight at least two wagon lengths before turning to navigate this bend in the canyon. New handlers have trouble every year."

"That's what I told Erik." Al said.

The other handlers said, "What?"

"That's what I told him."

They looked at each other and shook their heads. The boy on the left shrugged his shoulders.

Great, they didn't understand either. Al pointed for them to yell the command. He said, "You tell him."

One boy said, "Do you know what he said?"

The other boy rubbed the back of his neck and shook his head. "Maybe this guy can't talk."

"Well, they shouldn't have put him in the caravan if he can't talk."

Al pointed to his lips. "Swollen."

"Yeah, he can't talk. See, he pointed to his lips and mumbled again."

Al pointed at the boy and pointed to the wagons stuck in the canyon. "You."

"I think he said, 'you.'"

"What, he wants me to push the wagons? That won't work. Back em up. You reverse the load and re-position."

"Yeah," Al nodded his head. "You tell Erik." Why were these guys so dense? If they think I can't speak, then they should yell at Erik.

The wagons backed up and Al stepped aside to make room. Erik must have gotten the message.

Al said, "Move on back," and motioned with his hands.

"That's gratitude for you, we tell him what to do and he just shoos us away," one guy snorted.

Roden backed the wagons till three became visible on his side of the canyon bend. The wheels bounced over low rock outcrops as the hitches pivoted and zig-zagged the wagons. Al couldn't see what was happening, but the wagons then began to move forward. He waited and listened for the sound of wood grinding against rock, but he only heard the creaking of axles and thuds as the hitches engaged in the direction of travel for which they were designed. The wagons crept forward, and Al followed them farther into the darkness ahead. He found the sharp rock that had caught the wagons. It was studded with wooden splinters, large and small. He tried to determine if a touch of magic might make the pass easier to navigate, but he decided that rock supported the whole canyon wall. Maybe he'd leave it alone. His decision didn't matter anyway, since his magic was nonexistent right now.

CHAPTER 30

Zita ate her dinner in the wagon, concerned at what lay ahead that evening. A single candle glowed. Gadiel had warned her tonight they would practice advanced shape-shifting techniques, nevertheless, was it something she wanted? She spooned the stew into her mouth, not tasting the savory peas, carrots and potatoes.

For the next three days the caravan would ascend to the plateau. They neared their final destination, the Ice Castle and the Pit of Wretchedness. For Zita, this was her pit of revenge on Erik. When the boys entered the pit, Zita planned to shape-shift and follow them as an animal. The boys would grab the golden crown, and Zita would kill them or at least leave them in the pit, where they'd be unable to get out and take the crown back to Gadiel.

Gadiel walked into the cabin as Zita wiped the last of the stew from the bowl with a slice of hard bread.

Gadiel said, "Are you ready to begin your final and most important training?"

Zita's breath caught, her heart stopped, and then began beating again. She tried to control her shaking hand. It was fun to think of shape-shifting, but did she really want to change her own body?

Gadiel took her hand, "Relax, this first time I manage the process. I control the transformation, which allows you to come to grips with your body's changing shape. Without this first step, I've found that students panic and make things worse. Are you ready?"

The taste of bile rose to her mouth, and she felt nauseated. "Okay." She hugged her knees to her chest.

"What animal would you like?"

Zita thought back to the animals she enjoyed as a kid. The thought of being a magnificent mare sounded fun. "A horse."

Gadiel laughed, "A little big for our cabin. Let's begin with something smaller."

"A fox or a dog?"

"Let's start with a rabbit, so I won't have to worry about you biting me." He smiled.

A fluffy bunny sounded harmless enough. *Yeah, it might be fun to be a bunny and Gadiel is handling this first session. I won't have to worry about leaving myself in a horrible half-animal, half-human shape.*

"The first part of the magic for this step comes from you, when you execute the same steps used to shape-shift other objects. The other magic portion comes from the bond we created from the Fire and Ice ceremony."

Zita knew that connection. Gadiel could now read her mind, a worm digging through her brain, harvesting memories to use against her. Sometimes when she lay in bed on the border of sleep, he touched a memory and she re-lived a past event in her life. This last week he concentrated on memories of her mother. He invaded her privacy and her most cherished memories, but Zita was defenseless to stop the digging.

"Begin your meditation and focus."

Zita cleared her mind and targeted her attention at a single point of light in a dark, empty room. Her ability to focus improved since the early days when her mind wandered toward Erik. *Start with a large light the size of the white sun, and decrease the light into a pinpoint. Concentrate all thought on that tiny point.*

Gadiel spoke in a soothing voice, "Imagine a rabbit sitting at your feet."

In a moment a wild bunny hopped from the darkness of her mind, sat at her feet and watched her.

"Study its paws."

Zita picked up the cute bunny. Its light-brown fur felt soft as she handled the feet and legs. The feet had gray pads. She had never noticed that rabbits had claws.

"Imagine the bottom of your foot feeling like the rabbit's."

She sat on the bench in the cabin wearing a simple dress and no shoes. In her mind, she reached and touched the bottom of her right foot. Yes, the foot felt rough like the rabbit's pad. Zita stroked the rabbit's foot pad and then stroked her own, which felt the same.

"Picture the top of your foot the same as the rabbit's."

The transformation was amazing. Her foot tingled, and she rubbed out the funny feeling as hair grew on the top of her foot.

"Continue up the leg, but stop when you reach the hem of your dress."

Zita rubbed her legs as they grew more and more hairy until they were velvety.

"When you reach your dress, imagine the clothing integrating into your skin. The material will become a part of the transformation. We do that to make sure you don't transform back and find yourself naked."

She suppressed a giggle at the thought of being a bunny one minute and then naked in the middle of town.

"Concentrate."

She had mastered changing inanimate objects, and with a quick refocus the dress became a part of her skin.

"Touch the rabbit's body and your body becomes the same."

The transformation continued. A quiet feeling of excitement built in Zita's belly.

"Now the ears."

Zita pictured rabbit ears sticking out of her hair, and she laughed.

"Stay focused," Gadiel warned. "Work on the mouth."

Her entire body prickled and itched now as her hair changed texture and length. Zita touched the rabbit's mouth and nose. *Oh, rabbits have teeth. It makes sense, because they have to eat, but I never thought about it.* The mouth transformation challenged her, but in a moment her nose twitched and a small crevice connected the nose to her lips.

Zita sat on the bench as a rabbit, but a giant human-sized rabbit.

"Now we shrink you from the size of a human to the size of a normal rabbit." Gadiel touched the top of her head. "This can hurt."

Expecting a quick transition, the slowness of the change surprised her. Pain coursed through her body and she screamed as every molecule contracted. A vise squeezed tighter and tighter, each turn altering her body structure.

Then the pain subsided, and she sat panting and wriggling her nose. *Is it finished? Will shape-shifting hurt every time I transform?*

Gadiel found a mirror and turned it toward her.

The mirror reflected the pink nose and green eyes of a rabbit sitting on the bench. Zita had never seen a wild rabbit with green eyes.

Someone banged on the cabin door, "What's happening in there?"

Gadiel pointed at Zita and said, "Hold your concentration."

Erik's voice, she thought. Her skin itched.

Gadiel stroked her back. "Stay focused, maintain the shape of a rabbit."

Alpherge yelled, "Mr. Gadiel, I want my staff back."

"Ah, the boys have come back for their toys, a most inconvenient time to interrupt us." Gadiel stood and placed the mirror on the shelf. He looked at Zita the rabbit, "If I open the door, can you stay focused? We can't have you changing back in front of the boys."

Zita questioned whether she could hold this shape. Should she shake her head or was it okay to talk? Her voice? Could shapeshifters as animals talk like normal humans? She opened her little rabbit mouth to speak.

Gadiel put his finger over her lips. "Stay there and don't move."

Don't move? He's going to open the door while I'm transformed into a rabbit! Her eyes darted to the corners of the wagon looking for a hiding spot. *I can't let Erik see me like this, and I don't want him to even see me in the cabin. He'll know it's me.* Her body itched. Did that mean she was losing concentration?

Gadiel studied her. "Stay put and concentrate."

She turned her rabbit body to hop into a corner. It felt natural to hide.

Her teacher picked her up and placed her back on the bench where she had transformed into a rabbit. Gadiel raised his voice and spoke in the direction of the door, "Now's not a good time, let's talk tomorrow during the day."

Erik said, "No sir, we need to talk now. We're busy during the day leading the mastodons. Al wants his staff back."

"I'm still studying the staff. Give me a few more days."

"We're coming in now." The handle jiggled, but the door didn't open.

"I'm preparing for bed at the moment. It's an inconvenient time for me."

The boys pounded on the door, "Open the door, Gadiel."

Zita's body itched and trembled, and she concentrated to prevent her legs from dashing into hiding. She must hold the rabbit shape.

"Return to your wagon and sleep. You'll wake the mastodons with your loud banging. I can arrange more days for you to be chained to the wagons."

Silence. Were they leaving? Zita studied Gadiel.

He placed his finger over his lips.

A quieter tap, tap, tap on the door. "Please Mr. Gadiel, let's talk. It'll only take a minute."

Gadiel stared at rabbit Zita a moment, then moved toward the door.

He won't let them in, will he? She trembled and her heart raced. *They can't see me in this state. I can't hold this shape. What if I shape-shift back to human form in front of them? It'll ruin everything.* She ached to run and hide. The instinct was ingrained in her whole anatomy as a rabbit. *Why couldn't Gadiel have made me a dog? Then I could bark or bite them. Why a rabbit?*

Gadiel reached the door and loosed the lock, then turned the knob.

"No," a silent scream escaped her lips. They'll ruin everything.

The door swung open and Erik stood on the stoop.

She stared at him as he scanned the room.

Gadiel moved to block his view of Zita.

Zita quivered, but held her position. *Don't move, don't run, and don't hide. Stay still. They won't see you unless they come too close. Wasn't that the mantra of every wild rabbit she had ever encountered? Stand your ground. If the predator doesn't approach, then the animal is safe. How do rabbits do it?* The fear and desire to run became intense.

Erik said, "I heard a woman scream."

Gadiel laughed. "No woman, just me and my rabbit." He altered his position and pointed at Zita. "You must have heard a night animal. We are getting close to the wolves. They roam at night, looking for small animals like my rabbit."

"No, it came from this cabin. A woman is with you."

"You're wrong and are irritating me. Go back to your wagon and sleep before tomorrow's arduous journey."

"Show me."

"Is that necessary? Don't you trust me?"

Al spoke from behind Erik, "Don't trust him, get inside so I can get the staff."

"I'm still examining the staff, my young wizard friend. I'm opening secrets that may prove useful when I have time to train you."

Yes, Zita thought, don't let them enter. Send them back to their wagon.

"I want to verify that you still have the staff and haven't given it to Wagner to sell."

"Ah, you want to see the staff." Gadiel glanced at Zita.

Zita wanted to yell at Gadiel. *No, don't let them near me. I can't hold this shape if they're in the room.* Zita's body shivered and vibrated. *Focus on the light. Don't change shape.*

Gadiel stepped back from the door and the boys entered the tight quarters of the cabin. The room consisted of a single narrow space with benches on either side. The staff stood in a corner far from the doorway.

Gadiel stepped to the staff and held it. "Here it is, secure in my cabin. It's too valuable to allow Wagner to sell. I promise to keep it safe."

Al stepped toward Gadiel and the staff, ignoring Zita the rabbit.

Erik said. "What a cute bunny. Can I pet it?"

CHAPTER 31

Z ita glared at Gadiel. *Don't let Erik pet me. I can't hold this shape if he touches me.* She begged the old man with her green rabbit eyes.

Gadiel said, "Sure, stroke the bunny's fur, she likes that. She won't bite." He glared at Zita.

She wanted to scream, "No, don't let him touch me." She didn't have to speak the words, Gadiel knew her thoughts.

Erik stroked Zita's back.

Zita's body tingled and her chest tightened. She concentrated on holding her form. She couldn't let Erik ruin this.

Erik lifted her off the bench and held the rabbit to his chest, caressing her back with a gentle touch.

Her ear felt funny. Was she changing back? Zita focused on the tiny pinprick of light, ignoring Erik's tender strokes. His body was warm and his heartbeat comforting.

Gadiel pointed, "See, the staff is safe." Then he placed it back in the corner, out of Al's reach.

"May I touch it?" Al leaned forward. He had to hunch slightly to prevent his head from rubbing the cabin ceiling, which he knew made him look silly, and put him at a disadvantage. Gadiel shifted to block the move.

"There's a minor spell on the staff that allows me to search its inner magic. The spell takes time to work. You can't touch it for another twenty-four hours. Otherwise, I must start over."

Al's Adam's apple bobbed, and he moved his lips as if getting ready to say something.

Zita's rabbit ear drooped against Erik's chest and changed back to a human ear. *No, I must concentrate.* Taking in deep, slow breaths, she attempted to relax and focus at the same time, not an easy feat.

Erik stroked her back using long, relaxed strokes. "Relax little bunny, I won't hurt you. Aren't you a little furry ball of anxiety?"

Erik had a tender touch, and she felt safe next to his body. Zita's ear resumed its rabbit shape. She was pretty sure Erik hadn't noticed.

Erik's caresses reminded her of times with her mother at the Velidred Castle. After dinner, her mom had said, "Go get a book." Zita raced up the castle stairs into her room and came back with a handful of books. The leather covers, stained and scratched, were covered with drawings made by a village artist. The books contained simple pencil drawings of animals or citizens of the village. There was an occasional colored image. Mom pointed to an animal, and Zita would yell out its name. Or Mom pointed to the picture of the blacksmith and Zita said, "Horse-shoe maker." Mom stroked Zita's black hair and said, "You're right, honey."

After a moment to reminiscence, Zita checked her focus and concentrated on staying in a rabbit form.

Al said, "You've had plenty of time to research the staff, I want it back."

"Relax friend," Gadiel put his hand on Al's shoulder. "I promise to return it at the proper time. Have you taken the Fire and Ice challenge?"

Zita couldn't believe Gadiel brought this up with Al. She stopped thinking of Erik and concentrated on the new conversation.

"I've never heard of it."

"Maybe I shouldn't mention it. Many wizards take the challenge, and I thought, a mighty wizard like you, must have already received the initiation."

"Why would I want to?"

"The Fire and Ice challenge helps you become a stronger wizard, allows you to work with this staff and gives you wisdom of your past and future."

A smile brightened Al's face as he leaned in toward Gadiel and repeated, "Wisdom about my past and future?"

Zita glanced at Erik, who had stopped stroking her fur, his attention focused on Al and Gadiel. *Is this the man that will kill me? According to Forest River Blossom it is.* Not death from a simple arrow, her future said, but that a man will hold her under water until she drowned. She pictured her mom in the rain, an arrow through her heart when the castle guards shot her as she tried to escape Zita's dad. Memories returned of Erik killing her dad at the volcano, memories of the hours she sat alone on the side of the volcano afterwards, crying. Erik didn't come for her. Zita bit his hand.

Erik yelled, "Ow, why did you do that?" He tossed her to the bench.

Zita ran into the corner. *That will teach the troublemaker.*

Pain burst in her brain. Gadiel punished her when she didn't do what he wanted, a side effect of their connection from the Fire and Ice experience. He obviously wasn't happy with her interrupting his sales pitch to Al.

The old man continued talking to the young wizard, "The process involves a little magic, meditation and herbs."

"Is it safe?" Al rushed the words together, so they were well-nigh unintelligible. He bounced on his toes with excitement.

"Slow down," Erik said, "let me tell you about my experience with Cugbert before you do this tonight."

"Oh, it won't be tonight." Gadiel smiled. "We'll reach a frozen lake in a few days."

Erik touched Al's arm. "Come back to the wagon. Let's talk about the experience before you decide."

Al's mouth opened and closed as if he was too confused to find the right words. He pinched his lips and raised his eyebrows and said, "Come staff." Al raised his hands to receive the staff. It didn't move.

"Be careful, my friend. Do not disturb the staff. It sleeps for the moment."

"I don't know what you're doing, but I want it back."

Gadiel said, "In three days we reach the plateau and soon, the lake. Yes, the lake will be perfect for our purposes." He rubbed bony hands together.

"The staff."

"I promise to return the staff after the Fire and Ice ceremony."

Yes, Zita thought, and then Al will be his forever.

The boys left the cabin with assurances from Gadiel that Al would get the staff back.

The door shut, and pain spread through Zita's body.

"I told you to behave." Gadiel said.

The pain forced her to curl into a ball. She wanted to scream, but only emitted a tiny rabbit screech, high and thin. Her rabbit body wouldn't transform back into a human although she tried to mutate back. What game was Gadiel playing?

"You want to learn how to shape-shift your body?" He picked her up and placed her in a wooden cage. "Stay inside this cage for the rest of the night. You almost ruined everything. That boy must take the Fire and Ice experience. We can't let Cugbert brand him."

Zita peered through the wooden slats. She remained a rabbit in a prison without her magic. Erik's fault.

CHAPTER 32

For two days, the caravan ascended the mountain, winding back and forth across the rocky terrain. The only relief to the climb and rest for the mastodons occurred in meadows scattered in the mountains. On the morning of the third day, Erik stood next to Roden as Obadiah doled out fur jackets, hats and fur-lined boots to the handlers.

Erik breathed in the sharp, brisk mountain air. "Why do we need these? Aren't we just going to cross over the mountain peak and descend?"

Obadiah said, "We continue the ascent for half the day and then reach the plateau. Nothing blocks the wind up there, and where we used to get rain, you can now expect snow."

Erik shook the fur jacket, and dust and hair flew around him. "Do you expect me to wear this smelly old thing?"

"You can wear it or freeze, I don't care." Obadiah continued, "The first trip I took with the caravan I was skeptical about the jackets, too. You work hard walking up the mountain and don't think you'll get cold, but you will."

"A plateau? This whole Ice Castle deal is making more sense now. How high is the plateau?"

"Two miles or more."

Erik said, "Even though it's summer, the Ice Castle might be high enough in the mountains to never melt, assuming they made the castle of ice."

Obadiah smiled and said, "You're a mug, aren't ya?"

Erik wondered what he meant.

"When you reach the plateau, you need to tie yourself to the mastodon. The winds are brutal. Where's Al?"

"He's not feeling well. He's sleeping."

"Well, that's just too bad, ain't it? I'll show you and you can teach Al."

Obadiah grabbed a leather strap and tied a complicated knot to the mastodon's harness. "Make a knot like this that will keep you attached to Roden." Obadiah patted the beast's side. "If the straps are in the wrong place, one shake of Roden's head will fling you in the air and to your death. Give it a burl."

Erik tried to tie the knot the same way Obadiah had.

Obadiah yelled. "No, too close to his tusks, Roden will whack you into tomorrow."

Erik untied the knot and moved it behind the animal's ears.

"That's better, but place the knot along this section of leather strap." Obadiah pointed to two locations on the strap. "The belt slips along here. The wind blows so hard you'll want to move behind the mastodon for protection from the wind. To direct Roden, you will have movement along this tether to get close to Roden's head."

Again Erik tied the strap.

"See how it doesn't slide? You tied it too tight."

Erik gave an exasperated sigh, "I can't get the knot right."

"Your life depends on it; pay attention." Obadiah untied Erik's last attempt and slowed the movement. "Cross the two lengths here and push this loop through this hole." The knot locked in and he showed it sliding on the leather strap. "Give it a burl."

Three tries later, Erik mastered the knot and watched it slip along the strap.

"That's a brilliant start, but practice today and teach Al. Work together or Roden bolts. One walks with the mastodon while the other walks along the wagons. The goal is to work together and stay warm."

"Where do I attach the other end?" A large, metal loop was riveted to the other end of the strap.

"Put this around your waist." Obadiah handed Erik a belt.

The four inch wide belt had corresponding snap hooks on the left and right sides. This allowed him to walk on the right or left sides of Roden and lock the strap's metal loop in tight. Erik saw how the strap attached to the animal hooked into his belt. He pulled hard against the strap. "Holds nice."

"Put on the jacket."

Erik shook his head, reluctant to wear the nasty, smelly jacket. Then he shook the jacket once again in hopes of removing whatever caused the nastiness and put it on. It was baggy, but warm.

Obadiah grabbed the side of Erik's coat. "See, a hole in the jacket allows the strap to hook into the belt." Obadiah dug through the heavy fur, found the hole, and poked Erik in the side. "Here."

It was more difficult to clip in the buckle with the coat on, but Erik managed it.

"Practice these knots before we reach the plateau. This all becomes difficult with cold, numb hands."

Erik hung the coats on a wagon and tucked the leather boots into the large coat pockets. He shook Al awake and began hooking Roden to the wagons.

* * * *

The caravan started up the mountain and Erik educated Al on the mechanics of the strap, knot and belt systems. Al learned quickly as a school student, but not today. "What's wrong?" Erik asked.

Al said, "I feel terrible. I have a headache, I'm nauseated and I'm having trouble breathing. I don't know if I'll make it."

Erik said, "Think about it. This plateau must be higher than Denver, Colorado. Are you getting altitude sickness?"

"Maybe."

Erik thought Al ran out of inhalers weeks ago. If he's experiencing asthma induced issues, there were no self-remedies Al could do. Erik doubted the locals had medicines to help.

"Learn these knots before we get to the top of the mountain. According to Obadiah, our lives depend on it."

"Just let me die. It hurts too much to breathe."

"The higher we travel, the less oxygen is available, which explains your breathing problems," Erik said. "Do you want me to heal you or see if Obadiah has a local remedy?"

"Forget the local medicines. He'll try bloodletting or give me a concoction made from crazy insects and plants. I'll take my chances with death."

Erik attempted to put his hands on Al's head, and Al jerked away. "I'll be all right."

Al's face was pale and splotchy. The thin wizard had suffered on this trip, for the food was scarce and rationed. Al's weight loss looked extreme. His skin drew tight over his skull.

Erik wondered if Al could survive this trip. But he said, "Whatever you want is fine with me."

Roden's speed increased as they crested a hill, and the pine forest ended abruptly. They entered an area of shrubs, hardy cactus and creosote bushes. The flat plain spread before them. They had topped the plateau. The colors changed from the forest greens and blues to desert reds and browns. In the distance, tall jagged hills rose from the plateau, giant sentinels guarding the desert. The wind blew strong and brisk from the north.

Erik shivered and reached for the jackets.

Al vomited.

CHAPTER 33

Erik woke the next morning to wind howling around the wagons. Dark clouds hung low enough to touch, and they carried the whisper of snow. Erik wore the smelly fur jacket, boots and a fur hat. The mastodons gyrated their heads and bellowed. Two of them engaged in a pushing match. Obadiah blamed it on the weather change. Erik hoped there weren't going to be many days as dangerous as this was shaping up to be.

Erik watched his friend take a bite of beef jerky. Obadiah had watched the boys, recognized the problem, and recommended Al eat more to help counteract the altitude sickness.

Al ate three bites and vomited again. Unless Al solved his altitude issues, he would die. He needed to drink more water and eat more, but nothing stayed in his stomach.

"Are you okay, buddy?" Erik asked.

Al said, "No."

Obadiah walked by. "Get moving. In about five hours we'll reach the lake where we'll swap out the wheels with sled runners and continue the journey."

"Sleds?" Erik asked. He pictured images of Scandinavians from the eighteenth century pulling wagons over frozen winter lakes.

"It'll be faster on the ice."

Al said, "You're gonna put the weight of these wagons and mastodons on a frozen lake? You guys are crazy."

Obadiah checked Roden's harness, nodding in approval. "It's the only way to the Ice Castle. Do you want to get caught on this mountain during the winter? It'll take six months to go around the lake hiking up and down four mountain peaks. The lake's faster. Move."

Erik commanded Roden to move, and they fell in behind the caravan.

Obadiah walked away and yelled, "The weather only gets worse, so when the snow flies, strap into Roden if you want to survive."

Erik couldn't imagine it getting colder, though he remembered the frigid Montana winters on Earth where he drove the car on snowy roads and shoveled snow off the driveway. There were times his feet and fingers were so numb, they became useless. Then he had entered the warmth of the kitchen where Mom made cookies and hot chocolate, and his fingers hurt with a million pinpricks as his body warmed. He didn't know what to call these feelings. Was he homesick?

For the first two hours, the caravan proceeded without incident as the land lay flat with huge monolithic rocks poking toward the sky. Dark tattered clouds lowered as if drawn by the monoliths.

The wind, frigid and brisk, intensified, and hard wet sleet slashed their faces.

The path changed direction, and the caravan turned straight into the wind and driving snow. Erik huddled next to Roden for heat and protection from the stinging snow pellets. It can't get worse than this, Erik thought. He pulled the foul-smelling fur hat, still greasy from the hair of the person who wore it previously, lower on his ears.

An hour later, the caravan rounded another bend in the landscape. Erik lost the protection Roden provided and now pellets landed on his neck, melted and trickled frigid tentacles down his back. The sleet changed to heavy, wet snow. Not yet blizzard conditions, but Erik watched Roden's direction to make sure he followed the wagons ahead of them. As the snow deepened, he struggled to keep the wagon wheels in the tracks of the wagons in front of them.

Two hours later, they stopped.

"Let's get a move on." Obadiah shouted commands as he staggered through the snow, addressing the line of mastodon handlers. "Remove the wheels and attach the sleds."

"Are we at the lake?" Al asked, his voice a hoarse, weak whisper.

Obadiah said, "Not yet. The snow slowed us, and we're still two hours out. But it's deep enough for sleds, and the scouts we sent out this morning say the rest of the trail to the lake is snow covered."

Three men arrived at Erik's wagons. One carried a long wooden handle, jointed to a wooden square base. The other two hauled long, wooden sled runners. The first man placed the base part of the jointed tool under the wheel axle. With a mighty jump and downward shove on the wooden handle, the wagon wheels rose four inches off the ground. The deep snow barely touched the bottom of the raised wheel.

A second man produced a wrench, a square metal opening on a sixteen inch handle, and took off the wheel nut. They worked with efficiency, reminding Erik of an Indianapolis Five Hundred race-car pit crew. In less than thirty minutes they swapped out the four wheels for two runners for each of the four wagons Roden pulled.

The oldest man said, "Okay, rest time is over, move these wagons."

Erik stood on the side of Roden that offered protection from the blowing snow. He shouted, "Fo," and the sleds glided across the snow.

Roden easily advanced the sleds, forcing Erik to jog. The mighty mastodon's eyes squinted against the blowing snow. Erik attempted to guide Roden to stay in the tracks from the sleds before him. The deep snow became a hindrance to the humans, and Erik was forced to stay in the tracks of the previous wagon as the sled tracks changed to slick ice. Erik imagined being trampled by Roden or slipping under the wagon sleds.

Erik yelled, "Are you okay, Al?"

Al didn't respond.

"Al?"

Erik had strapped into the harness, following Obadiah's instructions. Had Al? In his weakened state, could Al keep pace? How could he check on Al, without stopping Roden and the wagons? Maybe they needed extra stopping space in the slick snow to prevent the animals behind from running into them.

"Al, answer me, are you okay?"

The wind blew harder, making a high-pitch whine as it blew around the animal and wagons. Was it the howling wind preventing Erik from hearing Al's answer or his weak voice?

Erik tried to look underneath Roden's belly to glimpse footprints or legs on the other side, but the straps prevented him from leaning down far enough.

Roden grunted and pulled to the right as Erik leaned, driving Erik into a pile of snow.

"Whoa boy, back on the track, big fella." Erik guided Roden back to the sled path.

"Al?"

At the speed Roden was pulling, Erik didn't have time to un-strap from Roden and race to the other side to check on Al. If Al hadn't strapped in and lost contact with Roden would another team behind stop and check on him? He knew the answer.

The snowflakes grew bigger and stuck on Erik's beard and eyelashes. The wind blasted over the top of Roden and around his sides, pounding Erik with its ferocity. *Mastodons are made for blizzards. Al and I aren't.*

Erik ignored the flakes and wondered what Al was experiencing on the other side of the animal. In Al's weakened state, he might not be walking, but just hanging from Roden and dragging in the snow. If he'd remembered to clip in.

If they reached the Ice Castle, but Al died on the way, should Erik capture the golden crown by himself? The crown didn't matter, Al was his friend and Erik couldn't let his friend die.

Erik shouted at the top of his voice, "Al. Are you okay? Do we need to stop?"

Then the sled lurched on Al's side, the wagon tilted as it wobbled over an object and then whacked the ground as it cleared.

"Al!"

Roden continued to charge ahead.

CHAPTER 34

Erik yelled into the wind, "Al! Are you okay?" Roden stomped through the mounting piles of snow.

The second wagon bumped, tilted, slid and plopped back into the track.

Erik suddenly didn't care if the caravan lost speed or the back wagons smashed into him, he commanded Roden to stop. At the speed they were moving, the wagons slid. Wagon number three in the train bumped, angled and slid, but didn't return to level. Roden came to a halt, and the wagons stopped. Wagon three was tilted.

"Come on Roden, that's Al under that wagon. Move." Erik nudged Roden until the third wagon slid into the rut.

Erik removed his straps and slogged through the snow until he reached wagon number three. He stepped into deep snow, slid over the wagon tongue, fell, recovered and reached the other side. A large lump lay un-moving in the snow behind the wagon.

Erik reached out. "Al, are you okay?" How could he be okay? He just had three heavy wagons slide over him. He had to be dead.

Brushing the snow away, Erik found only a boulder. Where was Al? If he was all right, he should have checked on the problem, too. Erik tramped up the line of wagons, fighting through the biting blizzard.

The blowing snow made visibility difficult, but he reached Roden and found Al, strapped in, but hanging at a precarious angle as his feet dangled in the snow.

"How long have you dragged like this?"

Al didn't answer. His ice-covered, cracked lips moved, but no sound emerged.

Erik unbuckled his friend and helped Al out of the wind. Al staggered through the deep snow as Erik half-helped and half carried him.

Sheltered behind a wagon, Erik looked into Al's eyes. There was life, but it was weak.

Two handlers arrived next to Erik. "Why did you stop?"

"I hit a boulder." Erik said.

"They designed the sleds to slide over them."

"Well, it didn't."

"We have to move this caravan, we're falling behind the rest of the group and in this snow we don't want to lose contact and miss the trail. We're near the ice and once you lose the trail in the ice, you can count yourself as dead."

Erik yelled, "Well go look at the boulder and figure out how to get around it, I need to care for my friend."

"You know Hadrian, leave your friend, he's dead weight. If he can't make the trip, he gets left in the snow. No exceptions."

Al said in a whisper, "Leave me, I'm ready to die."

"I'm not leaving you. I'll tie you to the sled. You can rest."

"That's not how it's done," the other handler said. "Either he leads the animal or he dies. A person is expendable. We have to keep moving, or we all die."

"My friend isn't dying on this trip." Erik wasn't sure he believed that.

Erik examined Al's eyes that contained no passion or will to live. The altitude and blizzard were too much.

Erik grabbed his friend and dragged him to the first wagon where he placed Al's feet on the sled runners. He found two cleats where he could tie in Al's straps.

"Hold these straps and keep your feet on the sled no matter what. Do you understand?"

Al mumbled something which Erik took as affirmation.

Erik yelled at the other handlers, "Get back to your mastodons and let's go."

They scowled, but Erik didn't care.

He strapped into Roden and shouted, "Fo."

Roden peered at Erik with a forlorn expression as if to say, "I want to ride, too."

Erik didn't care, "Fo, now." He smacked Roden.

The animal leaned forward and pulled. They went three feet and stopped. Despite Roden's straining, the wagons didn't move. The boulder prevented forward motion. While in motion they slid over the boulder, but without the speed they couldn't get the momentum to negotiate it.

"Hold." Erik squawked, and the beast relaxed.

Erik removed his straps and ran back to the third wagon again, repeating his steps over the wagon tongue. The sled, pinned behind the boulder, could not slide over the top despite the curl of the sled.

The other handlers approached, "Get moving."

"I'm stuck."

"They're idiots, these two, we should go around them and catch up with the caravan or we'll lose the path," the taller of the two handlers said.

"No," the other let out a deep breath, "they carry too much of the mastodon's food. We have to help. Move the wagons back and we'll try to guide it around the boulder."

Erik sprinted in the deep snow, sliding and slipping to reach Roden. He guided the massive beast backwards, trying to push the wagons back.

One handler who had stayed with Erik said, "Give me ten seconds then charge forward, we think we have enough space to guide it around the rock. Ten seconds." The handler ran back to the boulder.

Erik counted to ten, trying not to hurry. Then he slapped Roden and said, "Fo."

Roden strained. The row of wagons increased speed, slowed and then with a final jerk, they accelerated. Wagon number four angled over the rock, straightened, and they pushed forward.

The blizzard pounded, and the snow drifted higher, making it difficult to see the tracks left by the caravan. Erik coaxed Roden to move faster in the white-out conditions and hoped they were following the others.

CHAPTER 35

The blizzard pounded Erik, and he shaded his eyes with his hand, trying to see farther ahead. The path ahead was filled with snow, only faint outlines showed the sled marks of the caravan. Erik slapped Roden's shoulder, "Hurry."

They needed to find the lake while the path was visible and catch up to the rest of the caravan. He worried about Al tied to a wagon behind him, but if they didn't find the rest of the caravan, they both died.

The snow pummeled Erik's cheeks, the wind howled, and he thought he heard voices. He couldn't see through the blizzard, but he hoped they were getting closer.

Erik didn't know if he was maintaining the proper course, but the voices encouraged him. They sounded human to him, but on this planet he didn't know for sure. Wolves howled in the distance. Would there be a nice, simple transition to the frozen lake, maybe a boat ramp or slope?

The storm weakened, and the voices sounded closer, but so did the wolves' howls. The landscape changed abruptly from level to a sharp downhill, and Roden picked up speed. Eric ran, slipping and sliding in the snow, trying to stay upright to keep from being dragged.

His neck was stiff and strained. If they went too fast, he thought they might crash into the ice, break through and fall into the icy water. Erik wanted to catch up with the caravan, but didn't want to slam into the others if they waited on the lake for him. The wagons' speed scared him, and he knew this was madness. Erik ran to keep pace with the beast. He had to slow Roden down.

He hollered at Roden, "Stop. Stop. Stop!" Over and over, pulling on the harness. He dug his heels in the snow.

Snow sprayed from Erik's heels, their momentum building as they raced downhill.

A red glow appeared through the blizzard as if a lighthouse burned in the distance, and Roden and Erik were headed straight for it.

"Stop you crazy beast."

Roden was out of control, a massive frightened beast trying to escape from a screaming human. No yelling, cajoling, or cursing slowed his pace. Erik felt small; his one-hundred-fifty pounds was nothing compared to the trampling multi-ton mastodon. *We have to stop before we reach the lake.*

Then he knew he was hearing shouts. The red glow grew bigger, closer and brighter.

Erik worked hard to control the careening creature. Roden's feet thundered in the snow as he ran, the sound of a herd of buffalo instead of one solitary mastodon.

The red glow turned the blowing snow into a dull, reddish-gray haze, and Erik smelled smoke in the air.

Roden, Erik and the wagons passed a group of people who scrambled out of the way yelling, "Are you mad? Stop!"

Roden didn't stop. Images of fatal outcomes flashed through Erik's mind. They could run straight into the fire. Smash into other mastodons and wagons. Trample handlers who didn't move fast enough. Roden could lead him and the wagons past the caravan onto the ice, maybe many miles away before Roden stopped. Doomed. No scenario ended in survival.

They had reached the safety of the caravan where warmth, food, fellowship and help for Al were expected, but instead of comfort, death would be their fate. He dug his heels in harder, running a few feet, then planting his heels, but his leather boots slid and did little to slow the panicked Roden.

He pounded on Roden's shoulder, which didn't help. Nothing helped. Erik lurched, stumbled, and slid toward the fire.

Mastodons bellowed. Handlers jumped from the careening beast. Erik and Roden continued toward a giant bonfire. Now he could see logs piled ten feet high, burning yellow, red and blue.

Heat from the fire reached Erik a hundred yards away. He yearned to stand near it and warm himself, but Roden might fly through the logs and carry them two to three miles on the ice before they burned to death. Ash rose from the burning fire and blew toward them mixed with the snow.

Roden slowed, but it seemed too little, too late. Now they were thirty yards from the burning tower. Erik was sure they couldn't stop in such a short distance.

Handlers ran in front of the careening beast, waving their hands in Roden's face and yelling, "stop," and then they threw themselves sideways to keep from being trampled.

Little by little, Roden slowed.

Erik said, "Easy Roden." He rubbed the beast's shoulder.

Suddenly, Roden halted, ten yards from the bonfire. The abrupt stop threw Erik in the air. His strap, clipped to the beast, kept him from flying into the flames. Erik cried out in pain as the belt strap, wrapped around his waist, compressed his organs. He felt skin rubbing on his clothes under the belt. The burn of a road rash spread around his midsection.

The sledded wagons didn't stop, their momentum carried them into Roden, and they zig-zagged as they continued to slide, pivoting on the hitches. Even Roden couldn't hold steady against the combined weight. Erik, Roden and the wagons skidded one yard, two yards, five yards and came to a stop near the enormous bonfire.

The beast bellowed. His sides cascaded in and out, moving massive amounts of oxygen, while Erik felt like a rag doll thrown from a moving car.

Obadiah ran up to Erik, "G'Day, Cobber. That's an amazing entrance."

Erik doubled over and clutched his knees, gasping for oxygen. Then he remembered Al. In the hurry to get to the caravan, Erik forgot Al.

"Quick, check on Al."

"Where is he?"

Erik struggled to unhook the straps from Roden. In between gasps he pointed to the wagons, "Over there." Adrenaline coursed through his body, as sweat puddled in the small of his back, turning cool in the blowing snow.

They trotted back to the wagon and found Al, straps wrapped around his wrists, and he leaned back, inert. The clip still secured him to the wagon.

Is my friend still alive?

CHAPTER 36

A group of handlers untied the straps holding Al to the wagons, and removed Al's limp body from the sled. They wrapped him in a blanket and carried him to the fire. The bonfire had been built on a minor slope, still on land and not on the ice.

Obadiah asked, "Doesn't look good. He's half-a-crook or more."

"I don't know." Erik held Al's stiff hand, trying to discern some warmth. He felt a finger twitch. "He's still alive."

Hadrian bellowed, "If he can't travel, we leave him here, otherwise he's dead weight."

Erik looked at his friend. No way could he leave Al to die alone on this plateau. *How could Hadrian even think of treating Al like a broken wheel or something you threw in the garbage?* He pictured an old snow shovel he used to use on Earth until the metal bent in so many directions it became unusable, and he had tossed it in the trash. But his friend still had life in him; he wasn't a broken shovel. At least Erik hoped his friend would make it. They needed Al to complete their mission

Al's eyes moved beneath his closed eyelids as if he dreamed, and a moan escaped his lips.

"See, he's still alive." Erik said relieved.

Hadrian grunted, "When the remaining sleds arrive, we rest an hour and then we leave. He better be ready." The caravan leader walked away.

Who is cruel enough to leave a person lying near death in the middle of frozen nowhere?

Obadiah brought a bowl of hot soup for Erik. "Better eat this before you suffer like your friend. You need water, protein and fruit in these extreme conditions."

"Thanks," the soup contained small pieces of meat and Erik enjoyed it better than the beef jerky the handlers received each day. "How many days to the Ice Castle?"

"Five days usually, but we're way behind schedule. Hadrian now plans traveling eighteen-hour days and resting the animals six hours."

"That's brutal on the mastodons." Erik said. He thought of Al. Could Al recover if they walked eighteen-hour days?

Erik rubbed his hands as he sat on a log near the fire. Pins and needles pain electrified his fingers as his blood began to circulate better. The hot soup tasted delicious and warmed him.

"Will Hadrian abandon Al?" Erik asked.

Obadiah said, "I've seen it happen. A broken leg, an illness or someone too tired to continue produces the same result. He leaves them to die. We never find the bones on the return trip. The winter wolves eat them."

This is a brutal world. Erik didn't remember Earth being so raw, but they grew up in a tiny little town in Montana. They didn't see the hardships and senseless murders in the large cities or the rest of the world. Maybe nature wasn't like the Disney movies he'd seen.

He thought of Mom. What was she doing right now? Did she know they had traveled back to the world she'd purposely left? Did she miss him? He pictured her alone in the house sitting at the kitchen table with a cup of coffee in her hand, looking at photographs of him.

Al coughed and Erik appraised his friend. The warmth of the fire had melted the snow off his beard, and some color was returning to Al's face. The boy gave a start and then opened his eyes.

"Al." Erik touched Al's shoulder as he tried to rise. "Relax."

"Where are we? Are we at the Ice Castle?" Al asked.

"Take it easy. Obadiah, bring soup."

"I've had bad dreams with monsters chasing me, volcanos exploding, wolves tearing my flesh, and fish eating me. I'm so hungry." Al whispered the words in a gravelly voice.

"Rest. I have soup coming. How're you feeling?"

"Just leave me to die."

"No way; we're going to the Ice Castle and —"

Al collapsed to the ground.

Erik touched his friend. The warm soup had renewed Erik, and now he needed to revive Al, to give him a chance to live and realize his dream to capture the golden crown. Al never allowed Erik to heal him before, but Al couldn't say no this time.

He settled his hands on Al's forehead, the way Cugbert taught, and explored deep into Al's body. Nothing was broken. Broken bones were easy to heal. This was different. Healing required help from the sick person who needed to respond and help the body heal. Erik received no response from Al. Had Al lost the will to live? His body refused to help.

Erik hadn't yet learned what to do in this situation. He sensed a malnourished, frail and emaciated body, unable to bring energy to the technique. Cugbert once said the mind required healing in cases like this, but the procedure was dangerous and required more training.

Erik didn't care. Al needed mending. They couldn't release his father and the other stone warriors without the golden crown, and they needed Al's help to capture the crown. Sure, other wizards might have the magical ability, but Erik knew this was Al's quest.

He placed his hands once more on Al's forehead, and Erik took a deep cleansing breath. One more breath and Erik delved into Al's brain; he would either help his friend or kill him.

One section of the brain appeared alert and responsive, but toward the back of Al's skull darkness reigned. Erik sensed no vigor or energy from that region. Erik searched deeper and found a wall, hard as bricks. He sensed a squishy brain in the front, but the back seemed frozen or like concrete. Should he break through the wall? Was it supposed to be there? He'd never searched a brain. Did the wall serve a natural purpose to the body? If he broke the wall, what damage might he cause?

Obadiah touched Erik on the shoulder. "Here's the soup. Hadrian says we leave in ten minutes."

Erik broke concentration with Al. He needed more than ten minutes to plan a strategy to handle the wall. What would help? Force soup into Al and see if the added nourishment helped?

"Come on buddy, eat this soup." Erik lifted Al, helping him sit straight. "Eat, it will help."

Al opened his eyes, "No! No more food, it makes me barf." Al tried to nudge the spoon away, but his hand just dropped to the ground.

"Eat, you've got to warm up."

"Let me sleep."

Erik needed to force food on Al to prevent hypothermia in the frigid mountain air. In this weather a cold core meant death.

"One spoonful will be okay." Erik shoved the spoon into Al's mouth.

He tried again and Al sucked the liquid into his mouth. The vomiting didn't always happen right after he ate. Sometimes Al lasted thirty minutes before he emptied his stomach. Spoonful after spoonful, Erik fed his friend the broth but none of the meat in the soup. The next feeding they'd experiment with meat.

Color returned to Al's face. "Al, wake up and eat."

Hadrian strode by and said, "Harness the mastodons, we're heading out. Leave the boy, he won't make it."

"He'll make it." Erik snarled.

"Slow us down, I'll leave you both." Hadrian stalked away barking to other handlers, "Hitch the wagons, and let's get out of here."

Erik said, "Obadiah, help me tie Al into a hammock, so he can stay warm."

"We don't have time for that; leave him."

"We make time." Erik grabbed the younger boy by the coat and forced him over to Al, "Help me carry him to the wagon."

They each grabbed Al under an arm and dragged him through the snow to the wagon. The air was raw and wintry away from the warmth of the fire. Could Al survive the rest of the journey or even persevere through the next twelve hours?

With Obadiah's help, Erik rolled Al into the hammock. They covered him with two blankets and secured it all with rope.

The snow stopped, the wind blew the clouds apart, and stars twinkled in the night sky. Two moons provided light on the ice.

Erik hooked Roden to the wagons, working in double-time to keep from feeling Hadrian's wrath.

Hadrian shouted, "Move out."

CHAPTER 37

The sleds ran ten hours straight, long into the night, and the wind died and the snow stopped. A million stars shimmered in the darkness. A comet brightened the northern horizon with a tail that covered a quarter of the celestial sphere. Erik gaped at the comet which was illuminating the sky, brighter than any planet, trailed by a massive blue tail.

After the moons set, Hadrian called a halt as darkness slowed movement on the ice. Erik removed Roden's harness and fed the beast. Even Roden looked tired, probably because Al couldn't help lighten the load with magic.

He finished his chores and checked on Al. "Hey buddy, you awake?"

Al opened his eyes and blinked. "Erik, is that you?"

"Yeah, you okay?"

Al squirmed in the makeshift hammock. "Where am I? What am I doing in this cocoon? Get me out of here, I'm being eaten."

Erik chuckled, "It's not a cocoon, Obadiah and I put you in the hammock. Do you want help?"

"Yes, help me out of here, I'm starving."

That sounded encouraging. Erik struggled with the hammock. Al's weight in the hammock made it difficult to untie the knots. He didn't want to drop his friend on the ice.

Kenneth Brown

In a few minutes Al wobbled to his feet, swayed back and forth, and steadied.

"Where are we?" Al asked.

"We've traveled for ten hours on the lake. The sleds just glide."

The other handlers huddled around a fire.

Erik said, "Fire on the ice, isn't that dangerous?"

"Ha," Obadiah said, "to you summer-lubbers it might seem dangerous, but educated winter anglers won't have problems."

The fire was built of five logs arranged in a row on the ice, topped by another layer of five logs arranged perpendicular to the first row. Then a row laid in the same direction as the first row, while a fourth crisscrossed row blazed on top.

"Won't it burn a hole in the ice?" Erik asked.

"No worries, mate, she'll be right. The coals soak up the water and as the logs burn they fall on the wet ash and coals. This will keep us toasty the rest of the night."

They sat on a log and warmed themselves by the fire. Obadiah handed them an orange and a slab of beef jerky.

Al peeled the orange. He took off part of the rind and threw it on the ice.

"Hey what are you doing?" Obadiah asked.

"Peeling the orange so I can eat it."

Obadiah said, "No, eat the whole thing, peels and everything. We don't leave waste on the ice. Winter wolves find the food and pursue us like home-sick puppies."

Al gathered up his orange peel and chewed into it.

Obadiah said, "Al's appetite is back."

Al finished the orange in a few seconds and chomped on the jerky. He gazed skyward and asked, "How often do you see that comet?"

"What do you mean?" Obadiah passed a cloth bag filled with walnuts around the fire. Everyone took a handful and passed it to the next guy.

"The comet. How many years before it returns?"

"Every year."

Erik thought back to his studies of Halley's Comet that returned for a vacation to the sun every seventy-five years.

One handler said, "The comet represents the birth of a new dragon. A flying dragon lays an egg in the sky and as the comet nears the sun, the baby dragon cracks the egg and releases fire from his belly. The comet tail is the dragon shooting fire into the night sky, and the meteor showers that saturate the planet after the comet passes are pieces of the broken egg."

"What?" Al asked. "The comet is a flying dragon egg?"

"Yeah, that's what I said. The dragon flies around the sun and descends to earth in the southern hemisphere."

"That's a doozy." Al said.

Erik touched Al's arm and whispered, "Easy Al, remember these people have different beliefs than we do."

Obadiah said, "The caravan has to worry about the asteroid shower after the comet disappears. That's why Hadrian pushes the caravan hard. We have to reach the shore before the asteroid showers pummel the ice."

Erik said, "What do you mean asteroid shower? That would be a wonderful experience, sitting on the ice, far from light pollution, watching asteroids streak across the sky."

"Yeah, we did that at home a few times; woke in the middle of the night and watched the meteor showers." Al tossed walnuts into his mouth.

"No, these asteroids crash into the frozen lake." Obadiah threw another small log on the fire. "A meteorite can hit you, or the ice explodes and you drown in the freezing water."

"Are you serious? The meteorites land on the ice?" Erik asked.

Obadiah sat on the log, "Land on the ice, explode on the ice, break the ice, and if you're still on the ice, you probably die."

"Cool. We could locate a ton of meteors to study. You think they come from the comet? Or should I say from the dragon egg?" Al smiled.

Obadiah said, "No, he's wrong about the dragon egg."

"Yeah, what do you think?" The other handler asked.

Obadiah said, "My dad told me the god, Velidred, sends a message to his followers showing his dominant power over the planet and the skies. Velidred is all-powerful and shows his influence each summer to control the people of Aloheno."

Erik asked, "Do sacrifices occur when the comet arrives, like the eclipse of the moons?"

"No, nothing like that. Our village throws parties and a week-long celebration. In our town, men wear animal skins and women chase after them, and when they capture them the men become their servants for one week. Many people marry after the celebrations finish."

"A courting ritual rather than make this man my slave?" Erik took a bite of jerky.

"Yeah, it's all fun and games. We drink a lot of Ouuzool and the town has fun.

Erik looked at Al and they both smiled. Erik was glad to see Al smiling. Maybe he was feeling better.

Another handler commented, "There's no dragon. A wizard in the mountains has magnificent powers, and displays his wizardry by firing powerful energy into the heavens, exploding a star. The star's energy dissipates each night until it disappears. The next night the wizard explodes another star and we see the comet."

Al said, "Those are marvelous stories, but comets are balls of ice, rock and dust that circle the sun and as they near the sun the ice and dust break off the rock to form an ionized gas tail in the solar wind."

The three handlers glanced at each other, waited a second and laughed.

Obadiah said, "A good one, mate."

Erik stared into the night sky, looking at the stars. A band of many stars in the sky resembled the Milky Way. "Al, would you say we are in a spiral galaxy?"

Al studied the night sky, "Yeah, for sure a spiral galaxy."

"Do you think it's the Milky Way?"

"It makes sense we're still in the same galaxy, but I couldn't point to Earth."

A dog howled in the distance, followed by another dog and then others.

"Are those dogs on the ice?"

Obadiah said, "Not dogs, winter wolves. That's why we traveled so far tonight, to distance the caravan from them. Normally, they stay near shore, but if food is hard to find, they chase us. Don't leave food out, and make sure you stay with the caravan."

"How far from shore are we?" Al asked.

"I would say thirty to forty miles at least."

"And the winter wolves follow us, in case we drop food?" Al rubbed the back of his neck.

Kenneth Brown

"A pack of fifteen winter wolves can slay two mastodons in minutes. Be careful, they like the taste of humans even better, so stay close to people who can help you."

CHAPTER 38

The next day, Erik convinced Al to stay in the hammock. Al said, "Come on, I feel better, I can walk with you and Roden. The food I ate stayed down, I'm fine."

Erik said, "Let me check your vitals, and he tried to place his healing hands on Al."

"No, I told you I don't want you to heal me."

"Come on, man. I promise not to heal you, I wanna do a wellness check."

"It's unnecessary. I'm fine."

"I checked you out before we reached the ice. You're malnourished, weak, and you haven't gained enough strength to walk with Roden."

"Nope. I don't want you using your hocus pocus magic healing inside my body like that."

"I thought you were dying."

Al said, "I don't care, ask me first."

"You were non-responsive, almost dead."

"I'm here now, and I don't want you touching me. You might break something."

Erik gazed at his fur boots, "You have a wall."

"A wall?"

"In your brain."

"You were in my brain with your healing powers? Why?" *There's a wall in my brain? Is that what prevents me from doing magic and using and communicating with the staff?*

"Yes, there's a wall in your brain. I didn't touch it, but it didn't look right."

"I'm walking with Roden today." *Erik delved into my brain when I couldn't do anything about it? Is that the source of my strange dreams?*

Al walked with Roden for several miles, but he didn't last the full eighteen hours. After four hours on his feet, he returned to the hammock and slept six hours. They repeated that pattern the rest of the day. Al walked as far as he could and then clambered into the hammock. The weather was frosty, but sunny, and Erik didn't need Al's help to guide Roden on the ice.

The following day, as Al walked next to Roden, he said, "Tell me about the wall in my brain."

Erik said, "Nothing to tell. Imagine a brick wall around a patio."

"A brick wall around a patio?"

"Yeah, but it's high. The wall prevents light from entering or information from leaving."

"Like a computer firewall?" Al asked. *A firewall that prevents access to parts of my brain. Did the staff create the firewall or is it from something Gadiel did?*

Erik said, "Yeah, your brain lit up like a map showing all the city lights in the United States during the night. There was a network of lights and movement between different parts of the brain, but they were all blocked by this wall, and nothing occurred behind the wall."

"What did you do?"

"I wanted to probe the wall. A little, but someone interrupted me."

"I'm really glad you stopped. Some friend you are. You might have left me brain dead."

On the morning of the third day on the ice, before the caravan started, Gadiel walked by the boys and invited them to dine with him that night.

Al and Erik continued guiding Roden and the wagons over the ice, a monotonous journey with no change in the scenery except for the changing cloud shapes. No trees, birds, landmarks, not even mountain peaks in the distance.

"How big do you think this lake is?" Erik asked.

Al said, "A little math to determine miles traveled each day and the number of days traveled, we'd get close. Knowing the circumference of the world and planet curvature might give us an answer. Imagine being on an ocean so far from land you don't see landmarks because of the curvature of the planet. I'm not sure what Hadrian uses to plot his course. Are we walking in circles?"

"They must have a compass or something similar on this planet," Erik said. "Why do you think Gadiel wants us to dine with him?"

"Maybe he's finished studying my staff and wants to give it back."

"Will he give it to you?"

"He better or I will zap him."

"Can you zap him?"

"Probably not, my magic comes and goes. Sometimes it surges and I have magic and other times nothing."

Roden hitched his shoulders and snorted.

"Is there a pattern?" Erik asked, "Hey did you see that?"

"What?"

"A puff of smoke in the distance, is it another caravan or land?"

"Where?"

"Over this way, on my side of Roden."

"Land would be nice. This landscape is so boring, I'll take anything."

They traveled on as the sun drifted in the sky. Today, Al didn't need to rest in the hammock. He beat the altitude sickness and didn't die. They changed sides after a brief break, and Al decided the puffs of smoke originated from a volcano spewing mini eruptions of ash. The cone of the volcano took shape as they traveled.

Erik said, "Gadiel mentioned the Fire and Ice experience to you. Will you take it?"

"If he returns my staff, I'll consider it. I need the staff to be a proper wizard." Al thought, without the staff I'm just a dude, but with the staff, people respect me as a great and mighty wizard. I need the staff back.

"I took the Fire and Ice experience from Cugbert."

"Yeah?"

"He made me walk over burning coals."

"No way. How did that go?"

"I can't tell you."

"What?"

"Cugbert told me it's bad form to tell others about the experience."

"Come on, man. At least tell me about walking across a bed of coals. There's no way I'm doing that. Get my feet all burned. I just got so I can walk again, I don't need third-degree burns on my feet."

"It's weird, the coals didn't burn my feet, and after four steps, I entered a dreamlike experience."

Al said, "Tell me about the dream experience."

"No, I've said too much already."

"Did you have any adverse effects from doing it?"

"Well, Cugbert mentioned I might die if something went wrong."

"Die? Nope, not doing it."

"That's probably the right decision, because the fire section was the simple part. And I get . . . this feeling . . . that Cugbert is always in my brain. Just sitting and watching."

"Hah, it's settled, I'm not doing it." Al said.

CHAPTER 39

That night, Al sat on the bench next to Erik beside a fire near Gadiel's wagon cabin. Hadrian sat opposite them. Al thought it strange that Gadiel ate outside when he could eat inside. The outside temperature had to be zero degrees Fahrenheit, if not lower. Crystals formed on Al's beard from his breath. His hands never warmed and his fingers cracked and bled in the dry air.

Wagner offered Al and Erik Ouuzool, but both refused the intoxicating liquid. He followed with a bowl of sauerkraut, a handful of raisins and a pickle.

The fire blazed in a metal burner and it sat on a wooden platform like a factory skid that didn't allow the heat to sink into the ice.

Gadiel's wagon door opened, and a dog rushed through the door. The shaggy-haired dog had black hair. Al guessed it weighed thirty to forty pounds and thought it looked similar to a chow-chow on Earth.

The dog approached Erik and sniffed his boots and legs and did the same to Al. *This dog better not pee on me.* It sat on the ice between Al and Erik. The dog didn't bark or beg, but stared intently at Gadiel as if daring him to say something.

Wagner brought the boys a bowl of soup with peas, carrots and meat flavored with hot peppers and onions.

Gadiel said, "Young wizard, Obadiah informed me that your health has improved."

Al thought, nothing escapes the old man. "Yes, the altitude sickness only lasted a few days. I thought I was going to die."

"That would have been unfortunate."

Well, he said the right words, but it didn't sound hopeful. Doesn't he care whether I lie dead on the ice or if I help retrieve the golden crown?

"Yes, I'm alive and it's time we discuss the staff. You've had days to study it and I'm ready to have it back," Al felt happy he managed to confront Gadiel without stuttering or stammering.

"Exactly why you're here tonight. Yes, it's time for you to reclaim your staff. I extracted secrets from the wizards encased in the staff."

"Have you found out why it stopped talking to me?"

"Troubling news about that."

Not what Al wanted to hear. "What do you mean?"

"I'm still examining why the staff isn't communicating with its master."

"I'm still the master, right?"

"You will be its master until you die. This leads me to the Fire and Ice experience we talked about . . . ."

"I'm not doing it," Al blurted, "I spoke with Erik and I don't want to walk on coals."

Gadiel gave Erik a questioning look.

Erik glared at Al and whispered, "I told you not to say anything."

But Gadiel didn't yell at Erik or criticize him. In a soothing voice Gadiel said, "I understand you have concerns, but the ceremony is safe for a wizard of your caliber. It's infrequent that I lose a student."

Al doubted the caliber of his own wizardry. Magic appeared and disappeared with little understanding or control. He experienced days where magic permeated his body and other days where he struggled to light a candle with magic. He didn't know what caused his trouble. The disorder began when the staff stopped talking to him. *I need the staff back. I should have stayed with Sherry and Lily and enrolled in a wizard school instead of taking this trip. How can I get the golden crown when I can't do magic?* He hadn't told Erik his problems, afraid his friend might leave him on the ice to die and be eaten by the winter wolves.

Still talking in the soothing voice, Gadiel said, "I guide with great care, and the process allows you to join other wizards, better wizards than Master Wizard Ishwa. You're welcomed to a society of strong, elite wizards able to do magic beyond simple parlor tricks."

"Before taking this trip you told me you would study my staff and train me in magic, but all you have done is take my staff. Hand back the staff and then I will consider taking the Fire and Ice thing."

The dog next to Al howled, stuck out its purple-black tongue and panted.

Erik rubbed the dog's ears.

Gadiel said nothing for a moment.

Al stared into the fire, afraid to peer into Gadiel's eyes.

Hadrian said, "If you two plan to leave the safety of the caravan to do whatever crazy thing you wizards do, you must understand we are near the volcano and the closer you get to the volcano the thinner the ice."

Gadiel glowered at Hadrian for a moment as if thinking to cut the man's tongue out for talking, but returned his attention to Al.

Nearby handlers laughed, probably at a lewd joke, and the sound traveled in the frosty night air.

Gadiel's eyes turned blacker than normal and a red dot formed in a corner of his left eye. He said, "You understand not all wizards are equal. The survivors of the Fire and Ice experience are members of a select group. A few hundred wizards have participated and survived out of thousands of wizards on the planet, making us an elite society."

Al asked, "Survive?"

The red dot floated across Gadiel's eye and turned into a red scorpion.

The total experience of sitting in the dark night by a fire, yet freezing, with a million stars overhead and the comet plummeting out of view, forced shivers down Al's back.

"Anything worthwhile has risks. There might be pain. Maybe you make a wrong decision and something goes awry. I won't deny the risk, but think of the glory. You'll usher in the return of Alpherge the Great."

"I want the name, Alpherge the Mighty. So people know I'm not my grandfather. I aspire to magnificent accomplishments, too."

"I've heard of your conquests. You mastered the Black Castle dungeon."

Al nodded.

"You killed the Mountain King, did you not?"

Al sat taller on the log. "Yes."

"You freed the Kallurians."

"Yes."

"Then join the Great Wizarding Society. Take the Fire and Ice experience and become Alpherge the Mighty. Grab the opportunity for the respect you deserve if you . . ."

He didn't say anymore. Time seemed to stop. Silence settled around the caravan. The mastodons didn't grunt, the handlers stopped laughing and talking, even the logs on the fire didn't crackle. Gadiel stared at Al.

Al studied the scorpion dancing in the old man's eye. The scorpion waved a claw at Al, as if to say, join the society, and take the challenge.

* * * *

Erik rubbed the dog, a good-looking animal. What attracted Erik to the dog were its green eyes. How did the dog open the door of Gadiel's cabin? There was no dog in the cabin when the rabbit bit him. The rabbit had green eyes, too. Would the dog bite? No, it sat panting, and didn't even sniff at the food Hadrian gave the boys.

What magic did Gadiel possess to generate the different animals? That must be how they originated. Did they travel through a portal in the cabin or materialize from another dimension? He remembered D&D games where wizards summoned objects from other dimensions and spiritual planes.

"Hey Al, can you summon objects from another dimension?" Erik asked.

Al gazed steadily at Gadiel, a staring contest, which made Erik laugh, because Al had trouble looking anyone in the eye.

Al's attention shifted to Erik, "What?"

"Can you conjure objects from other dimensions? You know with magic?"

Al sniffed.

Gadiel said, "The Fire and Ice challenge will lead you to these new capabilities."

"You mean, after the challenge I'll have the ability, or you'll teach me these techniques after I take the challenge?" Al's eyes narrowed and he pressed his lips tight.

"The experience itself won't give you the ability." Gadiel rubbed his trimmed beard.

Erik considered that too. How come the handlers in the caravan have scraggy, wild beards, but Gadiel's beard is coiffed to perfection?

Al said, "Yeah, I thought that's what you would say. I pass on the challenge. It sounds dangerous, and the advantages you claim aren't real."

"The advantages are subtle. A wizard who grew up on a farm would think you were normal in wizardry skills, but then when you use your magic skills you demonstrate extra ability a surprise of the craft the other wizards didn't expect. You display more magic, stronger magic, and even exceptional magic. You won't know your new found power until you do it and see for yourself."

Al put his chin into both hands and rubbed his eyes with his fingertips. Erik knew this meant Al couldn't decide. He had watched Al do this while taking tests in school.

Erik said, "Make a decision already."

Al said, "I decided, and I'm not doing it. Now leave me alone." Al stood and rubbed the back of his neck. "I've decided."

Erik said, "It's getting late; we should head to bed."

Gadiel asked, "How long has it been that your magic hasn't worked?"

"You lost your magic?" Erik asked. "No, that's not true, you've helped Roden by lightening his workload each day."

* * * *

Al moved closer to the fire to warm his hands. What would Erik think? Al had masqueraded as a wizard for weeks, performing what

Gadiel called, "parlor tricks." The great Alpherge the Mighty outed as a fake master wizard.

Erik said, "Tell him how you're using magic every day."

Al studied the stars. He wanted to scream or yell or shoot a fireball into the sky. As a child, he had poured his milk into the cereal bowl and it flowed over the table, spilled into his lap, onto the chair and splashed to the floor. He remembered being so helpless. Mom had comforted him, but only after she yelled in surprise as the milk cascaded off the table. The only reason he attempted to pour it himself was to prove he was a big boy. He could pour his own milk.

Now, he remembered strutting through the village, staff in hand, as a great and mighty wizard to prove his worth. Instead he was masquerading as a wizard, a fraud.

"Don't we need your magic to get the golden crown?"

He felt his throat closing. He turned toward Erik. How could he prove that his magic was real? A fireball thrown into the sky and exploding into a hundred colors would show Erik. Al closed his eyes and tried to relax the tightness in his chest. Nothing. No magic.

Al rolled his shoulders, gazed at his feet and took a deep sigh. At that moment he wanted to be with Sherry, to hug her, get a word of encouragement or a smile, but they had left Sherry hundreds of miles away, angrier than a hornets nest.

Al said, "I don't have it, Erik. I can't work magic. I'm a fraud."

The black dog barked and the winter wolves howled an answer in the distance.

CHAPTER 40

adiel, Erik, Al and the dog stood a half-mile from the caravan where campfires glowed. The volcano loomed in the distance, a red glow near its peak. No wind stirred the frosty night air, as the Velidred moon cast an eerie red pall over the ice. Al shook. Was it from the chill in the air or his decision to take the Fire and Ice experience?

Gadiel directed handlers on setting up a row of burning embers across the ice. Al assumed magic prevented the embers from burning right through the ice. How much magic did Gadiel possess? Al felt the man lacked meaningful power, yet he used magic in ways that others didn't or couldn't.

Erik slapped Al's back. "This won't be a problem for you, buddy. Take the challenge and your magic will return, we'll reach the Ice Castle, find the golden crown and return to Sherry and Lily as heroes."

Return as heroes? I hope to survive the night. Walk across hot coals and then walk all day tomorrow. It was late, they grabbed four hours of sleep a night, and tonight they might only get two hours if they were lucky. He should tell Gadiel to forget it. He would take the challenge when they returned home, yet he seemed powerless to refuse, despite his protests.

Gadiel said, "The boys finished their preparations. Now it's your turn."

Al shook his head. "No, I don't want this. I'll take it when I get back to Velidred. There's no hurry. Right?"

Gadiel took Al's arm. "You're here, and the process has begun."

Al relaxed at Gadiel's touch.

"Drink this vial."

"It's not Ouuzool, is it?"

"No, a little mixture to help you relax."

"No, I don't—"

"Drink it."

Al looked at Erik, who nodded. "Go ahead, you'll be all right. I'm right here with you."

Gadiel said, "The drink contains properties to lead you into the spiritual world."

Erik survived his Fire and Ice challenge. Will I?

Al tipped the vial to his lips. A sweet mixture emanated from the bottle. He tipped back his head and drank the liquid, which resembled blue mouth wash. He stuck his tongue out and shook his head, trying to purge the nasty taste.

Gadiel said, "Remove your shoes and jacket for this part of the journey."

A "journey" to walk ten yards across hot coals? Not a journey, torture. Oh, and before walking on the hot coals they freeze me to death.

"Okay, Time to relax. Close your eyes and take a deep breath, then exhale long and slowly." Gadiel guided Al in relaxation techniques.

Al felt his hands relaxing and calm flowed to his shoulders. Long slow breaths, in and out.

Gadiel spoke softly, his voice hitting the low notes on a bassoon, "I'm putting an incense burner near you, sniff and breathe easy."

The frigid, dry air froze Al's nostrils. Then an aroma of cinnamon and honey suffused the night air, a pleasant, soothing, calm and comforting aroma.

"Keep your eyes closed. It's a short walk to the coals. Walk forward, never stopping."

Al took a sharp breath when Gadiel mentioned the coals.

Then a touch from Gadiel. "Breathe in, breathe out. The first step is the Fire Challenge. It's designed to rid you of sins you have committed against others."

Al felt the heat near his feet. Why was he doing this against his will? Apprehension flooded his mind and his body stiffened.

Gadiel said, "Open your eyes and concentrate on your friend Erik at the end of the bed of coals. Walk toward him and focus on him the whole way. Never stop walking."

Al gazed at Erik.

Gadiel nudged Al, and Al stepped onto the coals. He walked fast with long strides to reduce the number of steps needed to reach Erik.

The heat ascended from the coals, and he approached Erik who was ten yards away, nine yards, eight yards, then the sky flashed and he stood on a volcano with Sherry by his side. What was she doing here? The volcano spit fire high into the air. "Sherry, you're here."

Sherry moved toward the Mountain King standing near the volcano. Al couldn't stop her movement. Then he remembered the vial in his pocket. Yes, drink the vial Zita gave him and he could have extra power to fight the king.

Sherry pleaded with him not to drink the vial. "Save me."

Al thought he needed the extra magic. He removed the cork from the vial and drank the liquid. Magic came easily to Al, and with the extra power from the liquid inside the vial he could be invincible. He needed more magic to save Sherry, but where did she go?

He remembered passing out after drinking the liquid and losing sight of Sherry. Al didn't gain extra magic. Sherry stood next to the king, trapped in a transparent magic prison. It was Al's fault. His greed for increased power had backfired. Magic and treasures weren't the most important things. Spending time with friends and staying near them to protect them was more important.

A dark cloud closed around Al, the sights and sounds of the volcano and the battle faded from view, and Erik stood before him.

Erik said, "You did it, buddy."

Al remembered Sherry and how he had failed her on the volcano, because he desired more magic instead of her company.

The comet blazed near the horizon, its long tail stretched across the night sky. He imagined his magic resembled the comet, a brief, bright light at the moment it nears a planet and then gone. Was that to be his own fate, a moment of fame, and then his magic extinguished?

Gadiel said, "The next challenge is smoke. It's designed to show you present day sins. Drink this liquid to feel your loved one's presence."

He handed Al another vial. The glow of the Velidred moon cast a red gleam on the brown vial. Would this second potion taste as disgusting as the first vial? What strange chemicals were contained in this mixture? He didn't want to know. A quick un-corking and Al tipped back his head and downed the drink in one gulp.

"Bleah, that's horrible, is that sour milk?" Al wanted to spit.

The handlers sprinkled incense powder on the coals, and smoke billowed from the burning embers with a scent of pine and ginger.

"Walk through the smoke and remember loved ones in your life. Breathe deeply." Gadiel shoved Al into the smoke.

Al sucked in a huge breath and stumbled through the smoke, coughing.

He thought of his mother alone on Earth. She couldn't know where Al and his friends had gone. Did she think bears ate them in the forest or they fell off the mountain cliff? Had rescue parties searched for their bodies?

He choked on the thick air. There was no oxygen, and he wheezed and puffed. His asthma might kill him if this didn't end quickly.

Al entered a room, a den or living room. The smoke cleared, and the room transformed as his eyes focused. Yes, the room included a coffee table with magazines on top and a Lazy Boy recliner in the corner. A couch faced the window, and an electric keyboard sat next to the stairs.

This was the home Al grew up in on Earth. Everything looked familiar. Where was his mother? She always sat in the recliner, reading or working needlepoint.

Al called out, "Mom, are you home?"

He stepped into the kitchen. "Mom?"

She sat at the kitchen table and next to her were Erik's mom and Sherry's mom. They examined paperwork on the table.

His mom said, "According to my documents, the cave won't open naturally for four years."

"We can't wait four years to find the kids. We didn't prepare them enough, they weren't ready." Erik's mom said.

"Patricia, we did the best we could. A person or persons on Aloheno betrayed us. You know Duke Larrabee plotted to maneuver them off Earth."

"I trusted him."

"Can they still be alive?"

The image went blurry, the smoke returned, and Al entered a small cabin which had no candle or lantern. He blinked his eyes.

Then he heard her. Sherry. She talked to someone in the darkness.

Sherry said, "The boys aren't coming back."

Lily said, "How can we escape without the boys?"

Al's eyes adjusted to the darkness and he noticed both girls chained to the wall. Where were they? Who captured them and why?

"Our captors will make a mistake, and we'll take advantage and free ourselves."

"Do you think we'll survive?" Lily asked.

Sherry said, "We will. Someone will make a mistake. We just have to be ready for it. We'll figure out a way to escape. I promise."

Al walked to Sherry and stood before her.

Sherry glanced at her feet. Al tried to touch her face, but his hand passed through her.

Lily cried and Sherry said. "Prince Krunal will be sorry when I get my hands on him."

The smoke entered the room and Al yelled, "Erik and I are coming for you. We'll help." But he knew she didn't hear him.

The room faded from view and Al stepped through the smoke into the thin night air. He gasped in the wintry air. The sharp pain of cold stabbed his lungs.

Gadiel said, "You survived. Good, many have problems with the smoke."

Al thought of the girls. Were Sherry and Lily going to be okay until they returned?

Gadiel took out a small jar and unscrewed the lid. The jar reminded Al of the makeup jars his mom stored in the bathroom cabinet at home. Gadiel dipped his thumb into the cream and made three marks on Al's face. One long mark across his forehead, another beneath his right eye and the third across the beard on his chin.

"Let the oils of Velidred heal you from your sins. May you learn from your mistakes in the present day to guide you to a better future."

Al didn't know if the substance left a mark on his body or not. Was this war paint like football players applied to their faces before a game or a step of the Fire and Ice ceremony?

Al said, "Erik, the girls —"

"Quiet." Gadiel's voice broke through the silence. "Never repeat this experience to anyone."

"But my friends, Sherry and Lily."

"You cannot help them. Return to the present."

"My mom."

Erik said, "You saw your mom?"

"Yes, and your mom too."

"Quiet. If you share too much, you may not survive the next."

Erik said, "My mom?"

Gadiel said, "Now the last experience, the Ice challenge."

"What is that, you pour ice over my head?" Al asked.

"No. They submerge you in the lake." Erik said.

"This lake?" Al stomped his foot on the ice. "Are you crazy? I'm not doing that."

"It's necessary to finish the ceremony. Then your magic returns."

"A quick in and out, right?"

Kenneth Brown

"I can't dictate how long the ceremony takes. As long as is needed to cleanse you. I must mention we lose most candidates during the Ice challenge. It's difficult. Drink this hot tea and strip to your small-clothes."

CHAPTER 41

Al thought he must be intoxicated to agree to continue. But, he peeled off layer after layer of clothing, shivering. Al finished the honey flavored tea.

Gadiel moved him to a section of ice where the handlers had drilled a hole large enough for Al to enter the water. Gadiel said, "The Ice challenge permits you to see a future sin against your fellow man.

The handlers tied a rope around Al's mid-section. Al hugged his chest with his arms to stop shivering and said, "I don't want to do this, I'm already cold, and I'm not a strong swimmer." He leaned away from the hole and shook his head. *Nothing good can come from this experience.* The newspapers back on Earth related many stories of people drowning in seconds after hitting water at near-freezing temperatures.

Al remembered visiting a local lake in Montana to watch a demonstration of an icy water rescue by the local Fire Department. The announcer at the demonstration said the volunteers that jumped into the water needed rescuing fast if they weren't wearing a life-vest. If the victim didn't get rescued in seconds, then blood moved to the body's core and the extremities used for swimming didn't get enough blood to help the victim stay above water. They quickly drowned.

Al asked, "Do I pull the rope to give a signal for you to rescue me?"

Gadiel said, "I'll know when to pull you out."

Al didn't want to entrust his life to this man, but he continued as if controlled by another person. The old man had confiscated Al's staff, and Sherry is in danger. He rubbed his arms hard as they grew white in the bitter cold. Not even in the water yet, and his extremities were losing blood. He felt lightheaded, unsure if it was from the temperature or fear of jumping in the water.

Gadiel sprinkled powder on Al's head, "Show us this man's future sins." Two handlers standing by pushed Al into the water.

The water was one degree warmer than ice, and Al thought his heart stopped beating. The boys submerged his head, and he wanted to gasp but feared drowning if he took in water. Al bobbed to the surface and sucked in a vast quantity of frigid air. He wanted to scream, "Help me," to Erik or anyone willing to save him, but the freezing water grabbed him and squeezed his lungs so tightly he couldn't make a sound.

Thinking back to the Montana winter-water demonstration, the announcer said, "twenty percent die in the first two minutes, either from drowning because they panic, or they have a heart attack." Al sucked in more air, but grappled to breathe. He was sure he would die of a heart attack and needed Gadiel's mercy to rescue him in time.

Gadiel said to the boys, "Shove his head under water."

Dizziness overwhelmed Al as he realized Gadiel planned to kill him. Would Erik rescue him? Al shivered and his sluggish brain labored to discover a way to deliver him from a watery death. He struggled to swim to the surface, but the boys held his head underwater. *I should have died from the altitude sickness instead of this. Television shows say drowning is the worst way to die.*

He flailed in the water, his arms losing the battle against the boys shoving his head underwater. Al beat his arms harder to regain control, but his cells consumed the last of the oxygen in his blood.

A moment later he stood in a building where thirty girls sat on the floor. A red- headed woman wrote words on a chalk board. She said, "Who can tell me this word's definition?" She pointed at the word.

Eight hands rose into the air and one girl yelled, "I know."

"Easy Clarice," the teacher pivoted to the class, "let the other children have a chance."

The teacher, it was Sherry, wore a smile as she studied the girls on the floor. She pointed to one near the front, "Rita, can you try?"

The girl examined the floor.

Al stared. Sherry looked happy teaching the children. Is her future to teach on this planet? But he thought the ice experience was supposed to show his future. Did this mean that Sherry and he were to live in a village together? Maybe Sherry taught while Al practiced magic.

A man wearing fine clothes strode through the open door. An inch taller than Sherry, the man had a receding hairline that extended to the middle of his head. He strolled to Sherry, hugged and kissed her and said, "How are your students today?"

Sherry beamed, "They're all so smart, and will have a wonderful future because of this opportunity."

Al's eyes widened. He wanted to scream "no", but his mouth didn't work. He backed up, running his hands through his hair.

Then the scene shifted to a dark forest. Al searched for his staff, but it wasn't within reach. A man twenty feet away pulled a bowstring and loosed an arrow.

Al twisted to avoid the shot as the arrow flew inches from his chest. He attempted magic, but nothing happened. He raced through the forest, and the man chased after him.

His breathing became labored. Without magic, Al couldn't defeat the man. He realized his torn and sweat-soaked clothing indicated he'd been evading the man for a while. Al lived in the forest as a hermit to prevent the man from finding him. Food was scarce, but Al needed little.

Another arrow flew past as he dashed to safety, and his heart raced and his lungs burned for more oxygen. Al turned to locate his pursuer, but nothing moved in the dark shadows of the forest. Leaves rustled behind him. The man was closing the distance.

Should he zig and zag or rush straight? Were there places in the forest to gain leverage over his adversary? Yes, there was a rock ledge a hundred yards away. Get above the danger.

How did the man discover Al's hideaway? A local person must have sold him out. Yeah, a wizard in the woods living by himself . . . if a pursuer asked enough questions of enough people he could discover Al's location.

He needed twenty yards, and then take a sharp right up onto the rocks. The wizard gown might make it difficult to leap onto the ledges, but that was the one place Al knew he would have an advantage.

An arrow hit the tree next to him just as he spun behind it. Too close.

The man yelled, "You can't escape, wizard. Your magic has vanished. You're a failure as a wizard, and you left all your friends to die on this world."

"It's not true. I didn't leave them, they left me."

"The girls are fending for themselves and not getting enough to eat."

Tightness clasped his throat. He knew his friends were fine. He saw Sherry in the classroom, teaching, something she always dreamed of as a career. The man she kissed must be her husband. Al had left her to assure her a happy life without conflict. "Leave me alone."

"No, I won't leave you alone until you're dead."

Al leapt to the ledge, but moss covered the rocky surface and he slipped, falling to his back. His head bounced off the rock, and he struggled to regain his feet.

His pursuer, a muscular man with blue eyes and a dark beard, reached the rock. Al recognized his pursuer.

"Your moment to die has arrived, wizard." The man drew back the arrow.

"Don't do this. I didn't mean to leave my friends. My magic failed me." Al's head hurt where it had hit the rock, and his chest muscles were tight. He failed his friends, because of this stupid magic.

The archer, too close to miss a shot, said, "Your magic won't fail you when you're dead."

Al's body tingled, and the tension released in his body. Magic from the rocks surged through him. He smiled and discharged a fireball at the archer.

The man never saw it coming. The fireball exploded on the archer's chest and knocked him to the ground.

Al glanced to the sky, rose from the rock and stood over the archer. The archer's clothing smoked where the fireball hit, the exposed skin red, raw and charred. The stench of burned flesh replaced the fresh, forest-pine scent. Al had killed his friend, Erik, the archer.

CHAPTER 42

Zita watched as Al flopped, wet and raw, out of the water onto the ice. Gadiel had completed the Velidred Fire and Ice experience on Alpherge the Mighty. She knew Alpherge was Gadiel's property now, just the same as she belonged to Gadiel. Al was no longer mighty, and she imagined Al's grandfather, Alpherge the Great, turning over in his grave. The last step of the ceremony involved branding the Velidred brand onto Al's shoulder blade.

Zita maintained the form of the black dog during the entire night. Her shape-shifting powers grew every day under Gadiel's tutelage. She howled at the blood-red Velidred moon, and a chorus of howls returned from the winter wolves following the caravan on the frozen lake. With Alpherge under the Velidred brand, the only remaining step was to kill Erik. She concocted a plan, but first she needed to witness whiny Al cry from the branding.

Gadiel walked Al to the brazier where coals burned fiery blue, heating the branding iron.

Al said, "Are we done now? Can I put on my clothes?"

"In a moment, one step remains."

"Haven't you made me suffer enough for tonight?"

"The last step is the brand."

"Brand? Like cattle?"

Gadiel smiled and cocked his head, "Like cattle, if you wish. The brand allows entry into secret rooms where like-minded wizards share information and knowledge."

"Do you brand me on my butt?"

"No, we're more civilized than that."

"Don't let them brand me, Erik."

Erik said, "It's okay. The pain only lasts for two or three days."

"Three days!" Al struggled, but the other handlers held him.

Gadiel donned leather gloves and with both hands pulled the glowing iron from the brazier. "Position him face down on the ice."

Al screamed, "Erik, help!"

Erik moved toward Al and held his friend's legs to the ice.

Gadiel stood over Al, placed a foot on Al's back and pressed the hot iron flat onto Al's left shoulder.

In the quiet night air, the branding iron seared Al's skin, and the muscle sizzled as Al wailed in pain. The smell of burned flesh filled Zita's dog nostrils. She sneezed.

Gadiel pressed hard for two seconds and then removed the iron.

Zita howled with delight.

As Erik helped his friend back into clothes, Zita determined her next steps. She needed to separate Erik from his friend.

Still in dog form, she neared Al, who now sat on a log near the fire, and sniffed at his shoulder. Erik stood next to the fire.

Al said, "Get away, dog."

Zita barked.

Erik said, "Go on, shoo." He waved his hands at her.

Zita trotted to Erik and sniffed his leg.

"Get out of here, shoo."

Zita bit Erik's ankle.

"You rotten, stinking dog."

Zita howled at the moon.

"I'll get you for that, you worthless mutt."

Zita barked at Erik.

Erik darted toward her.

Zita scampered out of reach.

He chased.

Zita increased speed and raced around the wagons in the caravan.

Erik continued his pursuit.

Zita slowed to make sure Erik thought he could catch her, but stayed out of reach.

"Come on, you lousy mutt."

Zita slowed further to round the mastodons, and Erik dove and grabbed her hind leg.

"Ha, gotcha now," he said as he slid on the ice.

Zita wriggled to get free, but Erik had a firm grip on her leg. She twisted and bit Erik's arm, which caused him to let go.

Erik examined his arm and scowled at Zita.

Zita barked as she waited out of Erik's reach.

Erik halted the chase. He returned to the fire, but it was a feint. He pivoted and sprinted after Zita.

Zita darted around one wagon and looked back to make sure Erik still pursued. He did. She changed directions and headed toward the volcano. This next step was crucial to her plans. Erik needed to think he could catch her while she lured him onto thin ice. The winter wolves bayed in the distance.

For the next few moments she slowed, let Erik get close, but not close enough to catch her, and then sped up to re-start his pursuit. Twice, Erik appeared ready to give up, but Zita barked, crouching on her front paws, and the boy followed.

She headed straight toward the volcano and hoped that Hadrian was right, that the ice thinned as you neared it. Zita stopped to look at the red glow around the mountain top. Then the ice cracked behind her.

*****

Erik heard the cracking and had a sudden empty feeling in his stomach. He stopped chasing the dog. A fall into the freezing water would mean death without the magic of the Ice challenge. How to capture the dog without chasing it farther? He turned toward where the caravan should be but didn't see the wagons, animals or fires. Had he chased the dog that far?

He was enjoying the chase and knew the dog was playing with him, but now felt a harsh reality in the game. Erik's mind plunged to the worst probable outcome. Lost in the middle of nowhere, ice cracking under his weight with Gadiel's dog in a precarious position on even thinner ice, what should he do?

His heart beat hard, though he couldn't tell if it was from exertion or the panic that vise-gripped his organs.

Erik said in a high voice, "Come on doggie, playtime is over, let's go back to the caravan. I'm done with this game, it's dangerous out here." The Velidred moonlight reflected a wavy red pathway, and Erik wondered if there was melted water on top of the ice.

The dog barked and moved farther from Erik.

"No, no, no. Not that way. Come back to me, I won't hurt you."

The dog barked and wagged its tail.

Erik slid one slow step after another toward the dog, "Come on doggie, play time's done."

The dog moved toward the thinner ice, and there was another sharp crack. Weird, but the dog appeared to be getting smaller.

Is this magic that makes the dog smaller? Will leaving the dog here on the ice upset Gadiel? I won't do it, leave a dog out here in the below-freezing temperatures. What if the dog falls into the water? It's certain death. I have to capture the dog.

Erik pressed his lips together and tried to whistle for the dog. In the wintry air with his dry, cracked lips, only a faint hiss sounded. He shuffled closer.

The dog scooted back and became even smaller.

The ice cracked under Erik's weight again. *No. Easy.* "Come little doggie. I'll give you a treat. Let's return to the warm toasty fire and eat jerky."

Erik inhaled and choked, as the frosty air burned his lungs. If he fell into the water, they both might die. He inched closer.

The dog turned into the size of a Chihuahua, although it was still black with curly hair. It barked, but its previously deep bark was now sharp and yippy.

"Listen little doggie," Erik couldn't move closer without grave danger, "I can't get closer or one of us splashes into the water." He knew he'd be the one.

Wolves bayed in the distance, and Erik wondered if they were nearer. *Will wolves team with the dog or eat the little bugger?*

Erik pleaded, "You don't want to be dinner for the wolves, do you?"

Another move toward the volcano by the dog, and it reached the section of ice that clearly had a surface layer of water. The little animal lifted its paws and danced in the water, attempting to keep its feet dry.

"Ha, out of space." Erik laughed, "Return to me and I'll take you back to the caravan." He inched closer, but the dog stayed put. The ice thinned under his feet. This size dog worried him less if he could capture it. His ankle sill smarted from the bite.

Ten feet from the animal, in a soothing, placating voice, he said, "Nice and easy, come to me and I'll take you home."

The ice cracked, and Erik held his breath. He saw a dark line start five feet from his legs, break and barrel toward the dog. The crack grew wider with each foot. The dog sensed the impending catastrophe, and jumped. But it had nowhere to go and splashed into the icy water. The sound of the cracking ice echoed off the volcano and surrounding mountains. Then complete silence.

*****

Zita splashed into the frigid water. Her breath caught and her heart raced as the near freezing water battered her core. Shocked, her head went under. She paddled her arms, came back to the surface and gasped.

No, she thought. Not like this. Then she smiled at her predicament. If she died, she knew Erik perished too. Who dies first, she wondered? She listened for Erik's screams for help.

"Little doggie, are you okay?" Erik cried out.

She wiped water from her eyes and realized that she had shifted back into human form. Ha, she thought, Erik will know who his killer is before he dies. Maybe she could escape from the water and reach the warmth and safety of the caravan. Zita paddled toward the broken edge of ice. She must hurry.

The first piece of ice she reached broke in her hands, and she struggled to reach stronger ice. She worked hard, adrenalin pumped, but the bitter temperature of the water relentlessly bore down to silence her. Icicles dripped from her hair as the water froze in the night air.

*****

Erik stood on solid ice, his mouth opened in wonder, and watched the dog transform into a human. How could this be? Who was the dog? He bit his lip, disoriented by the change, and feared to move on the cracked ice.

Then the human was struggling to reach firm ice. He must save them. Think. How do you save someone in the water? He remembered TV shows at home and the ice rescue techniques they taught in middle school in Montana. Drop to your belly and spread your limbs, putting less weight on each square foot of ice.

Erik yelled, "I'm coming for you."

*****

He's still alive and not in the water? Zita examined the ice and saw Erik standing ten feet from her. She tried to throw a fireball, but the intense numbing water sapped her magic. Then she remembered Forest River Blossom's prediction that she would drown. This was that moment. At most, she had two minutes.

*****

Erik didn't recognize the person in the water. Long, wet icicles dangled over the person's face, obscuring the shape in the darkness. He removed his coat and pushed it in front of him as he lay on the ice. He slithered forward like a four-point starfish.

"I'm sliding my coat to you, grab it and I'll pull you out."

"You stay away from me. You're not drowning me. I'll get out myself."

That voice sounded familiar, and he tried to figure out who it was. Not a mastodon handler from the caravan, but a female and a voice he should recognize.

"You only have a minute to live, grab the coat." He pulled it in and then tossed it toward the woman while holding onto one sleeve.

The coat landed on the ice near the woman, close enough for her to grab it. But instead, she moved to another section of ice which broke away as she struggled.

"It doesn't work that way. Let your legs float to the top of the water and then belly crawl out."

The woman didn't listen, and the ice broke as she attempted to grasp it with stiff hands.

"Stop struggling or you'll break the ice I'm on, and I won't be able to rescue you." He shivered, lying on the ice without his jacket. *The warmth of that jacket can at least keep me alive. I should give up. We both don't need to die.* "Come on woman, don't be pigheaded, let me help you so we can both return to the caravan. Grab the jacket, I'm freezing here."

*****

Zita labored to reach ice that would hold her weight. With Erik on the ice and her in the water, she would die first. She couldn't let him touch her, because once he recognized her, she knew he'd drown her. He killed her dad and wanted to kill her, too.

"Beat it, I can get out myself." Water splashed as she struggled for a handhold.

"Stop splashing and grab the coat."

"No. You want to drown me." Her face numbed and speaking became difficult. When she tried to flip the hair from her face, huge chunks of ice banged against her cheeks. They cracked and fell into the water with a plop.

*****

It was becoming difficult to understand the woman's voice, but Erik thought she said he wanted to drown her. He struggled to place the voice and became agitated because the woman didn't listen. His mind blanked. The woman's time in the water was becoming deadly. She'd at least have frostbite, might lose a finger, toe or foot. He had to help her.

Erik left the jacket where it was and slid toward the woman, figuring she'd soon be too cold to struggle. Then he could pull her onto the ice.

"Don't come closer."

"Don't be an idiot, I can save you. You have about one minute before you're dead; let me help." *Who is this woman?* He closed within a yard.

She moved into deeper water, away from Erik and the safety of the ice.

"Are you crazy? Come toward my hand."

The woman flailed in the water.

"Stop splashing." Erik bared his teeth. "Grab my hand, I can rescue you." His muscles quivered as every little movement on the thin ice scared him.

*****

Zita's arms and clothing, sodden and wet, dragged her deeper, her feet were numb. It couldn't end this way. Erik lives and she dies. There must be something to bring him into the water, but her mind seized as her extremities numbed.

Erik slid closer.

She wanted both to be rescued and to scoot further from her rescuer.

He reached an arm to her.

Zita slapped it woodenly. If she let him get close, he'd shove her head beneath the water. Then both her life and hopes for revenge would be squashed. Zita's normal rational thinking faded as she struggled to remain conscious.

"Take my hand," Erik insisted.

She floated farther away in the brutal, icy water.

*****

What's wrong with this person? Erik stretched dangerously beyond the ice edge, his chest a foot over the water, trying to reach the woman. If he slipped into the water, they both died. His back ached from the effort, and he pressed the toes of his boots against the ice to prevent from slipping into the lake.

If the woman drifted too far, there'd be no way to rescue her.

The woman's flailing decreased, but she refused Erik's reach.

*****

Zita's head dropped into the water and she fought weakly to reach the air. The frigid water clutched her chest as if a large vise clamped it and squeezed. Arms, fingers and legs went numb, and she couldn't think. She gasped for air as her head cleared the surface.

Erik said, "Give me your hand, you only have seconds left."

What was she supposed to do, die on her own or let Erik drown her? No, she needed to yank Erik under with her. She splashed toward Erik's hand and grabbed it and sank into the water. She pulled, but wasn't strong enough to drag Erik into the water.

He pulled her toward him.

Zita scratched at his arms to force him to let go.

"Stop it." He yelled, "Stop struggling."

She wanted to cry, but nothing remained. A lump grew in her throat. The spirit of death hailed her.

*****

Crazy woman, why won't she let me help? Erik's muscles stiffened and cramped. He thought about letting her go. The woman wanted to die, she didn't want help, and he didn't have the strength to keep fighting her. He wanted to live.

The woman bounced in the water. *Is she trying to pull me under with her?* Sometimes her head surfaced and sometimes her hair floated on top. She didn't have much longer.

The woman bobbed out of the water and she freed her hands from his.

Erik grabbed her hair, but slipped and pushed her underwater.

*****

Zita knew it. The fortune had been foretold even before meeting the teenagers from Earth; Erik planned to drown her. She closed her eyes as she slipped into unconsciousness.

CHAPTER 43

He gritted his teeth to the bitter air as his arms screamed for release. Even his teeth ached.

Erik held tight to the woman's hair. He worried about sliding forward, but when she bobbed to the surface, he scooted back and jerked. The woman no longer struggled. He pulled her to the edge, and walked his toes to move further back from the open water. He grabbed and yanked her wet clothing and she flopped onto the ice.

They weren't safe yet, and he knew it. The ice was too thin to just lift her and start walking, even if he knew which direction to walk. The extra weight with her in his arms and the weight of the water and ice on her clothing would shatter this thin ice.

Erik toiled with her dead weight for a solid two minutes. Scoot back and pull the lifeless body for a few inches. For a moment he abandoned her to test the ice's thickness. Still too thin, and he carefully lowered himself again to spread-eagle position and pulled more. He felt frozen himself, and thought he couldn't lie on the ice any longer, so he carefully stood and dragged her by her feet, too scared to risk carrying her in his arms until they reached solid ice.

He left her in a pile and returned for his coat. Erik wanted to put it on himself and warm up, but he brought it for the woman. With frozen fingers, he stripped off her wet jacket, boots and clothing and pressed her hypothermic body into his. Not much help, but maybe she was still alive.

Euphoria lifted him for a moment as he realized he had just made a successful cold-water rescue using the same techniques they taught in school. *Bet those instructors didn't have a scenario like this in mind.*

He stooped to pick up his coat, contorted at a wild angle, juggled the woman in his arms, balanced and then threw the jacket over her to trap any warmth her feeble body might produce.

The woman was small and though she weighed only about a hundred pounds, Erik's arms tired. He had handled Roden's food, equipment, and the wagon, which had strengthened his muscles, but fatigue and sub-zero temperatures sucked his energy.

The wolves howled and Erik suspected they were approaching. Did they know he was practically alone on the ice? How many wolves roamed in the pack, and could he escape attack? Now, which direction to the caravan?

The woman wiggled within the coat, and he peeked at her face, the icicles now melted from her hair, and he almost dropped the woman to the ice. His heart stopped and then pounded as blood rushed to his face. Zita!

CHAPTER 44

Al woke to the sound of handlers shouting at mastodons. The first glimmers of sunrise brightened the eastern horizon. Didn't he just fall asleep? How late did they jump in the hammocks last night? Why didn't Erik wake him? He rolled to his side, craving more sleep. The caravan would move at daylight with or without Al.

Pain burned as his shoulder rubbed the rough hammock and he flashed back to last night's branding. His brain felt fuzzy and stuffy, the early stages of a head and sinus ailment disturbing his day. Vexing dreams flashed through his head, and the shoulder pain impeded his thinking. He speculated on the branding logo, tore off his jacket and tunic and tried to look over his shoulder, but the brand's shape eluded him.

He lay another moment with closed eyes.

Obadiah kicked him and said, "Out of the mattress, bull dust."

"Yeah, I'm moving," Al moaned and climbed out into the morning air.

Last night was horrendous. Why did he agree to the Fire and Ice experience? Al thought the ceremony included Gadiel pouring ice water over his head, not realizing they planned to submerge him in the lake. He pictured a football victory dunking for the coach and got a near-drowning instead. Al shivered, covered his shoulders and tugged on his jacket. The freezing air penetrated to his inner core.

Memories of Sherry, huddling in the dark, held captive by Prince Krunal rumbled through his mind. Why imprison and chain her? Here he lay, hundreds of miles abroad, and they traveled farther apart each day. He should return, but he couldn't turn back now. They had no maps. No GPS. No way to tell north from south on this ice. He didn't understand the constellations on this planet, so he couldn't guide by the stars. They must continue with the caravan and travel at the speed and direction of its leaders who apparently knew where they were.

Al put his jacket back on protecting the tender shoulder. He imagined Gadiel still pressing the hot iron into his flesh and using magic to keep it burning deep into his muscle.

Then he remembered the staff. Had he recovered the staff? He looked under the wagon and in other places he used to store it as he slept, but found nothing.

Gadiel lied. The man promised to return the staff after the Fire and Ice experience. Was the entire ceremony a ruse, a prank to force Al to get this horrendous brand? Was this an initiation rite they applied to first time handlers to have fun, comparable to a college-fraternity hazing?

Then he remembered the out-of-body experiences during the three events, the fire, smoke and ice. So real. He sensed Sherry was actually captured and needed his help. The last experience, where he killed Erik, boggled his mind. He couldn't imagine killing the friend who had saved his life only days ago.

Al needed answers — answers only Gadiel could provide. Time to confront Gadiel and force him to return the staff before the convoy moved. Al's magic floated out of reach, like stretching for the TV remote and being forced to leave the comfy chair to grab the clicker.

That's it; he'd demand the staff back from Gadiel.

Al said, "Erik, wake up buddy, we have to get busy. Everyone else is almost ready to roll and I have another task to complete before we begin."

Al examined Erik's hammock, and it hung empty.

CHAPTER 45

Al called, "Erik, where are you? I need your help." He walked around the wagon.

Erik wasn't there.

Obadiah said, "Hook up Roden, it's time to get the caravan moving. Hadrian is in a restless mood this morning. He says if we don't move, we'll all die. I've never seen him this adamant."

"I need to find Erik first."

Obadiah moved closer to Al and looked up at the taller man. "Your task is to harness Roden."

"But, Erik?" *Where is Erik this morning? He helped brand me.* Al winced at the pain in his shoulder. After the branding, Erik comforted Al, but then disappeared. Where?

Obadiah averted his gaze and said, "Erik is probably flirting with the women. Harness the wagons." Obadiah darted a glance at the volcano. "Hurry."

Al shook his head. *That didn't sound like Erik.* Al shrugged to loosen his shoulders. The scabbing wound scraped against his tunic, but he began his morning tasks. He pondered the best way to approach Gadiel to return the staff. The Fire and Ice experience had not delivered the promised magic.

Roden acted agitated. He bellowed when Al approached.

"Not today," Al said. He patted the animal's flank.

Over the last few weeks of travel, Erik and Al developed a rhythm harnessing the wagons, and Al felt awkward doing the work on his own. It forced him to concentrate on the task at hand. The procedure took more time than when they worked together.

He threw the blanket and harness over Roden while the animal stepped left and right and wagged his head back and forth.

"Easy," Al soothed. He talked to Roden, "What's going on that's got everyone on edge?"

The animal didn't respond, but Al saw the tension in his fellow handlers. The mastodons bellowed more than normal. One mastodon jerked its head, and a handler flew across the ice, sliding twenty feet.

Pinpricks of nerves crept up Al's spine. *What's going on this morning?*

Obadiah and another handler helped the thrown handler to his feet. They argued with the guy for a moment and dragged him back to the animal.

Where's Erik? Even if he was off flirting with the women, he'd return to help with morning chores.

Winter wolves howled in the distance.

Roden stomped his feet on the ice.

"Easy."

Al moved Roden to the wagons and attached the wagons to the harness.

Obadiah walked by and said, "Good, you're loaded, we leave in five minutes."

"Where's Erik?"

He studied the ice a moment then adjusted his gloves, "Don't know, don't care."

"I need to find him."

"Stay with Roden. The mastodons are edgy and we can't afford to lose any more of them." Obadiah strode to the next mastodon and wagon.

Al guided Roden and the wagons into the caravan line. He searched the other wagons for a sign of his friend. He verified the security of Roden's harnesses once more and tested the connections between the wagons.

As Al reached the last wagon pulled by Roden, he looked off in the distance toward the volcano. He saw small dots that looked dog-like. Wolves were stalking toward the volcano. He wondered why they moved toward the volcano and not in the direction of the caravan.

On a normal morning, the wolves hung back then matched the speed of the caravan. When the caravan moved, the wolves trailed. This time the wolves were traveling in the opposite direction. Had an animal become stranded on the ice?

Another handler approached Al. "Strange morning, don't you think? What's up with the wolves?"

Al stopped staring at the circling dots in the distance, "Huh? Yeah, strange morning." He needed to locate Erik before the caravan advanced. "Watch Roden and the wagons for two minutes. I'll be right back."

The guy drew his mouth into a straight line and said, "Not supposed to watch yours."

Al didn't wait for any further guff, but he marched toward Gadiel's wagon. He needed answers. He checked wagons he passed and asked the same question, "Have you seen Erik?"

Each inquiry received the same response. "Nope, not this morning."

When he arrived at Gadiel's wagon, Al pounded on the door.

Gadiel opened the door, and his back stiffened when he saw Al.

Al paused a second, studied Gadiel's eyes and said, "It didn't work. My magic isn't back."

Gadiel waited a moment.

A brief sensation entered Al's brain. He felt a bug walk across his arm and he slapped his coat to kill the bug.

The man in black nodded and said, "It worked fine."

"I don't have my magic." Al stood on the ice while Gadiel protected his doorway, two steps higher. Al disliked staring up at Gadiel. "Can I come in and retrieve my staff?"

"You're not ready."

"The whole Fire and Ice experience was a scam. You promised."

"I made no promises."

Al clenched his jaw and breathed deeply. No magic, no staff and Erik missing.

Gadiel said, "Return to your wagons, we leave soon."

"I'm searching for Erik."

The old man appeared thoughtful. He glanced to his left, toward the volcano, though the volcano wasn't visible from inside the doorway. Gadiel shrugged. "Haven't seen the boy this morning."

Hadrian walked by, "What are you doing here? We're ready to leave; get back to your wagons where you belong."

"Erik is missing."

Hadrian grabbed Al by the coat with powerful arms and pulled him close. He smelled of sweat. "If Erik isn't with the caravan this morning, then he's lost and we leave him."

"I'm tired of your lack of respect for our lives. We have to search for him; we can't let him die."

"The caravan leaves with or without him."

"No, I'm not going without my friend."

"Look around, boy." He stretched his hand to the bleakness of the frozen lake. Snow swirled into small patterns on the ice. "If he isn't with the caravan, he's already dead. The ice is thin near the volcano and if he traveled in that direction then he's in the water, dead. If he headed in any other direction, the winter wolves ate him for breakfast. Also dead. Deal with it. Your friend isn't coming back."

"Then I ought to find the body and bring it home." *That was the right thing. Take what's left of the body and return Erik's remains to his mother.*

"Listen, if you want to be alive at nightfall, then you leave with us right now." Hadrian pointed to the comet low in the sky. "The asteroid shower begins when we lose sight of the comet today."

Al trudged back to Roden and the wagons. Everything that had happened this morning disturbed him. Erik had never wandered off without telling Al. He remembered Erik dashed after the dog last night, but he was smart enough not to chase the dog onto thin ice. Al rubbed his unkempt beard. His stomach quivered, and he wondered if the altitude sickness was returning.

Was his discomfort a result of the Fire and Ice experience or a general nervousness like the mastodons and other handlers showed this morning? The air felt heavy, as if a sack of potatoes lay on his chest.

Mastodons bellowed.

When Al returned to his wagons, the other handler said, "Roden is a pain this morning, watch yourself."

Al said, "Yeah," and waved the guy away. He scanned the horizon for signs of Erik.

Roden rocked his massive head and tusks back and forth in a figure-eight pattern, and Al stood back.

He couldn't risk getting knocked over by Roden or trampled by the beast, for fear of being abandoned by Hadrian.

Hadrian sounded the call to advance, which Obadiah repeated. The caravan stirred, resembling an uncoiling snake. The wagon in front lurched forward and Roden followed without Al's command.

Roden pulled the wagons, and Al shuffled alongside, searching in every direction for Erik. Could he leave Erik to die on the ice? He bit his bottom lip. If his magic worked, then he could rescue Erik. Ha! Rescue, he didn't even know Erik's whereabouts. Could Al leave the caravan to find Erik's body? If the wolves got to Erik on the ice, what body parts might remain? If Erik drowned, Al might never locate the body. What strange animals might live under the ice, waiting for humans as their next meal?

The volcano puffed an ash cloud. The winter wolves howled.

Strange, Al thought, the wolves rarely howled during the day. He tightened his coat. Had the wolves found Erik's body? If Al drove Roden toward the wolves, could he find Erik? There must be thirty or forty wolves in the distance between the caravan and volcano.

His chest constricted to the point of pain. Should he risk the wolves to recover Erik? What chance for survival did he have without magic against thirty wolves? Would Roden panic around the wolves and make things worse? What if the ice thinned and Roden fell through? If Al borrowed Roden to search for Erik, what punishment would Hadrian enact? Could Al find the caravan again after locating Erik? Is Erik in a wagon with a cook, sleeping off a batch of Ouuzool? The questions were making him crazy.

The caravan moved fast, a hard pace for the mastodons.

Al needed to decide before they went much farther.

CHAPTER 46

Erik carried Zita's slowly warming body in his arms. He held her tight to his chest and shared body warmth with her. For the hundredth time, Erik scanned the horizon for a sign of the caravan.

He walked away from the thin ice near the volcano as the sun rose in the sky. He heard the crack of breaking ice behind him as the warmth of the sun increased. Erik stopped.

Zita said, "Why did you stop, did we reach the caravan?"

"No. The ice is cracking."

"Don't drop me in the freezing water."

"I won't drop you."

"Promise not to drown me."

"Why would I drown you? I've searched for you for months."

Zita snuggled tighter against his warm body.

Erik's arms ached from his efforts and he wanted to put Zita down and take a rest, but her wet frozen clothing lay far behind on the ice where he had dragged her out of the water. They needed to find the caravan so Zita could warm up by the stove in Gadiel's cabin.

Erik asked, "Why didn't you tell me you were with the caravan?"

Zita's body tensed, but she didn't answer.

Kenneth Brown

She shape-shifted into a dog and bit my leg and arm, then led me to this dangerous ice. Is she trying to kill me? The winter wolves moved toward them, closing to two hundred yards.

Zita's green eyes darted from Erik to the wolves, reflecting emerald sparkles in the morning sun.

Erik edged across the ice, expecting at any moment for more cracks to open and plunge them both into icy water. Had the caravan moved on and left them to die on the ice? Would Al try to find him?

He looked at Zita and said, "You're beautiful."

She blushed, looked at his eyes and then struggled to free herself.

Erik held tight. "Stop struggling, or we'll both drown."

Zita said, "That's what I want," and shoved hard against his chest. She broke free, and fell onto the ice.

"What are you doing? I'm trying to save your life."

* * * *

Zita tried to stand, became entangled in the jacket wrapped around her and fell back to the ice. *Why is this so difficult,* she thought?

"Stop struggling."

"You killed my dad." Zita grappled with the jacket, freed one foot, tried to stand and slipped on the ice.

"I rescued my friend, Lily."

"Your girlfriend," she screamed, and flailed her arms, still wrestling with the coat.

"No." Erik said, "Well, I wanted her, and yes, I suppose now that we're on this planet she's —"

"Stop bothering me, and get out of my life." Zita freed an arm, kicked her left foot, unbound the other hand and rolled free of the coat onto the ice.

She stood on the ice and glared. "You stabbed an arrow into Dad and rolled him over into the volcano."

Erik spluttered, "No."

"I saw you, Erik, don't deny it."

"I rescued my friend, whom your father tried to sacrifice."

The wolves howled, moving closer.

"Come on, Zita, you knew what I was doing. Plus, your fireball made it possible for me to reach your dad."

"I aimed the fireball at you." The frozen surface stung Zita's naked feet, but she didn't care. The time had arrived to kill Erik. Blast a fireball into him and her pain could disappear. Then she would watch the wolves feast on his body.

Erik said, "Let's talk."

Zita's muscles cramped in the bitter air. She studied Erik. Dark circles colored the skin beneath his eyes, and the skin was tight across his skull. She didn't care how haggard he looked.

She was freezing. She wrapped her arms around her body for warmth and noticed for the first time that she wore only small-clothes that clung tight to the shape of her body.

"Where are my clothes?"

"They were sopping wet and you would freeze to death wearing them."

"I'll freeze to death without them."

Erik moved closer. "Yes, that's why I wrapped my jacket around you."

Zita noticed the jacket on the ice and took a deep breath. She tried to cover herself with her arms.

"Wear the jacket."

Zita continued to dance on the ice. She wanted to run, but not in small-clothes in the brisk wintry air.

Erik picked up the jacket and held it out toward her. "You're freezing."

"I . . ." She couldn't give Erik the satisfaction of knowing he helped her. She raised one numb foot off the ice and then the other. "Maybe it'll help."

He moved closer.

"No, stay away."

"You won't get far in these freezing conditions without covering, and you're not wearing shoes."

She pressed her lips together. *A dash to the caravan might warm me, and then I won't need the jacket.* She searched her mind for Gadiel's presence. Where was he? This entire trip Gadiel lodged in her brain and now . . . wait. She sensed him moving in the distance. Zita squinted toward the far horizon.

Erik stepped closer, holding the jacket.

Gadiel and the caravan didn't care enough to rescue me? My only friend on this planet is this outsider, Erik? My life depends on Erik?

"The jacket." He held it for her.

"On the mountain that day."

"The eclipse."

"Did you mean what you said?"

Erik lowered his gaze and pawed a hand through his hair.

"I knew it."

"Zita!"

She glared, and with an ugly twist of her mouth, snorted in disgust.

King Haskell had arranged with Kestrel the Falcon Prince to capture these teenagers from Earth and return them to their birth planet, Aloheno. He had spent months planning to celebrate the eclipse of the triple moons and to sacrifice Lily, the girl from Earth, to Velidred, thus breaking the prophecy. King Haskell always desired more power and magic. Before the teens had arrived, Zita lived a marvelous life. But now everything had turned bleak and frigid; she only knew pain, suffering, and dirt.

Erik made brief eye contact and then looked at Zita's feet.

Her arms felt heavy as a numbness rose in her chest. Zita's knees buckled, and she collapsed to the ice.

Erik rushed to her and with his strong, rough hands, adjusted the coat around her arms and snuggled the buttons into their loops across Zita's chest and legs.

Why can't he leave me alone, so I can flee from the pain Erik and his friends brought? Tears welled.

"Are you okay?"

"Yes, leave me alone."

Erik lifted her off the ice and held her close.

CHAPTER 47

rik held Zita and enjoyed the beating of her heart against his chest. He needed a drink. He laughed to himself, surrounded by water, and he was thirsty.

Zita snuggled against him.

How did he feel toward Zita? She was attractive, but they only talked during moments of crisis. Lily had been in his life since they were children and he felt comfortable around her, but with Zita, she either snuggled into his arms or threw fireballs at him. What kind of relationship was that?

A wolf approached and sniffed Erik's feet.

"Get away." Erik kicked at the wolf, struggling to maintain balance. "Any clues you want to share about these animals?"

The animal backed away from Erik's foot.

"Nothing," Zita said, "Hunt in packs and like to eat humans."

The animals weren't as large as the wolves in Montana. These resembled Earth coyotes. One near the back of the pack appeared larger, maybe fifty pounds. The others were in the twenty to thirty-pounds range. Size didn't matter. They were a pack of fifteen, and with another smaller pack approaching from the east, the two humans were in trouble.

Another wolf threatened, Erik kicked at it, made contact and sent it sliding back toward the pack.

Two wolves circled in attack mode, hackles raised, separating to opposite sides.

Erik said, "We might be in trouble."

"Doesn't matter."

He kicked at the wolf on his left, but the animal backed out of the way and howled. The rest of the pack followed suit.

"What do you mean?"

"We're going to die."

"I won't let you die."

Zita wriggled an arm loose from Erik's grasp and pointed at two more packs of wolves approaching.

"We just need to hold the wolves off until someone rescues us or we find the caravan."

Zita sniffed, "The caravan isn't coming for us."

"Yeah, they are. Gadiel won't leave you to die, will he?"

"The caravan's gone, and they left us on the ice for the wolves."

"How do you know?" Erik readjusted her weight in his arms and kicked another wolf as it snapped at his ankles. A third approached. What would happen when ten ambushed them at once? Wolves in Montana jumped for their prey's throat. He'd seen packs of predators using numbers to drop even a large animal. If multiple wolves jumped Erik and he tumbled to the ice with Zita, they were goners.

"Trust me."

"Did you see them?" He guessed that with magic she saw farther than he could.

"No, I didn't, but I'm sure."

Would Al leave Erik to die? He couldn't believe this to be true, but could Al locate Erik out here on the ice? He woke up every morning right next to his friend. He was confident Al had searched for him before the caravan moved. Erik surveyed the ice for rescuers, but only wind-whipped flakes of snow danced across the ice. The caravan had left and Al didn't say goodbye.

A wolf nipped Erik's ankle.

"Ow."

"Kick them."

"Throw up a shield."

"My magic isn't working after falling through the ice. I know, otherwise you'd be dead." Zita smiled.

Erik's neck stiffened and his arms strained to hold Zita as a wolf jumped and bit at the coat Zita wore. He twisted away from the animal, and the sudden movement upset his balance and he wobbled a moment, swinging Zita in his arms for balance.

"Careful," She said.

"Should I try to walk through them?"

Three more wolves spread out in attack formation.

"This is looking bad."

Erik saw no path to victory. He didn't have the stamina, strength or stability to hold Zita and fight through the number of wolves that surrounded them.

Erik said, "I think I like you."

She huffed, "That's romantic."

"No, I mean it. Oh, it's complicated."

"Love?"

He shook his head. "Don't change my words, you're difficult to love."

"Me?"

"No, that's not what I meant. Ow!"

A wolf nipped his ankle and then another caught the other leg.

Erik danced around with Zita in his arms as he tried to keep away from the nippy little creatures.

"What did you mean?" Zita asked.

Erik sighed. Why did girls make it so difficult to tell them you liked them? Why did they make it such a big deal? He always had trouble talking to girls and now he had an alluring woman in his arms and they were about to die, and he couldn't tell her his feelings.

"I'm waiting."

His head ached, "I'm busy trying to prevent being eaten at the moment." The wolves reminded him of a bunch of girls at school. Girls traveled in packs, making it difficult for boys to approach. He yearned for Zita, but regretted leaving Lily by herself with Sherry.

"Boys." She snorted and shook her head.

"Boys aren't the problem, we know what we want."

"Girls are the problem?"

"Yes."

Zita lowered her eyebrows and her face reddened.

"No."

Zita smiled, "Boys are like wolves. They keep attacking a girl until they get what they want and then charge another girl."

"No, that's not it at all. Girls are the wolves, traveling in packs and causing boys confusion and fear."

A white-furred wolf with a gray patch around his eye jumped, clamped its teeth on Zita's jacket and clung there. The extra weight added to Zita's caused Erik to lean forward.

"We don't have long." Zita said. "Wagner told me the wolves go for the throat and kill you before disemboweling you."

"That's comforting." Erik assumed he'd die on this planet, and yeah, on an adventure he shouldn't have taken. A wolf grasped his boot and yanked.

"I wanted a chance to date you, spend time with you and go places. I searched for you after the . . . incident with your father." Erik wanted to tell her he loved her, but with a dry throat and painful, slashed ankles where the wolves' nips were taking a toll, he stayed silent.

.

CHAPTER 48

Al's jaw throbbed from clenching it tight, and he touched Roden's shoulder once more. He shouldn't be forced to make this decision, but he had to rescue his childhood friend. Al knew Erik would rescue him in the same situation. In fact, didn't he do that just a few days ago, when he could have left Al to die? His gut ached, but he had to take action.

"Roden turn left." Al moved to the wagon's running board and guided the mastodon out of the caravan and toward the wolves.

Obadiah yelled, "Al, come back. Don't leave the caravan or you'll die."

Al kept Roden at a fast speed, as he wanted to outrun anyone who might try to follow him and bring him back. He didn't know what his friend's condition might be. Would he find a full carcass, only a bone or two picked clean by the wolves or even worse, nothing but a red stain on the ice?

The turn took them into the wind, and its speed coupled with the speed of the running mastodon froze his face. The wolves were at least a mile away

He thought back to the safe confines of the caravan. Now that he had pulled away from its protection, even if he rescued Erik, could they ever find the others? Where was the road to the Ice Castle and could they locate it without a map? He supposed he could follow the general direction the caravan had gone and find land, but how far might they be then from the actual road?

Roden pounded across the ice with long strides, and each foot landed with a dull thud. Obadiah had talked of thin ice near the volcano. Al shouted, "Slow Roden!"

Once Roden built speed, it took time to slow him down, just like a fast-moving train in the Montana wilderness. "Slow boy."

Al scanned the horizon and saw four packs of wolves moving in an attack formation toward a specific spot. Then Al saw a human standing in the midst of the wolves.

"Slow."

Roden's speed decreased to a walking pace. Still fast and dangerous if they hit thin ice. If the ice broke now, Roden might be able to swim at first, but attached to the wagons the animal would be dragged under the ice to its death.

He brought Roden to a halt a quarter mile from the wolves. The wolves hadn't noticed the mastodon, because it was downwind. Roden snorted and shook his ears.

Al realized Roden smelled the wolves, and he hoped the wolves wouldn't spook the mastodon, causing the animal to respond with the old fight-or-flight instinct. "Quiet boy, if you want to live."

Roden stomped his feet on the ice, nervous of the wolves.

Al felt nervous too. That many wolves, if they ganged up on Roden, the animal couldn't defend itself from an attack since he was hooked to the wagons. Plus, if Roden spooked and abandoned Al, then Al and whoever was in the center of the circle would be stranded. He hoped that person was Erik. *Who else could it be?*

He padded toward the wolves, searching for an advantage. The little itch in his brain vanished. It was a feeling that Gadiel touched and probed his brain, which came as a by-product of the Fire and Ice experience. Al inhaled, and magic flickered to life in his inner core, spreading throughout his body. His magic was back. If he had his staff, then he'd be whole. Was Gadiel right? Did the Fire and Ice experience bring back his magic or is something else in play here?

He drew the magic in as power flowed, as if a sluicegate had opened to release a heavy spring thaw. It warmed him.

He threw a fireball at the pack of wolves nearest him and watched them burn, but he noticed the ice melt into a puddle below the burning animals. Their burnt bodies smoldered on the ice as other wolves ran away.

Can't do that; it's dangerous to melt the ice around Erik.

He trotted closer and saw a lone human carrying something in his arms. He noticed black hair in the bundle of Erik's jacket. *Is Erik trying to save the dog from the wolves?* Al yelled. "Erik, drop the dog and make a run for it. The wolves will go after the dog."

No reaction from Erik, who danced around the animals trying to keep from being pulled down and eaten.

The stench of burned fur and flesh floated on the breeze, and Roden bellowed.

"Roden, don't you go running away on me," He couldn't lose Roden this near to saving Erik. At least Erik still lived.

Movement behind Roden caught Al's attention, and he stared as something large moved toward them.

"What's this?" Could he rescue Erik first and then vanquish whatever approached from behind? He needed a distraction to give Erik a chance to escape.

What does a wolf cat? Meat, sure, but are they more attracted by rotting meat or fresh kills? Al wondered if a whiff of bacon would lure wolves.

He decided on bacon. Al remembered the sizzle of bacon in the kitchen as Mom made breakfast and how the scent permeated the house. He pictured a point a mile upwind from his present position and used magic to send the aroma to that point. He grinned and tied off the magic.

The wolves nearest Erik kept barking, biting and jumping at him and whatever he held. But the others in the pack stopped and sniffed the wind.

The wind increased its intensity, and the wolves reacted to the strong bacon scent. The wolves barked and howled, and those nearest Erik stopped biting at him.

A human yelled, but the wind drowned the words.

Al yelled back, "I'll reach you in a minute."

Two wolf packs sprinted toward the bacon scent. The others acted confused and barked at each other. Maybe they were older and wiser and realized they had an easy meal in Erik, so why run off after some unfamiliar scent.

Erik raised one hand and waved at Al.

"I'm coming for you," Al shouted. He remembered something running toward Roden and prepared to face it before Roden spooked. He pivoted and prepared a fireball, but there was no pack of wolves. A mastodon and wagon pulled up and parked next to Roden, and Obadiah jogged to Al.

"What are you doing here?"

"To save you." The boy smiled.

"I thought you were another pack of wolves and I almost blasted you with a fireball."

Obadiah backed up a moment. "I yelled at you to let you know I had your back."

Al pointed at Erik. "There's Erik, and it looks like he saved the stupid dog."

The last pack of wolves scampered after the bacon scent.

Erik walked toward the boys with his bundle in his arms.

The bundle in the jacket moved.

Erik said, "Easy Zita. I'll carry you."

Al thought, Zita, out here? He exchanged a glance with Obadiah.

A big, black dog wriggled free of the jacket and ambled to the boys.

Al laughed, "Oh, you named the dog Zita. Funny."

Erik appeared dazed as he squeezed his eyes shut for a moment. Then he smiled, starting with pursed lips that built into a smile showing all his teeth, followed by a bark of laughter.

Al couldn't imagine being stranded on the ice surrounded by wolves hoping a rescue party found him. Erik must have gone a little crazy while abandoned on the ice and threatened by the wolves. But why did he save the stupid dog or name the mutt, Zita?

CHAPTER 49

Erik hugged Al and said, "Thanks for saving me, buddy. Zita and I were goners out there."

The black dog barked.

Erik guessed she warmed up after she shape-shifted into the dog.

Obadiah said, "We have to move."

"Will you be able to get us to the Ice Castle?" Al asked.

"Yeah. But you won't be happy when you get there. Hadrian will tell us to rock off after he has a gutser and we'll be lucky to live through the beating for leaving the caravan."

"That's okay; we're not going to the Ice Castle as handlers. We're going for the golden crown," Al said.

Obadiah snorted and rolled his eyes. "Ah, the infamous golden crown. Every year we get a wise guy wizard in the caravan who knows how to find and secure the golden crown. They reach the Ice Castle and disappear forever."

"Well, not us," Al boasted. "I'm a wizard and I'm confident I'll bring back the crown."

"Yeah, right. To find the crown, you're sent to the Pit of Wretchedness, where an old, ruined castle sits in an overgrown jungle. You're both lucky you're still alive right now, and we're not even at the castle. If we don't get to land soon, we'll all be dead."

Erik arranged the hammock with several blankets and placed the dog, Zita, in the hammock. He kissed her on the snout and she licked his face. Erik said, "I won't tell these guys unless you agree."

She nodded.

"Okay. The hammock and blankets should keep you warm until we check in at the Ice Castle."

They started the trip, walking the mastodons carefully over the thin ice until it thickened and then urging the mastodons to full speed. Erik didn't understand the concern for the asteroid showers, but if Obadiah believed them an issue, then they would run the mastodons.

Al said, "What were you thinking chasing off in the night after that dog?"

"The dog bit me and I ran after it, I wasn't thinking. Then the next thing I know we're on thin ice and the dog goes into the water. But it wasn't a dog it—." Erik stopped talking.

"Why didn't you let it drown?

"I thought Gadiel or Hadrian would be mad at me if it drowned."

"Well, they're mad at us now, especially since Obadiah joined us."

Erik smiled, "It looks like your magic returned."

"Full power, baby. Now I go to Gadiel and demand my staff."

"Will he give it to you?"

"He won't have a choice. I'm stronger than he is in magic. The staff is attuned to me, or at least it should be if he hasn't altered it. When I call it, the staff flies into my hands."

"What if he locks it in a cabinet?"

"Hah, I break the lock."

Erik said, "Gadiel? Good guy or bad guy?"

"He promised to tease mysteries from the staff and teach me the staff's magic, but he's taught me nothing. He hinted of secret magic I could learn, but again, nothing. I'm leaning toward bad guy."

"We're counting on him to lead us to the golden crown; should we trust him?"

"I think he wants to get his hands on it, but we're going to grab it and not let him touch it."

"He has a lot of tricks."

"We'll outsmart the old geezer."

Erik chuckled, remembering past exploits where Al boasted of victory before the event but failed miserably. They shared similar conversations on Earth. Al would explain why his new design for a space ship could outperform any current design. He'd brag that he was smarter than the engineers at NASA, and to prove it he made prototypes of his designs. They transported the rockets to their favorite open space and set up the launch. With a camera to record each momentous occasion, Al ignited the rocket fuel, the prototype rose a few feet and then crashed or exploded in the sky. Three rockets never left the ground, instead each burst into flames on the launch pad. Erik hoped Al's confidence was accurate this time.

They traveled in silence for an hour as the mastodons hauled the wagons effortlessly on the ice. Once they built momentum, they kept the energy going and Roden didn't have any problems with the speed. An hour later land stretched before them, a valley between two mountain cliffs.

Obadiah yelled, "There's the path to the Ice Castle, only five miles to go."

Erik waved him to continue and high-fived Al. "We're gonna make it."

Erik thought, ah, a castle. No more sleeping on the ground, or in hammocks or being hunted by cats and winter wolves. They should have better food at the castle, fruit, vegetables and real meat, not the jerky they'd eaten for the last five weeks. He imagined the taste of a fresh apple. His mouth watered.

He dreamed of a hot bath and, thinking of Zita, he'd splurge for a shave. Could he arrange a date with her? He laughed. Where did teenagers go on this planet? No movie houses, no restaurants or fast-food places. The things he knew of dating were nonexistent on Aloheno. How did teenagers get acquainted?

Erik said, "Where do you take Sherry for a date?"

"What do you mean?"

"On Earth, where did you go?"

"Movies and ice cream after the movie."

"What movies?"

"Sci-Fi, and Sherry likes shows with super heroes."

"Okay, now give me dating spots on Aloheno."

Al whistled, "Yeah. A restaurant? No. Don't have those."

Erik said, "I know. Right? What's the dating scene on this planet? How do you meet girls?"

"I don't know. Maybe parents introduce the boy and girl, or rich people go to a masked ball at the castle."

"Sure the rich and powerful, but poor mopes like us, how do we hook up with the opposite sex?" Erik thought of Zita riding in the hammock and then pictured the two of them sitting in a dark restaurant enjoying a hamburger and a pop and staring into her emerald eyes.

"Are you hooking up with someone at the castle?"

Erik blushed, "No, I wondered how teenagers on Aloheno date. Just something that crossed my mind. What are you planning on doing about Sherry when we get back? Will you two marry on Aloheno?"

"Hah, marriage? Me?"

"Someday, Sherry might want to get married."

"I suppose."

"This culture might think she must marry before she turns twenty or nobody will marry her. Will you lead her on until she's past marrying age and then—"

A whistle, as of fireworks on the fourth of July in the U.S.A. on Earth, screamed across the sky. Erik searched the sky for fireworks, and the ice exploded a hundred yards in front of him. Ice and water blasted upward and rained on the wagon and Roden.

Roden panicked and tried an abrupt detour that slung the end wagon into a spin, which soon affected the rest. Roden lost his footing from the centrifugal force and landed on his side. The wagons stayed upright a moment and then the harness rolled with Roden forcing the wagons to tip as well.

Pandemonium erupted around the boys. Their wagon spun like a summer carnival ride, frictionless on the ice. Erik held tight to the wagon. He looked for Zita and the hammock which rode atop the side of the wagon. Good, she was safe.

The wagon spun but still moved toward the open crater in the ice.

Erik hollered, "Al, this would be a great time for some magic."

Al looked shell-shocked and clung to the wagon with closed eyes.

They spun three times and Erik watched them approach the crater. Maybe two more spins and Roden, the wagons, Zita, Al and Erik would be thrown into the water.

A second and third whistle screamed through the air, and two asteroids crashed into the ice behind them. Ice heaved into odd shapes, then cracked into smaller pieces.

On the next rotation, the wagons slowed, and they finished their spinning and sliding a few feet from the open water.

Erik said, "Al, you did it."

"I did nothing, I was holding on for my life."

The dog barked.

"Oh." Erik said.

Obadiah stopped and helped the boys get Roden back on his feet, which was difficult to do as the explosions rattled the animal. Roden bellowed and stamped his feet.

The wagons weighed too much for the boys to boost upright; they needed the mastodons to lift the overturned wagons.

Obadiah said, "Unhook Roden from the wagons, we'll use his strength to set these upright."

The boys jumped as another asteroid crashed into the ice three hundred yards away.

"Hurry,"

Erik unhooked Roden from the thills and the mastodon turned toward land and appeared ready to bolt, but Erik touched him on the rump and calmed him with his healing power.

He walked Roden to the first wagon and said, "Wait, let me remove the dog from the hammock. We don't want her getting hurt."

Zita jumped into Erik's arms.

Erik asked, "Are you okay?"

She shivered.

Another asteroid shattered a section of ice in the direction they needed to go.

Obadiah shouted, "It's not getting any quieter boys; let's right these wagons."

They worked fast, and Roden cooperated despite another four asteroids crashing into the ice and creating waves underneath the ice, bouncing the wagons and boys into the air and causing terrifying cracking sounds.

Erik hitched Roden to the wagons, and checked the harness, thills and wagons for damage. "Okay, it's done," he said.

Obadiah beckoned, "Follow me."

They were forced to take a crooked path to the shoreline as asteroids were crashing in the direction Obadiah wanted to go. Peering behind, Erik watched twenty more smash into the ice one mile or more from the boys. The ice waves rose and fell five feet.

Al said, "I remember watching the asteroid showers at home and they can last several hours. We gotta get off this ice."

The boys guided Roden and the wagons around widening cracks and holes as if meandering through a corn maze. Though it was important to get off the ice, they had to pick their spots.

Geysers of water erupted in every direction as rocks barreled out of the sky.

One minute, they guided the wagons south and east and then pivoted back west to navigate. Roden bellowed and rolled his eyes in apprehension at each explosion.

Erik squawked, "We're getting further from shore."

"It's the only way." Obadiah answered.

Ten minutes elapsed, and the boys made progress of only a hundred yards in the desired direction with a mile to go.

Erik muttered and rubbed the back of his neck. This close to shore and yet not making progress. He worried an asteroid might actually hit them or damage the ice so badly they wouldn't be able to reach land. Had he rescued Zita only to be annihilated by a meteor shower?

"Al, can you make an ice path for us?"

"What do you mean?"

"Can you freeze the water, fill the holes as we move so we travel straight? We'll never make it to shore at this rate."

"Freeze a path? Yes, Zita did it in the dungeon at the Velidred castle."

"Do you remember the incantation?"

"I think so." Al raised his hands with fingers pointed to shore, "Wind will blow with temperatures low."

The wind picked up and Erik shivered inside his coat.

Al stopped. His hands above his head, but he interrupted the spell.

"Is that it?" Erik asked.

"No, give me a second. I need something to rhyme with freeze."

"What?"

"I forgot part of the incantation, and I need something that rhymes with freeze."

"Any word?"

"No, a specific word."

Erik rattled off words that rhymed with freeze, "Breeze, bees, knees, trees, threes, peas, please."

"No, no. None of them."

Obadiah said, "You're not worth a Zach, man."

"Keep em coming."

The dog barked.

Oh great, Erik thought. Zita knows the word. Would she expose herself to Al and Obadiah? If she knows the word, why not shape-shift back and let them know? Their life depended on Al succeeding.

Al said, "Not fleas. Not cheese."

"Oh, come on already," Obadiah raised his hands in exasperation.

Twin asteroids streamed across the sky blazing red and orange screaming loudly. They landed close. Too close.

Erik said, "Running out of time.

"It's a simple word. Don't pressure me, I don't work well under pressure."

"How about sleaze?" Obadiah asked.

"No."

"Flees?" Erik asked.

"You already said fleas."

"Not the insect. As in a criminal flees the scene of a crime."

"It doesn't matter, it still isn't right."

Obadiah said, "The asteroid strikes are getting more intense."

Erik said, "Is it frieze?"

"That's the word we're trying to rhyme."

"The art spelling. You know a . . . oh what is it? Art on a wall. Architectural thingy."

"Nobody rhymes the same word. Frieze and freeze? Who creates an incantation like that?"

"I'm trying to help here. I know nothing about incantations."

A whistle of an asteroid, then a kerthump as it smashed into the ice. The ice they stood on heaved with the movement of the wave.

The dog sneezed.

"That's it." Al exclaimed.

"What?" Erik asked.

Al set his feet on the ice, "Fall's sneezes lead to winter's freezes. Ice, ice, ice," he trumpeted into the wind.

The holes in the ice firmed and a path between the mastodons and the land transformed into a bluish, green color.

Erik said, "Sneezes? That's the word?" He shook his head. Wizards were strange. He whispered to Zita, "Thanks."

They tested the ice before moving, and finding it firm, raced to shore.

CHAPTER 50

Al said, "With my magic back, we need to reclaim the staff. Once we reach the Ice Castle, I'm marching to Gadiel and demanding it back. If he doesn't give it to me, I'm calling it or using magic to get it."

Roden lumbered up the mountain pass, dragging the wagons through the slushy snow. Asteroids whistled and exploded on the lake behind them.

"How close do you have to be to call it?" Erik asked.

"I don't know, I don't sense a connection where we are now, but that might be Gadiel's doing. He better not bond with the staff because I need it to get the crown."

Rocky domes, none higher than one hundred feet and covered with snow, dotted the surrounding landscape. Snow hid the underlying rock formation, and Al wondered about the geology of the land. Two glaciers flowed parallel to each other in the distance. A mountain ridge separated the glaciers.

Al asked, "Do you think we can find the crown? Everyone says other adventurers tried and failed."

"We've traveled hundreds of miles in rough conditions to give it our best shot. Remember, the goal is to rescue my father so he doesn't hate me anymore."

"Yes, but we're kids from Montana. Do you think all the D&D games we played at home are the same as real adventuring?"

Erik said, "You're Alpherge the Mighty, and I'm Erik the Healer, we can do anything in this world."

"Have you given yourself a nickname now, Erik the Healer?"

"I'm testing it, to help me awaken the adventuring spirit."

A bird of prey screeched in the sky and dove toward a stream.

Half the time this land scared Al with its strange monsters, mastodons, and three moons. Even handling magic scared him. Was this a horrible, fascinating dream, and did they have what they needed to capture the crown? He hoped his magic would last and that it would respond when he needed its power. If he couldn't control it when he needed it to fight a monster, could they survive?

Obadiah guided his mastodon and wagon over the crest and stopped. Erik steered Roden to pull up beside the other mastodon.

The land opened into a lush valley where two waterfalls cascaded off the mountain cliffs in the distance. A green meadow gleamed between the sheer rock walls. The waterfalls fed a winding river flowing through the meadow. Mastodons grazed at the far end of the valley and sheep were held in a pen next to the mastodons.

Erik said, "Wow."

A storybook castle stood in the middle of the valley, its three large spires climbing to the sky from the middle of the whitewashed building.

Al cheered, "Is that the Ice Castle?"

"Yep," Obadiah said.

"No ice?" Erik asked.

Obadiah smiled, "I enjoy watching people's faces when they see it for the first time. It's three miles down into the valley, and the air warms the closer we get."

"Why warmer?"

Al said, "Geothermal power? Does the valley sit on a volcano or near a lake of molten lava?"

Obadiah shrugged and sauntered back to his mastodon, "Time to move. I'm hungry, and the food in the castle is excellent. Fresh lamb barbecued with amazing spices. You can't get these flavors anywhere else in the world. That's why I make this run every summer. It'll be rough as we can't change the sleds back to wheels."

They traveled the three miles more slowly, concerned about the sleds. Roden seemed as excited to reach their destination as the boys. The trail hair-pinned around the mountain, descending until they reached the valley floor.

The aroma of hot lamb filled the air and made Al's mouth water. The grilled food smelled so much better than the jerky they'd eaten for weeks. This place had possibilities.

As they reached the meadow, they became aware that water also splashed behind them from another high waterfall. The sun shone in the valley, and the troubles of the trip melted from Al's mind.

Zita, as a black dog, bolted toward the village.

"There goes your dog," Al said.

"Yep. I wonder if we'll ever see her again." He had a distant, empty stare in his eyes.

Obadiah showed them where to take the mastodons, and they still had two hours of work to park their wagons of mastodon feed and dung, brush Roden and help Obadiah unload his wagon of supplies for the Ice Castle. They had brought sugar cane, processed flour, and honey, which would be stored in huts within the valley.

After the last load, Obadiah said, "Before we return to Velidred we'll load the wagons with spices, lamb's wool and goods the locals make which sell in Velidred. We have five days before we leave, until then we celebrate with baths, barbecue, drink and music. The local girls are quick with a kiss." Obadiah winked at the boys.

Al's shoulders ached and his beard itched, and he wondered when he should confront Gadiel. Should he do it before they ate? Was there time right now?

Erik sidled up to Al and whispered, "When do we search for the crown?"

Al shook his head, "Don't know. But I want the staff first. Plus, where do we start? Look at this valley, it's huge. We gotta find somebody who knows where to look."

Obadiah said, "I'm going to the hot baths and I'll meet you guys in the tavern over there." He pointed to a building where flute and lyre music trilled across the meadow.

The boys walked to the castle doors, uncertain where to find Gadiel. Guards stood at the door.

A guard with a handlebar mustache and lance said, "Where're you two heading? Handlers bunk in the tents over there." He pointed to a group of fifteen green tents near the sheep pen.

"We need to see Gadiel."

"He's talking with the king. Now get out of here."

Al saw the perfectly manicured guards with their tall bearskin hats pulled down near their eyes, and their pressed uniforms of red and black. They stood at perfect attention. Al understood why they'd perceive Erik and him to be bums. The boys hadn't bathed in days. Their beards were scraggly, and they reeked of too many days on the road.

"Handlers can meet with Gadiel in his cabin tomorrow."

Erik asked, "Where's Gadiel's cabin?"

The guard pointed with his lance to a well maintained cabin in the shade of a large cedar tree on the other side of the river.

Erik looked at Al, raised his eyebrows and nodded to the cabin.

"Thank you officers, fine job," Erik said. He poked Al in the side. "Follow me."

They strolled from the castle toward a bridge which crossed the river. Erik stopped Al on the bridge.

Al said, "Why'd we stop?"

Erik said, "What if the staff is in Gadiel's cabin?"

"We wait until Gadiel returns and ask him for it."

"No, we locate it and snatch it now!"

"The guards will shred us with their lances."

Erik grabbed Al's shoulders, "Listen. Every time you've asked Gadiel for your staff he's refused. He buffaloes you with different reasons, and you don't stand up for yourself. Then you walk away empty handed. The staff is yours, and you deserve it."

"Yeah."

"We're going to the cabin and grabbing it."

"Just sneak in and steal it?"

"The staff is yours, we're returning it to its rightful owner. Look, it's a nice, warm day, people open windows to air out their houses on nice days. We sneak in a window, nab the staff, and head to the tents. Then a hot bath, yummy food and sleep."

Al's stomach tensed and he tilted his head side to side, weighing the options. He liked the plan, unless they got caught. "What if the guards catch us and throw us in the dungeon or something? Then we'll never get the staff and can't retrieve the golden crown."

"No worries, I'll go in, and you keep watch. They'll only throw me in the dungeon."

It was a perfect day in the valley, comfortable temperatures, with the sun shining on green grass. After long days on the ice, the warmer temperatures felt fantastic.

Erik said, "It'll be easy. No worries. We'll hide the staff until it's time to search for the crown. Gadiel will never find it. When we go for the crown, we retrieve the staff."

"Might work." Al didn't relish stealing the staff, but didn't fancy Gadiel having it one day more than necessary. Erik was right, Gadiel never planned to return the staff to Al.

They drifted toward the cabin, observing the river, and discussing the surrounding mountain peaks. They didn't want to appear in a hurry, nervous or shifty. Simple, Erik knocks on the door. If someone answers, then they ask for Gadiel, since he isn't there, then they leave and try another day.

As they approached the cabin, Al scratched at his beard and chin with trembling, tingling fingers. The skin under his beard near his Adam's apple itched in the heat. He jerked his head right and left, patrolling for people.

"Stop looking guilty," Erik whispered.

Al's stomach tightened and flopped, and he thought he might vomit, "I'm not looking guilty."

"Walk normal, we're knocking on the door and leaving a message. That's all. Relax."

"I can't relax." Bile rose in his throat, and Al expected to heave on the meadow in front of everyone. Al envisioned the guards waiting until Erik broke into the house and then capturing them in the act and executing them at dawn using a guillotine. "Let's not do this, we'll talk to Gadiel, he'll return it."

Erik grabbed Al's arm. "Quit making a scene, we're doing this." He dragged Al toward the cabin.

Erik took a deep breath and knocked on the cabin door. After a long wait, he knocked again. No one answered the door.

"Not a big cabin, so no one's home."

They scrambled to the back of the cabin and checked for open windows. The back of the house sat thirty feet from a sheer mountain face which hid the window from view.

"The window's open. Stand by the cedar over there and come and get me if you see anybody." Erik pushed Al toward the tree.

Erik climbed through the window.

Al's body shook as he surveyed the castle grounds for people heading toward the cabin and thought for a moment. *Wait, I should be able to sense the staff. Erik doesn't have to sneak through the window because I can call the staff with magic.*

He took a deep breath and sought the staff using magic. Yes, the staff responded; he felt its presence in the valley, but not at the cabin. No, it was at the castle in Gadiel's hands. Al darted to the window and whispered, "Erik, it's not there."

Erik didn't answer.

Where was he, the cabin isn't that big. He tried again, speaking louder, "Erik the staff's in the castle, get out of the cabin."

There was no movement in the cabin.

"Come on, where are you?" He heard two voices, a male and female. He yelled, "Erik, get out of there."

Al perceived Gadiel's presence in his brain a moment before he was paralyzed with pain. His brain felt like it exploded. It was as if a thousand bombs of migraines attacked his synapses at once. He slumped to the ground holding his head. He blacked out.

Al didn't know how long it took for him to recover, but when he did, three soldiers held the points of their lances to his chest. Hadrian stood behind the soldiers, holding Obadiah tightly.

Erik backed through the window. "The staff isn't there."

CHAPTER 51

Zita watched through the window as Hadrian and the castle guards marched the boys to the castle dungeon. There were severe penalties for stealing objects and breaking into homes, and the boys might lose a finger or hand to the executioner.

It'd be a shame if Erik lost a hand. She loved his strong shoulders and rough hands. They better not damage his wonderful lips, because the kiss he had given her moments earlier, lingered. She brushed her lips with a finger.

She had prepared a fireball to throw at the man who entered the room, then she realized who it was. Erik searched for the staff, but it wasn't in the cabin. Gadiel had it with him. Then they had talked, and he gazed into her eyes. And when he sat next to her, she kissed his tender lips. Zita closed her eyes, remembering the moment.

She shook her head from the reverie, and prepared herself for the banquet, an event that happened every summer when the caravan arrived. The party celebrated the delivery of fruit, vegetables and supplies to the castle. It was a joyous time with plentiful food, music and dancing, and she could meet the new king.

* * * *

An hour later she entered the castle banquet hall, where huge red and white banners decorated the walls. She meandered through the room, meeting the local dukes and duchesses. She listened to music played by three musicians on flute, zither and lyre. A serving girl handed her a mug of the local drink. Zita drank a sip and coughed at the tartness of the atrocious champagne. The atmosphere in the room radiated fun and frivolity as the band played a lively tune.

Zita watched the local dignitaries dancing in the ballroom. She searched for people she recognized from previous visits, but saw no one, not even Gadiel.

A young man in his twenties with bright blue eyes and dark eyebrows approached her. He bowed deeply and said, "I am Lawrence of Holden Keep."

Zita curtsied and decided not to let these people know her true identity. She hoped no one recognized her. She extended a hand to the man. "Clarice of the Open Plains Province,"

He took her hand and gently kissed it.

"Did you come with the caravan?"

"Yes, I'm traveling with my Uncle."

"How was the journey?"

If she was honest, she'd tell the man what a dreadful, boring journey it had been, stuck in a cabin, doing nothing but watch the caravan travel over various terrains, but said, "A normal journey."

"I'm imagining traveling the long distance from Velidred castle, seeing unfamiliar landscapes over the mountains, plains, ice and prairies, and encounters with wild beasts. What an exciting trip."

Zita smiled and said, "Not much excitement on this trip." *Yeah, there'd been that brief encounter with wolves and drowning, but Erik saved me. I learned how to shape-shift.* She wondered if she should surprise the young man by shape-shifting into an animal right in front of him. *That would be a good way to anger Gadiel.* She drained the remaining liquid in the mug and grimaced.

"The drink is awful, isn't it?" Lawrence asked.

"Can I say it's vile, without offending you?"

"We had a hard frost just as we harvested the grapes last fall. The entire crop was ruined. We dug up this barrel from twenty years ago. I agree; it's vile." They both laughed.

An obese man and two plump women walked into the hall. The man's garments were ill-fitting, unable to cover the expanse of his waist. The robe was woven in a garish green and purple pattern.

"Who are they?" Zita asked.

"Heathcliff and his sisters, Verde and Rose." Lawrence said. "An ugly lot of hoarders."

Zita thought the sisters had eaten less than their brother, but not by much. "Is their father king?"

"No, their father used to be king, but he died a year ago. A new king from the southern provinces has taken residence in the Ice Castle. These three were allowed to stay in the castle. The new king was injured in a battle, a skirmish he lost. People I've spoken with say he has wizarding skills, but I guess they weren't sufficient to protect him."

"Interesting." Zita smiled and snatched a mug of ale off a nearby tray offered by a servant. Could Erik become a prince or duke? That would make him more appealing. She scanned the banquet hall for Gadiel.

"Did you hear the news?" Lawrence asked?

"What news?"

"Two caravan handlers broke into a home. The guards caught them red handed and threw them into the dungeon. Rumor has it the executioner sharpens the guillotine."

Zita gasped.

"Don't worry, my lady. The guards captured them. You'll be safe. I'll protect you from those ruffians."

"Did they take anything?"

"Didn't have a chance the way I heard it. The guards had their eyes on them from the moment they reached the valley. Long, dirty hair and beards, easy to see they were ne'er-do-wells. Surprised Hadrian brought them this far north."

Zita's stomach hardened. How could she keep Erik alive? He saved her. Was it her turn to save him?

The music stopped mid-song. Two dancers completed their twirls and their dresses swished back and forth, but the music had died.

A castle servant raised his voice. "Prepare for the king's arrival."

The people turned toward the great hall entrance and ended their conversations.

A shorter gentleman, dressed in royal finery of purple and yellow, walked into the room. Burns splotched his face, and his left arm hung limp by his side.

A squeak escaped Zita's lips as she covered her mouth with her hands.

Lawrence said, "Don't be frightened. He's the new king of the Ice Castle."

The servant announced the king, "King Haskell, from Velidred Castle."

Zita's heart drummed hard against her chest, and she didn't know whether to laugh or cry. Thoughts bounced around her brain. *Should I run to him? No, he'd expect me to walk with royal posture and poise.* Her legs trembled, she couldn't move.

"Are you all right?" Lawrence asked.

"What," she stammered. Tears pooled in her eyes and then overflowed and streamed over her cheeks.

Lawrence offered Zita his handkerchief.

Zita didn't notice, She wove between the dancers, as she approached the king. She worried her legs might collapse.

Two guards saw her coming and stopped her progress. "That's as close as you get, lady."

The king scanned the room, a gleam in his eye and a knowing grin on his lips as the guests clapped at his arrival.

Zita tried to push through the guards, but collapsed to the floor instead. She extended her hands toward him and said, "Daddy?"

The king looked at her as if he didn't recognize the young girl sitting on the floor.

The guards looked confused, as if wondering whether to help her stand or capture her. They looked to the king for instructions.

King Haskell pushed through the guards and said, "Zita, is that you, Baby?" He reached out his good hand.

Zita blinked tears from her eyes and grasped the king's hand as he helped her to her feet.

Then King Haskell did something Zita remembered from years ago. He hugged her.

Warmth and love flowed over her. Was this the man she threw the fireball at just months ago? Had he changed?

He kissed her on the forehead, "It's wonderful to see you, Zita. I missed you."

She took large, deep, savoring breaths. Was it possible he didn't realize the fireball came from her? Should she tell him? No, enjoy the moment.

The king held her back from his body with his one good arm, "You've lost weight. Was the journey difficult?"

"Daddy, I'm so happy to see you're alive. Those burns look painful and infected." She reached out to touch his face, but he turned his head.

In a low menacing voice he said, "Did you think you could kill me with a simple fireball, the great wizard-king of Velidred?"

She felt heat rise to her cheeks, and she couldn't look into her father's eyes. She knew him to be a vengeful king. Would she join the boys in the dungeon?

Gadiel padded to the king's side. "Good, you've re-connected. We have things to discuss."

"It can wait," King Haskell said.

"No, it can't wait. We talk now, before someone does something stupid." He glowered at Zita.

What stupid thing did Gadiel think she had planned?

"We must retire to your chambers, Your Majesty, for a few minutes, to discuss strategy for the safe deliverance of the crown into our hands."

Zita remembered her dad, the king, in similar circumstances when underlings attempted to force him to action he didn't desire at the moment. He'd fly into a rage and rebuke the offender. She would enjoy such a show of power over Gadiel.

Instead, the king perused the banquet hall and made a slight gesture to the musicians, and music once again filled the room. He smiled at Zita, nodded at Gadiel, and escorted Zita from the hall.

* * * *

They sat in the king's antechamber and servants brought them food and drink. The king sat in a large chair, much larger than his compact frame required. The back of the wooden chair extended two feet above his head. It was carved with the image of a mastodon.

Zita was surprised at the paintings on the wall. They appeared to be of previous kings and queens. There was also one of men hunting. She thought it odd that her father hadn't replaced those paintings.

"How did you get here, Daddy? I looked for you at the volcano, but I didn't find you."

Gadiel answered, "Magic my child. Deep magic power from the depths of the volcano and Velidred Moon allowed your father to transport here. No mere feat with his injuries."

King Haskell nodded. "A trick Gadiel taught me years ago. A compounding of different forces prevented me from shielding the attacks. My injuries were too severe to fight back."

Dad had never been a humble man, but the eclipse experience weakened him, and Zita now recognized his humanity.

The king continued. "I understand you're under Gadiel's tutelage; he can teach you Velidred's secrets. Be forewarned, the old magic is great wizardry and requires tremendous power. I'm afraid the injuries and power used to transport me to the Ice Castle have depleted my magic."

Zita said, "A boy that traveled with us has power to heal, like Cugbert. Maybe he can—"

Gadiel interrupted her, "Yes, let's talk about the boys. We didn't bring them here to heal anyone. They're here to capture the crown. They think it's a golden crown. Everyone who seeks it is deceived by this image. I knew they'd be easily swayed by the mention of a golden crown."

"I heard the guillotine is being sharpened." Zita sipped her champagne.

"To keep the populace under control, my king," Gadiel said. "We'll release them into the Pit of Wretchedness and see if they have the magic to return with the helmet of justice."

"Helmet of justice?" Zita asked.

"Yes. There is no golden crown, it's a leather helmet with a gold dragon upon it. It's known as the helmet of justice and was last worn by King Stephen III."

"And if they retrieve it?" Zita asked.

"That's your role, Zita," Gadiel said. "Once they find the helmet of justice, you'll take it and kill them, or leave them to die."

Zita felt a shiver race through her body as she lifted her chin in a royal gesture. "Do you expect me to go into the Pit of Wretchedness with them? What if I choose not to kill them or leave them to die?"

Gadiel smiled and pain flooded Zita's brain as if lightning bolts bounced in her skull.

"Argh," Zita flinched and squinted against the pain.

"Enough," the king bellowed.

The pain subsided in slow waves, like ripples in a still pond. *Here was the truth then, Gadiel controlled her and most likely controlled Dad, too.*

"When do we send the boys into the pit?" The king asked.

Gadiel answered. "They must leave at night. The scroll is explicit about the timing, 'near midnight on a moon-less night in the height of summer.'"

Zita said, "What makes you think these boys can find the crown? Oh, excuse me, the helmet of justice. Haven't others tried and failed?"

"People come through here year after year, a few with magic, others seeking glory, all have failed to return from the pit. But these boys have something extra, and it's going to require both of them to find it. One without the other is useless."

Zita stood. "And yet you abandoned us to die on the ice?"

"Zita sit." Her father commanded.

"Daddy, this man left me to drown. Without Erik, one of the boys in the dungeon, I wouldn't be here. The other boy, Alpherge, rescued both of us from the wolves." She stood defying Dad and Gadiel. "Now you want to dispatch me . . ." her voice cracked, "into the Pit of Wretchedness never to return?"

The silence was stifling as Gadiel and King Haskell exchanged glances.

"I'm to wander in the Pit of Wretchedness or worse, be eaten by wild monsters, ghosts or undead creatures? Is that the fate you've assigned your only child?"

The king rose from his chair, a difficult task as he had to brace himself with his good arm to force his bruised body out of the chair.

Had her father become a crippled and aged old man? What game was Gadiel playing? What games had he played his entire life, manipulating the people around him as if they were pieces on a child's board game? And now she was falling captured in the spider's web. The Fire and Ice experience sealed her life to his.

Her dad placed his hand on her shoulder. "Zita, this crown is important to us all. Gadiel believes that the boys can find it and return it to us. They have the power, and ancient scrolls speak of their ability."

"Can't we let them return with the crown and then rejoice with them?"

He gripped her shoulder. "We can't let them live."

"Can't Gadiel kill them? Alpherge took the Fire and Ice challenge, too. Certainly, Gadiel would take pleasure in delivering the final blow to Alpherge the Mighty."

Gadiel looked pleased. The man appeared dangerous when he smiled. "I fear that with the helmet of justice, Alpherge might thwart my," he paused, "touches."

"Daddy, I know you want me to kill Erik, but I can't."

He kissed her forehead. "Do it for me."

She hesitated, weighing her words. Would she make it worse for Erik or could she convince him that she didn't have to kill him? Despite Gadiel's control over her or Dad's desires, she couldn't kill Erik. She blurted, "I love him."

The two men exchanged glances as King Haskell pursed his lips.

Gadiel said, "I believed you wanted revenge on these boys because of what they did to your father."

"Dad is alive."

"Injured and with only minor magic remaining. I knew he was here because I sensed his movement and use of Velidred's power. Now, you can resurrect him to his full glory."

The king studied Zita.

Zita scowled at her father. "How can you do this to me? Everything I've wanted you've killed or kept from me. Now, when I thought you dead, you're plotting to kill someone I love."

"I love you, Zita."

Her father had never said those words to her. Seventeen years she yearned for those words from his lips. "Didn't you love Mom, too? Where is she Daddy? Where?"

Gadiel said, "Should I?"

King Haskell shouted, "No!" Then his control returned, and he said, "Leave her for the moment, but at the proper time, we'll use your skill." The king flicked his hand and Gadiel left the room.

The king moved to embrace Zita with his good arm, but she rebuffed his advance.

Zita repeated, "I can't, Daddy, I love him."

CHAPTER 52

A l asked, "When will they kill us?"

Sweat rolled down his back into the open sores from the flogging he received before being chained in the dungeon three days ago. The sores hurt and itched, but that was nothing compared to the pain inflicted by the rat creatures in the dungeon when they licked and bit the sores.

Erik responded, "Any day now."

The dungeon had been built near a volcanic hot spot in the valley that kept the walls too hot to touch. Al couldn't tolerate the walls, and the heat of the floor caused his feet to blister. He hadn't slept since they were locked in the dungeon because of the heat, for fear of the rats, and fear that at any moment they'd issue his death sentence. The guard told them the penalty for breaking and entering was the guillotine, and the blacksmith had been told to sharpen the blade.

Al said to Erik, "I wish they'd do it already."

"Come on, big guy, stay strong. Have you tried to break the spell Gadiel placed on you?"

"Yes, two minutes ago. Get off my back." *Break the spell, get the magic back. Get us out of the dungeon. Break us free.* "Have you learned how to heal me without touching me?" Whenever Al complained, Erik revisited that task.

"Don't be so testy, Al."

"Really? We haven't eaten or slept in three days, my back is killing me, and the vermin only make it worse, and you say don't be testy?"

"We're getting out of here." Erik said.

"Do you have magic now? I sure don't. Do you plan to beat up the guard and steal his keys? How are we getting out?"

They repeated this conversation every hour. Al could detect Erik by sound and smell in the darkness, but light never reached the dungeon. They didn't know for sure how many days passed, but had tried to ark time by the changing guards.

"I don't expect Gadiel to kill us. He wants the crown as much as we do."

"If the caravan leaves without us, even if we find the crown, we're stranded here until next summer."

Al squirmed as something ran across his back, but it was only sweat rolling into the deep gouges made by the leather straps. "Is that his plan? Sequester us in the dungeon until the caravan leaves and then send us after the crown?"

"Maybe."

"It doesn't matter, without magic and my staff, we can't find the crown." Every time Al attempted to break through the barrier, Gadiel discharged waves of pain into his brain.

"He's gotta give us water if he wants us to leave the dungeon alive." Erik rattled the chains attached to his arms. "Let us out!"

"I can't even yell at the guards anymore, it makes my throat hurt. I'm surprised I still sweat. I sure hope when the sweating stops my back won't sting as much."

"When you stop sweating, that'll increase the rotting of our flesh, and the vermin will swarm us like the first time."

Al recalled when they were first thrown into the dungeon and shackled, the rats appeared immediately and bit deep into the cuts.

They even chewed healthy skin on the boys' arms and legs. Al and Erik had fought them off as best they could. Since that time, only one or two rats had attacked every few hours. The rat bites hurt worse than the flogging.

Erik asked, "I wonder if the portal to Earth opened while we were traveling and if Lily and Sherry are home eating ice cream."

Al recalled his Fire and Ice experience, where Prince Krunal held Lily and Sherry prisoners. He wanted to tell Erik the story of the girls and their captivity, but Gadiel had forbidden him to repeat what he experienced during the trial. *What difference will it make if we're doomed? Won't Erik want the truth before he dies?*

"Ice cream would be good," Erik said. "A double-scooped chocolate cone."

Al's mouth watered. "Don't do that; it makes it worse."

Erik said, "We gotta consider possibilities. Look, we're getting out of here. Gadiel needs us to locate the crown and believes we can bring it back."

"What power does Gadiel have here? The castle king has the power."

"I assume Gadiel can rescue us. He acts humble, but he's wily and intelligent. There's a reason we're trapped here instead of dead. Was there anything we're missing in what they told us about the crown? Obadiah mentioned the Pit of Wretchedness. I feel wretched in this dungeon. Is this dungeon cell the Pit of Wretchedness? Maybe the crown is near and we only think we're helpless?"

Could this be the Pit of Wretchedness? Al's mind raced through the possibilities of escape. They hadn't seen a guard for a while, so no chance of knocking one out and stealing the keys. The best he could figure, the room was four stone walls with a metal door. A single guard was posted just outside. Al shook his chains in frustration.

Erik said, "Tell me about the magic barrier."

"I've told you a thousand times. Why won't you leave me alone about the magic?"

"If you missed something I can help."

Al shook his chains. "Leave me alone."

"I'm not asking you to do magic, because I realize it's painful when Gadiel . . . corrects you. Just tell me what emotions the barrier generates."

"Like someone fired a thousand volts of electricity through my brain."

"Not that—that's not an emotion. The barrier. Talk to me about the barrier itself."

Al tried to swallow, but couldn't produce enough saliva to swallow. He struggled to stretch his shoulders to their full length, but the chains were too restrictive. *What does Erik hope to gain by this new tactic?* He breathed a deep sigh. "No."

"Don't be like that, I'm trying to help."

"In a priestly role?"

"I'm your friend, Al!"

He wasn't sure if he said the words in anger, frustration or just to be mean, but Al blurted, "Prince Krunal is holding Sherry and Lily captive."

"How do you know that?"

"I encountered them in my Fire and Ice experience."

"Why didn't you tell me?"

"Gadiel told me not to."

"Sherry and Lily? Are they chained like us?"

"Yes, in a cabin."

"Why?"

"Not sure, but if I die and you make it back, rescue them."

"You're won't die."

"You don't know that."

"Promise me."

Erik snorted, "Yeah, okay, whatever, when you die, I'll rescue the girls. Stay strong and focused. If you lose the will to live, you will die."

"I'm ready to die."

"Listen, talk to me about the magic barrier."

Al mumbled in a mocking voice, "'Talk to me about the magic barrier.'"

The silence in the room comforted Al. Erik didn't realize how frustrating it felt to have magic ability and yet not be able to practice the skill. Sure, he feared the times Gadiel inflicted pain when he attempted to use magic. But sensing the magic, and not touching it, ached like when he was a kid gazing through a glass counter at candy and his mom telling him he couldn't have any. So close, but not allowed to consume its pleasures.

Al heard Erik sucking moisture into his mouth, which meant he expected Erik to talk again. "Don't ask," Al said.

"What else can we do? Communicate with me. Let me help."

"Because you have magical abilities and can snip the threads that are preventing my magic?"

"I might view the problem from a fresh perspective. You're great at chess because you've memorized all those different chess moves, right? When we play war games, I perceive human nature better and can predict an opponent's movements. Give me a chance to try, buddy."

After several deep breaths through his nose, Al said, "Okay." Al relaxed his jaw and facial muscles, releasing the built up tightness.

Silence for a moment.

Al said, "Remember two years ago when I got some of those three-dimensional metal puzzles, where you pivot the pieces and slide them just right to make them work?"

"Yeah."

"Remember the childhood game, Operation?"

"I loved that game."

"Envision a combination of those two. I manipulate the puzzles in my mind and then if I make a wrong move, or I touch the sides, Gadiel feels my presence and squashes the attempt." Just recalling lightning bolts stabbing his brain made Al flinch. "He's got me worried about the pain, and I'm afraid to try anymore."

"Do you get further each time or does the trap spring and stop you in the same game location?"

"It's not like a video game where you master the moves and advance to the next level where you can use those and learn even more. I'm presented with the same puzzle three or four times, make progress, and then on the next try face a different puzzle. But I'm forced to start over, never to come across the original puzzle."

Erik said, "Does the barrier have concrete walls?"

"It's hard to describe the experience. Imagine being inside a bubble with the puzzle. I'm certain if I solve the puzzle, the bubble will burst. Outside the bubble, magic streams, the same way the magic swirled on the volcano. It flows like a liquid spilling through space. Like the Northern Lights. But I can't get to it."

"Can you manipulate the puzzle?"

"When I search for the magic, the puzzle appears in my mind."

"What if you reach the point where you see the puzzle, and instead of solving the puzzle, just visualize the puzzle gone?"

Chains rattled, the door squeaked open, and a hand poked a burning torch of light into the room, followed by a familiar face.

"Hi boys," Wagner said.

The aroma of roasted chicken replaced the stale stench of the dungeon. The rats rustled in the dark corners of the room.

"What are you doing here?" Al asked.

"Bringing food and water to strengthen you for the journey."

"What do you want, Wagner?" Erik growled.

"Aren't you boys hungry?"

Al hoped Erik didn't say something stupid to make Wagner take the food back. "I'm hungry."

"Will the king let us go?" Erik rattled his chains.

"Not yet. Gadiel has a task for you after dark," Wagner said.

"A task for us? It's dark here all the time. What can we do for Gadiel?" Erik asked.

"Not in the dungeon. It's time to earn your keep. He's sending you for the golden crown."

"Who says we want to search for it instead of enjoying these plush living arrangements?"

"I can give the food to the rats, they sound hungry." Wagner pushed his torch toward one corner and twenty hunched-back, gray rats scrambled back and forth along the wall to avoid the light.

"No, give me the food, I'll go for the crown." Al said. "Don't ruin this opportunity for food, Erik."

Erik said, "What's preventing the king from chopping off our heads after we get back, even if we find the crown?"

"Gadiel assured me when you return with the crown, he'll let you return home with the caravan. We need you two to handle Roden." Wagner tossed a drumstick in Al's direction. Al fumbled it in his left hand, the chicken caromed off the chain holding him to the wall, and bounced into his right hand and he made the catch.

"We'll need a map," Al mumbled over a mouthful of chicken.

"I'll supply you with a map and a rope." Wagner moved to toss a chicken leg to Erik, but stopped. "Promise me something."

"What?" Erik growled.

"Be nice to me, boys. I'm happy to let you stay here and die. One prisoner didn't cooperate, and we rubbed bacon grease all over his body. The rats loved the feast."

"What do you want?" Erik tapered his anger.

Wagner waved the chicken leg in his hand as if wielding a sword, "The legend speaks of a broadsword hidden with the crown. Promise to deliver the broadsword to me, and I promise the wizard's staff to you before you enter the pit."

Al didn't wait for Erik to counter offer. "Done."

CHAPTER 53

Six hours later, Obadiah opened the dungeon door, and the guard released the two prisoners. Al rubbed his wrists and legs where the shackles had held him and stretched his long arms to release the ache in his shoulders and back. Obadiah gave the boys more water and food and led the boys up the stone castle steps, which cooled Al's blistered feet. Reaching the outdoors, he took long, deep gulps of fresh air.

Obadiah led them to the fortress walls where an elderly man with a donkey and cart was parked. The man's beard extended to his waist, and he stunk like the dungeon.

"This is Larry." Obadiah said, "He'll lead you to the path that drops into the Pit of Wretchedness."

Larry smiled with a near-toothless grin.

Obadiah took shoes from Larry's wagon and handed them to the boys. "Here's your shoes, you're gonna need them." Then he pulled a scroll from a pocket. "Here's a map and directions to the treasure." He handed the scroll to Erik.

Erik rolled it out and examined it in the dim light. "It's faded. I see markings, maybe words, on the map, but I can't read it."

Obadiah peered at his feet. "That's what I told Gadiel, but he said you'll be able to read it in the pit."

Al shook his head, "How can we trust him? Wouldn't it be easier to put our heads into the guillotine and forget all this drama?"

Erik said, "Relax, big guy. Who knows if they're lying?"

Larry put in his opinion, "No one returns from the Pit of Wretchedness."

"There, he said it," Al said. "The first truth anyone has spoken to us since arriving at the castle."

Obadiah said, "Follow the path into the great pit until you reach the first marker, the remains of a gargoyle that once guarded the castle walls. Turn right at the gargoyle and continue until you reach the geyser. Near the geyser is an entrance into the castle. After that you can read the scroll."

"Have you been there?"

"No. The pit is a death hole," Obadiah said.

Larry cackled, "No one returns from the Pit of Wretchedness."

Obadiah cocked his head, "I have given these instructions to other . . . recruits."

Al flapped his arms and hollered, "You've sent others to their deaths?"

"They searched for the golden crown, and I offer advice on the path to take. That is all."

Al started to hyperventilate. *This isn't happening. We're entering the Pit of Wretchedness, and no one returns.* He couldn't blame Erik for this decision, as he wanted the golden crown as much as Erik did. Even if they find the crown, would it really work to transform the stone soldiers back to their former selves?

Obadiah said, "The caravan leaves at first light. If you want to return to Velidred, be back in time to leave with the caravan, otherwise you're beyond the Black Stump."

Al looked at Erik and shook his head. "We're gonna die."

"A grand adventure, just like the games we played at home," Erik said.

"Larry will give you a rope and two torches."

Erik raised his eyebrows. "That's it? No bows and arrows, lances, or swords?"

"Wait." Al raised his hand. "Wagner promised to meet us here with my staff."

Obadiah hunched his shoulders. "Don't know. I'm responsible for Larry and the torches."

"I shouldn't have trusted him," Al said.

Erik hoisted an unlit torch into the air. "Tell Wagner we aren't returning with the broadsword."

Larry cackled, "There's no broadsword. It's a myth."

Erik pulled Obadiah close. "Run, tell Wagner without the staff we aren't bringing back the broadsword. We'll wait for his answer."

Obadiah sprinted to the castle.

"The wheels are falling off this adventure, and we haven't even started." Al rubbed the back of his neck. "No staff, no magic, a broadsword which may not be real, and no one returns from the Pit of Wretchedness. I'm not going."

Erik said, "I'm going in no matter what you do, I'm here to save my father and show him I'm not a cowardly priest."

None of the three moons showed although stars sparkled in the spiral galaxy.

Heaviness settled over Al's body, and he blew his cheeks out and released in slow, noisy breaths. "Sorry for wanting to back out. I'll admit I'm scared. Our lives are in danger and we aren't playing a game in Mom's basement. There are consequences if we do something wrong. What monsters and beasts inhabit the pit?"

Larry answered, "No one knows for sure. Jaguars, monkeys, giant spiders, alligators, snakes, members of the undead, ghosts, and rumors of wraiths."

"If no one knows, then who created the map?"

"A mystery." Larry cackled.

Al disliked Larry. He held out his hands, lifted his right hand and weighed his options. "We can stay here and take the caravan back at first light, in which case, we'll still be alive." Then he lowered his right hand and lifted his left. "Or enter the pit and die."

Erik said, "Or we go into the pit, return with the crown, victorious, and save the stone soldiers which includes my father. Remember, you talked us into this journey. Sherry and Lily didn't want you to go. It's your idea and your goal—to find the golden crown. This is your adventure. Own up to your destiny, Al."

Larry cackled.

"It doesn't look like Wagner is bringing the staff now or after we return," Erik said.

"Then it's decided; we don't bring him the broadsword. I know you're all gung-ho about the crown, but remember, I have no magic. If we need magic to protect ourselves or a magic spell to open a door, I got nothing."

For once Erik didn't look confident as he stared into space. He lowered his head to the horizon. "We should leave soon. It's no good if we get back with the crown after the caravan leaves. Plus, it's summer, sunrise will come early."

Al's stomach did flips.

They waited a few more minutes for Obadiah or Wagner to return, but no one appeared. They started the journey. Larry walked them to the path that led into the Pit of Wretchedness.

Al tried to reach out for his magic as they walked. He thought maybe as they got further from Gadiel, the wizard's ability to disturb Al's brain might lessen. He worked the puzzle from a dozen angles, solved one part of the puzzle as he manipulated the pieces. Then as the puzzle flipped, Gadiel shocked him with the force of a Taser. Al fell to his knees as the aftershocks bounced in his skull.

"You okay, buddy?"

"Yeah," Al said in a lifeless, unenthusiastic voice. Larry and Erik were leading him to his death. He was determined to enter the pit with his magic, and he tried again. What did Erik say, 'try to make the puzzle disappear?' The puzzle floated in emptiness in his mind's eye. How to make it disappear? He couldn't detect how it appeared. As he concentrated on the puzzle while trying not to trip on the uneven ground, the best he managed was to get the puzzle to flicker.

Larry stopped the donkey and wagon when they reached a forest. The old man lifted the remaining torch from the wagon and handed it to Al. Using a flint and steel, Larry lit Al's torch. The torch's heat forced Al to hold it away from his body.

Erik touched his torch Al's torch to light, and then Erik threw a coiled rope over his shoulder. "Ready?"

Larry cackled, "No one returns from the Pit of Wretchedness."

"Yeah, we know," Al said.

They entered the forest on a narrow path. The path was steep and dropped off a cliff on the right. Encroaching large leaf plants on the left forced them to walk in single file. Erik led the way. The farther along the path they went, the darker it became, despite the torches.

"How far down does this take us?" Al asked.

Erik stopped and raised his torch over the cliff. "I don't see the bottom."

They walked for a while and a mosquito bit Al on the cheek and he slapped his face. "Ow, what was that? What are mosquitoes doing out in the night?"

Erik wiped sweat off his brow. "It's weird. It's like we're walking right into the rim of the volcano."

From the right came a loud echoing rumble. It changed to the bubbling sound of boiling water, then came a swoosh, followed by the sound of falling rain. Then there was silence.

A loud rumble started to their right. It changed to the sound of boiling water, then a swoosh, followed by the sound of falling rain and then disappeared.

Al said, "Sounds like the geyser is in that direction," he pointed toward the sound.

"Locate the gargoyle first."

The chatter of monkeys echoed. The forest turned into a jungle as ferns, large-leafy plants, and thick fog replaced the forest trees.

"Fog in a volcano?"

"Let's hope fog and not volcanic fog or vog, which I believe will kill us in seconds."

Al said, "I suspect dying by the volcanic fog would be better than being eaten by a pack of monkeys."

A movement on the left caught Al's eye, and he stopped. "Erik." Al's voice rose.

"Yeah." Erik trudged forward.

Al whispered, "Stop."

Erik didn't stop.

"Stop!"

Erik halted, though Al had trouble seeing him in the fog.

Erik asked, "What's happening? Why did you stop?"

Al pointed at the bushes. "Check the bushes," he whispered.

"Speak up," Erik snapped.

Al slapped his arm where a mosquito bit him, "In the bushes, do you see it?"

"What?"

Two large greenish eyes shone through the branches and leaves of the bush nearest Al.

"Don't you see those eyes?"

The animal meandered parallel to the trail, disinterested in the boys. In a moment, its black-spotted, golden body disappeared into the fog.

"A jaguar," Al whispered.

They waited a few moments to give the animal plenty of time to pass. They had enough troubles without becoming a meal for a large cat.

Again, a swoosh sounded in the distance.

Al pushed Erik. "That's the geyser; find the gargoyle so we can get inside the castle walls."

They traveled along the path and Erik waved his torch back and forth as he searched for the gargoyle. "There!" He pointed with the torch.

A granite statue lay on its side. Long ears protruded from its tiger head, and long incisors framed an open mouth. Broken wings lay in the decaying leaves. A green, twenty-foot long snake slithered across the top of the gargoyle.

Al clenched his jaw and scouted the jungle for other dangers. Snakes didn't help his peace of mind. "Turn right."

Monkeys chattered at the boys from the nearest tree.

"Erik, I don't like it here. Find the geyser."

Erik said, "I thought they designed gargoyles to be good spirits or moral angels to ward off evil."

"I don't care, just keep moving."

The geyser sounded louder.

"Close." Erik advanced along the path.

The jaguar slithered in and out of Al's vision. He held his torch on the same side as the jaguar had been, an attempt at protection if it changed its mind and began to stalk them. He tripped on a root and stumbled but managed to keep from falling.

Al said, "Tell the jaguar to disappear."

Erik laughed, "I don't think it works that way."

"Did you see its size?"

"It won't follow us into the castle."

"Right. Or maybe that's its home where ten or twenty of its closest friends are waiting to devour us."

The bubbling and swoosh sounded, and as they rounded a corner, a column of water was falling back toward a rocky crevice, and they heard the rain-like sound. Steam filled the air, and Al struggled to breathe in the oppressive humidity. As the steam cleared, a stone wall was exposed. The water gurgled and dripped back into the geyser's mouth.

"There, we can sneak through that crack in the wall," Erik pointed his torch at a black shadow.

Al swore his insides quivered. "We have to cross the geyser's mouth, hoping it won't shoot off boiling water to disfigure our faces. Oh, and yeah, don't fall into the geyser mouth. Then we have to get over to the crack and squeeze through that tiny space."

"Sounds right," Erik said.

"Right for you, your shoulders aren't as wide as mine and you're smaller." *Why did I agree to this?*

The geyser spouted, and the boys jumped back from the boiling water, holding their torches well away from the spray.

Al said, "The geyser isn't consistent when it vents. Didn't it erupt about once every ten minutes before, and now it's spouted three times in a minute?"

CHAPTER 54

Al said, "I'm gonna die."

"Don't be so dramatic, we can get past that no problem."

Al asked "How? The geyser's eruption pattern is not predictable. We might think we have it, and then just as we step across the hole, it scalds us with boiling water."

Wild vegetation, trees, bushes with large leaves and vines blocked the way to the wall except for a bare twenty-foot circle surrounding the mouth of the geyser where scalding water splashed and prevented plant growth.

"You can't walk right over the geyser, the ground might not be solid, and you'll fall into the magma heating the water."

Monkeys chattered in the trees.

Erik said, "Remember the Tarzan movies, where he flew through the forest on the vines? We can do that."

"Vines?"

"Yeah, like this one." Erik grabbed a vine and pulled hard. The vine separated from the tree and fell to the ground. "Okay, not that one."

Al shook his head, "Let's stay on the ground and move fast around the geyser."

"You're the one who's concerned about falling into molten lava."

"What if the vine fails like that one just as we swing over the geyser, and we fall directly into that hole?" Al asked.

"This one seems secure. Hold this." Erik handed his torch to Al and pulled hard on a green vine hanging from a tall tree. He climbed five-feet and jerked the vine.

"What about the torches?"

"I'll go first, and then you toss me the torches."

"Toss our only light over the geyser and hope you catch it? This plan won't work. Why not walk around the geyser? We can follow the path on the right and reach the wall."

"Hand me the torch." Erik dropped to the ground, grabbed the torch and moved in the direction Al recommended. After ten-feet he stopped. "Hey look at this."

"What?"

"Come here, You gotta see this."

"Why can't you just tell me? The geyser's gonna blow any second."

"Hurry."

Al trotted to Erik while monitoring the geyser. "What is it?"

Erik shoved his torch and exposed a giant spider web glistening between two trees. "Want to go in that direction?"

Al retreated to the safe spot. "Okay, how about the vines?"

"It's easy, start a little way back like this," Erik grabbed high on the vine and prepared to race toward the wall like a pole vaulter.

"Wait."

"What?"

"Wait for the geyser to erupt."

They waited a minute. The geyser didn't erupt.

"I'm going, it won't erupt."

"Wait." Erik was always so impatient. Just let it happen, thought Al.

Another minute passed without an eruption.

Erik lowered an arm and shook his head. "Should have jumped."

"Like you always tell me, relax."

Al caught a glimpse of a tawny shoulder as the jaguar rustled through the bushes, fifteen-feet from the boys.

Al touched Erik's shoulder and stammered, "Mayy…be you should go."

The jaguar swiveled its head and watched the boys.

"Time to go, Erik."

"Relax, the jaguar won't hurt you."

"It looks hungry." Al backed away from the jaguar.

The cat's green eyes glowed.

The geyser erupted with a ka-whoosh, scaring Al back toward the jaguar.

Al said, "Go, Erik, go."

Erik waited for the water to stop spraying, stepped back two steps, held tight to the vine, got a running start and swung over the geyser doing his best Tarzan yell, "Ah-a-a-ahaha." He reached the wall and dropped from the vine to the ground.

"Here, catch." Erik threw the vine back toward Al.

Al had to catch the vine with his elbows since he had the torches in his hands. He stepped on the vine with his foot, and with a glare at the jaguar and a gander at the re-charging geyser said, "I'm throwing the first torch."

In a moment both torches were in Erik's hands and darkness surrounded Al.

The jaguar became invisible except for its glowing green eyes floating between the bushes.

Erik yelled, "Wait for the next eruption.

"I can't wait."

"Two minutes."

"The jaguar looks hungry."

"Don't risk it, man, it's not worth it."

Al stepped toward the jaguar with the vine in his hand. *I should wait for the geyser to erupt.*

The jaguar roared.

Al ran toward the geyser and jumped. He floated by the geyser, which didn't erupt.

Erik put up his hands to catch Al. "Let go."

Al didn't let go. He hit the wall and kicked off, back toward the geyser. He rode the vine back toward the jaguar. The jaguar opened its jaws as Al's momentum stopped him. He reversed direction toward the geyser.

Could he get lucky with another pass over the geyser's mouth? Why hadn't he dropped at the wall? The vine rotated as Al again rode it toward the crack. Al kept his eyes on the hole beneath him. If it did start to spout, he had no good plan for how to save himself.

Time stretched, and Al drifted as in slow motion. He lost focus on the wall as the momentum of the vine twirled his body. Al wanted to shut his eyes as he swung over the geyser for the second time. *Remember to let go when I hit the wall.*

A slight catching sound arose from the hole beneath him and a bubble formed in the water.

He looked in horror at Erik. He wouldn't make it. The vine carried him closer to the wall.

The geyser erupted in a giant swoosh, shooting steaming water twenty-feet into the air.

Al wanted to scream; his heart raced in his chest. He held tighter to the vine, and closed his eyes. His breath burst in and out, and he mumbled, "Hold tight, don't let go."

Erik grabbed Al's legs. "You're okay, buddy. Let go and slide to the ground."

Al opened his eyes and slid down the vine. "That was close."

The geyser bubbled and spurted water. The boiling liquid pounded the rock like heavy raindrops on a rooftop. The boys huddled just beyond its reach.

Erik picked up a torch from the ground and handed it to Al. "The cracked wall is here." He pointed his torch at an uneven gash in the castle wall.

Erik squeezed through the crack first with some difficulty. Then Al followed, manipulating his tall frame through the irregular, tight space that had opened between large cut stones.

Al swallowed hard, choking a scream as the stones scraped his flailed-raw back.

"Do you think an earthquake caused this?" Erik asked.

Al shrugged.

The room smelled of ancient alcohol. Al held his torch high. Barrels rested on their sides in one corner, their lids broken into shards. Wooden staves littered the floor, and metal hoops that had once secured the barrels lay twisted into snaky shapes.

Erik asked, "Wine cellar?"

"Let's see the map. Where's the crown?"

Erik opened the scroll while Al held both torches. "Hey, look at this. I can read the names of the rooms now."

Al peered over Erik's shoulders.

Erik continued, "According to the map, the treasure is in the bell tower here. We're in the wine cellar, which means we follow these stairs into this room here." He pointed at the map. "Up these steps into the banquet hall."

They trotted up the stone stairs, the edges worn from people ascending and descending for centuries, and entered a room where torn and rotting tapestries hung at odd angles on stone walls. The room contained a broken table, but nothing else.

Another set of steps took them into the banquet hall, where a mess of pottery shards littered the floor. A large, rectangular wooden table stood surrounded by overturned, broken benches. The scene resembled the remains of a defeated army. A fireplace large enough to stand in gaped vacantly in the wall, and a musty wild boar's head filled the space above the mantel.

Erik unfurled the scroll on the table and studied the map, orienting it to fit what they'd seen so far. He placed his index finger on the banquet hall space and moved his finger along a hallway to a set of rooms in the map's corner. "We walk through this hallway, up these stairs, then back through this hallway to the chapel and bell tower."

"Why keep the golden crown in the bell tower?" Al asked.

"It's difficult to reach and easy to protect?"

A man slipped into the light. "I can answer that question."

Al jumped, dropping his torch. "Who are you?"

"Oh, didn't mean to frighten you. I'm Lord Randall of Beddingstine. Here for the banquet." The man wore a burgundy beret on his head. A tapered, gold, brocaded shirt with a high burgundy collar hugged his body. The sleeves of the shirt puffed out at the shoulders and were striped with gold and burgundy. Below the elbow, the sleeves were tight, and embroidered gold scrolls circled the sleeves to his hands. Tight black pants and high black boots completed the ensemble.

Al's heart thumped against his chest as he stepped back from the man. "How did you get here?"

"Been here a month. Are you new arrivals? The king didn't say he had more guests coming."

"Who is this guy?" Al mouthed.

Erik lifted his shoulders.

Lord Randall touched his closely-shaved, oiled beard and pointed across the room. "Lady Charlotte is looking fine tonight, don't you think?" He winked a steel-blue eye.

No one was in the room except the three of them.

Erik said, "Yes, a lovely lady."

The man slapped Erik on the back. "I must speak with her." He nodded his head at the boys, strode into the shadows and disappeared. The sound of boots shuffling across stone lasted a moment longer.

Erik said, "That was weird."

"Was he a ghost?"

"I don't know. You'd think so, but I felt his hand on my back." Erik straightened his back and mimicked the man, "I'm Lord Randall of Beddingstine and I must talk with Lady Charlotte."

Al gave a nervous laugh, "Yeah, let's get out of here." He retrieved his torch from the floor and Erik helped him to re-light it.

They hurried through the hallway where empty armor lay dismembered across the floor. A silver-coated battle helmet lay bruised and beaten, and Erik placed his torch in a wall sconce designed for that purpose and picked up the helmet.

"Don't touch that, you don't know what magic or evil it contains." Al's stomach churned.

"Maybe it's the crown we seek." Erik pulled it over his head.

"What are you doing? How many crown-seekers have entered this castle? We don't know why they failed. Maybe it's because they picked up random objects, like helmets destined to kill them. Take it off."

Erik put his hands under the helmet and lifted, but it didn't move. "Al?"

"Don't mess with me."

"I can't get it off." He lifted the helmet at the base of his neck, but it didn't move. "Al, help," Erik's voice sounded muffled.

Al couldn't do much. He needed to hold the torch in one hand, and couldn't get any leverage with the other. Erik's eyes showed as black dots through the faceplate.

"Hurry, it's tightening around my neck."

"What can I do?"

"Use magic. Anything. Help, I can't breathe." Erik's gasped through the face plate.

Al searched for magic. His many attempts and failures in the dungeon flittered through his mind. Would his magic now work in the castle? The puzzle floated in mid-air, but appeared weak and distant. He imagined it gone.

Erik gagged and wheezed inside the helmet.

CHAPTER 55

Al stretched his mind toward the puzzle. He needed his magic to save Erik from the attacking helmet. How could he make the puzzle disappear and not alert Gadiel?

Lord Randall padded up to Al and said, "I say chaps, do you know the direction to Lady Charlotte's chambers?"

The man startled Al. "We're busy at the moment," Al gave Lord Randall an exasperated look.

Erik laughed in the helmet.

"The cute serving girl with the blonde hair told me the lady's chambers were in this hallway. Do you know her?" Lord Randall asked.

"Erik?" Al ran his free hand through his hair. "Are you laughing?"

Lord Randall said, "You're not much help, I'll ask the knight. Sir Knight, are you aware of Lady Charlotte's private chambers?"

Erik pulled off the helmet with a wide grin on his face. He said, "Lord Randall, the lady's chambers are the third room down the hall." Erik pointed in the direction they had just passed.

"I knew I could count on a knight to help me instead of this poor servant." Lord Randall jerked his head in Al's direction. He did a slight head dip and flourished his burgundy cap toward Erik. "Thank you, Sir Knight," and he headed in the direction opposite to where Erik had pointed.

Erik laughed as Lord Randall disappeared.

"I should whack you or turn you into a frog."

"Is your magic back?"

"Don't know. I was almost there when Lord Randall appeared. Why were you messing with me?"

"Having fun. It's a creepy place, and I thought I could lighten the mood. Then Lord Randall started asking questions and made me laugh."

"The next time you run into trouble, I'm not helping, You can die for all I care." Al sucked in deep breaths to release the tension in his neck and shoulders.

They followed in the direction Lord Randall had gone and reached a circular stone staircase at the end of the hall.

"Do you think it weird Lord Randall has appeared to us twice?" Al asked.

"Hard to say. A ghost might repeat a specific pattern of steps and questions every night. I wonder how he died."

"I'm guessing poison."

Al clomped up the steps behind Erik as the torches threw shadows on the walls. The insides of the steps were too small for Al's feet, and the outside edges weren't much better. He kept his free hand on the inside brick walls. As they ascended a sweet scent filled the air.

"The man doesn't have his head in his hands, a knife in his gut or blood spurting out his chest. I figure Lady Charlotte's husband or boyfriend dropped poison in the Lord's drink or food. Never saw it coming."

"Plausible." Erik slowed as he reached the next floor. "Do you smell that?"

"The incense?"

"Yeah, who's burning incense?"

"Another ghost, adventurers, or someone who lives in the castle?"

This hallway had an arched ceiling and was narrower than on the lower floor. Every third step a painted line across the floor extended up both walls, and connected at the ceiling. The lines, the width of a man's hand, varied in colors of purple and pink. Several niches in the walls held three candlesticks each, and incense burned in silver thuribles.

Al said, "Somebody must be here." He examined the candles which hadn't burned down far. "Why didn't we think to bring weapons with us?"

"Did Lord Randall light these candles?"

"Or magic, if Gadiel is helping us."

"How does he know where we are?"

"He knows my exact location at all times better than a GPS system." Al shook his head, but he still felt Gadiel's presence. He stopped in the hallway and prepared his mind for magic. If the room contained magic, he should be able to sense it.

"There's a lighted chamber up ahead."

Al took a deep breath and held it. He counted to ten and blew out loudly. He closed his eyes. He did a quick search for the puzzle in his mind, but it wasn't there. The flow of magic swept into his body, and he gasped and coughed.

"Al, stop messing around, here's a room."

After being without magic for so many days, Al enjoyed the power that surged through his mind. He welcomed it into his being with the same pleasure as finding a cool creek on a hot day. The magic splashed over his skin and refreshed his core.

Al marched toward Erik with confidence, "I sense magic in the hallway."

"Are we in danger?"

"I don't think so, but let me check the room for traps before we enter."

Al reveled in the flowing magic and from the hallway reached out with a spell to check for traps. He sensed searching tentacles of his magic as he examined the room's walls, floor, and ceiling.

"It's okay." Al entered first into what turned out to be a chapel. It was a large chapel, the length of a classroom with a vaulted ceiling. An altar stood at the front of the room. A gold statue of a large frog, the size of a bulldog sat atop the altar.

Erik said, "Do these people worship those pink and purple frogs we encountered that first day on this planet?"

Paintings of the garish frogs covered the walls, floors and even the arched ceiling.

Erik approached the gold frog and reached out toward it.

"Wait," Al yelled.

Erik stopped.

On the floor next to the altar lay a human skeleton.

"I thought you said it's safe."

"No magic. Doesn't mean the place is safe. We have limited information about this chapel. Powerful wizards practiced their magic here, and I might not recognize their conjuring. Touch nothing, and wait for my all clear signal."

"What if the crown is underneath the golden frog?"

"The map said the treasure is in the bell tower."

Erik placed the map on the altar, next to the frog, and unfurled the scroll. "The bell tower should intersect with the chapel. It shows an accessible space to the bell tower from," he spun toward the rear of the chapel and pointed to the corner, "there."

Al and Erik walked to the corner and examined the walls for a door or some kind of opening.

"There's no door here," Al said as he rubbed his hands across the walls.

"Magic?"

Al raised his hands and cast a spell to find secret doors, "Alfar eldur."

A bright red light shone as if a laser burned an outline of a door.

Erik slapped Al on the back. "You da man."

"Opio noonya." Al waved his hands in front of the door.

The wall creaked, and the boys shuffled back as the door opened into the chapel. A stuffy, dusty wind blew into the room and the air warmed.

Al stepped into the tight space. "It's an empty closet." He examined the tiny room and finally looked up into a dark space that extended beyond the light from his torch.

"Use magic to see if there are more hidden niches," Erik said. "The crown must be here."

"Not here. Any half-baked wizard could uncover it here."

Lord Randall stepped next to Erik, "Ah, looking for the treasure, boys?"

Erik squawked, "Stop sneaking up on us, man."

"Many an adventurer has searched this bell tower. They each carry a map, but never find the treasure. You may access the bell tower with that rope you carry."

Erik touched the rope draped over his shoulder.

"Fine, chap, then scurry up the bell tower and grab the treasure for us."

"For us?" Al asked.

"Well, I get part of the treasure if I help you pinpoint its location, right lads?"

Al glanced at Erik, who nodded. "I'll shoot a fireball up this shaft, and you watch for somewhere to attach the rope."

Erik squeezed into the room with Al. "Get out of the room to throw your fireball; I need space to toss the rope."

They wiggled and scooted until Al stood in the chapel and Erik in the closet.

Lord Randall said, "Be careful with fireballs, you might burn down the castle."

"I can produce a light ball that'll hover at the right spot." Al stuck his head into the space and created a lighted sphere in his hand. The sphere floated up the shaft.

"Why didn't you produce that light in the dungeon?" Erik asked.

The light ball drifted up the shaft, ten-feet, fifteen, thirty, and then the bells became dimly visible. The roof that once protected the bells was splintered. A large gash opened to the sky. A metal rod supported four bells in varying sizes.

"I think I can throw the rope over the rod."

Erik tossed the rope up the shaft, but missed and it plopped back around him. He rolled it and stood half in the chapel and half in the closet and gave a mighty toss. The rope struck the largest bell, which rang once, a deep sound vibrating through his bones.

Lord Randall lowered his voice to a whisper, placed his hands in his armpits and peered around the closet door, "Don't ring the bells."

Al touched Erik's shoulder and whispered, "Be careful."

"Careful? I have no control over where the rope goes. I'm just tossing it and hoping it wraps around the rod."

"Try not to hit the bells."

"Are you serious?"

Lord Randall took off his burgundy cap and hissed, "Quiet, they're coming."

"Who?" Al asked.

The lord's arms shook and beads of sweat formed on his forehead. He whimpered, "They're coming."

Al held his breath trying to hear, his stomach clenched rock hard. Who was following them through the castle? He nudged Erik, "Try again."

Erik wound the rope and bent his knees. Then he jumped off the ground as he tossed the rope upward. The rope flew straight, and it hit the smallest bell, which swung back and forth, pealing four times. The rope landed hard on the closet floor.

Al scanned the chapel for Lord Randall, but the man had disappeared again. Al pushed Erik into the room.

"What're you doing?"

"Get in there." Al squeezed into the tight space with his friend. Then he commanded the door, "Hooro Naletay."

The door closed.

"What is it?" Erik whispered.

"Not sure, but it spooked Lord Randall."

An animal growled in the chapel.

Al said, "Is that the jaguar?" A chill ran up his spine.

Noises emanated from the chapel as if an animal sniffed outside the door.

They hunkered in the small space, waiting for the animal to leave the chapel.

Erik whispered, "What time do you think it is? We need to hurry if we expect to return with the caravan."

"We gotta get the crown first."

"Clear my space so I can throw the rope."

"Let me try magic."

"Now you're using magic? Why didn't you do that before I hit the bells?"

"Thought of it while waiting for the jaguar to vamoose." Al cast a spell on the end of the rope and lifted his hand toward the bells. The rope responded by snaking upward. With a wave of his hand, the rope tied itself tight, not against the bell rod, but to the wooden framework that held the rod in place.

Erik grabbed the rope and tugged hard. "Solid, let's go." He scurried up the rope, curling his legs around the rope and trapping it between his feet to propel himself to the tower.

Al used magic to send the torches to Erik.

Al grabbed the rope and scooted up, but his feet and the rope twisted the wrong way. He hung twelve feet above the floor while he untangled his feet. The method that worked for him was to place his feet on the wall and walk the wall while pulling toward the bells with his hands. This was more work, and he was gasping for breath when he finally reached the bells. Erik helped him over a rail onto the bell tower floor.

Two human skulls lay on the floor. Al lifted one and said, "This adventure is turning bad."

"Use magic and search for hidden doors again."

"Alfar eldur."

A light beam searched the platform, scanned inside the bells, and checked the busted roof. No hidden doors.

The boys examined the map. Al pointed to the bells. "The map shows the treasure on that wall."

"How do you know?"

"The bells, small to large, the treasure shows on the large bell side."

They ran their hands over the wall, but found nothing.

Erik sat on the floor. "Any magic that identifies a hidden panel?"

"Nothing." Al sat next to Erik. "Let me examine the scroll."

The small sphere of light still glowed and it hovered over the scroll. The boys studied the document.

"I can't read these words. Is it a foreign language?" Al rubbed his head. "I remember a rhyme Forest River Blossom told me, maybe we need that to reveal the treasure."

"What's that?"

Al stood and faced the wall. "Oona ganna takkay goota, Nekkay akkay pakkee soota," He didn't know what the spell or rhyme did, and he wondered how safe the words were to speak in the bell tower. It might be a spell that rings the bells or sends bats into the tower, but Al sensed it would expose the treasure.

"Keep going." Erik stood.

"We don't know what it does."

"We're running out of time."

Al whispered, "Airay voomay meesay ketch." He pressed his lips tight.

He heard the closet door open, and then the rope shook.

Erik whispered, "Someone's coming. Stop!"

"It'll be worse if we leave the incantation hanging. I have to finish the spell." The time walking around the village flashed through Al's mind. *Rather than showing off to the villagers and entertaining the children, I should have found a wizard to teach me needed wizarding skills and magical language. Then, maybe, I could read the scroll or find the hidden niche and treasures. Instead, the spell I blurted out might kill us both.*

The rope swung for a moment, and then a human form crawled over the rail and dropped to the floor.

"Nekkay ekkay moosmay wretch." Al finished the spell and touched his fingertip to his nose.

CHAPTER 56

l demanded, "Who are you?" The shape struggled to its feet. It was a man's body, but he hid in the shadows, and Al couldn't determine the person's identity. He backed closer to the wall.

The man glided toward the boys, keeping his face in shadows. "Did you find the crown? The treasure?"

Al breathed a sigh of relief, "Lord Randall, is that you?"

"Lady Charlotte agreed to meet me in the bell tower, have you seen her?" He moved closer.

Annoyance tinged Erik's voice. "Didn't you find her on the third floor?"

"How's the search for the treasure?" Lord Randall asked. "It contains many riches."

Al glanced at Erik. "We haven't found it."

"Did you say the right words?"

"Thought I did."

"Are you reading the scroll right?"

"We can't read it because we don't know that language."

Lord Randall squinted at Al and laughed, "The grand wizard, Alpherge the Mighty, can't read a scroll?"

"You know me?" Al noticed Lord Randall wasn't wearing his burgundy cap.

The man coughed lightly. "Uh, yes, the other wizards told me to expect you, and I'm here to assist. I'm familiar with the ancient languages."

Erik handed Lord Randall the scroll.

"Move that torch closer," he said.

Al peered over the lord's shoulder, trying to decide if he was a specter or a manifestation of magic. It was no coincidence that the guy kept appearing now, when they were close to the treasure. Was the man created by Gadiel to keep an eye on him? A shiver raced down Al's back.

Lord Randall pointed to the scroll and said, "This line mentions the treasure in the bell tower and three keys which are needed to open the hidden niche."

"We don't have keys." Al shook his head. This was not going as planned. "What keys? Where do we use them?" He pointed to the blank wall.

"Not physical keys. Magic keys," Lord Randall laughed.

"Is there a magic spell I need to cast? A chant, what is it?"

"Slow down my tall friend." Lord Randall glanced up from the scroll and winked a green eye, "It's a simple manipulation of wind, water, and fire."

Could Al influence those three basic elements? He recalled his wish for more training. If he had his staff, then the wizards within the staff could help.

"What do I need to do?"

"Use three elements to ring the bells in a specific order and tune."

"You worried about ringing the bells before, but now it's safe? The rules keep changing."

"Uh, yes, go ahead. Not a problem."

Al exchanged a worried glance with Erik.

Erik shook his head and shrugged.

The smell of sandalwood incense drifted up the shaft.

"Lord Randall, did you shut the door before you came up the shaft?"

He squinted and tugged his lower lip while tilting his head side to side for a moment, "Doesn't matter does it, chaps? Execute the magic."

Al whispered to Erik, "I don't like this."

Erik whispered, "We're running out of time, do you have other ideas?"

"This first line is hringo mey-o lit-loo bow-jollunni fimm sinnum mey-o lofti."

"Which means?" Al asked.

"Oh yes, young chap. With air, ring the small bell five times."

Al remembered his training on the rooftop at the wizard school. Air. He had learned this in the class and thought it could be accomplished. He imagined a breeze blowing in the still night jungle air. The castle had become stifling. Hot, damp air smothered him, and the linen clothing he wore stuck against his skin.

How hard did he have to push the bell? "What happens if I ring it more than five times?"

"Five times."

Al managed to produce a directed stream of air. But the bell didn't ring. He increased the pressure, and the bell moved, but the clapper didn't strike the side.

A wailing, as of many voices, emanated from the chapel, rising in the steamy air.

"What's that?" Al asked.

Lord Randall said, "Ignore it. Keep going; can you do this or not?"

"I'm trying not to ring it too many times. Let me concentrate." Al breathed deeply and closed his eyes. Stretching his right hand, he gestured to the bell, and it rang. Once, twice, three times. He reduced the pressure, and the bell rang once more.

"Five times," Lord Randall said.

"I can count."

The wailing voices increased in volume, and shimmering waves of light formed in the bell shaft.

Al pressed a channel of warm air at the smallest bell and it rang once more.

Erik said, "Do you guys see that wavering light? I think it's coming from the chapel."

Al nodded as beads of sweat formed above his lips.

Lord Randall's forefinger touched a line on the scroll "Next it says, 'hringdoo ee pree-ohu bow-jollunni fra vinstry viso-var mey-o vat-nee.'"

"Which means," Al watched the shimmering light grow dense as the wails increased in volume.

"Yes, yes, just a sec while I translate it. OK. Ring the third bell from the left two times with water."

Al noticed for the first time his parched mouth. This heat sapped his energy. He stared at the bell next to the small bell.

Erik poked him. "Do it."

There were kids at the wizarding classes who managed water with ease, but not Al. He had never mastered the water element in class, but fog worked for him. Could he move a bell with fog? What's the distinction between fog and rain? Beads of sweat formed on his forehead from the stifling heat.

"Is the spell for water unknown to you?" Lord Randall tapped his foot.

"Give me a minute."

The wailing increased and the shape from the chapel coalesced into a dark, opaque shape that floated above the bell tower.

Al sucked saliva into his dry mouth. His solar plexus cramped at the pressure from Erik, Lord Randall, and the shapes materializing around the bell tower. How could he create magic with this stress? Al shook his hands, trying to relieve the mounting heaviness enveloping his body.

"A little magic soon, Alpherge the Mighty."

"Get off my back," Al shouted. "Do you know magic?"

"Well, no." Lord Randall blustered.

"Then let me think."

"Relax," Erik patted him on the shoulder, "you got this."

Al thought of a garden hose at home lying in the summer sun. Turn on the spigot and water flows through the hose. That's it. He shaped his hands as if holding a hose and imagined water surging through the hose.

A few drops of water dribbled past his fingers and dripped to the floor.

Al shook his head.

A second shape formed in the air around the bell tower.

Al spit on his hand and visualized the water flowing through the hose. He turned the spigot on high. The imaginary hose wriggled in his mind as the water streamed through the spigot. Water gushed from his hands.

"Woo-hoo," Erik yelled.

The water splashed around the bell tower until Al gained control. He placed his thumb over the imaginary hose to build pressure and pointed it at the third bell from the left. He released a directed jet, and the bell rang once. He moved his thumb back and forth to ring the bell a second time. The sound was tinny. Was that good enough? Al slowed the stream and took a drink of the water. He spit it out. "Yuck."

Lord Randall said, "Ring the large bell only once with fire and let the sound drift into the distance."

A third shape formed from the shimmering waves.

Erik said, "We have a problem."

Lord Randall said, "Ring the last bell, hurry."

Al raised his hands with fingers pointed at the large bell and sent a fire blast.

The large bell rang once, a low, rich sound that reverberated for twenty-three seconds. He counted.

The sound resonated throughout Al's body, and the wall opened with brick rubbing against brick, exposing a large wooden chest in a niche in the wall.

CHAPTER 57

Al wanted to look at the chest sitting in the bell tower niche, but the luminous objects had materialized into skeletons wearing dark, torn robes with hoods over their skulls. Their wails pierced his brain, and he covered his ears to lessen the intensity.

"What are those things? Al asked.

Lord Randall said, "Shadow spawn."

"Are they friendly?"

"Friendly? They're the dead souls of evil wizards that caused the collapse of this castle and the surrounding countryside. Your life and soul will drain from your body where they touch you, and over time the process consumes your body and you become one of them." Lord Randall backed closer to Al and Erik. "Don't let them scratch you."

Al ignored the chest and focused his attention on the shadow spawn. "How do you kill them?"

"You can't kill them. The best you can hope for is to drive them back to their lair." Lord Randall raised a sword at the creatures.

Erik asked, "Where did you get that sword?"

"I, uh, always carry one with me."

"Can I use magic to stop them from killing us?"

"They don't kill you, at least not your inner self. Only your body. You'll wander the castle forever, feeding on other adventurers."

Al gasped. "What magic do I use?"

"How should I know? I've never seen them before today. All I know is family folk tales, and I never believed the stories."

The shadow spawn flew above them, swooping toward the trio in the bell tower. Their yellow eyes shone with a nebulous glow.

Lord Randall waved the sword at the creatures, but they flew around the sword as if it wasn't even there. He backed to the wall next to Al.

Al said, "Erik, look in the chest for the crown. Maybe that'll give us the advantage we need."

Erik jumped into the niche and tried to open the chest lid. "It's locked."

"Break the lock," Lord Randall called out.

"With what? Give me your sword."

Lord Randall stabbed and waved his sword in the air, with no apparent results against the creatures. "No."

"Is the lock magical? What does the scroll say?"

"I'm a little busy here, boys."

"Give me the sword, and you read the scroll for the needed magic."

"Not now."

Al's heartbeat thrashed in his ears, and he tensed as a creature flew near his head.

Erik said, "Al, say the words."

"What words?"

"You know the nursery rhyme."

One shadow spawn member rubbed a bony finger across Al's left arm and he cried out in pain. "What nursery rhyme?"

"I don't know, hickory dickory dock. No not that." Erik rattled the lock on the treasure chest. "Eeny, meeny, miny, moe. Yeah, that one."

Al's arm numbed where the shadow spawn had touched him. He raised his right arm but could only partially lift his left toward the treasure chest. He exposed his back to the evil, flying creatures.

"Oona, ganna, takkay, goota." He flourished his right hand. "Nekkay, akkay, pakkee, soota," A phantom's finger sliced across his back and he arched in agony.

"Finish it," Lord Randall said.

A wave of pain, doom, and loss swept through Al's brain. They were going to die. Well, at least he and Erik, Lord Randall was probably already dead.

Al glanced over his shoulder and turned back to the chest. "Airay, voomay, meesay, ketch,"

Lord Randall said, "Duck."

The ragged robe of the creature scraped across Al's head, and a thousand souls wailed in the night. Hope faded; why finish the magic chant? His skeleton was destined to float over this abandoned castle forever, attacking adventurers seeking the crown. Doomed to an eternity of anguish, sharing the pain and suffering of the lost, wailing souls.

Erik said, "Finish it, Al. Say the last line." He touched Al's shoulder.

Al flinched at his friend's touch and ducked lower to the ground. "It's finished."

Lord Randall turned his sword on Al. "I'll kill you myself, if you don't say the words."

Al stared up at Lord Randall and saw a brief flicker in the man's image, and Al thought he saw a different version of Lord Randall. A shadow spawn swooped low over Lord Randall, and he turned his sword to shoo it away from his body.

Could it be? "Erik," Al said.

"Say the words."

A shadow spawn aimed a bony digit at Al's right eye and Al tipped back his head exposing his neck for the creature; he was ready for the pain and agony which would end his suffering. His muscles felt weak. Surely the creature could sense Al's defeat. Al saw the creature face to face as it hovered over him. Its white skull peeked from inside the cowl of the hood, yellow eyes glowing hot. The creature stabbed at Al's eye, but some invisible barrier stopped its progress.

"Whoo-hoo, that's it Al, fight the creature." Erik whooped from inside the niche.

Al knew he didn't create the shield, someone else did. It couldn't be Erik, so it had to be Lord Randall. Did Gadiel control Lord Randall more than he had imagined? The old wizard knew they hadn't located the crown yet. Gadiel couldn't let them die yet. Not until they secured the crown.

Al rolled to his knees, confident of the protection presented by Lord Randall and finished the chant, "Nekkay, ekkay, moosmay, wretch." He watched the lock on the treasure chest.

Erik fiddled with the lock, but nothing happened. "It didn't work. That wasn't it. Lord Randall, read the scroll. There must be a different spell."

"You're not in danger, Lord Randall. I know you created a shield to keep the shadow spawn from touching us. Read the scroll." Al stood next to Lord Randall. "Read the scroll," he repeated.

Every time the shadow spawn swooped toward Al, their wails grew louder and Al's arm and back flared in pain as if someone had jabbed him with a hot, dull knife in the same location. The throbbing pain was tormenting, and he ached to acquiesce to the skeletal creatures. Just surrender to them and the pain would cease.

Lord Randall opened the scroll and muttered under his breath as he read the words, searching for the proper spell to release the treasure in the chest. "Try this."

"What do you mean, try this? Are you guessing? It might make things worse."

"Say these words, 'finna kho bao.'"

Erik said, "Go ahead Al. You might as well, since it's not looking good at the moment."

Two of the spectral creatures hovered near Al's face, trying to break through Lord Randall's protecting shield. Despite the shield, Al's injuries burned, and surrender flared in his mind.

Al said, "Finna kho boo."

"Not boo, bao, as in the bow of a ship," Lord Randall said.

"You said, boo."

"Don't argue, Al, say the right word."

Al, unable to lift his left arm, raised his good hand to the chest. "Finna kho bao." He emphasized the bao stretching it out.

Erik rattled the lock, but it didn't open. "That's not it."

"Are you trying to kill us?" Al asked. "Are you even reading that scroll or just making up garbage?"

"I'm doing the best I can." Lord Randall waved the scroll at Al. "You read it if you know so much."

"Think about it, the word finna either is finish or find, but not open the lock. What else does the scroll say?"

At the next swoop of the creatures, the shield fluttered. Lord Randall's skin flickered for a moment.

"The shield is dissipating," Lord Randall said.

"Can I send a dispel magic chant at them?"

"I don't know, I told you I've never encountered them."

Al shouted, "Don't lie to us. When we first opened the bell tower door, you ran away because something was coming. What was it? Why are you helping us now and not running?"

Al faced the creatures as they tried to bore into the shield. He raised his right arm and twisted a cupped hand toward the sky, "Aveexe togafiti."

The shadow spawn stopped breaking through the shield.

Erik high-fived the air and said, "Way to go, Al."

Al stood taller as the thrill of triumph raced through his body.

Then the shadow spawn returned, angrier than before as they scraped with bony fingers against the weakening shield.

"Do your fables and legends mention how to kill these creatures?"

Erik said, "Shouldn't we concentrate our attention on opening the chest? We're running out of time. The crown could help us."

One shadow spawn hand broke through the shield and grabbed at Al, but Al moved closer to the niche.

Lord Randall took a deep breath and sighed. "There's one way to remove them, but if the story turns out to be only a fable or child's tale, this might not work."

"Tell me."

"A dictum chant might eradicate them, but . . ." Lord Randall stopped.

"Continue."

"You won't like it."

"Tell me."

"The dictum chant works, but you have to touch them when you say it."

The remaining energy to struggle against the shadow spawn left him, and Al slumped. Hopelessness overcame his mind. How could he touch those creatures? They might reach him and consume his soul. His strength was sapped.

Lord Randall said, "You have to touch their bones, not just their robes."

Al shook his head. "I can't do that. You do it, you know the chant."

Lord Randall said, "In my present form, I don't have the power to touch them."

Erik spoke from the niche, "Do it, Al."

"There's one more thing," Lord Randall said.

Al moaned, "No."

"You touch them four times, touch the shadow spawn and say the words."

"Four times? To each one?"

"No, just to one of them."

"The same one each time?"

"No, they're interconnected, you can touch the same one or four different ones."

"Can I grab one arm and just say the chant four times?"

"Nope."

Al had trouble breathing and his stomach clenched, "Give me a break." The darkness surrounding him increased. A hot sauna of moisture shattered his will to live. Was it the creatures manipulating him or just the knowledge this quest would kill him?

"Here are the words you use, 'Dictum daemonium sancti videbunt lucem.'"

Why not release my soul to the creatures and escape from my problems? I don't have to do this. Who am I kidding? The grand wizard, Alpherge the Mighty, is a caricature, a high school kid who got absorbed in the magical possibilities on this crazy world. I can't fight these phantom creatures.

Erik said, "You got this Al. Grab the arm that's poking through the shield right now."

Why were they on this trip? To find the crown to save Erik's dad. A noble quest. When they played fantasy role games at home, the best adventures included a noble quest. Yes. This is a noble quest. Save Erik's dad and discover a way to open the portal to Earth. We need the crown.

Al grabbed the bony arm sticking through the shield as it reached back and forth to rake its finger across his body once more. He screamed the magic words, "Dictum daemonium sancti videbunt lucem."

The three shadow spawn howled as one, no longer the wailing of the souls lost in their evil, but a scream of terror. The one Al had touched shook its arm free and backed away.

"Yeah! Three more times." Erik cheered.

Lord Randall said, "The first time you do it, you deafen them."

The shadow spawn retreated from the shield as if re-grouping to plan another attack.

Al said, "Read the scroll and find the chant to open the chest. We're running out of time." It was impossible to judge how long they had been fighting the shadow spawn. They still had to return to the caravan before dawn.

The specters swooped toward Al in a movement designed to draw him out of the shield. They passed near but not close enough for Al to grab an arm or leg or even part of a robe. He stretched out his arm but yanked it back when he realized he couldn't reach them.

Lord Randall muttered the words as he read, nodded and said, "Ah ha, try this."

One creature hovered near the weak spot in the shield while a second extended an arm toward Al.

Erik said, "Grab his arm,"

The creature jerked its arm back as Al reached for it, and a second shadow spawn raked its finger across Al's forearm.

"No," Al screamed. That was his good arm. How could he defeat these creatures if he couldn't use either arm? His other arm hung by his side, useless in this battle for his soul. And now his good arm had only minutes before it failed.

The shadow spawn tried the same technique to trick Al into exposing his arm again.

Al waited for the bony fingers to come near, and then he jumped at the creature which pulled back. Al continued into the air, ignoring the first shadow spawn. He grabbed the exposed arm of the second. "Dictum daemonium sancti videbunt lucem."

The second scream from the creatures caused both boys to cover their ears, but Al could only protect one ear. The shadow spawn flew into the darkness, away from the bell tower.

Lord Randall said, "Say these words, hurry. 'Tatala ley locaa.'"

"Why?" Al examined his good arm. How much time remained before both arms became useless?

"It opens the chest."

Al scanned the dark, expecting the return of the shadow spawn then turned toward the chest. "Tatala ley locaa."

A flash of light appeared around the lock, and it broke free. Erik removed the shackle and opened the chest.

The shadow spawns' wails increased in volume as three attacked the shield at once. Their fingernails seemed diamond sharp. A piercing screech filled the air, like a student running his fingernails across a chalkboard. Al turned his head from the sound.

Al felt the effects of the evil encapsulate his right arm. How much time did he have? If he didn't finish this fast, they had no chance to survive.

CHAPTER 58

One shadow spawn made an upward long cut into the shield, and Al thrust his arm through the slot and grabbed its exposed leg. "Dictum daemonium sancti videbunt lucem."

The ghostly skeleton exploded in fire; the bright light blinded Al for a moment.

The other two floated, immobile.

Lord Randall said, "They're paralyzed, hurry finish the spell."

Al jumped at the one closest to him, but wasn't able to reach it.

Erik yelled from the niche, "Jump higher."

Al tried again and missed. "I'm jumping as high as I can."

One skeleton's leg twitched.

Black liquid oozed from Al's right arm, and his strength ebbed.

The shadow spawn stretched their limbs as if just waking.

"Now," Erik said.

With a mighty leap, Al lifted off the floor and stretched as far as possible. He grabbed a shadow spawn's foot and pulled hard, bringing the creature to the floor. He shouted, "Dictum daemonium sancti videbunt lucem."

The creatures disappeared.

Al looked at his empty hand. "What happened? Where did it go? Why didn't it explode like the other one?"

Lord Randall patted Al on the shoulder. "They're banished back to their evil lair for a while."

"You mean we didn't kill them?"

"No, they'll be back."

"How long?"

"The tales of old never say."

Erik said, "Look at this treasure."

He dug into the items in the chest and brought up a handful of gold coins, necklaces, and diamonds. "Wow. Behold my treasure."

"Do you see the crown?" Lord Randall asked.

"The crown is ours." Al glared at Lord Randall.

"We'll see."

Al's arms ached, and the black liquid oozed from the wounds and dripped onto his hands. They had traveled months to locate the treasure, and now he wouldn't make it back to Velidred and Sherry. His feet numbed in his boots, and his ability to think became difficult. He felt as if his brain had been replaced with cotton balls.

Erik flung coins and gold nuggets out of the chest, pitching gem-studded knives, gold and silver bracelets to the floor. He stopped at a pearl necklace and stuffed it into his pocket.

Lord Randall said, "Keep nothing from the chest except the crown. Everything else will kill you when you leave the castle."

"Don't worry about it. The necklace is for a friend."

"Go ahead and keep it, but you'll die."

Erik threw a handful of coins to the floor and said, "The crown isn't here."

"You must be wrong. It has to be in the chest," Al said. He looked at Lord Randall and wanted to grab the man by his fancy embroidered shirt and shake him, but Al was struggling to even lift his arms. "You lied."

Lord Randall presented the scroll to Al. "Read it yourself. I followed the instructions, I have no reason—"

Al's hands were useless and it fell to the floor

"You knew from the start the golden crown wasn't in the treasure chest. Go back to your Lady Charlotte; we don't need you." Al stumbled and fell. He smacked his head on the floor.

Erik dropped the gold he was holding and said, "Are you okay?" He jumped out of the niche and turned Al onto his back. "You're looking bad, buddy."

Al's blood seeped from the shadow spawn scratches. It was tainted black and flowed as unusually thick goo from his body. The shadow spawn had won, and Alpherge the Mighty's fate and future was as a shadow spawn to roam the jungle and castle, consuming the souls of adventurers for eternity. He didn't care about the golden crown, but he thought of Sherry. Where was she? Was she a prisoner? Al wanted to hold her hand and talk with her one last time.

Erik mumbled words while pressing on the gouged slits in Al's arm. "Heart so pure, wisdom and healing, cure the fever and restore to health this wizard's arm, clean the wound, seal the injury, heal this man and stop the misery."

Al remembered this chant from their old games at home. He snorted. There was no way an incantation from a child's game would heal people on this planet. What healing powers did Erik actually possess? He had healed the lumberjack, and the child that fell, but did his friend have power over demonic curses designed to send Al to the soulless underworld?

A chill ran through Al's body, and he imagined the death knell had arrived. Life completed. No crown and no returning to Earth. He collapsed into darkness.

* * * *

Al came to, lying on a stone floor in a room gleaming with candlelight. He smelled sandalwood incense. His body felt both weak and chilled. He wasn't in the bell tower anymore, but where was he?

Lord Randall said, "According to the scroll, there's a crypt in the chapel."

"A crypt in the chapel? Where?" Erik asked.

"The body of King Stephen III lies in the crypt."

"Is the crown buried with the king?"

"It doesn't say. The scroll reads like a historical document, telling about the king's adventures and how well he treated his subjects. It says as he lay on his death bed he gave three hundred gold coins to each village resident. Oh wait, the scroll says the king's skill as a wizard helped him convince the wizarding community to assemble as a nation, uniting for the good of wizards and non-wizards."

"How does that help us? Are the items we seek with the king?"

Lord Randall waved the scroll in the air. "It doesn't mention any treasures with the king."

"Where's the crypt?"

"Why won't you listen? The scroll doesn't show the crypt's location."

Erik ran a hand through his hair. "Does this chapel have a burial crypt?"

"It's either in the chapel or in the castle's lower recesses."

Erik said, "No. I am not going into a dungeon. No good can come from that. Plus, I don't have the strength to carry that tangle of arms and legs to the dungeon. If he doesn't recover—"

Al opened his eyes and noticed the pink and purple stripes running across the chapel's ceiling. His arms felt weighted, and his mind wrestled with his muscles to move his body. He tried to talk, but nothing happened.

Erik said, "Did they bury the crown with King Stephen's remains? Does the scroll talk about the crown and king together?"

"It doesn't talk about the crown at all."

That makes no sense, Al thought. They're supposed to use the scroll to find the crown, yet it's not mentioned in the scroll. The treasure chest inspired adventurers to search for the treasure, and the searchers discovered the chest, took gold coins and died from the evil specters in the castle. Or maybe Lord Randall or the wild animals in the jungle killed them as they tried to leave. They all died or were consumed into evil.

Al screamed, but produced no sound, not even a mumble. Paralyzed. His friend saved him from the soulless shadow spawn, but at what cost?

Erik said, "Back on Earth they buried bodies in the floor of cathedrals. Did they bury King Stephen in the floor?" Erik stomped across the floor.

Al listened to the stomps. Hard surface. Hard surface. Then a hollow sound.

"Here. Underneath Al."

Lord Randall said, "Let's drag him out of the way."

They grabbed Al's legs and dragged him across the rough stone floor. He scraped against each imperfection in the stones. Al wanted to yell. It's me, I'm awake. Help. He worked moisture into his mouth, but he was still unable to swallow. Now he worried he'd drown in his own saliva.

"It's here. The inscription's cut into the stone. 'King Stephen III, righteous leader of justice and freedom,'" Erik said.

"Open the crypt," Lord Randall said.

"With what? Where's your sword?"

"Huh, oh I left it in the bell tower."

"Why did you do that?"

"I helped lower your dead friend down the rope."

"He's not dead."

"Examine him. The man's dead."

"Grab a candlestick."

"I don't trust the candlesticks. I think there's a curse on them."

Al thought of the nursery rhyme. That's it, King Stephen's crypt. When he tried to talk, he couldn't utter even a moan.

Erik said, "Climb the rope and retrieve the sword."

Lord Randall said, "I'm not climbing the rope, I barely made it the first time. You go."

"I'm staying with my friend."

"Your dead friend."

"He's not dead."

"Your healing spell didn't work; you tried your best."

The bickering continued, and Al was glad Erik hadn't left him alone to die. Time was running out. Was daylight minutes or hours from now? When did daybreak arrive? Neither of them wore a watch, and their cell phones were long gone. If they were even a few minutes late, the mastodons and caravan could travel out of sight with no hope for Al and Erik to catch them. Al struggled to say something, anything.

Lord Randall said, "Why did you take the necklace."

"None of your business."

"It will call up goblins and magical curses against us."

"I'm saving it for a friend."

"Who."

"None of your business. Retrieve your sword."

"Not until you tell me why you took the necklace. Is it for your girlfriend from Earth, Lily?"

"How do you know about her?"

"Tell me!" Lord Randall screamed.

"Stop it," Al whispered. He tried to yell, but managed only a whisper.

"Hush! Did you hear that?" Erik asked.

"What?"

"Al's alive." Erik knelt next to Al and lifted his friend's head. "Are you okay?"

"No, everything hurts." Al stopped talking, closed his eyes and breathed slowly. Then he said, "The nursery rhyme."

"What about it?" Erik asked.

"The nursery rhyme opens the crypt."

"Does your magic work?"

Breathing the sandalwood scent from the incense was calming Al. He had been considering his magic as he recovered. He couldn't sit up without help, and talking was difficult. His brain worked, though the back of his head hurt from being dragged across the rough floor.

Al said, "Swivel me toward the crypt."

Erik dragged Al's upper body to reposition him facing the crypt.

"Hold up my arms so they are pointed at the crypt."

"Lord Randall, help me with his other arm."

Al felt magic enter his body when Lord Randall touched his arm. Who or what was this spirit? How could a ghost control magic or, for that matter, lift Al's arm?

Al took a deep breath and said, "Oona ganna takkay goota, Nekkay akkay pakkee soota, Airay voomay meesay ketch, Nekkay ekkay moosmay wretch.

Al felt additional magic flow from Lord Randall as he cast the spell. Was it good magic, evil magic, or a curse that would bite them later? Al didn't know.

The lid of the crypt slid open as the marble panel glided across the floor.

CHAPTER 59

s the lid of the crypt of King Stephen III opened, Erik returned Al to a reclining position on the floor. Erik then peered into the opening and said, "There's a skeleton holding a broadsword, and the skull is wearing a leather helmet with a gold dragon attached to it."

Lord Randall reached into the crypt, yanked the helmet off the skull, displacing the bones, and placed it on his head. "This is the crown we seek. The helmet of justice is real."

"Where's the golden crown." Erik asked.

"There is no golden crown. The magic is in the helmet of justice and now it's mine."

"What do you mean there's no gold crown?"

"Just what I said, it's not a gold crown. Gadiel tricked you into helping me get the helmet of justice.

The helmet reminded Erik of an old, leather football helmet. A small, gold dragon sat upon leather strips of blue and red which crossed the helmet's top. The dragon appeared ready to fly, wings outstretched, and mouth opened showing many teeth. Scales were intricately carved into the body, and its tail swung alongside the helmet and ended above the helmet's left ear hole. Red rubies served as the dragon's eyes.

Erik stared at the sword lying in the burial chamber in the hands of the skeletal remains of King Stephen III. The sword extended the length of his arm and glowed green, like the Aurora Borealis with a pulse. A black leather grip wrapped the handle with a scrolled, silver cross guard to protect the hand.

Erik grabbed the broadsword, ripping it out of the king's dead fingers, and tested the weight and grip in his hand. He pointed the business end toward Lord Randall. "That's not yours."

"You're wrong. With this crown, I can restore my rightful place in the Velidred Castle."

This castle isn't Velidred, so where did this ghost originate? Has the helmet given Lord Randall enough magic power to allow him to transfer himself from this castle to Velidred?

A second Lord Randall, wearing a burgundy cap, entered the room and brandished a sword at Erik. "I challenge you to a duel for dishonoring Lady Charlotte."

Erik's heart beat faster. He cocked his head at the new arrival and raised the sword, but not in an aggressive posture. "Let's talk first."

"No one dis-honors Lady Charlotte." The blue-eyed, second Lord Randall jabbed the sword at Erik's belly.

Erik danced backwards and used the broadsword to block the thrust. Metal clanged against metal. How did this Lord Randall acquire a sword? He's a ghost. Erik had assumed the Lord Randall in the bell tower wasn't in actual danger because he was already a ghost. But the sword this one wields is real, and the other Lord Randall just placed the helmet on his head. What strange magic is this? Which one of these guys is the real Lord Randall?

"Al, buddy, I need a little help here."

Al moaned, but didn't move.

The second Lord Randall and Erik parried, but the long broadsword was difficult to use in the enclosed chapel space. Lord Randall backed Erik into a chapel niche, and Erik knocked over a table that held a burning candle. It bounced to the stone floor and went out. There was no room to maneuver, and Lord Randall was fast and efficient with his sword-play. Erik worked hard to keep from being impaled as he swung his sword in defense.

Metal pounded against metal, echoing in the small chapel like a blacksmith's forge, and green sparks exploded in tiny fireworks off Erik's sword. He wondered if the blade held magic. *That would explain Wagner's interest in the sword.*

Al moved on the floor, managing to roll from his back. He muscled to his hands and knees.

Lord Randall thrust at Erik.

Erik blocked, and the ghost's sword slid toward Erik's hand until it locked against the broadsword's guard. Erik used the leverage and shoved Lord Randall, providing him space to maneuver out of the chapel niche.

Sweat beaded on Erik's forehead as he danced forward and flourished his weapon. How can a ghost use a real sword, Erik wondered? "Al, I need your help."

Al swayed like a sleepy toddler, unable to stand or to engage with the actions in the chapel.

Lord Randall moved with speed and agility as he parried, thrust and danced in the small space. He sliced his sword toward Erik's mid-section, and initiated a rapid sequence of swordplay.

Erik Blocked.

Stabbed at Erik.

Blocked.

Then Lord Randall spun three-hundred and sixty degrees and sliced a two inch wound in Erik's upper left arm.

Erik gasped and jerked back from the blow. A sudden coldness hit his core as he realized this match was for real. He didn't have sword skills beyond backyard pretend fights with wrapping paper tubes, and there was no way he could survive an attack against a superior opponent.

Lord Randall's attack increased in speed.

Erik's heart thundered in his chest. He tried to predict Lord Randall's moves as the sword, which had seemed light when he first hoisted it, grew heavier in his tiring arm.

The green-eyed Lord Randall, with the helmet still on his head, stood watching the action.

Al appeared ready to stand, but he suddenly mutated into a monkey.

Erik blinked in disbelief and distraction, he missed a blocking move, and Lord Randall's sword cut Erik's upper thigh.

The monkey raced around the room and circled Erik and Lord Randall as they exchanged blows. Al, the monkey, chattered and hooted, then stopped behind Erik and howled.

Lord Randall said, "I warned you not to visit the lovely Lady Charlotte."

"I haven't," Erik said. Could Al manage magic as a monkey? Erik hoped so, because Lord Randall's exceptional swordplay meant a victory strike soon for the ghost.

"You directed me to her bed chambers, knowledge a lover holds close to his heart."

The green-eyed Lord Randall gasped, "What are you saying?"

The monkey jumped on Erik's shoulders.

"Get off me Al, I don't have time for monkey business."

The monkey grunted and hooted while waving its arms.

"I'm clueless what you're saying, Al, I hope it's a spell to disarm this Lord Randall."

The cloying sandalwood incense burned heavy in the chapel; tendrils of smoke swirled in patterns as the men brandished their swords.

The Lord Randall with the sword stood at attention for a moment, took a deep breath and said, "With deep regret, I must kill you now. You were a friend, ally and a worthy opponent, but Lady Charlotte's honor, you see."

Everything happened fast. The lord started a furious flurry of sword strikes.

Erik blocked and gyrated, though several strikes hit him, ripping his tunic and slicing into his arms. The monkey screamed in his ear as Erik parried. "Stop it, you wacky monkey, I can't think."

Lord Randall moved in close.

The monkey leapt from Erik's shoulder and landed on Lord Randall's face.

Lord Randall stopped his attack as he wrestled the monkey off his head.

Erik raised his sword and stabbed Lord Randall in the gut. The broadsword slashed through his opponent and came out red. Blood dripped onto a purple stripe that ran across the floor.

Lord Randall dropped his sword and put his hand to the wound in his belly. He stumbled back into a chapel niche. The color drained from his face and his chin trembled as he gaped at Erik with wide, unbelieving eyes. "You were my friend, why did you betray me?" He tumbled onto the table and collapsed to the floor.

The green-eyed Lord Randall, still wearing King Stephen's helmet, asked, "You and Lady Charlotte?"

"Give me a break," Erik said. "I haven't been in the castle long enough to even meet Lady Charlotte, and she must have died decades ago. But then you already know that, don't you?"

The monkey chattered at the remaining Lord Randall.

Green-eyed Lord Randall smiled, "You took a necklace from the chest. Why?" He sent a fireball toward Erik's feet.

The fireball exploded in front of Erik.

Erik shuffled back, using the broadsword as a shield. He didn't know Lord Randall's story, nor the history of either one, but the man was delusional. It was luck that allowed Erik to kill the other guy, but he had no chance against a wizard. What should he do? Should he try a mad dash at Lord Randall and attempt to stab him before being blasted with a fireball? Was either one of the lords a ghost? Should they run away?

Al the monkey ran behind Erik and howled.

"I need some ideas, Al," Erik yelled over the screaming monkey.

The monkey chattered back.

"We can't leave without the helmet, and Lord Randall is acting insane. He's got the helmet crown thingy and is tossing fireballs at us." Erik edged further from Lord Randall and toward the altar.

"You two don't have a clue, do you?" Lord Randall asked.

"Listen, just give me the helmet and we'll leave you and Lady Charlotte alone. We aren't seeking trouble."

Lord Randall began to melt before their eyes. The sandy colored hair became long and black. The beard transformed into smooth skin and the tight fitting embroidered shirt changed into a dress. His body shrunk a few inches and features became delicate.

Erik felt disoriented for a moment as he recognized the woman that stood before him.

"Who's the necklace for Erik?" She advanced toward him.

CHAPTER 60

Erik blinked and wiped a sleeve across his forehead to sponge away the sweat streaming into his eyes. Blood from the battle with Lord Randall smeared on the fabric. The woman before him was gorgeous. But was this person a trick, yet more magic within the castle?

Erik said, "What are you doing here?"

The monkey chattered, darted to the altar, bounded onto it and howled.

The woman pushed hair from her eyes, tucking it inside the helmet. She smiled at Erik and moved closer. "I'm here to retrieve the helmet of justice for Gadiel."

Erik's heart hammered as he stood fast at the woman's approach. "The helmet isn't yours to give."

"Lord Randall injured you." Zita stroked his arm near the lacerations the lord inflicted during the skirmish.

"Give me the helmet."

"You and the little monkey? The helmet won't fit the monkey's head."

Erik stared into Zita's green eyes and breathed deeply. She was so near.

She stroked Erik's chin, rubbing her hands through his beard.

Zita's touch sent a tingling through his body, and he stepped closer to her. He still held the sword in his right hand, but with his left arm pulled her tight to his chest.

"Who's the necklace for?"

"You. I could have told you in the bell tower, but," he chuckled, "I didn't realize it was you. If I'd known, I'd have kept your secret."

Zita laid her head on Erik's chest.

The monkey howled and hopped on the altar.

"How do I know you're real? Strange things are happening in this castle."

She stood on her toes and gave him a light kiss on the cheek. "You rescued me from the water."

His chest tightened. Should he believe this woman? Do dark magic creatures perceive inner secrets and thoughts? Where was Zita if she wasn't in this castle? He hadn't seen her since he kissed her inside Gadiel's cabin.

"Don't give the helmet to Gadiel."

"He promised to release me from his magical enslavement."

Erik's tone hardened. "We came here because Gadiel told us the crown had the power to release the stone warriors. I can't let you deliver it to Gadiel."

"Gadiel used you to seize the crown. He has no intention to let you keep it. In fact, he says he won't allow me to leave this castle without killing you both first."

Erik clenched his teeth, stepped back and raised the sword.

The little monkey raced back and forth on the altar, chattering and howling.

The noise from the monkey, the incense, and loss of blood had Erik's head aching. "Shut up, Al."

Zita smirked at him with sorrow. "That sword won't hurt me." She had no affection of love or passion in her voice.

"It will if I ram it through your heart." He brandished the long blade in the air.

She gave him a long, pained stare and then broke eye contact. Zita shook her head, and when she gazed at Erik again, tears glistened in her eyes.

This time Erik looked away and peered around the room, blocking out the sound of the monkey. His head reeled from the purple and yellow stripes in the chapel, the swirling smoke from the incense, and the monkey's antics on the altar. Images of frogs on the walls and ceiling, and the golden image of the frog on the altar seemed grotesque, too alien to process. How could he convince Zita to reunite with them and keep the helmet?

Erik said, "Return to Velidred with us and bring the helmet, and I'll introduce you to my father."

"I've met your father, Commander Jack Anderson, a great military leader that King Haskell turned into stone along with the thousands of warriors that marched with him." She moved toward Erik.

Erik stepped back.

Zita said, "My father is still alive."

Erik's mind shifted through images of the volcano, the eclipse, and Lily's sacrifice. The Mountain King was alive? Did Zita already know this when he rescued her from the ice? Is that why she took the trip? Was this her betrayal?

The monkey leaped high into the vaulted chapel and landed on Erik's shoulder with a thud. Alpherge, the monkey, dug his claws into Erik's shoulder to keep from sliding to the floor. Al resumed his chattering, waving monkey arms at Zita.

She said, "I can't kill you, my love. I told Gadiel and Dad I didn't have the heart for it. However, I figured you two can kill each other."

She waved her arms and extended her fingers in a sensuous dance.

Erik's body changed. His legs grew wider and hair exploded over his entire body. "What are you doing?" He yelled.

His arms grew longer and his hands became claws, too clumsy to hold the broadsword, and it clanged to the floor. His nose converted into a snout and his body weight forced him to his hands which had turned into claws.

Zita completed Erik's transformation into a bear.

The monkey leaped off Erik's shoulders and bounded to the altar.

Zita snickered. "A bear fighting a monkey won't do. I need a fair fight." Her arms performed a similar dance as before, and the monkey changed into a tiger. "Perfect."

Erik yelled, but the sound came out as a bear's roar.

The tiger growled behind Erik.

Erik turned toward Al with an instinctive urge to fight the tiger. The part of him that was still Erik tried to reason with Al the tiger, but the words came out as grunts and growls.

* * * *

Zita moved to the doorway to watch the fight between the two animals. *This should be interesting.*

Erik, the bear, rushed the tiger. Al, the tiger backed up, claws extended, and then the bear retreated.

The tiger roared and stalked toward the bear, seeking a vulnerable place to attack.

Without retreating, the bear kept its face toward the tiger. With agility, the tiger sprang toward the bear, and the bear reared up on its back legs and bulldozed the tiger to the ground. The bear slashed at the tiger, and the tiger scooted backward.

The tiger turned and attacked the bear, swiping a claw across the bear's back.

The bear screamed in pain.

Zita's heart was raw, and she wished for a different outcome, but she knew her father and Gadiel wouldn't allow the boys to live. It was hard seeing Erik die, but she had to ensure both boys died before she left the room. She hoped Erik died first. She was sure she could kill Al, but not Erik. She closed her eyes for a moment as the tiger slashed the bear.

The animals growled and circled to gain leverage in the small chapel. The bear rose above the tiger and raked long claws across the tiger's side.

With a loud roar, the tiger attacked again and rose on its hind legs to stand taller than the bear, but the bear was more comfortable on two legs and pushed the tiger onto its back. The tiger rolled and faced the bear once more.

The bear attacked over and over with a constant charge and used its superior frame and weight to overpower the tiger and force it against the wall. Returning quick blows and raking its claws across the bear's face, the tiger kept the match even by its agility.

Zita had trouble breathing while watching the battle. She remembered the wonderful experiences with Erik, the first time he kissed her and how the action surprised her. He had a sweet soul and didn't deserve to die.

The chapel filled with the raw scents of fear and blood overpowering the incense. The bear and tiger rolled against the walls. Locked in a clinch, they backed into the altar, moving it against its stone legs. The golden frog wobbled for a second before settling.

She tried to pay attention; she didn't want to become a collateral casualty of the battle. She needed to prepare to move if they reached her position.

Grunts and roars reverberated in the space. Again the bear bulldozed the tiger into the wall. The tiger crouched low and pounced onto the bear's back, digging its claws deep into the animal's leathery shoulders. It opened its jaws to deliver the fatal bite to the bear's neck.

The bear roared and rolled onto its back forcing the tiger to release its grip. The tiger retreated to the other side of the chapel.

The blue-eyed Lord Randall that Erik had defeated still lay in the chapel niche. Inexplicably, he sat up and twisted his burgundy cap back and forth in his hands.

Without pause, the bear charged the tiger, forcing the animal onto its back legs, but the larger bear stood above the tiger. They clawed at each other, striking air more often than landing a blow.

The bear forced the tiger onto its back, raking its claws against the tiger's belly. The tiger released a primal scream of pain and rolled from the bear.

Zita put her hands over her ears to keep out the noise. The bear might win this match. It looked like its superior size and weight would overcome the agility and cunning of the tiger.

The blue-eyed Lord Randall stood in the niche. Blood dripped from his wound, but despite this, the castle lord replaced his burgundy cap on his head and adjusted it.

The bear approached the tiger, but the tiger lowered its head as if surrendering to the bear.

"No, no, no. Don't surrender. Kill each other." She cast an air spell at the bear and broke its left foreleg.

The bear grunted and hitched a step on the leg.

The tiger noticed the pause and rose into attack posture.

The bear tried to charge but the pain in its leg hampered its movement.

In a split second, the tiger swiped the bear's face, slicing long, red stripes across the bear's snout.

The bear retreated from the tiger.

Lord Randall limped toward Zita.

Zita was watching the animals, but Lord Randall stepped closer and she couldn't avoid seeing his shape change.

Beyond his shoulder, she saw the tiger jump onto the bear's back, and the bear had no answer for the move.

Lord Randall's face transformed from the handsome face of a castle lord. His ears lengthened, his teeth became thinner and sharper, his lips turned pale and thin, and his face became gaunt and took on a greenish hue. His garments fell away, leaving only a loin cloth over a green body with taut muscles.

The tiger sank its teeth into the bear's shoulder and the bear cried out in pain.

With a speed Zita didn't expect, Lord Randall, now a goblin, jumped on her, knocked her to the floor and plunged his teeth deep in her neck.

Zita tensed, her skin tingled and her eyes bulged. What had just happened? Lord Randall, a goblin? *Once bitten by a goblin, no one ever survives. A goblin gains its strength from its victims, sucking out their blood and their life source. Their attacks are overwhelming and invincible.* Zita struggled to force the goblin off, but thrashing and flailing only made the goblin bite deeper.

CHAPTER 61

With a mighty heave, the bear threw the tiger off its back. But it wasn't a tiger; Al transformed back into his own body, hit the floor and lay still, gasping for breath. Al didn't know why things changed, but he gratefully ran his hands over his body, making sure he was whole.

Erik lay opposite Al, his broken left arm bent at a strange angle. He was scored with gashes, and his clothing was shredded and blood-soaked. What was left hung at strange angles on his frame.

Al said, "What happened to us? How you doing, buddy?" He rolled over and crawled to his friend.

"Not good." Erik lifted his arm.

"Can I help?"

"Yes," Erik said, "set the bone for me."

"I'm no doctor."

"You're all I got."

"Can't it wait until we get back to the castle? Don't they have a healer?"

"Please, yank it until it snaps into place and then we'll wrap it."

Al grimaced at the broken arm and pushed his long hair out of his face. He considered the task. He'd never felt comfortable when people were ill or unhealthy. What was he supposed to do? A chill shuddered down his back.

Erik said, "Do it quick, and then I can heal you."

"Why not heal yourself?"

"Healing doesn't work that way; healers can't heal themselves." Erik rubbed his injured arm, trying to ease the pain. "Please, do this."

Al grabbed Eric's hand and avoided looking at the bone sticking out of the wrist. Then he shook his head. "I can't."

"Pull on the hand, it'll be fine."

Al looked at the frog on the altar and pulled Erik's hand.

Erik screamed, "Ahhh."

Al stopped.

"No, keep pulling, you're almost there."

"Stop screaming."

"It hurts."

"Do you want me to fix it?"

Erik gritted his teeth and grunted as Al pulled once more.

A click sounded as the bone snapped into the irregular broken slot.

Erik wriggled his fingers. "Okay, that will have to do. Find a cloth to wrap it."

"Where?" Al waved around the small chapel.

"Never mind." Erik tore his tunic, using his teeth to help shred the cloth. "Wrap it with this."

Two minutes later, the arm was encased in a makeshift cast and Al helped Erik to his feet.

Erik lifted the broadsword from the chapel floor.

Al asked, "What happened to the helmet?"

"Zita had it. Where is she?"

* * * *

Erik scanned the chapel and noticed strange shadows by the chapel doorway. "Over there." He trotted to the doorway.

Zita lay on the floor, her face pale and gaunt, with a green monster at her throat. She was alive. Her breath was low and raspy, and her eyes bulged in terror. She blinked at Erik and her lips moved, but the only sound was the horrible rasping.

Erik stabbed the sword into the green goblin. The creature waved it off with a long, green hand as if it were of no consequence.

Al said, "The helmet is over here." He lifted the helmet and shoved it onto his head, the gold dragon leaned to one side. "Let's go."

"We can't."

"Why not?"

Erik's eyes felt gummy and his chest ached at the sight of Zita. "We have to save Zita."

"Are you crazy? Look at you. She caused all those wounds. Zita broke your wrist. Why save her?"

Erik's heart hammered in his chest. As the goblin sucked on Zita's neck, Erik clasped her hand.

She smiled at the touch.

Al said, "We don't have time for you two to make goo-goo eyes. Look at her. She's as good as dead."

"Kill the monster."

"You can't kill a goblin. It's impossible."

"Does the helmet give you extra power?"

Al closed his eyes and moved his hands while mumbling words, too indistinct for Erik to understand.

The pale green creature continued to suck at Zita's neck.

Zita pleaded with her eyes.

Al said, "Like I said, you can't kill goblins. Grab the sword and let's go. This helmet doesn't fit my head, it's too small. I'm not feeling any magic in it."

"We can't leave her like this."

"Look at her. She's as good as dead. Even if you healed her, she'd still die."

He appraised Zita and shook his head. How could he help her? The goblin sucked more life from Zita, leaving her body shriveled, her skin tight against her skull.

"She's too far—"

"Don't say it." Erik grabbed the sword and brandished it at Al. "Kill the creature."

"What are you doing? I'm telling you, goblins are impossible to kill with magic."

"Kill the goblin." Erik thrust the sword at Al.

Al moved back. "You're being unreasonable. Let's leave; we have the helmet and the sword." Al tried to deflect the sword which hovered near his gut. "Dawn is coming, and we have to reach the caravan before sunrise."

Erik waved the sword, "Save her, don't let that creature kill her."

"She's evil. Even if you saved her, she would turn on you. She broke your arm and tried to kill you; why heal her this time? If she doesn't die now, she'll only try to kill you again."

Erik bared his teeth and moved closer to Al. "I will kill you with this sword right now if you don't use magic to get the goblin off of her."

Al's eyes widened, and he drew in a deep breath. "Are you listening to what you're saying? We have what we came for, leave Zita, she's nothing but trouble."

Blood pounded in Erik's ears as the sword twitched in his hands. Why did his friend act this way? Erik charged Al with the sword.

Al blocked the sword with a magic shield and used air to throw Erik across the room, bouncing him against the altar.

* * * *

Al's stomach hardened as fatigue gripped his body. What was Erik doing? Why didn't he see the truth? With the helmet in their possession, it was time to flee the castle. He had never seen Erik this angry.

Erik stood and picked up the frog statue. Carrying the object over his head, he ran, screaming a war cry, toward Al. Then at the last minute Erik tossed the statue at Al.

Al blocked the flying frog, and it dropped to the floor. "Take it easy." How did his friend have the strength and mobility with a broken arm to pick up and throw the statue?

Erik's muscles and veins bulged on his neck as he screamed, "I'm not taking it easy, you're letting a person I love die."

How can I calm Erik when he's being totally unreasonable? Al needed to take Erik's mind off Zita. "We have the helmet. We can save your father and all those other stone warriors. I beg you, let's go." Al pointed into the hallway.

"Go, if you won't help." Erik crumpled to the floor next to Zita and the creature.

"No, please don't stay, the goblin will suck your blood next. They're insatiable. We've learned about goblins from the games we use to play. One victim is never enough. Grab the sword, and come with me, I'm leaving."

"If Zita dies, then we die together." Erik's eyes glistened; he balled his good hand into a fist and raised it at Al. "Leave."

Erik's optimism had always pulled them together, the two of them and Sherry and Lily. Al had no magic for this unprecedented behavior. To stay in the castle and die wasn't an option. He had the helmet, the object of his quest, and he needed to return to Sherry. To survive, he must leave Erik with Zita and let them die. "I'm leaving."

"Then go!"

Al shook his head and the weight of the gold dragon atop the helmet made it wobble. Where was the magic in this helmet or crown or whatever they called it? It was small, heavy and uncomfortable on his head, and he could sense no magic. He wanted to help Erik, but couldn't come up with any answers.

Al searched the room one more time before leaving. The altar lay bare. The purple and yellow stripes hadn't changed. Two more candles had burned out, and the room had grown dark. The crypt lay open; the skeletal remains of King Stephen III were exposed. The room offered no answers, no clues to save Zita or to convince Erik to leave. Al staggered from the chapel into the hallway.

* * * *

Erik held Zita's clammy hand and looked into her green eyes. Her eyes had attracted him when they met on that first day on the mountain when Erik and his friends traveled through the portal to this planet. Now her eyes bulged in terror. He thought of the events that transpired in the months since meeting Zita, and he hated to lose her.

She moaned and clenched Erik's hand tighter.

Her skin was blanched, ashen white, and he wondered how she could still be alive.

"I'll stay with you." He patted her arm with his left hand, ignoring the pain it caused. With a deep sigh he said, "You won't die alone. I love you."

Zita blinked in anguish.

Erik considered the trouble this woman put him through, and yet he yearned for her. He scooted closer, so they were touching.

The goblin snarled and slurped at Zita's neck.

Erik took the necklace from his pocket and pushed it into the dying girl's hand. "This was always to be yours. I didn't want Al to know that you were still alive and so near to us. I hoped on the return trip we would tell Al about your shape-shifting and we could enjoy each other's company."

She grasped the necklace in her fingers, and her lips parted in a slight smile.

Erik needed to kill the goblin. He wanted time to heal Zita, but knew Al was right. You can't kill goblins. How long had this creature roamed the castle killing adventurers that wandered into the chapel looking for treasures?

He pulled on the goblin's leg.

The creature growled, and cast a sidelong glance at Erik. Its black pupils swam in pale yellow orbs. The goblin threw out an arm, and with a long pointed fingernail sliced across Erik's chest. Zita's blood dripped from its long pointed teeth.

This is it, then. We die together at the hands of this creature. Why didn't it react at all to the sword, yet when I touched it . . .

* * * *

Al hurried along the corridor, located the circular stairway, and descended the small stairs to the lower floor. Did he really intend to leave Erik with that creature? He thought back to the crazy things that had happened to them since arriving on Aloheno. Erik rescued Al in the dungeon at Velidred castle. His friend saved him on this long trip with the caravan when Hadrian wanted to leave him for dead because of altitude sickness.

Why did his friend work so hard for Zita? Now his impulsive friend would die with Zita in a goblin's death embrace.

Al once more wished he had the staff. He wanted to converse with the wizards. Maybe with the ancient magic from the staff he could kill the goblin and save Erik and Zita.

He reached the banquet hall and didn't see any ghosts or goblins, a good sign. Al realized Zita pretended to be Lord Randall in the bell tower. Funny how tired that Lord Randall was climbing the rope, though Al couldn't think why a ghost had to climb the rope instead of flying to the bell tower.

Al muttered, "We wouldn't have found the treasure or the helmet without Zita's help." He rubbed the back of his neck. *Is Erik right? Should we comfort her as she dies? Is she dead now?*

He took a deep breath and closed his eyes. It would be crazy to come on this arduous journey, find the crown and lose Erik. He imagined Sherry and Lily's reaction if he came back without Erik. *What kind of person am I if I leave my best friend to die?*

With a loud sigh Al said, "Oh great magical crown, how do I kill the goblin and save my friend?"

A moment later, Al charged back up the stairs.

CHAPTER 62

Erik said, "I'm attempting to change the balance in your favor, it's our only hope to defeat the goblin. Are you ready?"

Zita's eyes teared, and she answered weakly, "Yes."

He examined Zita's withering body and wondered if his idea to save her was too late. Maybe he would just make matters worse. His plan might leave Zita a shapeless blob. Had the goblin's bite infected her so badly she would be transformed into a goblin? He resolved to try to rescue her anyway.

He stood over the goblin's body and held his hands above the creature. Erik didn't know if his strategy had merit, but it was his last hope.

Al raced into the room, a wide grin on his lips. He held the loose helmet on his head with one hand. Panting for air he said, "I know how to kill it. Just—" He stopped. "You figured it out didn't you?"

Erik hoped he had the answer. He remembered playing a dungeon game with his friends years ago and using this ploy to drive away a goblin. It doesn't kill the goblin, everyone knew you can't kill them, but it drives them away.

"Go ahead, you're right." Al nodded and gave his friend a goofy grin.

Erik combined skills Cugbert taught him and words from the Earth game. Erik grabbed the goblin's arm and chanted, "Healing power, force of good, heal this soul from foot to head, enter its body and baffle the dead."

The goblin stopped sucking Zita's neck and snarled at the boys. The creature yanked against Erik's grasp, but Erik held tight. It struggled and shook, thrashed and flailed to loosen the healer's touch.

Erik's healing power flowed from his inner self. A stream of goodness and purity flowed into the goblin. This force was intolerable to the creature.

The goblin jerked away from Zita's body and tried to bite Erik, but the healer held firm. The goblin was strong and with a mighty shove against Erik it attempted to dislodge the vice-like grip. From where it braced a hand against the boy, tendrils of smoke arose.

Calm and focus exuded from Erik as the power of purity rushed through his fingers. Pustules, like smallpox, appeared on the goblin's arms and from these tiny volcanoes, fires erupted.

Erik drove the creature into the hallway and shoved him away.

The goblin faced his attacker, and they postured for dominance.

Had Erik released the creature too soon? Should he have pushed the goblin further or locked it in a closet or something? Erik's muscles tightened in readiness for a new attack.

Then the goblin's demeanor changed, its long green arms flopped limply, and it broke eye contact with Erik.

Erik marched toward the creature with hands lifted in defense, prepared for the goblin to counter-attack. Could he stop it?

The creature gave a blood-curdling scream, frightening Erik. Suddenly it turned, bolted down the corridor and hurtled through the window.

A fifty-foot fall wouldn't kill the creature, but Erik hoped it had bought him time to save Zita. He rushed back into the chapel.

Zita lay on the floor, pale and weak with smears of wet blood around the ragged bite on her neck. Another candle guttered which left only one weak candle still burning.

Erik's heartbeat quickened, and his body shook. "Zita, I'm here."

Her eyes were closed, and she lay unmoving.

Al said, "Does she have enough strength left for healing? What if she comes back as a goblin?"

Erik leaned down and put his ear to Zita's mouth. "She's still breathing. Not much time."

He rubbed his hands together to stimulate the healing power. "Please let this be the right thing." He took two deep breaths and placed one hand on the top of Zita's head and the other on the goblin bite.

A weak pulse beat in her neck, and it encouraged Erik to continue.

The flame of the last candle flickered, then died. Darkness enveloped the room and the entire castle was quiet. Cloying incense hung heavy in the room, already oppressive with the heat and humidity of the surrounding jungle.

Erik's breath bottled up in his chest. Was it too late? He could barely sense Zita's life force. Had she surrendered to death? He said, "Thank you for being a part of my life Zita. You challenged me, and my heart beats for you." Heat flushed from his neck to his face, and he worked to clear his throat. He thought of Zita's pink lips, green eyes and flirty smile and how much he wanted her to live.

The healing procedure imparted to Erik a hyper-awareness of his own body. Each skin cell tingled, each heartbeat was pronounced, and he even became aware of the synapses of his brain firing. He entered into union with Zita, searching her inner core for a spark he could kindle. He said, "Heal the arms, legs and heart, heal the child here before me. Nature's strength weave its caress and saturate her wounds with sparks of life."

Zita's heart beat faster and stronger, but still weakly.

"Give me light," Erik yelled at Al.

Al whipped up a blue globe that radiated light in their part of the room.

Zita's eyes stayed closed, her skin pallid and reflecting only the ghostly blue of the globe.

Erik didn't have enough experience, strength, knowledge or power to heal Zita. She was too far gone, and she couldn't bring enough strength to the table for healing. He might make her stable, but in the long term his skills would only give her extra moments before she died. He was too late.

Al said, "How's it going?"

"It's not. She's dying." He was light-headed in the hot, stuffy room. Suddenly, the heat and fatigue of the last three days hit him like a sledgehammer. In that demoralized moment, a thought drifted through his brain. This room contained extra healing power he might tap. But, the more he struggled to recall the thought, the farther away the important clue drifted.

Erik poured out another stream of healing, this time concentrating on the bite, a jagged mess of goblin tooth marks, widened by Zita's thrashing to escape. Maybe he had used too much of his reserves to remove the goblin and now didn't have the strength to heal Zita. That'd be perfect. Remove the goblin, but lose the patient.

"What do you need?" Al asked.

"I don't know." He needed peace and time alone without pressure.

"Maybe the helmet can help." Al removed the helmet and placed it on Erik's head. It didn't fit his head any better than Al's. The golden dragon cocked at an angle.

"What are you doing?" Erik threw the helmet to the floor.

"I'm trying to help."

"Well, stop it." Again a thought nudged. This room contained a healing icon. What was it?

"Do you want the sword?" Al asked. He squirmed. "Then if your healing doesn't work, you can kill her before she transforms into a goblin."

"No, I don't want the sword. I want you to be quiet." Was that Zita's fate if she died right now? Would she turn into a creature wandering the castle halls looking for adventurers' souls she could suck dry? She'd blame Erik for the rest of eternity.

Erik felt a tired brain synapse fire, and a memory sparked his thought processes. *The healing charm Cugbert wore around his neck that saved the logger. Yes, he needed something in the room.* "Find the frog."

"What?"

"The frog. The golden frog I tossed at you."

Al scurried away, taking the blue globe of light with him.

Zita's still face appeared calm and peaceful from Erik's healing, as if a person sleeping in the light of a full moon. He placed one hand on her forehead and the other over her wound.

Al returned, struggling with the heavy frog. "How did you throw this at me with a broken arm?"

"Put it next to me on the floor, over here." Erik pointed to his left, near Zita's head.

Erik removed his hand from her forehead and placed it on the frog's back. His body trembled. "This will work." He wished he felt as confident as he tried to sound.

Curing a patient using a healing object required saying particular words and a change in technique, Erik lifted his hand from the frog, sighed and spit into his palm.

"Why did you do that?"

"For luck," Erik grinned at his friend. "It adds no value to the healing process."

He slapped the frog on the back with his slimy hand and said, "Heal this body, heal her wounds, and return her to full health."

Erik sucked in a deep breath. "Whoa." The healing power gushed from the statue as if a spigot had been turned to full blast, pumping vast curative properties.

Zita's body jerked.

"Hold her legs,"

Al jammed her legs to the floor.

"Look at that." The wound beneath Erik's hands mended, and Zita's body re-filled with blood and fluids. The tight skin across her skull regained elasticity and color. Her cold body warmed beneath his touch. "Do you see? She's returning to us Al, we did it."

CHAPTER 63

Zita opened her eyes and screamed.

"It's okay, Zita, it's me." He lifted both hands, uncertain what to do next.

Zita stared at Erik, no expression on her face.

Erik smiled and licked his lips as his stomach fluttered. "How are you feeling?"

She lifted the hand with the necklace and stared at it.

"It's yours." He reached out, took it from her and gently clasped it around her neck.

She smiled and put her hand in his.

Al said, "Remember, we have to return to the caravan before sunrise."

Erik had forgotten about the caravan. Did they have time? How long had it taken them to travel to the ruined castle from the Ice Castle?

The sound of wings fluttering, small squeaking noises and scratching sounds came from the bell tower.

Al said, "It sounds like bats are coming in to roost. That means daylight is close. Hurry." Al stood. "Plus, we have to navigate through the jungle and escape the jaguar."

Zita said, "Don't worry about the jaguar, it won't bother you."

Erik now realized the jaguar had been Zita and he chuckled, "Can you stand?" He helped Zita to her feet, but she wobbled and crumpled into his arms.

He laid her again on the floor.

Al grabbed the helmet and placed it on his head.

Erik said, "Take the sword, too."

"Don't you want it?"

"Yes, but my hands will be full."

"Oh, you're taking the frog."

"The frog is amazing, but no, the frog stays."

"Why?"

"Because it's too heavy for you to carry to the caravan." Erik lifted Zita off the floor and snuggled her close to his chest.

"What are you doing?" Zita asked.

"You're coming with me to the caravan and I'm not letting you out of my arms."

Zita no longer struggled.

They traveled out of the castle and through the dark forest. Monkeys chattered and birds whistled around them.

Erik listened to the bird's whistles and songs, which brought back memories of Earth. The birds had wakened him in the early morning darkness as they sang their songs to each other, thirty minutes before sunrise.

He said, "We have a half hour. Let's hurry." They could make it to the caravan. They had the helmet, the broadsword, and he carried Zita in his arms. "Al, our first adventure, and we captured the treasure."

Erik thought Al looked funny holding the sword while he used his other hand to balance the helmet perched on his head at an odd angle. The helmet didn't fit Al, and the weight of the golden dragon caused it to tip sideways. They hoped to use it as a great magical item to rescue the stone warriors, and yet, it didn't fit the wizard. Erik shook his head at the irony.

They ascended from the depths of the Pit of Wretchedness, the jungle changed into forest and then to grass, and the glow from the rising sun was visible on the horizon. Dawn had arrived.

Erik adjusted Zita in his arms.

* * * *

They reached the caravan where a crowd of townspeople had gathered to watch the handlers arrange and harness mastodons to the wagons. The mastodons bellowed. Breakfast smells drifted on a slight breeze. Hadrian was shouting commands to break camp.

Al couldn't believe it. He stood taller and stronger than ever as he inhaled deep breaths in satisfaction. The great adventurer, a mighty wizard, had defeated the mysterious castle magic, retrieved the helmet of justice and returned to the townspeople in victory. Al stopped, threw back his shoulders and stuck out his chest. His magic had returned victorious.

Obadiah sprinted toward them. "You found it."

It was a glorious morning. Al, tired but fulfilled, watched the bystanders' reactions as he raised the helmet and shouted, "The helmet of justice."

The townspeople looked confused, and a murmur of conversation drifted on the air.

Al expected the people to cheer, but maybe they didn't realize the helmet's significance. "Come on people, Alpherge the Mighty, wizard extraordinaire, has defeated evil and returned with the treasure."

Obadiah gawked in wonder. "Is that the crown? Was it difficult? Did you slay monsters? Tell me."

Erik helped Zita to stand, but kept an arm around her waist.

Al announced, "We have stories of an adventure to last a bard's lifetime." He scanned the scene. It didn't look right, and the reactions of the people differed from what he imagined. *Come on people, we're hero adventurers, celebrate our victory.*

The first rays of the sun brightened the field, and Al could distinguish faces.

Gadiel stood near his wagon with Hadrian, Wagner, and another man. The man looked familiar, but injured. Gadiel held Al's staff.

Hah, with my magic back, I can call the staff, and no one and nothing can stop me. He placed the helmet lopsided on his head and said, "Come staff."

Al fell to his knees, the helmet and sword dropped to the grass, and he clutched his head.

"What's wrong?" Erik asked.

Al moaned, "Gadiel," but couldn't say more. A thousand pinpricks of pain exploded in his head. He curled into a ball on the wet grass, powerless in Gadiel's presence.

* * * *

Zita, standing next to Erik in the cool morning air, was enjoying his warm body touching hers. The heat of the jungle in the Pit of Wretchedness was replaced by a normal spring morning at the Ice Castle. Erik had saved her again and professed his love for her. *This is the best day of my life.*

Then she saw Dad next to Gadiel, and Al writhing on the ground.

Energy gathered above her father. The potential of lightning that makes your hair rise in a thunderstorm. "Daddy don't," Zita screamed.

King Haskell raised his good arm to shoulder level as a fireball formed above his hand.

Her muscles cramped; her body was not fully functioning. How could her father execute Erik now, after the boy from Earth had rescued her twice? Her mind saw each action in slow motion. She glanced at her father and then at Erik, who wore a wonderful smile.

Erik stared at Zita, his eyes wide. A boyish grin lit his face, and he leaned into her, tugging her close.

Zita's legs went weak. She wasn't sure if it was from fear of watching Erik die or the joy of having Erik so close. She shoved him to save him from the first blast of the fireball, but he held tight and drew closer.

King Haskell released the fireball.

She wondered if her magic still worked after her battle with the goblin. It had sucked so much from her she realized if Erik let go she'd collapse to the ground, but she had to save him. She conjured a shield to stop the fireball.

Erik gave her a kiss on the cheek.

A jolt of pleasure surged through her body as her heart banged in her chest. Zita's shield faltered as the fireball rushed toward the young couple. She screamed.

Erik turned his head to the danger, and his mouth formed an O.

Zita found the magic she needed, either from Erik's kiss or her own resources, but the shield re-formed and the fireball exploded in reds and yellows as it curved around the shield.

She didn't have strength to return fire. Al still rolled on the ground in pain. The helmet lay on the grass near her feet. She didn't understand what powers the helmet contained but wondered if it could give her the strength she needed.

Erik held her tight, too tight. She pushed him away. The world spun, and Zita fell to the ground, unable to support herself. The helmet lay at an odd angle on the ground, the dragon on its side within inches of her hand.

Can I protect Erik from Dad's wrath?

* * * *

Erik stood in disbelief as the blast split and streamed around the shield. He gawked at the man who released the fireball. Al claimed Gadiel wasn't strong, yet Erik noticed the old man holding Al's staff. Had that given Gadiel the extra power to blast them?

Who was the short man next to Gadiel that fired the initial shot? The man looked familiar, but why did he want to kill Erik and Zita? Then Erik recognized the man, King Haskell, from the volcano. Zita's father. King Haskell was still alive? Did Zita know her dad lived? Why hadn't she told him?

Another fireball from King Haskell streaked high over Erik's left shoulder.

Erik yelled, "Al, do something." Despite the quest they had just survived, without his friend's magic, their lives still hung in the balance.

Al moaned and wriggled on the grass, holding his head.

Erik dove to the ground, and grabbed the broadsword.

CHAPTER 64

The pain inside Al's head smothered his ability to think. How to stop the torture? What had Erik said? Visualize a shield within his brain, but that never worked. He realized the three of them were nothing more than Gadiel's tools. Gadiel could not recover the helmet himself, so he had forced them to do his dirty work. Al opened his eyes.

Erik was clutching the sword in his hands and lay on the ground next to Zita.

Zita held the helmet of justice.

Al's throat burned as bile bubbled into his mouth. They shouldn't have saved Zita. She planned to take the helmet and give it to Gadiel. She was the old wizard's pawn. Why didn't Erik listen to him? He spit out the bile and struggled to his feet. Millions of tiny bright dots sparked behind his eyes, and he pressed a hand to his stomach.

Electrostatic energy crackled as a fireball formed near the wagons. He didn't see where the menace originated but sensed the danger and formed a shield.

The impact of the fireball striking the shield knocked him to the ground.

The pain in his head increased.

Al needed to shield himself from Gadiel's control if he expected to survive this ordeal.

Kenneth Brown

* * * *

Zita wrestled the helmet toward her, its weight surprising her. The way Al wore it and hung onto it to keep it from falling from his head, led her to believe it was heavy, but its weight was trivial.

A fireball flew by and exploded on the grass behind her. The sound of the exploding fireball was deafening. She hoped the helmet gave her protection. What was its power, and why did Gadiel want it?

Erik lay near her with the sword in his hands, but he kept his head pressed to the ground.

Zita sat up to put the helmet on, but wobbled in the effort. Without Erik she would have died in the Pit of Wretchedness, and she couldn't let Gadiel and Dad kill Erik now.

She lifted the helmet as Gadiel bludgeoned her brain with his Fire and Ice connection. The inflicted torture tore through her body, and she swooned, the helmet of justice rolling into the green grass.

Erik crawled on elbows and knees to reach her, the sword in one hand. He grabbed her arm.

His healing power surged through her, imparting internal strength, and he comforted her against Gadiel's incursion.

* * * *

Al had a thought. Does this connection with Gadiel operate in reverse? Maybe he could control Gadiel. In earlier attacks, he merely shielded. What if he attacked through the shared bond?

King Haskell sent a fireball screaming over their heads.

~ 434 ~

Despite the pain pounding through his skull, Al sent feelers along the connection with Gadiel. Tendrils of Al's thoughts snaked through space and time and landed on Gadiel.

Gadiel assaulted Al's mind with increased ferocity.

Al held true. He realized that despite Gadiel's knowledge and skill with the techniques, Al's strength was greater. The puzzle he tried to solve while in the dungeon was unsolvable in his own mind, because the puzzle foundation and the last piece lay in Gadiel's brain.

Al attacked Gadiel. He severed the link of pain being served by Gadiel and sent his own onslaught against the old man. Al delved into Gadiel's brain and identified points of pain and concern in the old man.

Gadiel attempted to block, but Al pursued, changing directions when Gadiel erected barriers before him. Al mentally chased the man through the Ice Castle. Gadiel raced through the halls.

Al followed, staying close.

The elder wizard ducked into a castle room and shut the door. Locks clicked.

Al exploded the door.

The scene changed, and Gadiel darted into a garden of flowers and rebuffed Al with an attack of bees.

Al realized he didn't need to envision chasing after the wizard. He only had to think where he wanted to be and he landed in the proper location. He imagined the bees removed, and they disappeared.

Gadiel entered a hedge maze, and Al lost him for a moment.

Trying a different tactic, Al searched Gadiel's brain for weaknesses. He found an injured knee and shot a point-of-attack spell to the man's right leg. Gadiel collapsed.

In an instant, they were back in front of Gadiel's wagon by the caravan.

Gadiel lay on the ground with Al's staff in his hand.

Al said, "Staff come."

A morning breeze was fluttering leaves in the fresh trees. The summer morning sun rose golden in the blue sky. A mastodon bellowed.

The staff flew toward Al.

* * * *

Zita gained enough strength to sit up and attempted to place the helmet on her head again. Despite Gadiel's unrelenting bombardment of pain, she adjusted the helmet of justice on her head and tucked wisps of hair behind her ears. When she fastened the strap under her chin, the wisdom of eternity swirled in her mind like planets around a sun, and it took her breath away.

What is this magical helmet that allows me to visualize rays and auroras of magic? With the helmet, she understood the powers, reading the trails and currents of magic being used.

King Haskell prepared another fireball.

Zita didn't need to point her fingers and hands, she didn't need to chant an incantation, and she had no need to use her arms to toss a magical spell. She had only to think of the magic her dad prepared to use. She simply snuffed it with a thought, as easily as extinguishing a candle with her breath. One moment, the fireball formed in King Haskell's hands, and the next moment an ocean wave of magic destroyed it.

CHAPTER 65

Zita stood. She took Erik's hand, and reached out to Al. They rose together, and Zita led them toward Gadiel and her dad. Her breath came light and easy, the pain and sorrow from the night's struggles had washed from her body. The pain her father had caused her throughout her life dissipated. Her obsession with his neglect was gone. She now walked with friends, and she pressed against Erik, enjoying his touch.

The three arrived at the wagon. King Haskell's shoulders slumped as he brought a shaky hand to his brow to wipe away beads of perspiration.

The king said, "Zita, what have you done?"

Zita said, "I'm charging you both with crimes against the populace."

Gadiel shuddered on the ground, but he wasn't giving in. "By whose authority do you make that charge?"

"By the people."

Gadiel laughed, "Ha. What do villagers understand of the actions and schemes of kings and wizards? How will you stop us?" He struggled to his feet, and Hadrian helped the old man stand. "King Haskell, alert the guards and have these children arrested and thrown in the dungeon."

King Haskell clenched his jaw tight, the muscles in his neck rigid and stiff. He said nothing.

Gadiel's nostrils flared, and he bared his teeth. "Hadrian, send someone to fetch the guards, I want these kids in the dungeon so we can start our journey back to Velidred. Move, we're losing daylight."

Hadrian moved hesitantly toward the castle, and Zita watched him go. She sensed Gadiel in her brain, tentative tendrils searching for a pain center. She squashed it.

Gadiel's eyes narrowed, and Zita saw the red scorpion cross Gadiel's pupil. Through all the months of traveling with Gadiel, she had never realized what the scorpion meant, but the helmet of justice gave her insight. The scorpion, the mark of corruption, the evil of Velidred, gave Gadiel dominant power to manipulate those who fell under its spell. And yet, now, wearing the helmet, she was the dominate one.

Gadiel said, "Erik, give the sword to Wagner."

Erik walked to Wagner.

"Erik, no!" Zita screamed.

Wagner said, "We agreed, if he found the sword he promised to give it to me."

Al said, "That agreement was valid if you acquired the staff for me, but you failed."

Gadiel repeated, "Give the sword to Wagner."

Erik licked his lips, smiled and shifted the sword in his hand, preparing to hand it to Wagner.

Zita thought fast; she couldn't let Erik give away the powerful sword. But Gadiel could still control Erik with his hypnotizing power.

There was a way to remove the scorpion, Gadiel's mark of corruption, but she couldn't do it herself. They needed the sword. "Erik, stop."

He stopped and looked at Zita, as a puppy dog wishing to please everyone.

Wagner moved closer and reached for the sword.

Zita used a puff of air to push Wagner back.

She whispered, "Al, wrap Gadiel in air."

Al swiftly murmured an incantation and Gadiel stiffened, his arms locked tight by his sides.

"Erik, I need you and Al both, we have to . . . operate."

Gadiel said, "What are you doing?"

"Removing Velidred's corruption from your body."

"No, don't, I will die."

"So be it."

"For six weeks on the journey, I cared for you, trained you in magic and I could squash you like a bug. Now this is how you treat me? Haskell, do something."

King Haskell stood silent and unmoving.

Zita said, "You took care of me to use me, just like you've done to these boys. We're nothing but puppets to use and discard. I say, no more."

She led the boys to Gadiel and had Erik stand directly in front of him. She positioned Alpherge on Erik's right, and then she stood on Erik's left. She didn't know where the knowledge originated for what she needed to do, only that the helmet's power and wisdom guided her decisions.

"The sword and Erik's ability in healing will remove Velidred's corruption from Gadiel's body."

Al fidgeted, "Are you sure about this? The corruption won't flow into Erik, will it?"

"He will be safe," She said. "Al put your hand on Erik's shoulder and if Gadiel tries to influence him, you block it. We don't want Gadiel to twist the sword's power at us."

Al placed his hand on Erik's shoulder.

A black cloud appeared in the east and darkness shrouded the caravan.

"Okay, I sense Gadiel coming through Erik."

Erik slashed at Al with the sword.

Al shielded.

Gadiel screamed in pain.

"I can make it worse," Al said.

Zita placed her hand on Erik's shoulder.

* * * *

Two wizards' energy flowed through Erik. He couldn't believe the power.

Zita said, "Do you see the red scorpion in Gadiel's eye?"

"Yes."

"Place the tip of the sword on Gadiel's eye."

"Do you want me to ram the sword through his brain?"

"No. A gentle touch. A healing touch. Use your healing power to extract Velidred's corruption from his body. The sword is required, and Al's and my magic will aid your ability."

Handlers and townspeople huddled closer, sensing something unusual was about to happen.

Erik took a deep breath. "And I'm not in danger?" He gazed into Zita's eyes, glowing green in the cloudy darkness.

At first, she didn't answer but then nodded. "Yes. You're safe."

He was tired. The long trip, the days in the dungeon, the long night in the jungle, gashes on his body and his broken arm weighed on him. The sword was heavy and awkward "And what happens if I push too far?"

Gadiel gasped, but still wrapped in air, he couldn't move.

"We're with you." She gave Erik a kiss on the cheek. "Though if you break through the eye's surface, then you'll release the corruption to nearby villagers."

A groan arose from the handlers and townspeople near enough to hear this, and the closest people shuffled backwards, jostling those who stood behind.

Erik coughed. "A drink of water would be nice,"

Zita said, "Wagner bring water."

Erik downed the water and gazed into Zita's eyes.

She nodded at him and squeezed his shoulder.

His breathing accelerated as he lifted the sword toward Gadiel, the fatigue of the last few days causing his arm to shake. Erik didn't know if he would be able to gently touch the man's eye with the tip of the sword.

Someone in the crowd called, "Here come the castle guards. Make way for the guards."

The guard commander ordered, "Drop the sword and release Mr. Gadiel." He approached Erik, but a shield blocked his progress.

"Daddy, have the castle guards stand down."

King Haskell said meekly, "Commander, let the teens continue."

The commander looked from King Haskell to the teens and back. He elevated his hand, "Withdraw."

Zita said, "Everyone stand back. This will be dangerous."

The guards retreated to a safe distance and reassigned themselves to crowd control, pushing the on-lookers back.

"You can do this Erik."

Erik studied Gadiel. The wrinkles on his face were more pronounced. The man appeared infinitely tired, but a trace of defiance waged in his eyes.

Al said, "Finish it."

Erik lifted the sword. He guided the blade with slight movements toward the man, and as the tip moved closer, Gadiel closed his eyes.

"Al, can you keep his eyelid opened?"

Despite Gadiel's furrowed brow, the eyelid opened.

Erik searched his mind for a frame of reference. Friends at school on Earth sometimes took out their contact lenses, refreshed the contacts with liquid and put them back into their eyes. He needed a soft touch, a gentle touch like refreshing contacts.

The sword moved closer to Gadiel's eye. The crowd hushed. Even the mastodons were quiet.

How would he recognize the moment when he touched the eye with the sword? He didn't sense motion, smells, or sounds through the sword. The sword grew heavy. Maybe they should put Gadiel on the ground to make it easier? The sword tip brushed Gadiel's eyelashes, and Erik edged the sword closer.

Erik held his breath and calmed himself, though a knot of concern clenched his chest. He pursed his lips and forced the tension to subside.

Before the sword touched the pupil, at the last micro-distance possible, Erik became aware that within Gadiel's eye, a hundred two-legged winged dragons roared and screamed. Their hind parts writhed as serpents with barbed tails.

Erik eased back. "What are those things?

Zita said, "We felt it too. They're wyvern, from the caves of the Velidred Volcano. We can't let them escape. Al, can you create a vessel within the sword to contain the corruption?"

Al's lips drew into a straight line.

CHAPTER 66

The wyverns screamed, but the villagers didn't move. Couldn't they hear the angry creatures? Al thought.

Al tried to invent ways to create a vessel inside a sword that would capture evil. *How am I supposed to do that?*

The people's silence unnerved him. He thought his role was to keep Gadiel in check, and now Zita asked for more magic. Al checked the air flows holding Gadiel, and wished for help to guide his actions, because he didn't know the proper steps to create a container within a sword. In fact, it seemed like a ridiculous idea. Who could do such a thing? Where was the internet when you needed it?

He wanted to walk around and free his mind, to gather his thoughts and decide on a course of action. Then he realized what he held in his hand. What he had longed for since before joining the caravan. The staff of Ishwa contained three trapped wizards with decades of knowledge of magic, though the staff hadn't talked with him in six weeks.

He didn't have to verbalize the question. He reached out with his mind and asked, "How do you enclose corruption in a vessel and store it in a sword?" *Would they answer him?*

Isabel, the witch, responded, but she didn't have a clue. Callahan, the curious wizard, found the question interesting, but asked for additional time to plan a method to create the vessel.

Al turned to the elder of the staff members, the wizard with the long beard. "Can you help?"

"What is the purpose of such a vessel?"

"We want to contain Velidred's corruption from Gadiel's eye in that sword."

"Ah, Velidred's corruption. We longed to resolve that issue years ago, yet Gadiel disappeared each time before we vanquished the evil."

"Can we do it?"

"What do you perceive when you interrogate the evil?"

"A hundred wyverns roar."

"Velidred's evil. How secure is the sword?"

Al replied, "My friend Erik holds the sword. We are protecting it."

The staff responded, "How many corporeal wizards help you?"

"One other. Princess Zita."

"Little Zita, Queen Noreen and King Haskell's daughter?"

"Yes. Do you know her?"

"Only as a baby. Do you trust this woman? Are there other wizards to help? We found with twelve wizards we had the ideal flow of magic and control."

"No, but we have you, and Zita wears the helmet of justice."

The staff didn't reply, but a rush of excitement emanated from it, an awareness of a great mystery of the universe.

"Can we do what she asks? Can we lock the corruption in the sword?"

"Make a vessel."

"How?"

No verbal answer came, but the staff guided Al's magic into the sword. A transparent crystal sphere formed on the sword guard. The sphere rotated and reflected sunlight as it grew.

The staff said, "That is sufficient for our purposes. Nudge the sword toward the eye, but don't touch it."

Al said, "Erik, move the sword closer, but don't touch the eye."

Sweat formed on Al's brow as he managed the different flows of magic, one flow encasing Gadiel in air, another holding the man's eye open, and controlling the sphere.

The sword shook in Erik's hands.

"Hold it still."

"I'm trying."

The staff said, "Open a window in the sphere. The corruption will be sucked into the vessel."

Knowledge to perform the steps entered Al's mind. One moment the sphere was whole, and then in the next, a window formed on its surface. Al imagined a vacuum inside the vessel that cried for indulgence.

"This next part is tricky and dangerous. If you get it wrong, the corruption spills out among the people."

Al nodded at Erik. "Ease the tip to touch the eye. No matter what you see, sense, or hear, maintain the connection."

Erik said, "Make it fast."

"It takes as long as it takes."

The sword touched Gadiel's eye, and wyverns roared and shot fire from their mouths.

Al's connection with Erik's shoulder jiggled causing a slight interruption. Twenty-two variegated, fire-breathing wyverns, expanding in size as they escaped, flew to the field where the caravan and townspeople congregated.

Villagers bolted in every direction.

Al's muscles tightened as he thrust out his chest and increased his resolve.

The staff said, "Increase the vacuum, force the wyverns into the sphere."

Gadiel stood comatose; his mouth hung open, his only support coming from Al's air which secured him upright.

Al yelled, "Zita increase your magic."

Al felt the magical surge, as of hot water from a hose in the summer sun. He perceived his magic as blue, while Zita's rushed into the sword in a deep emerald color.

The wyverns in the field spit fire, stabbing at the villagers with their barbed tails.

Zita cried out, "Erik, heal the wound in Gadiel's eye. Stitch it up like a cut. We can't let the wyverns return to Gadiel."

The colors changed and a yellow glow emitted from Erik.

The wyverns screamed, one spewed fire, and a wagon burst into flames. Mastodons roared and stomped in the confusion.

Erik said, "Make this fast, I can't hold on much longer."

The staff guided Al, and the colors congealed, forming a white laser light, true and steady. Al made the globe grow and sucked the wyverns into the sphere one by one. He didn't know how long it took, but the sphere grew to fifty feet in diameter. As the sphere sucked them in, the wyverns wriggled like snakes in a den. They squirmed and writhed, but couldn't escape.

"That's all of them. Hurry," Erik said.

Al focused. He closed the window, but wondered how to shrink the globe. The auroras ebbed and swelled a fiery blue, and the sphere gradually diminished on its own. Sparks flew from the sphere.

The sphere shrunk to the size of a diamond on an engagement ring, and Al forced the object toward the hilt. When it reached the sword's hand-guard, Al heated the hilt.

"Hey what are you doing, it's getting hot."

"Hold." Al forced the diamond into the middle of the hand-guard and rapid-cooled the metal, permanently setting the diamond into the sword.

"Okay, remove the sword from Gadiel's eye."

Zita yelled, "Wait."

CHAPTER 67

Al asked, "What's wrong?"

Zita said, "You have to release the flows before he pulls the sword back."

"Please hurry. I can't hold the sword much longer," Erik said.

Al saw the tension in Erik's body. His neck muscles corded tight, and his face scrunched in concentration. Al separated the flows, and the hot white laser light dispersed into blue, yellow and emerald.

Al commanded, "Erik, release your healing flow. Slowly."

Erik's yellow flow vanished, leaving the blue and emerald flows of magic coursing through the sword. Al jerked at the sudden release of Erik's flow. Al took a deep breath and swallowed, "I said, 'slow.'"

"Zita, go ahead." Al didn't really want to tell Zita to pull back as the energy of the linked magic was powerful, and he desired even more.

Zita sighed and answered with a small nod. The emerald flow dissipated.

Erik said, "Faster."

The blue magic bled from the sword as Al relaxed his hold on Erik.

Erik jerked the sword back and the point dropped to the ground.

"Is it safe to release Gadiel?" Al asked.

Zita closed her eyes and nodded.

Al took a breath, his cramped muscles relaxed. He released Gadiel from his chains of air, and pain flowed through Al's body at the sudden loss of tension. However, it was the clean pain of physical exertion, not the evil pain of magic control.

Gadiel fell in an untidy heap.

"Is he dead?"

Erik checked, "He's alive."

Zita said, "Hadrian, get Gadiel to his wagon and put him in bed."

Handlers moved Gadiel to his wagon.

* * * *

Zita approached her dad.

King Haskell backed away, his arms at his side. He didn't make eye contact.

She stood in front of her father and lifted his chin, "Daddy, I'm stripping you of your magic, but will leave you to reign as king of the Ice Castle."

"Why do you have to remove my magic?"

"Ambition forced you to take immoral and unethical actions. If I strip your magic from you, then you will understand others and serve the kingdom with concern for others instead of force."

King Haskell released a long sigh.

Zita studied her father, a defeated man, still with unhealed injuries from the battle at the volcano. Most of the wounds would haunt him the rest of his life, but Erik might heal him of the most painful. She loved her dad, always had, but their differences had led them to fight more than show love and respect to the other.

She touched him, but he jerked away. "Daddy, I love you."

He smiled, "You remind me of your mother. I miss her."

"I miss her, too." Zita's eyelids were hot and gummy, and the field spun in her vision. She wanted to hug her dad, but he stood distant and defiant. "Are you ready?"

King Haskell nodded and placed his arms across his chest.

The helmet of justice guided Zita as she thought of the proper steps to conjure a permanent shield between him and magic. It required finesse. She pressed her hand to his chest, chanting words of magic, touching her other hand to the dragon atop the helmet. Then she squeezed off the flow of magic and twisted until it snapped.

When she twisted and shut the flow, King Haskell turned his torso as if blocking a blow.

Zita used more magic to cauterize the breakpoint within her father. The technique left him some power and would prevent his desire to die. He would be weak against wizards but manage skills above that of a commoner.

King Haskell stumbled when Zita was finished, and he careened into a guard who saved him from crashing to the ground.

"Erik, can you heal his wounds?"

Erik rubbed his hands together, placed them on the king and after eight minutes, the burns had faded to a pale pink, and the king's wounds had healed.

Zita felt calm but empty. She moved closer and placed her hands on the king's arm. "I'm returning to Velidred with Erik. Will you be okay here?"

He nodded. "Thank you, Zita."

Kenneth Brown

She commanded the guards to lead him to the castle.

* * * *

The caravan departed two hours later than Hadrian desired. Fatigue washed through Erik's body, and he somehow convinced Wagner to give them food before the journey. Erik wished he had two or three days' rest at the Ice Castle, but accepted what Hadrian gave them.

Erik smiled at his reunion with Roden. He'd come to enjoy the beast's company, calm compared to tigers and goblins. Roden gave him a playful shove. He and Al guided Roden as the convoy started its return journey to Velidred.

Zita handled Gadiel's wagon. The old man's energy level had diminished, and Hadrian managed many of the tasks Gadiel supervised on the trip to the Ice Castle.

He thought of the journey to Velidred and wondered if the helmet would really allow them to release the stone warriors. Erik had imagined Al wielding the helmet's magic, but Zita now commanded the helmet. He hoped she'd help release his father from his stone prison.

They reached the frozen lake later that same day. The meteors had stopped while the caravan rested at the Ice Castle, and the ice had re-formed on the lake. Hadrian pushed the caravan hard and long into the night.

Erik ate dinner with Al, Gadiel, Obadiah, Wagner, Hadrian and Zita. She sat next to him wearing the helmet. "Will you wear that helmet everywhere?"

"I might." She slid closer to him on the bench.

They kissed, a slow, deliberate and satisfying smooch. Erik wondered how he was going to explain this to Lily.

* * * *

Zita thought of Erik, Gadiel, and Dad as she lay in her cot in the cabin that first night. She had started this journey to wage revenge on Erik for killing her dad. Yet, King Haskell lived, and rather than killing Erik, she had teamed up with him to prevent her father's wrath from causing greater harm and to vanquish Gadiel's influence on her.

She had changed. She now wondered how she could use the helmet of justice to serve others. The King and Gadiel had influenced townspeople by force and fear over the decades, but now she wanted to rule with peace and justice. The helmet exposed truths about the people she observed. Truths and secrets that they held in their hearts. Erik loved her, but he hid desire for another woman, Lily. Zita needed to crush this problem when they returned to Velidred.

* * * *

Five days later, the caravan slid off the ice onto firm ground. Al guided Roden, using a touch of magic to make the task easier for the giant mastodon as the wagons jostled off the ice onto the steep rise.

Al enjoyed his role on this planet more than he had since arriving. He spent time each night talking with the staff. Even before Al met Gadiel, the old man had cast a spell on the staff that reduced its ability to communicate with its rightful owner. This influence had now ended.

Each night, Al ate dinner with Gadiel and discussed the staff. Gadiel, now acquiescent and helpful, told Al of an old wizard in the mountains, Finn, who carved staffs and other magical items. This wizard might be a guiding mentor to learn the staff's secrets.

Kenneth Brown

They traveled ten days from the Ice Castle. Gadiel weakened each day after the teens removed the corruption of evil. Erik tried to heal him, but it appeared the man had aged a hundred years in just days. His last two days, the old man never left the cabin. When the stars shone in the night sky and as the wolves howled in the forest, Hadrian and Wagner carried Gadiel's lifeless body into the forest.

Wolves and wild animals snarled and growled through the night.

At sunup the next day, Hadrian forced the caravan toward Velidred Castle. The days were long and tiring, and Al thought of Sherry and wondered if she lived.

* * * *

Sherry's wrists were red and raw from the shackles the men had placed on her. Something had to be done to relax the tightness of the shackles around her wrists. Lily lay on the floor in the fetal position with her back striped red from the whipping she endured the day before. Sherry knew they had to get out of this cabin. Even though the mayor told her they would get an audience with Prince Krunal, she didn't believe the man.

When Lily roused, Sherry called out to her, "Are you okay?" Her friend had cried the whole night, and wouldn't talk with Sherry. She wanted to embrace her, but the chains didn't allow it. She never realized the dangers she had put them both in by starting the school. How could Lily ever forgive her?

Lily unwound herself from her position and let out a moan, "I'm sorry Sherry, it's all my fault." Lily didn't look at Sherry.

Heat rushed into Sherry's face, "No, it's my fault for starting the school." The little cabin smelled of sweat and fear.

Lily had an uncertain look on her face, "Kestrel told me it was dangerous for us."

"What are you talking about?"

"You know. Kestrel and me."

"This is about the school. It has nothing to do with you and Kestrel. The mayor and Mooney dragged me out of the cabin, and rode me through the town while the villagers threw rocks and eggs at me."

Lily turned away as if gathering her thoughts, "Kestrel warned me that seeing him would be dangerous."

"When did he warn you? We only saw him that one time." *What was Lily talking about? How could Kestrel warn her?*

A flush of crimson crept across Lily's face and her ears turned red, "I didn't want to tell you about us."

Sherry waited while Lily coughed.

Lily pulled her knees to her chest, "When you told me to leave the cabin, I decided to see if I could find Kestrel. I left the village and headed back into the forest where we first saw him."

Sherry gave a small gasp, "Are you serious?"

Lily swallowed as tears formed in her eyes. "He's cute."

"He's dangerous."

"I knew you would react this way. You don't know him the way I do. He's gentle and sweet."

Sherry shook her head, "He tried to kill you."

"He wanted to marry me, and tried to talk King Haskell out of sacrificing me."

"He almost killed Al trying to get the staff. And multiple times he threw fireballs at us on the volcano. He's not a nice guy."

"You don't know him the way I do." Lily said.

"Don't see him any—" *Who am I kidding? I have no control over Lily and her actions. If she wants to see Kestrel, I don't care.*

Let her, and this time I won't try to rescue her. It doesn't matter, as we're trapped in this cabin with no way out. "Listen, I'm sorry, if you want to see him—" Sherry couldn't say it. *I hate this planet.*

They sat in silence for a few minutes.

Sherry sighed and said, "I'm sure the reason we're both prisoners is because of the school. The tailor's daughter was a plant. They arrested us because I educated the girls."

The End

Thank you for reading my book. If you enjoyed it, won't you please take a moment to leave me a review at your favorite retailer?

Thanks!

Kenneth Brown

MORE FROM SERIES

The Mountain King Series by Kenneth Brown

Haskell – Orphan to King – Prequel to the Mountain King Series

Eclipse of the Triple Moons

Zita's Revenge

Go to https://www.adgitizepress.com for more details.

UPCOMING BOOKS FROM KENNETH BROWN

RESCUE OF THE STONE WARRIORS

Read more about Sherry and Lily's struggles while the boys were on their adventure for the golden crown. Sherry and Lily are captured for teaching girls in the Village of Crossroads. They have a chance for redemption if they can fulfill an insurmountable request. Otherwise they will be sent to the Gallows.

Zita and the teens from Earth have the Helmet of Justice. They hope to use it to rescue the Stone Warriors, including Erik's father. But it doesn't work, forcing Al and Zita to search for a man named, Finn.

Magic, determination, danger, and adventure will challenge the teens to survive against incredible odds.

Rescue of the Stone Warriors is scheduled for publication in 2021.

KENNETH BROWN

This is Kenneth Brown's third book in the Mountain King Series. He has been writing professionally since the release of his first book in 2018.

He loves to hike, spend time with his family and sings in the church choir. Even though he started writing late in life, he loves to create worlds, creatures and characters to have exciting adventures in those fantastical worlds.

Check out https://www.adgitizepress.com for novel release dates and details about the author.

ACKNOWLEDGEMENTS

I want to give special thanks to the people that helped make this book the best it can be.

Editor: Joan H Young, Author, Editor and famous Hiker

Members of the Poplar Creek Library writing group: Mary-Megan Kalvig and Susan Wells

Thank you all for your willingness to educate me on word usage, story flow and grammar.

The cover artwork was created by Kenneth Brown using an image from Tomertu from Shutterstock. Kenneth's creative director, Mary Brown, was instrumental in getting the final image into a format worth presenting to the world. We hope you like it

BONUS MATERIAL

Thank you for purchasing this book. We hope you enjoyed Zita's Revenge. Please take the time to write a review of this book on your favorite book buying website.

To find out more about the author, Kenneth Brown, and get advance notification about future books, check out the website, Adgitize Press, https://www.adgitizepress.com. Join the Adgitize Press Readers Group to receive these great benefits.

- Get the latest information on New Releases
- Insider Looks at Outlines, Plots, Characters, Deleted Scenes and Exclusive behind the Scenes Glimpses at Kenneth Brown's Writing
- Sneak Peeks of Upcoming Chapters
- Ask the Author Questions
- Exclusive Offers
- And MORE

Find out more about the exciting prequel to The Mountain King Series, Haskell – Orphan to King. Read the fantasy story of how orphan, Haskell, lost his parents, and rose from orphan thief to become King Haskell, the Mountain King. An exciting tale of intrigue, fear and magic.